To his left, a small dot glowed on the radar screen.

The target! Right on schedule!

Trans American Flight 902, a jet-propelled lamb to the slaughter.

The 707 seemed to be suspended in the sky, a tiny, motionless silhouette . . . full of life and activity.

If only he had a missile, the surgical procedure of destruction would be more acceptable, more like a military sortie. But aircraft manufacturers could not get their hands on such lethal hardware.

He reached forward and uncovered a guarded button on the instrument panel.

Six-point-eight nautical miles . . .

The jetliner seemed to swell as the distance shrank.

Five-point-zero nautical miles.

Oh God, forgive me, Mike screamed.

He depressed the red button. . . .

FLIGHT 902 IS DOWN!

HAL FISHMAN AND BARRY SCHIFF

FAWCETT CREST • NEW YORK

FOR OUR WIVES

1

NEAR COLORADO SPRINGS, Colorado, in the Operations Center hundreds of feet below the earth's surface, the North American Air Defense Command (NORAD) radar staff was in wild confusion. The fifty-six-foot-wide, nineteen-foot-tall electronic map of the world spanning one wall of the subterranean room showed no indication of a launch from any hostile nation. Yet several radar-detected targets were now coming in at various altitudes. From an assortment of directions. At incomprehensible speeds.

Colonel Wayne Phillimore, the officer responsible for the Pacific Air Defense Identification Zone, bounded from his glass-enclosed office in the corner of the immense Operations Center, which—according to some observers—resembled NASA's Launch Control Center in Houston. He ran past the computer banks with a sprint aimed at reminding others of his status—back in '63—as a star of Villanova's 400-meter relay team. He half-crouched beside one of his most experienced radar specialists as if readying himself to spring to the next radar position. There were twenty-seven radar screens in all, each monitoring a specified grid section of the Pacific.

"There it is, sir! There!" The specialist pointed at the computer-enhanced image on the screen.

Phillimore shook his head. "Something wrong . . . nothing flies that fast!"

"I know that, sir, but . . . Jesus, look! It's gone again!"

Phillimore blinked. The target had indeed vanished.

"Goddam equipment's screwed up, sir. Damn target keeps on coming in, then disappearing, then comin' back higher than before. It don't make no sense, sir," said the sergeant in an aggrieved tone.

Colonel Phillimore hoped fervently that it was indeed a case of equipment malfunction. But there was always the possibility that it was something else, something infinitely more serious.

"Sir, the target's headin' for Los Angeles . . . at about Mach five, according to this . . ."

"Mach five?" Colonel Phillimore stared at the flickering radar screen. What the hell kind of an airplane could fly at five times the speed of sound—about 3,500 miles per hour?

"This is crazy, sir. That altitude's comin' in at 107,000 feet!"

"Equipment malfunction," declared Phillimore with more confidence than he felt. "That is the only explanation."

"It was okay a minute ago, sir."

Phillimore bit his lip. Jesus Christ Almighty, a man's career could balance on a moment like this. And, damn it, there was no time to think . . .

He grabbed the hot-line phone.

General Blackman answered at once, his curt voice instantly recognizable. "Yes?"

"Sir, we have an unidentified target."

"And?"

"The computer displays it at one hundred seven thousand feet, sir, with a cruise speed of at least Mach five."

"What?"

"Sir, I said one hundred seven thousand feet . . ."

"And Mach *five?*"

"That's affirmative, sir."

"Course?"

"Presently one-six-five degrees, sir."

"Present position?"

"Sir . . ."

"Well?" General Blackman's voice had the snap of a whiplash.

Phillimore wondered for a moment if his eyes were deceiving him. Thank God Booth and the other radar operators were looking equally mystified. "It's gone, sir."

"*Gone?*"

"Now it's appeared again. But to the north . . ."

"What the hell is going on there?"

"Sir, now it's vanished again . . ."

"Targets only vanish if equipment is malfunctioning," the general declared resolutely, as if proclaiming a tenet of faith.

"Yes, I know, sir. You're right, of course . . . but as far as we can determine, all equipment seems to be working normally. "Jesus" he suddenly blurted.

"What is it now?"

"Sir, the target's reappeared."

Booth threw up his hands in the manner of a man who had done everything humanly possible and was now content to let fate have its way.

"What's happening now?"

Phillimore felt the rivulets of sweat beginning to roll down his neck; his collar felt damp and sticky. "It's gone again, sir."

"Gone, you say." The general sighed. Audibly.

"Yes, sir. And we've got the backup monitors and computers all showing exactly the same thing, sir. Er . . . that is, not showing it. I don't understand this, sir. I've never heard of anything quite like this before . . ."

Booth shouted and pointed at his radar console. "Got the bastard again! There he is!"

"We have the target again," Phillimore reported urgently. "My God, now the damned thing is *east* of Los Angeles. The speed is still being computed at about Mach Five . . . in fact, a little faster . . . with no change in altitude . . ."

"Yes?"

"Gone again, sir."

It was a clear night. From more than twenty miles above, the earth was blackness punctuated by smudges of light, smudges called San Francisco, Las Vegas, Phoenix, Bakersfield, Santa Barbara—and an even larger blur of light away to the right by the name of Los Angeles. The target. Down there, in the area the pilot could scan without moving his head, there were millions of people, loving and killing, hoping and despairing. But from this lofty viewpoint, it seemed so trivial. He smiled; the nearer you got to heaven, the more Godlike your thoughts.

There were also a few tiny specks of light in the west, far

out to sea. Ships, no doubt, still days away from shore, plodding along at only a few knots. His aircraft was traveling at almost one mile every *second*, gobbling up the distance three times faster than a bullet fired from a Smith & Wesson Combat Magnum. The pilot had to rely on his instruments to inform him of this; at such an altitude there was no reference— not even a cloud—by which to judge speed. The aircraft was rock-steady; no tremors, no wind sounds; even the twin jet engines were almost silent, their roar muted to a mere hum that seemed so distant that it might have belonged to another aircraft. But that was impossible for the simple reason that no other airplane in the world could fly this fast or this high.

An amber warning light blinked on the annunciator panel before him: *Nuclear Device Armed*.

Beside the light, two lines on a cathode ray tube angled toward one another. They crossed. The amber light vanished. A green, illuminated message appeared on the panel:

Nuclear Device Released.

2

"WOULD YOU HAVE a seat, Miss Dempsey? Captain Simpson will be right with you." Mechanical smile; weary voice. Pushing forty; starting to puff a little about the chin and cheeks; concerned about it but possessing insufficient will-power to do anything about it. Bored with her job—and probably with life in general.

As Karen Dempsey sat down, she chided herself for that less-than-flattering portrait of the chief pilot's secretary. One day, she told herself, someone's going to read your mind and clobber you one for what you're thinking. But noticing things about people was a habit, just as difficult to give up as smoking.

She looked calm as she picked up an aviation magazine and began to casually flip through its pages. In truth, she was nervous, both eager for her meeting with Captain Simpson and dreading it. A tough one, Simpson, according to one source; a pussycat, according to another. Whom could you believe?

All she hoped was that he would be fair. Not much to ask, but there were still many dinosaurs left on earth, in her experience. But she had a good deal of practice dealing with them. As if to emphasize the point, she raised her chin a defiant inch or two. It was a finely angled but surprisingly determined-looking chin that contrasted charmingly, if unconventionally, with her short, somewhat snub nose and her almond-shaped eyes of blue-green. Her auburn hair was cut short, framing a broad forehead. Perhaps her mouth was a trifle too prominent for Karen Dempsey to be classified as beautiful in the conventional sense; she was a decidedly attractive female, however,

5

and her coolly assured manner (which had caused her to be known among certain of her colleagues at Trans American Airlines as a cold fish) was an assiduously cultivated veneer, a protective device for the first female pilot at TAA.

"Captain Simpson will see you now."

The moment of truth. Karen smiled and nodded her thanks as she passed the plump secretary on her way into the chief pilot's office.

"It's a pleasure," said Simpson. And his smile seemed to add that he meant that remark. He indicated a chair. He was a man approaching sixty with a lean, weathered face and penetrating gray eyes. He shuffled some papers on his desk.

"Here we are—or, rather, here you are. Karen Jane Dempsey, twenty-nine, born in Santa Barbara, educated there and at UCLA in Los Angeles. Father owned a flying school, huh?"

"That's right, Captain."

"Bet you were flying long before you were legally old enough."

"I won't deny that," she said with a certain amount of pride.

Simpson grinned as he studied the file once more. "Joined TAA five years ago, based in Chicago." He looked up. "So now you've hit the big-time. Flight engineer to first officer. Did just fine during your training. You're the only one in captivity at TAA, you know: a lady copilot. You should feel pretty good about it."

"I'm delighted," she said, "though it's a lot more responsibility and I'm not sure how some of the captains will like having me in the right seat."

Simpson nodded thoughtfully. "My guess is, it depends on how well you do your job. Let's see, you arrived here from Chicago yesterday. I guess you're staying at the Holiday Inn until you find a place for yourself?"

She nodded. "I looked at a couple of apartments this morning before I came here."

"Find anything you like?"

"Not yet, Captain."

"There's plenty of time."

She smiled. "I'd like to find something soon. I won't feel I've really arrived until I get settled in my own place."

"I know what you mean," murmured Simpson as his eyes scanned her file. "Any problems while you were a flight engineer?"

"Nothing significant," she said. "I once had a run-in with a mechanic at Omaha when I insisted he replace a nosewheel tire during a snowstorm. I thought he was going to slug me."

"But he changed the tire?"

"Only after complaining to the captain."

"What did the captain say?"

"He said he would go along with whatever the flight engineer recommended."

"Must have made you feel pretty good."

"Yes, it was only my third flight and I wasn't too sure of myself."

"Are you sure of yourself now?"

Again the chin rose fractionally. "Ninety-five percent sure, Captain. I'd be lying to you if I said anything else."

Simpson nodded approvingly. "The training center considers you captain material. If it didn't you wouldn't have been promoted. Do you think you'll become TAA's first female captain?"

"If not, it won't be for lack of trying."

"How do you think the passengers will react to a female captain?"

"I think they'll react just as well as they have to female doctors and lawyers and judges. The important thing is to do the job well."

Abruptly changing the subject, Simpson asked, "Planning on getting married?"

"No, at least not in the immediate future."

"No steady boy friend, a pretty girl like you?"

She shook her head.

Simpson smiled. "Seems to me you just told me to mind my own damn business without saying a word."

"Sorry, I didn't mean to . . ."

"That's all right," Simpson assured her. "Don't blame you. It really isn't any of my business. But let's be honest. You represent a large investment for this airline. We have a lot of confidence in you and we think you're going to do a great job for us. If we didn't you wouldn't be here. But I tend to be a bit old-fashioned and in my experience attractive young women usually get married. And then they have babies. So why should you be an exception?"

Karen took a deep breath. "Would you feel better if I told you I was a lesbian?"

His silvery eyebrows arched. "A what? Listen . . ."

"It's all right," she said. "I'm not. And I very much enjoy the company of men. I was engaged at one time. I'd be less than honest with you, Captain, if I told you that marriage and children are out of the question. But I can tell you that they're not important to me right now. My job is. Aviation is. I've been crazy about flying ever since I can remember. It's always been the most important thing in my life. It's why I worked so hard to get all my advanced ratings, applied to almost every major airline and kept on updating my applications until one took me on and gave me a chance."

"And that was us."

"Look, I'll always be grateful. I know it must have created a lot of problems, hiring me. I've been very happy with TAA. All I can tell you is I'll continue to do the very best job I know how, and I hope I can keep on working for you until I retire. But it may not work out that way for me any more than it might for any other pilot you hire."

"Okay," said Simpson. "You made your point."

Karen sensed that perhaps she had made the point too forcefully. Maybe she had sounded a little too glib, a little too well prepared for the question. The irony was that she meant every word she said.

3

MACLEOD'S TEMPLES THROBBED. It felt as if there were someone inside his head, someone angry and frustrated, beating with clenched fists, desperately trying to pound out the truth. In vain. That son of a bitch cared no more about the truth than did Machiavelli; it was just a device, something to be twisted and distorted to achieve the desired results.

How, Macleod wondered, could anyone named Christmas be such a grade A, dyed-in-the-wool bastard? And how did he have the nerve to continue to wear that phony smile? Why didn't anyone else seem to notice that it was only his tight, narrow lips that smiled, not the rest of his fat, overfed face?

Ralph Christmas was Angie's attorney. You had to hand it to her, the bitch. Once again she had demonstrated her unerring instinct for finding just the right man at just the right time. There she sat, demure as Princess Grace. She should have been an actress. She would have won the ultimate Oscar: Greatest Performance of This or Any Year.

"Were you or were you not aware of your wife's fear of flying, Captain Macleod?"

"Fear? I wouldn't say that . . ."

"What would you say, Captain?" Christmas had a sort of condescending courtesy that made you want to knee him in the crotch.

"She was a little nervous at times."

" 'A little nervous.' That's the way you describe it. Don't you think 'terror-stricken' would be a more accurate description?"

"No . . ." After kneeing him, it would be intensely pleasing to let the smirking bastard have it in one, or preferably both, of his shifty, beady eyes.

"Is it not true, Captain Macleod, that you took your wife flying in your little, private airplane last September the eighteenth?"

"I'd have to consult my log book."

"You may recall the journey when I tell you that your destination was Lake Louise near Banff in Alberta, Canada, some one hundred and twenty miles west of Calgary."

"Okay, I remember the flight. We ran into some bad weather . . ."

"Were you not delayed and did you not have to spend a day waiting for the weather to clear on a small field in British Columbia?"

"Yes. We had to wait for weather . . ."

"And did your wife not plead with you to cancel the trip and go home?"

"Plead with me? No, I wouldn't say that . . ."

"But you insisted on continuing. And didn't you try to make her take the controls of the aircraft while you were flying over treacherous mountains?"

Macleod gripped both the armrests until his knuckles turned white. "I thought she'd enjoy flying more if she knew a little about controlling an airplane."

"You made her take the controls, didn't you? You actually took her hands, didn't you, Captain Macleod, and forcibly placed them on the control wheel . . .?"

"Well, yes. But . . ."

"You knew she was petrified, didn't you, Captain?"

"You see . . ."

"Please answer the question, Captain." Smoothly, politely. But mercilessly. "Was your wife frightened about taking the controls of the aircraft?"

"Yes, I guess you could say that, but . . ."

"Thank you, Captain."

Bit by insidious bit the lawyer constructed his case, fabricating the fiction of an insensitive, heavy-handed, sadistic airline captain subjecting his innocent young wife to unspeakable terrors in the cockpit. It was bullshit, of course. But Christmas did his job brilliantly, convincingly.

Afterwards, even Worthington, Macleod's attorney, had to admit that it had been a first-class performance. "Old Ralph can be quite spectacular when he gets his teeth into a case," he said, stuffing tobacco into that stinking pipe of his. "Of course it's no fun when you're his victim. But that's the essence of jurisprudence, isn't it? You win some, you lose some."

Macleod's cheekbones quivered.

"The bastard crucified me!"

"You might say that," Worthington agreed. "But, you see, I wasn't prepared for all that stuff about you forcing her to fly the plane against her will. Powerful argument. It had a lot of effect. It was a major factor in tipping the case their way, in my opinion. You should have told me about it. We might have come out a lot better if I'd been better prepared."

"How the hell could I prepare you? It never crossed my mind. I didn't force her to do a damned thing!"

"But you attempted to persuade her, didn't you?"

"Persuade her? Yes, but only because . . ."

"I'm sure you had the very best of intentions," Worthington murmured, alternately puffing and examining the bowl of his pipe the way a scientist might examine a potentially dangerous combination of ingredients in a test tube. "Unfortunately, intentions are difficult to prove."

Macleod heard his teeth grind. Which attorney did he detest the most? "Are we going to appeal?"

"We could," Worthington purred. "But I'm not at all sure I'd recommend it. Nothing really substantial to base it on, if you know what I mean. Shame we got Judge Greene, of course. Pure misfortune. He has a reputation for coming down mercilessly on husbands. I remember a case back in 'seventy-eight . . ."

"I don't give a damn about the case in 'seventy-eight! I care about this case! A goddam crime is being committed! A man is being ruined. *Me!* And for no reason. Mental *cruelty*, for God's sake! I've never been mentally cruel, or physically cruel, for that matter, to anyone in my life . . .!"

He had too many martinis for lunch. They invariably disagreed with him. You're a stupid bastard for drinking like this, he told himself. Just as you were out of your mind for marrying Angie. Damn her. He would be doing mankind a favor if he killed her. She was a predator. Warm, lovely, appealing as hell—with transistorized veins and a heart like an IBM computer.

She did one hell of a number on you, he told himself. She flattered you. And you fell for it.

"Watch out for women who flatter you," his father had once advised him. "The average man possesses no known defense against it."

Wise words. But unheeded. He fell for it all the way, every morsel of adoration. He had just made it to first officer when he met Angie. He was one of the youngest copilots in Trans American history. The three gold stripes looked magnificent on each of his sleeves. He looked magnificent in his uniform; she looked magnificent on his arm. Prince Charles and Lady Diana. She knew how to gaze up at a man, eyes liquid with admiration; she could make him feel as if he were something carved on the side of Mount Rushmore.

What had gone wrong? Even now he wasn't sure. No doubt some $100-an-hour psychiatrist could explain the whole thing, neatly categorizing every action, every incident. But to hell with having a shrink prodding his libido; to hell with everyone and everything. No wonder men used to run away and join the French Foreign Legion.

He felt depressed and empty. And abysmally ignorant. Why couldn't he understand life the way his father did? The old man had no college education, no fancy rank or uniform. He had left school at fifteen, back in Dundee, Scotland, just another working-class boy without privilege or promise. One of a family of nine, occupying a damp little four-room house the size of the average American garage. No one on the street owned a car, or even an inside toilet. He had emigrated to the United States just in time for the Depression; there had been years of unemployment, years of waiting and hoping, barely surviving; then years of working at a lathe to buy his son a better life than he had endured. The old man had had no advantages; no one had ever given him anything; he had been obliged to spend most of his life at dreary, repetitive labor. Yet he was basically a happy man, respected by everyone for his good humor, his wit and his innate decency. He was argumentative and opinionated—and usually right.

Macleod had inherited his father's raw-boned features, his bright blue eyes, his aggressive jaw. Tall and lean, he looked younger than his thirty-nine years, although a dusting of gray was visible in his curly, light brown hair.

He returned to his apartment, grimacing as he opened the front door. Stacks of unopened cartons reached almost from floor to ceiling, making the room look like a warehouse. He surveyed the place. Something had to be done to make it habitable. Pictures. He needed pictures. But did he have any? Or did *she* get them all? He couldn't remember. He shrugged. Why worry about pictures when financial disaster stared him in the face. From now on, enormous sums were to be sliced off his income, to go to her, to finance her parasitic existence. And what of the pathetic balance? Would it be enough to provide him with the essentials? With food, rent, transportation and clothing?

And Worthington's fee?

Why not sue the bastard for professional incompetence? If pilots could be ruined for pilot error, why shouldn't attorneys be destroyed for legal error?

The Cessna 182 would have to go. Or did she already own it? He couldn't remember, but he consoled himself for a few moments, picturing a takeoff in the single-engine Cessna, flying low over the city, buzzing houses and office buildings, waving at outraged policemen and federal aviation officials . . . spotting Angie driving along in *his* white Mercedes 450SL convertible. Target in sight! Wheel forward, diving like an avenging eagle, lining up the car through the whirling propeller, adjusting for the crosswind—a touch of rudder; the wings angled nicely; closer, closer, a glimpse of her pretty, terrified face. Then . . . smash! Direct hit, dead center.

Kamikaze, California style.

The marriage had lasted nine years less a few weeks. Shame the wedding and divorce anniversaries couldn't have been identical. It would have tied things up so neatly.

God, what those nine years had *cost* him!

The phone rang. It was Barney Young. "All over?"

"All over."

"How d'you feel?"

"Fine, Barney, just fine."

"You feel lousy. I know." Barney did know; he'd been through the process twice. Barney was in advertising. "Remember, it's the best thing that ever happened to you. It hurts for a while, but you'll get over it. We all do."

"I'm okay, I told you."

"It'll take a little time. The important thing is to get back into circulation, Mac. Start living again. Listen, there's this girl here at the office. In media. Very classy lady. Recently divorced . . .''

"No, thanks, Barney, not right now."

"Didn't you ever learn that when you fall off a horse, you're supposed to get right back into the saddle again?" Barney laughed lecherously. "Same thing now. Get back in there, swingin'—"

Macleod said he knew exactly what Barney meant.

"I'm serious," Barney said.

"I know. And I appreciate your concern."

"But bug off. Right?"

"Right."

"Don't say I didn't try."

"I won't. I promise."

"Maybe some racquetball?"

"I don't think so. But thanks."

Barney meant well.

The phone rang again. His mother. Was he all right? Eating properly? Getting plenty of rest? Why not visit his mother for a few days?

"I can't right now," he told her. "I'm flying tomorrow. But I'll come and see you soon. Really."

In the inevitable way of women she began to cry. "This is the first divorce in the Macleod family," she sobbed.

"I'll bet it won't be the last."

"That's the trouble," said his mother. "You never did take marriage seriously."

"I take the alimony seriously, very seriously," Macleod told her with conviction.

His father's voice cut in, the Scottish burr as pronounced as on the day he got off the ship. "All right, lad?"

"Sure."

"That's good. It'll turn out fine."

"Right."

"Will we see you soon?"

"Very soon."

"Good. Look, son, you take good care of yourself."

"I'll do that."

After he had hung up, Macleod felt a genuine desire to

pack his bag and take the first plane east, to New Brunswick, New Jersey, and spend some time talking to his father, sharing some homemade haggis and forgetting the appalling events of the past few days.

4

ERIC LOCKHART DETESTED politicians. Devious individuals, all of them, infinitely more interested in furthering their own ambitions than in the welfare of their constituents. They postured and pontificated for the media, diligently, painstakingly creating images to win votes. They all belonged in show business; charisma had come to count for more than integrity; a handsome profile meant more than a good record; personality had become more important than performance. Many of them were on the take. But aerospace manufacturers had to deal with politicians when military contracts were involved. They had no choice.

As Chairman of the Board of Lockhart Aerospace Industries, Eric Lockhart usually left such dealings to vice-presidents and technical marketing experts. But there were times when he had to be personally involved. This was such a time.

He was conscious of their penetrating stares as he settled himself at the table; he arranged his papers before him, the neatly typed rows of performance specifications, the charts, the graphs. All the information was at hand. The task was to convey it to them; to convince them; to make them *understand*.

The chairman of the Senate Armed Services Committee introduced him in predictably patronizing terms. "Like his father before him, Eric Lockhart has dedicated his life to producing the finest military and commercial aircraft in the world. He is one of those men who has succeeded in becoming a legend in his own time. As the leader of this giant corporation, he has an extraordinary record of accomplishment. We greatly appreciate his being here today and it is with great pleasure that I introduce Mr. Eric Lockhart."

16

Lockhart acknowledged the remarks, letting his gaze survey the curved row of faces. Familiar faces, most of them. He had a vociferous supporter in Senator David Walsh, sitting to the left of the chairman. They were not only close friends, but allies in a battle to rearm America. But the others? Some were dedicated opponents, others simply unknown quantities.

The job was to persuade this Senate committee to support the Lockhart project, certainly no mean chore. Attitudes were indeed changing. But for Eric Lockhart, an entire political philosophy had to be exorcised like an evil spirit that had possessed America for decades.

Deep-rooted prejudices against the military still existed. A few more Trident submarines and a hundred B-1 bombers did not constitute the national commitment to strength that Eric Lockhart espoused. For him, the issue was military superiority, not parity, with the Soviet Union. What some referred to as the rearming of America was totally inadequate. He felt that this was only a stopgap measure to provide minimal security in the near future. Lockhart's vision, however, transcended the nineties and extended into the next century. But the reality of the situation was that several of these interrogators disagreed with his position. They had virtually slandered the name Lockhart in their speeches because it had become fashionable to criticize military preparedness, a doctrine that had roots in the failure of America to achieve victory since World War Two. For many of these pacifists, it was a crime to seek military superiority.

Underplay. That had been the advice of Charlie Anderson.

Lockhart sat up, a stocky, vigorous figure. He placed his hands flat on the table before him. His voice possessed the confident tone of one who had been accorded the utmost respect and deference all his life.

"Basically, gentlemen, what I have to tell you about is a new airplane. But it is really much more than a new airplane. It is, in fact, a weapons system, the most advanced, most sophisticated airborne weapons system in the world today. No other nation has anything like it. You are undoubtedly aware that Lockhart Aerospace used this magnificent aircraft to conduct a simulated attack on Los Angeles nineteen days ago. Our military was totally incapable of defending against this attack, to take any sort of effective action. Had the attack been genuine, we could have obliterated southern California. The important thing to understand, gentlemen, is that this is not merely another evolutionary advance of military aviation; it is a revolutionary advance. This aircraft, the XB-3A, represents the kind of quantum leap that was taken when the jet airplane was introduced. But this, gentlemen, is a singular breakthrough that *only the United States possesses*."

Pause, he reminded himself. Let them absorb these crucial facts for a moment or two. He cleared his throat. "Simply put, gentlemen, there is no defense against the XB-3A and will not be in the foreseeable future. I realize that this is a far-reaching statement. But allow me to clarify. In the XB-3A— we've named it the 'Devastator'—the United States has an aerial weapons system that is overwhelmingly faster than anything else in the air, with greater range and more devastating firepower. It is the only aircraft configured for advanced particle-beam weaponry, the ultimate in military technology. It must be described as awesome. But of particular interest, gentlemen, is the electronic countermeasures we have developed for this weapons platform. We have on-board equipment capable of neutralizing every radar defense system in the world and rendering them completely impotent."

Again, a pause. Let them absorb *that* revelation. "We demonstrated system effectiveness when we flew the Devastator against the best defenses of the North American Air Defense Command. We were able to confuse these radar facilities completely, by taking their transmissions and *re*transmitting them. At the pilot's discretion, the Devastator became completely invisible to electronic detection. The net effect was utter confusion on the ground. NORAD knew they had a target, but they had no idea where or at what altitude. They couldn't launch interceptors from George Air Force Base because they had no idea where to send them; no doubt they thought their equipment was malfunctioning. Now, while some of you may criticize us for taking such a dramatic measure, I feel it was worthwhile to demonstrate just what a superior weapon our country now posseses. We know the Soviets are exploring similar areas of technology, but for once, we are far ahead of them; time is on our side. There is absolutely no doubt that if the United States Air Force were equipped with squadrons of Devastators, America's safety and the security of the entire free world would be preserved for the foreseeable future.''

He sat down. The room was electrifyingly silent.

''Excellent,'' whispered Anderson, the corporate legal counsel who had accompanied Lockhart from Seattle. ''Just right, Eric.''

Lockhart shrugged, studying the row of faces that constituted the committee. These were the men who wielded the power. They were pompous and vain, too, and probably saved pictures of themselves from newspapers and magazines, or stacked videotapes of their television appearances on shelves like library books. The question was, would they be motivated solely by the winds of political expediency or would they truly comprehend that with their votes, they controlled the destiny of the country?

Senator Joseph Pynes shuffled his papers and cleared his throat. He was a midwesterner and liked to create the impression that he had reluctantly exchanged jeans and checkered shirt for a pin-stripe suit and silk tie. Pynes had made a fine art of looking slightly uncomfortable in a collar; the act won him votes during every election. The senator had a phony, down-home quality to his phrasing that irritated Lockhart. He liked people to think of him as the simple fellow who can't be dazzled by big-city glitter, who sees things as they really are, and who pulls no punches when he sees something wrong, something in need of fixin'. Pure corn.

''No true patriot could ever deny the tremendous contribution made by two generations of Lockharts. Perhaps more than any other family they have helped to establish America's supremacy in the air.'' Pynes nodded, stroking his long chin in his practiced manner. ''I can remembered how comforting the sight of those Lockhart airplanes was when we were pinned down on Utah Beach on Six June, Nineteen Forty-Four. I can tell you I thanked God they didn't wear the Iron Cross.'' He waited for the rumble of approval. Pynes was a skilled orator. ''But,'' he said, ''I've got to say this, Mr. Lockhart: we've come to a time in our history when we simply can't always afford to keep on buying bigger and faster and more expensive military hardware.'' Now came the regretful shaking of the gray mane. ''We've got to be realistic. There aren't any magic solutions to the arms race. If we produce a bigger and better warplane, it's dollars to dough-nuts the Russians are going to bring out something even bigger and even better a few months later. Then we'll have to make ours better. If this airplane is as good as Mr. Lockhart says it is—and I've certainly got no reason to doubt his word—and if we go ahead and start production and spend God only knows how many billions of dollars equipping our air force with this new airplane, then, gentlemen, what we'll be doing is accelerating the arms race. An arms race that'll make the others look like a little friendly game at the bowling alley. It'll be an arms race that will be all but uncontrollable. Besides,'' he added with that down-home smile of sweet reason, ''let's face it, those tens of billions of dollars could and *should* be spent building a better, safer, saner society right here in these United States. We've got problems enough at home; we don't need to create more problems internation-ally . . .''

Senator Walsh cut in. A ruggedly attractive man who projected an image of authority, Walsh, like Pynes, had presidential ambitions. It was generally acknowledged that he would be the Republican standard bearer in the next election. He said, caustically, ''A lot of politicians said the same sort of thing in the thirties, Senator. And we wound up with World War Two.''

Pynes shook his head. He did it well, smoothly, effectively, like a dancer who has performed the same routine a thousand times and has it down to perfection. ''It's a matter of degree,'' he said, neatly managing to imply that David Walsh lacked the insight to perceive this. ''Have I ever suggested—even *intimated*—that we should cut back on the necessary defenses for our nation? Of course not. But what I am saying is that there must be a limit. We have to get our priorities in order. Urban problems. Unemployment. Inflation. Let's not get fur-ther into debt to give our air force even more glamorous toys to play with . . .''

''Toys?'' snapped Walsh.

''A figure of speech,'' smiled Pynes.

''This is far too important a matter to be the subject of frivolous figures of speech. We're considering a weapons system that can put the United States far ahead of any poten-tial adversary. We may very well be determining the future of our children and their children. It is self-evident that we need this weapon, gentlemen, because it is our duty to do everything in our power to ensure America's security.''

"But not to go broke in the process.''

They represented the two extremes: Walsh the Hawk, Pynes the Dove. The cartoonists had had their fun with both of them, exaggerating Walsh's somewhat boyish appearance, illustrating Pynes to look like something out of Li'l Abner. In between were the others, the fence-sitters, the senators who represented farming states, the senators who owed their careers to Lockhart's competitors. Some feared that an enormous technological advance in American weaponry would upset the delicate balance of world power. Others asked how many jobs the production of the airplane represented. Still others suggested that Lockhart was overselling the capabilities of his product. . . .

"They're idiots," Lockhart snapped as he flung his briefcase on the table of the hotel suite. "The obvious stares them in the face and they can't see it.''

Charles Anderson took off his glasses and cleaned the lenses in his meticulous, painstaking way. "The day was by no means lost, Eric. There was a good deal of support from some key senators.''

"But they wondered if it would be politically wise to agree with me too openly. That hillbilly, Pynes, is a complete moron.''

"I don't think they take him too seriously, Eric.''

Lockhart shrugged. "What a ludicrous world we live in. We wonder and worry about that incompetent committee when we have a weapon the country needs desperately. That's all that really matters.''

Anderson said, "The members of the committee have all the technical specifications of the XB-3A; they'll be examining the whole question in much more detail over the next few days.'' He hesitated, then said, "Can I order anything for you, Eric? Something to drink?''

Lockhart shook his head. He stood by a window overlooking the city; the White House could be seen between the freshly blooming cherry blossoms. Washington always seemed so fresh and innocent at this time of year.

Anderson withdrew. It was one thing that had to be said for Anderson; he usually knew when he wasn't wanted.

Lockhart closed his eyes. He felt weary, drained. Presenting your case—no matter how vital—to a roomful of incompetent senators was infinitely more wearing than going to the dentist for root canal work. The trouble was, the whole business of dealing with politicians was so frustrating; it left you with nothing but uncertainty. Should you have pounded the table? Should you have inundated them with charts and tables, motion pictures and slides, the whole paraphernalia of audiovisual wizardry without which most executives seemed to be incapable of explaining where the men's room is located? Lockhart had chosen to state his case simply, straightforwardly, but perhaps the sheer enormity of the subject demanded better packaging. Perhaps politicians can't appreciate the true significance of a subject unless it is wrapped in slides and rear-projection dissolves. . . .

The sense of impending failure was like a lead weight deep in his gut. He had seen it in the senators' eyes. They would turn down the XB-3A. The depressing fact was that the doctrine of military superiority was still somehow unpopular, almost unAmerican. Americans by the millions persisted in believing that if the United States sought peace, the Soviets would do the same. It was, he told himself, like posting a sign in your window saying that the front door is unlocked and if you don't burgle my house I won't burgle yours. Where did history teach that such a policy ever resulted in anything but defeat? Mankind always exploits weakness in others. It is the nature of the beast.

Had he failed more than Lockhart Aerospace Industries? Had he failed America itself? The truth was, America could be destroyed because of weakness. It could be saved by the Devastator. He had an awesome responsibility.

But he had to wait for the official verdict of the committee. Damn them.

The telephone rang. It was Mike, bright, youthful, enthusiastic as ever. "How did it go, Dad?"

"They listened politely. They thanked me for coming. Only our friend, Senator Walsh, was one hundred percent behind us."

"That was all?"

"That was all."

"They didn't turn it *down?*" Unspeakable eventuality.

"No. They're studying the specs."

"You don't sound optimistic."

"I haven't had dinner yet. I never feel optimistic before dinner. How are things back on the coast?"

"Okay. No problems."

"Your mother?"

"She's . . . so-so."

"She's at home?"

"I just called her."

"You talked with her?"

"Yes."

"Was she sober?"

"More or less. When are you coming home?"

"Tomorrow morning. I'll be landing shortly before noon. How about meeting me for lunch?"

"I'd like that, Dad. Thanks."

They agreed to meet at one o'clock in the lobby of the Seattle Athletic Club. Lockhart smiled as he hung up the phone. Thank God for a son like Mike. Thirty-one years old, a master's degree in aeronautical engineering from CalTech, one of the sharpest experimental test pilots in the country, good-looking enough to rival Robert Redford, yet levelheaded and deeply interested in the company. A man was lucky to have such a son, even luckier when that son was a friend, a colleague.

Lockhart ordered a Caesar salad from room service. He had watched his diet very closely since his mid-twenties, when he witnessed the passing of the company's chief designer. A brilliant man, yet a fool. He had diligently eaten, drunk and smoked himself to death. Here was a man who had so much to live for, so much to contribute. But he died at forty-two, a victim of his own insatiable appetites. Increasingly it seemed to Lockhart that the man had come to personify Americans as a whole: people blessed with an abundance of everything, yet becoming weak and sick because of that abundance. Mentally, physically, morally, the whole structure of American society seemed to be disintegrating. Self-indulgence, self-worship, self, self, self . . . and it led inevitably to self-destruction. Lockhart saw it happening everywhere; the greatest country in the history of mankind, *his* country, his fellow citizens committing suicide like the devotees of some crackpot religious cult. . . .

Eric Lockhart was fifty-eight. In excellent physical condition. He moved like a man at least ten years his junior. He exercised daily: fifty push-ups, three miles of jogging, a dozen laps in the pool. He thought of his body as a highly complicated piece of machinery that required the correct fuel, just the right period of rest balanced by exactly the necessary amount of movement in order to function with maximum efficiency.

He was an intense human being. That intensity was etched in his face, in the sharp, almost geometrically precise lines around his eyes and mouth. He was an individualist who demanded much of himself and his associates, a man possessing phenomenal ability and vitality, yet little humor or tolerance. His world was a place of black and white, right and wrong; there was no room for indecision or uncertainty, waste or inefficiency. A difficult man, a forbidding man, feared by many of his colleagues and competitors, but respected.

The XB-3A Devastator was his supreme achievement. He had inspired it, had personally overseen every aspect of its development, chaired countless meetings, considered all proposals, and constantly driven his designers and production experts to their limits. But what was going to happen to his creation? The questions seared him within like an ulcer.

5

THE IMPORTANT THING was not to get mad. You were being paid to do a job. All that mattered was doing it correctly—professionalism personified. But they could really get to you, those goddamn male chauvinists and their superiority complexes.

Karen Dempsey was in the right-hand cockpit seat of an intercontinental Boeing 707-320BAH belonging to Trans American Airlines. Her focus shifted from the instrument panel to the long ribbon of runway speeding before her.

The airspeed indicator read 140 . . . 142 . . .

Rotation speed.

"Vee-R," she announced, the phrase confirming to the captain that the airplane was now traveling fast enough to take to the air.

He was already easing back on the control column, bringing the nosewheel off the ground, exposing the broad underside of the wings to the speeding air. For a moment the 707 hurtled along, nose high, a creature still bound to earth but seeming to sniff eagerly at the sky.

Then the rumble of the main wheels ceased.

Karen glanced to one side; the runway dropped smoothly away as the big jet thrust itself into the air at a seventeen-degree angle, propelled by the herculean power of the four JT3C-7 engines that swayed in streamlined pods beneath the gracefully swept-back wings.

"Gear up," the captain commanded.

Her hand was already reaching for the lever. She pulled it toward her and then raised it. This brought three thousand pounds of hydraulic pressure into action, hauling the multi-wheeled landing gear into the three wells in the fuselage and wings.

"Flaps up," he called.

She moved the handle forward and felt the aircraft respond, shifting posture slightly as the broad trailing-edge flaps retracted neatly into the wing. The outside air suddenly became a blur of white as the jetliner sped blindly into the thick cloud 1,300 feet above Seattle.

This captain was a natural aviator, you had to admit that. Many pilots did nothing more than operate the controls correctly. They did a competent job. But a few had a way with them, a certain style that set them apart; to such pilots the controls were more than mechanical devices—they were extensions of their own limbs. Her father had been such a pilot: a natural, a man who couldn't be imagined living in an age before flight.

The captain glanced at her, his expression as frosty as ever, calling for the after-takeoff checklist. Did he hate all copilots? Or just all female copilots? Damn him, he made no effort to conceal his resentment. She was about as welcome on this flight deck as a leper. No doubt if it were up to Captain Frank J. Macleod she would have been banned from the cockpit of his airplane. But, fortunately, Superman Macleod had no choice in the matter. The company said that Karen J. Dempsey was capable of performing the duties of first officer on a Boeing 707, therefore he had to accept her as a member of his crew whether he liked it or not. Clearly he hadn't liked it when they had met in the operations office, and he liked it even less when they had boarded the aircraft and taken their seats. A deep-freeze condition had set in. And intensified. Was he at this moment hoping that she might do something, something terribly, unforgivably wrong? She knew his kind. Nothing would give him greater pleasure than having an excuse to go to the chief pilot and tell him about that silly bitch, Dempsey, who had the nerve to call herself a first officer, who should have stayed on the ground, in the kitchen and in the bedroom where all females belonged. . . .

The only way to handle the Macleods of this world was to be impervious to their hostility, to act as if it didn't exist.

And to be efficient as hell.

She half-turned toward Marriott, the flight engineer, sitting at his panel immediately behind the first officer's seat, and responded to his reading of the checklist.

"Rudder pump?"

"Off," she replied.

"Gear lever?"

"Off."

"Seat belt—no smoking sign?"

"Checked."

"Logo light?"

"Off."

"Landing lights?"

"Off."

"Ignition?"

"Off."

She turned to Macleod. "After-takeoff checklist complete, Captain."

The Incredible Hulk nodded and grunted an acknowledgement, cold eyes fixed on the instrument panel, his left hand moving the control wheel ever so slightly to maintain the desired heading and climb speed.

Karen pressed the transmit button on her microphone. "Departure Control, this is Trans American Eight-Two-Two out of seven for two-four-zero," she reported, informing the controller that the Boeing was climbing, passing through an altitude of 7,000 feet on the way to 24,000 feet, as decreed by the most recent clearance.

At least the controller seemed pleased that a woman's voice was emanating from TAA 822. His response to her was noticeably more animated, less matter-of-fact than his conversation with the male pilot on Western's Flight 640 a moment ago.

"Roger, Trans Am Eight-Two-Two, contact Seattle Center on one-two-eight-point-two. And have a nice flight."

"Roger, Eight-Two-Two changing over. So long."

The airspeed indicator read 250 knots. On the button. Not 245 or 255, but 250, the maximum legal airspeed when below 10,000 feet. A pro, this bristly bastard Macleod. Just her luck to get him for her first flight as an official first officer. During the last week she had taken two familiarization flights, like all new copilots, doing little more than observing and trying not to get in the way. Did they all want her to fail, all the male pilots? Did they regard her as an intruder in their cozy little world, their international private club with its esoteric jargon and arcane procedures? Did they feel threatened by her? Did they see her as an advance guard to be followed by thousands more of her kind, pilots in skirts, pushing and shoving the men out one by one? And if a female first officer was a fearsome prospect, what about Trans American's first woman *captain?* Were they already thinking of *her* in those terms? It was likely, wasn't it? After all, a male pilot who had just made it to copilot might reasonably expect to graduate to the coveted left seat in another ten years or so.

Ten years. My God, she would be thirty-nine. *Captain* Dempsey. Yes, she could make it. It would be worth it, and it was possible. If she didn't screw up. If she didn't goof. The trouble was, captains like Macleod could wreck everything by filing unsatisfactory fitness reports about her: "Just hasn't got what it takes . . ." "Can't handle the job when the going gets rough . . ." "Can't keep up with the airplane . . ." "Not captain material."

To hell with them. She'd show them all.

She had been flying airplanes since she was big enough to peer over the instrument panel of a J-3 Cub. Her father had fastened blocks of wood to the rudder pedals so that her short legs could move the controls. By the time she was thirteen she was a decent pilot; she had fifty-two hours in the Cub; she had even soloed the airplane a few times, which was strictly illegal for someone her age. On her fourteenth birthday, the minimum legal age for soloing a glider, she took off alone in a Schweizer 1-26 sailplane and spent three hours soaring above the desert. At seventeen, she obtained her private pilot's license and a year later was earning a living as a flight instructor. She then became a charter pilot for a local air-taxi operator and was even hired to ferry a few lightplanes to Europe. At twenty-five she was accepted by Trans American; she became a second officer, a flight engineer. She was the lowliest member of the three-man flight crew. Her duties consisted largely of monitoring engine performance, managing the fuel system and tending to air conditioning and pressurizing the 707s and 727s. She wasn't allowed to actually fly the airplane, but the job was an essential step up to the next level, occupant of the right-hand seat on the flight deck.

Next to God.

Karen Dempsey often considered herself extraordinarily fortunate. She was being paid well for doing what she enjoyed most. She simply loved airplanes and the way they looked. She loved their feel and smell, their promise of excitement and travel. The experience of flight never lost its magic for her. There was nothing in the world quite like that moment of lift-off when the airplane comes alive in your hands, when it becomes a creature of the air, a tiny, impudent world of its own, darting into an invisible ocean, eager to take on the vastness of space . . .

"Cruise power."

A grunted command from the left seat. Macleod seemed to possess only one facial expression: hostile.

Five hours later, he relented and allowed her to shoot the Canarsie approach and land the 707 at New York's John F. Kennedy Airport. She wanted it to be a greaser, main wheels kissing the concrete, tire rubber squealing softly, obsequiously. But fate wasn't that kind. The aircraft dropped the last foot or so, arriving on runway 13-left with a thump and a rattle. Nothing dangerous, nothing even wrong. It happened sometimes, especially when landing in a crosswind. But it would have been infinitely more satisfying if it hadn't happened during that landing with that captain sitting, watching, mentally criticizing and filing.

As Macleod taxied the 707 to the terminal building, she and Marriott read the after-landing checklist like priests intoning their scriptures: brake pressure, radar, transponder, DME, flaps, spoilers, ignition, anti-skid, turbocompressors, air source . . .

Macleod parked the aircraft at the ramp, bringing it to a halt so smoothly she couldn't feel when it came to rest.

No comment from the captain. No praise, no criticism. She might have been some mechanical device on the instrument panel. When they had shut down the engines and secured the cockpit, he simply rose, put on his jacket and cap, grabbed his flight kit and suitcase and stomped off to the exit.

Marriott unfolded himself from his seat and stretched. He was a curly-haired young man in his mid-twenties. "He's really a pretty nice guy when you get to know him."

"I'm sure he is," said Karen.

"Something seems to be bugging him."

I think I know what it is, Karen said to herself.

Marriott pulled his jacket on and adjusted his tie. "Personally I think it's just great having a woman on the flight deck."

She smiled. "Thanks."

"I mean it. You can get pretty damn tired of looking at the backs of balding, gray heads. Besides, it keeps the conversation at a higher level."

What conversation? she wondered. Karen nodded in the direction of Macleod's departure. "Have you flown with him before?"

"Mac? Sure. Lots of times. He's as good as they come."

"Is he always in such a lousy mood?"

"No," Marriott mused. "I've got to say that I've never seen him like this before."

Karen nodded ruefully. *She* was the reason for Macleod's savage mood. Marriott knew it just as well as she did, but he was too considerate to mention it. Macleod resented her; probably hated the sight of her. Was he at this moment calling Simpson, the chief pilot, and telling him to get this dumb broad off his airplane?

Macleod was a male chauvinist dinosaur.

The question was, how many more such creatures lurked in TAA captains' uniforms?

The bottle of Chivas Regal had been drained. The glass lay on its side, smeared and cloudy from excessive handling. Spilled whiskey had spotted the table. Incongruously, a radio was bleating some monotonous, mindless rock song.

Lockhart had found his wife asleep on the patio, sprawled on the chaise longue, another empty glass beside her. Dorothy awoke and shivered. She stared at him with bleary, blinking eyes.

"You're back," she muttered.

"How observant," he commented.

"You're such a shit," she said. "How was Washington? Did you give my regards to the President?"

"I didn't see him this time."

"Did you get laid?"

"What difference does it make to you?"

She shrugged, looked in the glass, then looked around for a bottle.

"I see you've been refreshing yourself," he said.

"Screw you," she said—which was what she always said when she was drunk and could think of no other response. Her eyes had that all too familiar, heavy-lidded look. She had been drinking for the three days he was in Washington, steady, mechanical imbibing, sloshing the stuff down until she passed out, then waking up and sloshing down more until she passed out again. And again. It was her standard operating procedure. The curious thing was how she always maintained a certain precarious dignity, never becoming unkempt, never losing her balance when she took a few steps. What's more, she was always able to enunciate clearly during her drinking sessions, which was a pity because the more she drank the nastier she became, bitter at life in general and at Eric Lockhart in particular. A strange, convoluted woman, Dorothy. Prior to this bout she had been on the wagon for two weeks. But it was a less than serene time. The tension had been building day by day. She became more acerbic, more sarcastic, venomously discontented with her existence, her clothes, her husband, her family. . . .

"What do you know about this girl Michael is seeing?"

"Not much," he said.

"Why not much?"

"He's over twenty-one. I don't pry into his private life."

"Don't bullshit me the way you do everyone else."

God, it was loathsome, the way her mouth twisted when she snarled, like some old witch in a children's book. "Sleep it off, Dorothy."

"I have a right to know who he's seeing. I'm his mother."

"I imagine that's a fact he'd rather forget," Lockhart said, as he turned away and leafed through the small pile of mail lying on a silver tray. He gazed at the envelopes without seeing them. Every nerve in his body seemed to be on fire. Damn her. What had he ever done to deserve such a bitch? Once, a lifetime ago, there had been excitement ("SOCIETY BEAUTY TO WED SON OF AVIATION PIONEER"); there had been tenderness and trust. But gradually, insidiously, the metamorphosis had taken place. The absurd thing was that she actually blamed *him* for the disintegration of the marriage, accusing him of caring more for his work than for her.

Still, she clung to him like a parasite. Presumably it afforded her some small pleasure to torment him, knowing that he detested the thought of divorce, with its publicity and inevitable baring of a thousand unpalatable truths, even more than he detested her. She understood him; she knew his phobias. Three years before, he had offered her a tax-free income of one hundred thousand dollars a year plus the house in Palm Beach plus a new car every two years. She could live in comfort for the rest of her life. She could keep the Lockhart name. But no.

"Is he going to marry that slut, Wanda?"

"I have no idea."

"Didn't you talk about her over lunch? You did have lunch with Michael, didn't you?"

"How did you know?"

"I have my ways," she cackled.

"I saw Mike when I got back from Washington. We had lunch at the Athletic Club. But we didn't discuss his sex life. For your information, men seldom discuss their sex lives, particularly over lunch."

"Except when you're boasting, claiming how many times you got laid last week, how the chicks can't resist you . . ."

"Knock it off, Dorothy."

"Where the hell is that woman? I need a drink."

He left her bellowing for more Scotch. He could still hear her when he was on the second floor, closing and locking the door of his study. He turned on the stereo; the Grieg piano concerto was a welcome tranquilizer.

He sat at his desk. To one side was a floor-to-ceiling bookcase, it shelves stacked with technical books on aviation and business, biographies, history, philosophy: the library of a consummate intellectual. The books were like old, trusted friends who never failed him, always waiting for him whenever he needed them. To the other side was a wall covered with photographs, plaques, awards, and documents: memorabilia of Lockhart Aerospace and its predecessors, Lockhart Aeroplane Company and Lockhart Aviation.

Across the room from the Chippendale desk that had once belonged to his father was a picture window framing the

Pacific. At any time of the day or night, the restless water could be heard, thudding on the rocks below. The study was Lockhart's sanctum sanctorum. It was a place where a man could think and be himself, a refuge from a world that seemed to be forever closing in on him.

The telephone rang. It was David Walsh; he was one of only a half dozen people who knew Lockhart's private number. As soon as Walsh spoke, Lockhart knew he had bad news.

"How are you, Eric?"

"The committee turned it down."

"No . . . no, Eric, don't jump to conclusions. No decision has been reached."

"But you're not optimistic, are you?"

Walsh sighed. "I must tell you that our initial discussions haven't been going as positively as I had hoped, but I'm doing my best. I'll call you later."

Lockhart hung up. He gazed at the telephone for a few minutes as if willing it to ring again, this time with better news. But the only sound was the unrelenting movement of the ocean far below. He took a deep breath and sat back; he found himself studying a framed charcoal sketch of the XB-3A, a gift from one of the staff draftsmen.

The artist had caught the essence of the aircraft remarkably well.

The Devastator was an airplane of superlative lines and unmatched beauty. And apparently no future.

He picked up the phone and dialed. She answered at once.

6

IT STARTED OUT so well. Macleod encountered her in the lobby of the New York Sheraton Hotel. At an acute angle. She had just lost a heel, and swayed, almost fell. He caught her by the arm. She turned, smiled. Pretty eyes, big and blue. Tiny nose. Dark hair falling charmingly across her forehead.

"Ruddy heel!" She had an English accent, crisp and clear. She grinned. "Thanks awfully. I nearly fell over."

"So I noticed," Macleod responded. "Can I help you put that back on?"

She shook her head, causing her hair to fall back into place. "Very good of you. But I'll just pop upstairs and put on another pair." She stood up. "I think I've got my key somewhere." She searched in her purse with the frowning concentration of a scientist on the trail of a rare element. "Isn't that ridiculous? I know I had it . . ."

"Perhaps you left it at the desk?"

She snapped her fingers. "Of course, that's it! What a chump."

"Are you staying here long?" He wanted to add "and alone?"

"A few days. Back to London on Friday. You're an airline pilot, aren't you?"

He nodded. No question about that. The dark blue jacket, the distinctive cap, the four gold stripes on each sleeve were quite an asset during chance encounters with the opposite sex. The uniform seemed to have an invisible sign that read: THIS IS A SOLID, RELIABLE INDIVIDUAL, TO BE TRUSTED ABSOLUTELY AT ALL TIMES.

He told her he flew for Trans American Airlines.

She nodded. "Good line."

"So is British Airways," he contributed.

"Ta," she said with a refreshingly frank smile. No coyness, no shyness with this one.

"Are you in New York on business?"

Another brisk nod. "I work for an import-export firm. Frightfully boring but it pays the rent. Do you live in New York?"

"Seattle," Macleod told her. "Flying back tomorrow afternoon."

"How nice," she said.

"If you have no plans for this evening, would you care to join me for dinner?" Just like that. Slick, smooth. A breeze.

And she said yes, she would like to very much indeed. She had to pop down to see someone on 42nd Street, but she'd be back in a jiff, which, translated, meant an hour.

He took her to a place he knew on Eighth Avenue where they served superlative lasagna, where the tablecloths were red-and-white check and the waiters were genuine Italians. He discovered that she was twenty-eight, was born in a place called Bury St. Edmunds, but now lived in a "flat" in South Kensington (". . . not far from the tube station, if you know the district"). Had been engaged to a budding actor but recently broke it off. Liked New York. Liked Americans, found them friendly and amusing. Fond of mystery stories, but thought English murders more stimulating than American murders. *Adored* Billy Joel and Neil Diamond. *Adored* Christopher Reeve and Michael Caine. *Adored Godfather* but considered *Apocalypse* somewhat self-indulgent. Drove something called a Mini, but relished the thought of one day owning a Jag. Father a bank manager; brother in oil, living near Bahrain. Worried about inflation. Bored by oil. And pollution. And strikes. She had a direct way.

"I like you," she said. "So I'd like to know if you're married. I suppose you are. It's almost inevitable, isn't it?"

He told her about Angie. She shook her head sympathetically. It was, she asserted, jolly unfair.

"I'd love to learn to fly," she said. "Is it difficult?"

"Not really, as long as you have a sense of balance and reasonably good coordination. Next time you come to the

States, stay over for a few extra days and I'll teach you some of the basics."

She thought that was a super idea. "Do you ever fly to England?" she asked.

"Once in a while. Mostly I fly back and forth across the United States. But occasionally I fly a polar trip, Seattle nonstop Stockholm. Nice trip. Spend a couple of days in Sweden and then fly home the same way."

They both agreed that it wasn't *that* far from London to Stockholm.

They further agreed that it was remarkable how total strangers could meet and there could be instant rapport between them. . . .

In the morning she left a note on his dressing table.

SORRY. REALLY.

Cash. Credit cards. Licenses. Rolex watch. Cross pen with which she had written the note. All gone.

"No," said the desk clerk, lip twitching into the suspicion of a smile, "there's no Miss Cranbrook registered here."

"But she said . . ."

What the hell difference did it make what she said?

The cop sounded bored, as if he'd heard the same story several times every night. "How long since you lost your credit cards?"

"I don't know. I woke up . . ."

"Uh huh. So it could have been most of the night, huh?"

"That's right."

"That's too bad. She coulda done a lotta damage in that time . . . and you an airline pilot, huh?"

The implication was that he should have known better. Goddam.

Then there was a call to the local office of the Federal Aviation Administration. Sorry about that, but he lost his pilot's certificate. And no, he couldn't wait for a duplicate to be mailed; he was scheduled to take a flight out of Kennedy this afternoon. Would they please send a telegram detailing the fact that he was certificated to fly 707s and that the wire was authority for him to take the flight. . . .

Then he had to call half a dozen credit card offices. To each one it was necessary to explain that, no, he didn't know the card number and, no, he couldn't look up an old bill because he didn't happen to be calling from home and, yes, he would reconfirm the loss with his local office when he returned to Seattle, advising the representative of his card number.

The assistant manager of the hotel said he was sorry it had happened. But his attitude was cool. No doubt he was saying to himself that men who struck up casual relationships and invited strange women into their rooms—when paying single rates—only got what they deserved.

Macleod was then obliged to borrow fifty dollars from another crew member staying at the hotel. Miss Cranbrook, or whatever her name was, had left him with the princely sum of forty-seven cents. Why hadn't she bothered with the change? Damn her. In every other way she had been so methodical.

Incredibly, he seemed even grouchier than he had been the previous day.

When Karen greeted him with a cheerful "Good afternoon, Captain," she got a grunt for her trouble. She observed him glancing at his wrist, then looking around for a clock on the wall of the operations office. Had the great man reported for a flight without his watch?

He studied the flight plan, breathing heavily, irritably. Then, without a word, he thrust the yellow, computer-spawned form at her. She heard him talking to another captain. Something about a third captain who had run into problems on his semi-annual physical examination. Heart murmurs. Forty-three—hell of an age to be put out to pasture.

She glanced over the flight plan at Macleod. Why was he always in such a rotten mood? Were the responsibilities of being a captain too much for him? Some men—and women—just weren't captain material. The responsibility of command was too much for them; it weighed on them, wore them down. Might Macleod suffer a cardiac arrest during a takeoff or landing? Would she have to take over the controls at an instant's notice? It was possible. Such things happened, just like the understudy suddenly getting the big opportunity to play the star's role. . . .

It would be a feather in her cap. Well done, Miss Dempsey; you saved the day. Trans American Airlines is proud of you—

and thank God we hired you . . . A female knight in shining armor.

She glanced again at Macleod. Still scowling at the world in general. Was he more easygoing years ago when he was a first officer?

A strikingly handsome captain said, "You must be Miss Dempsey. Or should I say *Ms.?* It's not *Mrs.*, is it?"

"No," she said.

"Thank God," he exclaimed with exaggerated relief. He called to Macleod, "Mac, you lucky s.o.b. How come you get the sexy first officers and I have to put up with guys like Bomberg here?" Without waiting for an answer he turned back to Karen. "I'm Harris. Clive Harris. I saw you in the St. Louis ramp office a couple of times. You were a second officer then, weren't you? I read about your promotion in the house organ." He grinned. He had a magnificent grin. And knew it. His wavy black hair was slightly gray at the temples. "That's a hell of an expression, isn't it? *House organ.* How are you enjoying life out on the coast? You're based in Seattle now, aren't you? I'm sure I read that in the, er . . . house organ. Flying back today, are you? Too bad. Lots of things we could do in the Big Apple. How soon will you be back?"

But this time he did pause long enough for her to answer his question. She told him that she had no idea when she'd be back because she was flying on reserve. Could be next week . . . or next year.

"Pity," he said, gazing at her. He had russet eyes and they crinkled neatly when he smiled. "But you've got to let me know when you're coming back."

"Maybe," she said. Every instinct commanded her to beware of this one.

"Maybe?" he said. "That's not much of an answer. Why don't you put it a little differently? Say, 'That's a great idea and I'll be sure to call you as soon as I find out when I'm flying this way again.' "

"I'll think about it," she promised without sincerity. No doubt he was handsome, but what an egotistical bore. He probably thought he could charm the pants off the Mona Lisa.

"Here, let me give you one of my cards," he said, reaching for his wallet. "We do have a lot in common, don't we?"

"We do?"

"Well," he said, flashing that seemingly artificial smile, "if we don't, we'll have to work on it until we do."

His card stated: CAPT. CLIVE HARRIS, TRANS AMERICAN AIRLINES. He had scribbled a telephone number in bright red ink.

"If I'm not there, my answering service will know where to find me."

Macleod materialized, smouldering, brows dark, jaw jutting. "If it isn't interfering too much with your social life, Miss Dempsey, I'd like to get this goddam flight underway."

Captain Harris told him to cool it; Macleod turned on his heels with an angry snort.

Karen attempted to apologize as they made their way out to the aircraft. "I'm sorry, Captain . . . but he talked to me . . . I couldn't just ignore him . . . we're not even friends . . . I really don't know him from Adam. . . ."

Macleod didn't respond; he continued to speed through the building, taking enormous strides, forcing her into a graceless half-run, half-march in an effort to keep up with him. When they reached the aircraft she was short of breath and feeling the dampness of perspiration sticking her shirt to her body.

Damn it, she wouldn't give in. She could be just as tough as he was. Think about the job. About the en-route weather. The hydraulic interconnect check, the Mach trim check, computing takeoff performance, obtaining clearances, turning on the pitot heat, reading the checklist, identifying VOR stations, reviewing emergency procedures . . .

"Watch out for that guy, Harris," advised Marriott during the stopover in Chicago. They were in the employees' cafeteria having coffee. "Hell of a hustler, they say. Girls at every layover, that kind of thing."

She felt the irritation rising within her. "I'm perfectly capable of taking care of myself," she told Marriott.

The flight engineer grinned. "Don't be so sure. He's *legendary*."

She pointed a lean finger at him. "Guys like you think that all you need is a good line, an expensive dinner, a few drinks, and it's Sacksville. This may come as a shock to you, but women can say *no!*"

Marriott reddened. "Okay," he said. "Sorry about that; just trying to help." He got to his feet. "I guess you can find your own way back to the airplane."

Karen found herself staring intently into her cup, examining the drops of coffee still clinging to the side, studying the small chip on the edge of the saucer. She had the uncomfortable feeling that everyone in the cafeteria was staring at her, silently castigating her for the way she had treated a pleasant and obviously well-meaning young man who had her best interests at heart.

The Chicago-Seattle leg was notable for the total absence of friendly conversation among members of the flight crew.

Karen intended to apologize to Marriott. And to explain to Macleod. But the opportunity slipped by. After landing, the crew members went their separate ways. Impatient to get away from her? She couldn't blame them.

7

LOCKHART AEROSPACE INDUSTRIES occupied almost two thousand acres about forty miles north of Seattle, Washington, only a few miles east of Puget Sound. The main office building had been constructed on the spot where Willard Lockhart had built his first aircraft, in a barn on an uncle's farm. The year had been 1911. Despite several crashes, Willard Lockhart succeeded in developing a successful design, a fabric-covered, two-place biplane trainer. When the United States entered World War I, he found himself in business. The government needed airplanes. Lots of them. Fast. Lockhart purchased his uncle's property and set up shop. He built trainers. Then he designed a fighter (or "scout" as it was then called). It was a speedy, agile little machine, and would undoubtedly have done well on the Western Front. But the war ended before the Lockhart LS-1 had progressed beyond the prototype stage. Within weeks of the armistice, lucrative military contracts for airplanes were canceled. Willard Lockhart shut down the hastily erected production sheds and assembly buildings; he paid off the just as hastily assembled workforce, thanking every man and woman for his or her contribution to the winning of the war. The Lockhart Aeroplane Company's brief season as a "cornerstone" of American industry had ended. The company's sole customer was no longer in the market for airplanes.

Willard Lockhart immediately set out to develop the LS-1 into a sportplane. It was handsome, but no one wanted to buy it. He developed a two-place version, then a three-place model with a sliding canopy over the rear cockpit. No one wanted to buy those either. Where was all the enthusiasm for aviation that the papers and magazines had so eagerly predicted? Where were all the Americans who were going to be flying about in their own private planes as soon as the war was over? The truth soon became apparent: the minuscule number of Americans who wanted to fly could pick up a government-surplus Jenny or Standard for a few hundred dollars, spare engine included. There simply was no market for expensive new airplanes.

For a few precarious years the fledgling company survived by turning out parts for automobiles and iceboxes. A movie company bought the prototype LS-1, painted it black, put Iron Crosses on its wings and fuselage, and used it in an aerial epic as the mount of the redoubtable Baron von Schmüller, the Black Baron. While impersonating an Albatross, the LS-1 collided head-on with a Thomas-Morse Scout that was impersonating a Sopwith Camel. Both aircraft vanished in a ball of flame. But the fiery footage was clipped from the final print of the film; the producer considered it too gory for family entertainment.

The LC-4 was Lockhart's first commercial success, a three-engine, high-wing monoplane, incorporating a revolutionary new idea: retractable landing gear. Many a film star and sports hero had his or her picture taken on the steps of an LC-4; soon it became fashionable to travel by air. The LC-4 carried a dozen passengers. In moderate comfort (but appalling din) it could transport them to their destination at close to one hundred and fifty miles per hour. Trans American Airlines purchased ten of the new airliners; the first was delivered the day of the stock market crash of 1929. Two years later, the U.S. Navy decided to buy Lockhart's sleek new monoplane as its primary carrier-based fighter. Then the French bought the type. An experimental Lockhart racing plane won the Bendix Trophy during the Cleveland Air Races; half a dozen long-distance flyers made record-setting flights in Lockhart planes. As the world's political situation deteriorated, the recently restructured Lockhart Aviation Corporation experienced increasing prosperity.

Eric Lockhart grew up with airplanes; one of his earliest recollections was crouching in an open cockpit battered by an icy wind, his mother clutching him, her eyes wide with terror. Something was wrong; he recognized that, but since he couldn't see over the side of the cockpit he couldn't tell what was happening. But he knew everything would be all right; his father was at the controls. Then came a sudden, splintering crash as the plane hit the ground. The world became a frightening place of bumps and bangs. Then silence. His father's assuring face looked in. Was everyone okay? Afterwards the story was related a thousand times: "There was little Eric, calm as could be, doing his best to console his mother who had burst into tears!"

He could fly a lightplane before he could drive a car. While a senior in high school, he began flying for the family firm; he put in time with the company even after he started college, working on a degree in aeronautical engineering. Nineteen when the Japanese attacked Pearl Harbor, he volunteered for the Army Air Corps. But the authorities told him to continue working with his father's company; they said he would contribute far more to the war effort by testing production aircraft than by becoming another combat flier. In 1942 he narrowly escaped death when the tail of a twin-engined night fighter prototype began to disintegrate during a drive test. He successfully wrestled the unwieldy machine to the ground, but crashed on landing and was dragged unconscious from the wreckage.

A year later he again came close to death during an inflight fire, the result of slipshod assembly work in the factory—an all too frequent problem in those days when there was unrelenting pressure to increase production. The fighter's engine burst into flames moments after takeoff. Too low to bail out, Lockhart had no choice but to stay with the blazing machine and bring it in for a crash landing. By the time he touched down, his flight suit was on fire; he could smell his own flesh burning. He spent six weeks in the hospital; nearly forty years later the scars on his neck and shoulders still reminded him of his brush with fate. And he still had nightmares about being trapped in burning aircraft, of smelling himself on fire, of desperately trying to open a cockpit canopy that wouldn't budge. . . .

His mother once declared that he had changed after that crash; he had become more introspective, quicker to argue and to take offense. It was nonsense, of course. Women, particularly mothers, were forever seeking significant moments in life to rationalize personality changes; they couldn't accept that people simply do change.

Lockhart Aviation was one of the first to experiment with commercial jet aircraft. The attractive LC-11 might have been the world's first jet airliner. But it was born too soon. The world's airlines weren't ready; their DC-7's and 1649A Constellations were still new—besides, no one was sure that the average passenger would ever accept jet travel; there was no telling what the speed, altitude and acceleration might do to those inside.

In 1946, Eric Lockhart married Dorothy Mitchell, the daughter of a congressman, the granddaughter of a general in the United States Army. It was the wedding of the year. Society columnists reported and photographed the event. The young couple honeymooned in Hawaii, cruising in Willard Lockhart's yacht, *Wings*.

Five years later Michael was born. Then, after two years, came Gail. But she died at the age of four months, a victim of crib death. Eric Lockhart had thought his wife was going to die of grief. She seemed to shrink physically. She wouldn't eat, couldn't sleep. Dorothy Lockhart blamed herself for her daughter's death, no matter how many doctors and psychiatrists assured her that it could not have been avoided, one of those things that happened no matter how careful a mother was. . . .

She began to drink two, three and four martinis before dinner . . . and then before lunch.

In 1963, Willard Lockhart died of a heart attack on the sixteenth hole at the Sea Island Golf and Country Club in Georgia, and Eric became president of the company. He was forty-one years old. Within five years Lockhart Aviation had become Lockhart Aerospace Industries. There were new divisions: Electronics, Microprocessors, Helicopters.

Time magazine did a cover story about Eric Lockhart, describing him as "the coolly efficient head of America's most diversified, most prosperous aerospace corporation." But although his company was successful, Lockhart was becoming increasingly disturbed about America's security. Early in the late sixties he began to speak out publicly against America's policy of rapprochement with the Soviets. The Communists, he said, were the antithesis of everything America stood for. He called for a strong United States—superiority, not parity with the Russians. The liberals accused him of right-wing extremism and warmongering. Soon the hippies and yippies were burning him in effigy as the personification of the greedy capitalist who would plunge the world into war simply to make money for the military-industrial complex.

Hate letters, mostly anonymous, arrived frequently. Comedians made jokes about "The *Lickhard* Aerospace Company" where sales meetings were war conferences, where field representatives were rewarded with cash bonuses proportional to the amount of civil strife they could stir up in various parts of the world, and sales managers produced elaborate charts to demonstrate imaginative, innovative approaches to the business of destroying major urban areas. Such humor faded with the disastrous U.S. retreat from Vietnam. Suddenly it wasn't very funny any more.

It was in the post-Vietnam era that the United States withdrew from its role as world policeman and retreated to the security of its own isolation. But as the Soviet Union filled the international power vacuum, Americans in significant numbers began to tell Eric Lockhart that they endorsed his views. One was Senator David Walsh.

"It's a goddam tragedy," said the senator as he sat in Lockhart's office. Walsh was a well-groomed man in his early fifties, still youthful in appearance but a few pounds overweight, his clothes wrinkled from travel. "I pleaded with them to be nonpartisan. There was nothing more I could do, Eric."

"Any chance of the committee reversing its decision?"

Walsh shrugged. "I'm afraid not. It's conceivable that the full Senate could vote the measure out of committee, but it's not very likely. We just don't have enough votes."

Lockhart studied the silver model of the LC-4 on his desk. It had been presented to his father almost half a century ago, a magnificent example of the silversmith's art, every rib and rivet painstakingly detailed, the tiny propellers and engines perfectly proportioned. The aviation business was simple and straightforward in those days: you made a better airplane than the competition and customers beat a path to your door.

Lockhart could feel anger and frustration creating a curious roar within him. He felt his flesh prickling, sweat forming around his collar.

He took a deep breath. Calm down, he told himself. Get control. More deep breaths.

"The committee believes that we can negotiate with the Russians for arms control."

"Those incompetents have no knowledge of history. Poland, Czechoslovakia, Hungary, Afghanistan. Won't they ever learn?" Another thought struck him. "Or perhaps they don't think the Devastator will do what we claim? We can arrange another demonstration . . ."

Walsh shook his head. "Eric, no one is arguing about the merits of the airplane or its capabilities. It boils down to two factors: a fear of setting off another round in the arms race with the Soviets, and cost."

"Cost? How much is the security of America worth?"

Walsh threw up his hands in frustration. "Eric, I don't know what the hell to do. I don't think anything will change their minds short of war."

"What about the President?"

Walsh sighed. "He's so obsessed with the treaty that . . ."

"Insanity!" Lockhart snapped. Mention of MARTY—the proposed Mutual Arms Reduction Treaty—infuriated him. "The Soviets must be toasting our President in the Kremlin. They want the treaty. And why not? They're so far ahead of us militarily, there's nothing they'd like better than to freeze us into a position of inferiority. They'll never abide by the provisions of the treaty anyway. But we will. It's that kind of policy that led to World War Two; and it could lead to another, one we wouldn't win!"

Walsh nodded. "I couldn't agree more."

"I know a lot of those senators hate my guts. But I don't count and neither do they. They're not important and neither am I. But America *is*. And that's the whole point. This decision is not only a disaster for the United States and its allies, it's also going to destroy our aerospace industry. Those damn pacifists have been whittling away at our military strength for decades. My God, we couldn't even mount an effective military operation to rescue our own citizens when they were kidnapped by a bunch of religious fanatics in the Persian Gulf. We get softer and more vulnerable every day. And our enemies get stronger and bolder. And why shouldn't they? We're living up to their charge that America is only a paper tiger.''

"I promise you, Eric, that the Devastator will be one of the most important issues of my campaign."

Walsh's presidential ambitions had already caused some pundits to consider him the leading contender for the Republican nomination. He had an impeccable, conservative image and that all-important TV charisma. Despite his hawkish stance, he was admired by people of all political persuasions; he had managed not to alienate too many kingmakers during his years in the Senate. He commanded respect—largely, in Lockhart's opinion, because he *looked* as if he should command respect. But like all politicians of Lockhart's acquaintance, Walsh was still more show than substance. Nevertheless, Lockhart knew that Senator Walsh held deep political convictions akin to his own.

When Walsh had gone, Lockhart turned his chair so that he could look out over the ocean, through the fringe of trees that his father had planted in the thirties. They were tall now, standing like sentries. Beyond the trees lay the Pacific, sparkling in the spring sunshine. He never tired of gazing at the sea, studying passing ships through binoculars or telescope, watching the shifting of the waters at the bidding of the weather, the anger and power of waves, the gentle shimmering of moonlight on a motionless surface.

The world beyond those seas was full of jealous men who hated America, who worked tirelessly, hoping, praying one day to bring this great country to her knees. How they would rejoice to see America in collapse, the last bulwark against the Communist revolution. The sickening thing was, those dictators could already see it beginning to happen. This once powerful, resolute land was undergoing a sad transformation. Where was the courage, the initiative, the power that had created this incredible nation?

Why could Americans no longer recognize the dangers that faced them? Were they so consumed by hedonism, so weakened by excess that they were blind to reality? The Communists could sniff out weakness, like foxes around a herd of sheep. Eventually, inevitably, the Soviets would make their move. In Europe. In the Middle East. The Far East. Perhaps on several fronts simultaneously. The contemplation was awesome. Lockhart shook his head, frowning, biting his lower lip, pained by these thoughts. America represents the ultimate achievement of mankind. Its citizens are the most creative, the most productive.

And, it seemed, the blindest.

He made a telephone call; then he told his secretary that he would be leaving for the day.

Eric Lockhart drove a plain blue Chevrolet, winding his way through the usual afternoon crush of traffic. He drove skillfully, with the economy of movement of a man accustomed to operating complex machines.

He drove for thirty-nine minutes, until he reached a middle-class, suburban neighborhood, a pleasant, unassuming area where bank managers and insurance agents built their homes. He turned onto Meadowlark Avenue, slowing down before reaching number 1727, and smiled as he observed the window. He reached into the glove compartment and pressed the button on the automatic garage-door opener. Judging it nicely, he was able to drive straight into the garage without stopping. Inside, he parked beside a Ford Mustang. Again he pressed the button; the garage door obediently closed behind him.

He savored this moment of privacy.

The door leading into the house swung open. She appeared. Tall and elegant, even in jeans and a sweatshirt.

"Glad you could make it. A surprise."

"I needed to see you," he said as he walked toward her.

They kissed, tenderly but passionately, smiling at one another for a long, delectable instant after their lips parted.

"How are you?" he asked her.

"I'm great," she told him in her measured way. Virginia had a low-pitched, somewhat throaty voice; it was exceptionally attractive and she used it well, enunciating every word. She was not especially beautiful, but there was a sensual quality about her. A very intelligent woman, Virginia Patterson, with a realistic attitude toward life. Formerly an employee of Lockhart Aerospace, she had spent half a dozen years in the late sixties as secretary to the vice-president of Corporate Communications. Then she had left to marry a university professor in Michigan. The marriage failed and she returned to Seattle. One afternoon Eric Lockhart had encountered her in the parking lot outside the executive tower. They exchanged a few words. She told him she had hoped to be rehired. He found himself physically attracted, but curiously, he had hardly noticed her when she had worked at the company previously. He suggested she call his office the following day. Within a month the arrangements had been made: she had a house and car; she did a little bookkeeping and secretarial work for him. At home. Her son, Robert, age twelve, was away at school. A pleasant boy, but in less than two months he would be home for summer vacation; it would be a bleak time for Lockhart because discretion required that he steer clear of the house when the boy was home.

"You look delicious."

"As a matter of fact, I feel kind of delicious," she said. "I just replaced a washer in the kitchen faucet. It doesn't drip any more."

"You should have called a plumber."

"And pay him thirty or forty dollars? Not on your life!"

They went into the house, his arms about her shoulders. She had a marvelous way of snuggling into him as they walked together. The sheer presence of her was almost intoxicating.

The curtains in the living room were open, as he had noted from the street. It was their signal. If for any reason he wasn't to stop, she would draw the drapes. He would drive to a phone booth and call. There was always the possibility of an unexpected guest; Lockhart had no desire to come into the house and be recognized by some gossipy housewife. No doubt Virginia's immediate neighbors were keenly aware that a man visited her from time to time, driving a blue Chevy. But that's all they knew. And since the vast majority of his arrivals and departures took place after dark, he provided little opportunity for them to find out more. A midafternoon visit was a rare occurrence.

"Tough day?" she asked.

"Tough enough," he admitted.

"I thought so. You look tired."

"It's old age," he said.

She shook her head. "Something wrong?"

He shrugged. "Just business."

"Nothing to do with home?" She uttered the word as if she hated it.

"No."

"How are things there?"

"The same."

She nodded, a wry smile on her lips. She indicated the sofa. "Relax. Take your shoes and tie off and I'll fix a drink."

"Don't bother with the drinks," he told her. "Just come over here and sit down."

She looked concerned. "Something is wrong, isn't it?"

"Just business," he said again. "Nothing more."

"Serious?"

"A disappointment," he said—and smiled to himself. It was like calling World War Two a difference of opinion. He put his feet on a hassock. She slipped his socks off and began to massage his feet, one toe at a time, working the flesh until the pleasure ran up his legs like a series of gentle, stimulating shocks. What a superb touch she had. There was a unique quality to her skin, something that rekindled old fires at will.

He said, "You make me feel like a kid. I love it."

"I love you, Eric. I love everything about you." There could be no doubt that she felt deep affection for him; God knows whether it could be classified as genuine love. That didn't matter. The closeness of their relationship was enough for the moment. He never pretended to himself that he was sexually attractive in the conventional sense. He had no illusions about his physical appearance, although he still possessed a moderately trim figure and a good head of hair. But there could be little doubt that Virginia was excited by him, or perhaps, to be more accurate, by what he represented. It was more than just his money. It was his influence, his power, his ability to shape world events, to make or break men. . . .

"Have you heard from Robert recently?"

"He called yesterday."

"And?"

"Needs some money. As usual."

"Does he still want to be a test pilot?"

"That's what he says. Funny, isn't it, that he should be so interested in aviation?"

"Do you think he knows about . . . us?"

She shook her head, slowly, thoughtfully. "But he might come to you looking for a job in a few years."

"Then he'd have one."

"It sounds like a plot from a B movie: son unknowingly works for mother's former lover."

"Former?"

She shrugged, smiling. "Sorry."

"I hope we're never former anything to each other."

"I'd like that, too. But . . . well, nothing lasts forever, does it?" She stood up. "Anyway, how about that drink now? The usual?"

"Yeah."

He heard her go into the kitchen and open the refrigerator; there was the clinking of ice cubes in glasses. Then she went upstairs, as he knew she would. At this moment she would be tugging off her clothes, dropping them on her bed until she was naked. She was probably going to glance at herself in the full-length mirror opposite her bed; perhaps she would accord herself a curt nod of approval at what she saw: no child-woman, but a splendidly mature female, strong and sensuous and intensely sure of herself. Then she would slip on the blue-and-white striped robe, fluff her dark hair, perhaps touch up her lipstick and treat herself to a touch of perfume.

He heard her footsteps descending the stairs. She went back into the kitchen. A moment later she emerged. But she wasn't wearing the blue-and-white striped robe. She wasn't wearing anything. And it suited her splendidly. She carried herself with such assurance, such pride; her enticing breasts swayed as she moved, nipples dark and erect.

"I slipped into something more comfortable," she said.

He laughed and suddenly realized it was the first time he had laughed in a long time. God, she was good for him.

He pulled off his clothes as she arranged herself on the sofa. She was marvelously shameless, enjoying nudity and intimacy as a gourmet might revel in a fine dinner. She liked to delay the actual coupling, savoring the anticipation, taking pleasure in delicate touchings and nuzzlings. But soon, inevitably, the pace quickened. How she could excite him. Amazing that Virginia and Dorothy actually belonged to the same species. In fact, Dorothy was the more beautiful; her figure was slimmer, more fashionable. But somehow she was like a remarkably attractive package that was empty. Sex with her had always been disappointing, incomplete, a necessary ritual, like brushing teeth, something that had to be done at intervals. With Virginia it was so totally different.

He buried his face between her breasts, breathing in the embracing warmth of her, the closeness of her. It was fantastically good to abandon oneself to passion, to allow oneself to be transported, reduced to a superbly elemental level. . . .

Afterwards, they smiled at one another like veterans who have come through yet another battle unscathed. She examined the hair on his chest, studying single hairs as if they were prize specimens. "You're a very gentle man, Eric— nothing at all like your public image. You know, I used to be terrified of you. Everyone told me what a tyrant you were and how the entire place quaked when you were on a rampage. But I found out that it was just stupidity and incompetence that made you angry."

"They still do," he said. "And that's why I was in such a lousy mood when I got here. That damned Senate committee rejected the most important weapons system we've ever developed, the ultimate example of stupidity and incompetence."

"I'm really sorry, Eric. How will it affect the company?"

"It's not the company I'm worried about. It's the country." He felt splendidly protective as alarm shadowed her eyes. He gently stroked the hair back from her brow. "You know about the Devastator. What you may not know is that the security of the free world could hinge on it. It's that simple."

"I had no idea it was that important."

"But it is enormously expensive as well. And with an election coming up, those penny-pinchers in Washington don't want to hit their constituents with any increase in the military defense budget that could lead to an increase in taxes. They're gambling with the security of the country. This attitude is incomprehensible."

"Maybe they'll change their minds."

"I'm afraid not."

"I wish I could do something to help."

"You just did."

He sipped the iced tea she always made for him. "I have to go to New Orleans next week. Can you get away?"

She nodded. "How long?"

"Four days. Starting Tuesday. I'll be at the Hilton."

"Great," she said. "I'll check in at the Sonesta."

"I was hoping you'd say that," he said. They wouldn't meet at the Sonesta; there was far too much danger of his being recognized. He would rent a car and pick her up. They would drive into the country, find a quiet restaurant and a motel, and spend the evening and the night together, returning in the early hours. The next night they would find somewhere else to eat and to stay.

"Are you going to New Orleans because of the new airplane?"

He shook his head. "It's an international organization of aerospace executives. We meet periodically to tell each other how clever we are and how we could solve the world's problems if only governments would allow us to do what we do best."

"Perhaps someone will come up with a way for you to get the government to change its mind about the Devastator."

He shook his head. "Virginia, I've got to face reality. Right now it's a dead issue."

"I'm sure you've done everything possible."

"Have I? I really wonder." He took her shoulders in his hands. "Sure, I've provided them with everything there is to know about the airplane and its systems. But apparently that wasn't enough. So maybe I should have grabbed them and banged their collective heads together until they saw reason. God, you keep asking yourself how far you should go . . . when the course of world events could be determined by this airplane."

He released her, shaking his head apologetically at the finger marks he left on her shoulders.

"I'm sorry."

"Don't be."

"I just had to let off some steam."

"I'm glad you did."

"The trouble with you," he said, "is that you're too damned easy to talk to. There's something about you that makes me want to unburden myself on you."

"And in me," she added, grinning wickedly. The grin

faded. "I'm very proud that you can talk to me about such things; you make me feel I'm an important part of your life."

"You are."

"If there's a way to solve this problem, you'll find it," she declared. "You can do anything, Eric, anything at all."

8

"SHE'S DYING TO meet you," Barney declared.

"But I'm not dying to meet her," said Macleod.

"Mac, you're becoming a goddam . . . recluse!"

"It's cheaper."

"Listen, buddy, I know you got taken by that English broad. It was a tough break, what with the divorce and everything. Look, I'll lend you a few bucks if you're short."

"Thanks, but no thanks."

"Mac, you've got to start circulating again. It's *necessary*. Snap out of it, ol' buddy. You've got to, for your own good."

Macleod sighed. Barney meant well in his own persistent way. And he was probably right. The last couple of weeks had been rough, day after day of wincing as the memories came back to haunt him, to mock him like taunting kids who were always just out of reach. A guy could get sick, brooding, snarling, trying to figure out how to make it to payday, how to swing yet another loan from the airline credit union—and how to pay the damned thing back when he did.

The English bitch had taken him for plenty in the early hours of the morning in New York. And the American bitch, his ex-wife, had taken him for a helluva lot more. Was that his destiny? To be a target for female vultures? *Women!* And that pain-in-the-ass of a first officer had been far more interested in her social life with priapismic Clive Harris than with getting the flight out on time. Typical female. No matter how they pretend to be professionals, the only important thing in their lives is sex. And screwing honest working men out of their last nickel.

"This one's nuts about airline pilots," said Barney. "Christ knows why," he added.

"Barney, you know I can't stand blind dates," Macleod said.

"Would I steer you wrong? Me? Barney?"

Macleod sighed in resignation. "Okay. Where and what time?"

Barney's girlfriend's friend's name was Elizabeth and she worked for a photo agency, a place that made available hundreds of thousands of photographs to advertising agencies and publishers. They had, she told Macleod, a lot of airplane pictures.

"They're big right now. So are crashes. Lots of calls for cracked-up airliners. Have you ever crashed? No, I guess not, otherwise you'd be dead, wouldn't you?"

"People sometimes survive crashes," he pointed out.

Barney and his girlfriend nodded. Barney called for another round of drinks.

Elizabeth said, "Some of the ones we have in the shop are the pits. Gross. Hardly anything left of anything. Little twisted bits of metal. Pieces of people lying around. Yech! I don't know how you can do that for a living. Don't you ever get scared?"

"No, not really," he yawned.

"I would be. But they don't have women pilots, do they?"

"There are a few," Macleod told her. "In fact I flew with one recently. But I think she may be going into another line of work soon. At least I hope so. Do you enjoy your work?"

She shook her head. She was a redhead; she had a large, sensuous underlip and eyes of remarkable vacuity. "People are always bitching. It's never the goddam picture they wanted. You go through the files and dig out the transparencies and send them off on approval—it's a hell of a lot of paperwork. Then they keep them too long or they say they've returned them when they haven't—and the trouble is, sometimes they're real good accounts so you can't call 'em deadbeats, can you?"

"I suppose not," said Macleod, wondering what he was missing on television.

"It's tougher than you realize."

"I'm sure it is."

"D'you want to ball?"

"Not especially."

"No?" She sounded incredulous.

"I never put out on the first date," said Macleod nonchalantly.

"What a comedian," said Barney, leaning across the table.

"Yeah?" murmured Elizabeth, obviously unsure. "So what're we going to do?"

"There must be something else," Barney assured her.

After interminable hours at a disco where the amplification was earsplitting and the lighting had apparently been designed to induce vertigo and permanent eye damage, they all wound up at Macleod's apartment. Elizabeth had a navy grog, her sixth of the evening, and promptly threw up on Macleod's new rug.

"I've never seen her do that before," said Barney's girlfriend. "You shouldn't have given her that drink."

"Now you tell me."

"You didn't ask," she replied with maddening logic.

"The stain'll come out," said Barney authoritatively.

At last they left. Macleod sloshed water and detergent on the mess. It was obvious that Barney was no expert; the stain was indelible. He was putting the pail and rags away when there was a knock on the front door. He opened it. A small, muscular man stood there, fists clenched, breathing fire.

"Okay, you son of a bitch, where is she? I know she's in there, so don't bullshit me. I've had it."

He pushed Macleod aside and stormed into the apartment, searching the bedroom, the closets, the bathroom and finally the kitchen.

Macleod asked, "Who the hell are you looking for?"

"My lousy wife," he said in a somewhat calmer voice. The man sounded less assured now.

"No wives here," Macleod reported.

"But I was sure this was the place." He snapped his fingers in irritation at his own incompetence. "Damn. I'm really sorry."

"Don't mention it," said Macleod. "It happens all the time."

The man sniffed. "Hey there's a funny smell in here."

"Really?"

"Yeah, it's really bad. I don't know how you can live in a place like this."

"I hope you find your wife."

The man shrugged. "She's not much. Don't know why the hell I get so pissed off. She isn't worth the aggravation. Screws around all the time. You think I oughta get rid of her?"

"Why not? Say, how would you like a drink?"

"That's real nice of you considering how I barged in here."

"It's okay. Would you like a navy grog? On second thought, how about bourbon and soda?"

"Yeah." The man looked around. "Just moved in?"

"Not really. But I haven't gotten around to unpacking yet."

"You married?"

"Used to be."

"Women are a pain in the ass, aren't they?"

"No doubt about that," Macleod agreed.

In the morning he unpacked books; dozens, hundreds of them, some Angie's, some his—some that he couldn't remember ever seeing before. He spent an hour lost in the pages of a long-forgotten volume about aerial battles over the Western Front. He was transported back to the era of biplane fighters, with their Vickers and Spandau machine guns, crates that were tricky to fly, inflammable as hell, and prone to structural failure. Their daring pilots huddled in open cockpits, sprayed by castor oil from the rotating cylinders of their rickety engines, frozen fingers gripping joysticks, aching lungs gasping for oxygen as they engaged in combat at altitudes up to 20,000 feet. Who would have the guts to do such things these days? Who would even dare to take one of those contraptions off the ground? The FAA probably wouldn't even allow it.

Sometimes he wished he had been born fifty years earlier, so that he might have grown up in what now seemed to have been the golden age of so many things that turned him on: flight, jazz, good novels, wit; it must have been reassuring to live at a time when you could readily identify the good guys and the bad guys, when good taste seemed to have some importance in the scheme of things.

He shrugged. It was foolish, aching with nostalgia for a time he had only read about. He had to cope with *now*, not the Roaring Twenties. And he had much to be thankful for, didn't he? There was every reason to contemplate a great future with TAA, flying all over the world for the next twenty years. And might there not even be an executive position waiting for him when his flying days drew to a close? In the immediate future, he would soon be upgrading from the 707 to newer equipment, the Lockheed L-1011 "Tristar" or perhaps the newer wide-body jets that Trans Am was considering. That was something to look forward to, right? And it would happen soon. In the meantime, however, he was content to continue flying the 707. She was an aging bird now, no longer the big moneymaker that she had been back in the days when kerosene had cost ten cents a gallon. But she wore her years with grace and style; her lines were still as essentially *right* as when the prototype first flew back in 1954. He felt a curious bond to the 707; both he and the airplane had been young together. When the last 707 vanished from service, his own youth would have finally, irretrievably vanished too. No! Damn it all, forty can't be considered old, not these days, especially to someone thirty-nine! He was still in the prime of life.

It sounded like a cut of beef.

He thought about Angie; he couldn't help it.

His jaw tightened; his fists clenched. Damn her, the bitch. What a complete job she had done on him. Had the whole thing been premeditated, right from the start? If not, when did she decide? What year, what month, what week? What goddam moment?

He shook his head, as if to toss the thought aside. He refused to think about it—or her—any more. The subject only made his guts churn.

And reminded him of money.

He had to visit the credit union office for a personal loan. Soon. He didn't have enough to make it to pay day. He considered his approach. Would he tell the loan officer that he needed the money for a new car? A new stereo? A vacation? Would they ask him for more collateral?

If he was honest he'd tell them he needed it for rent and food; he needed it because he'd been robbed, once by his ex-wife and once by a slick and lovely Limey. They were facts that couldn't be denied. But such a story would set the tongues wagging; the gossips in the credit union were never happier than when a captain—one of those pampered prima donnas—was in financial difficulties.

But the ordeal had to be faced. He hoped that the office would not be crowded with applicants at this early hour.

He set out, hunched uncomfortably in the slightly rusty little Honda.

It happened at the corner of Brenner Way and 20th Avenue N.E.

"That dumb broad!" he later exclaimed to Simpson, the Chief Pilot at Trans Am. "She ran the stop sign! Never even slowed down. I still don't know how I missed her. Honest to God, it was a miracle. I nearly flipped the car as I swerved to avoid her, almost ran head-on into a bus coming the other way. And off she went totally oblivious to what happened."

Simpson shook his head sympathetically. "That kind of thing can really shake you up."

Macleod's heart still pounded. The female sex seemed to be determined to destroy him, one way or another. Was it a conspiracy?

He said, "Women shouldn't drive. They have no feel for anything mechanical. Watch a man and then a woman parking a car. It's something to do with metabolism or the menstrual cycle or some damn thing like that."

Simpson said, "I've got to admit I've seen some crazy women drivers in my time too. But I've also seen some good ones."

"It'd be a safer world if they stayed off the road."

"And out of the air, Mac?" Simpson inquired with a wry smile.

Macleod nodded vigorously. "I'd buy that too."

"But what if a woman has earned her place in the air? Passed every test? Proven she can fly as well as a man—better than most? Should she be denied the right to fly?"

Macleod wagged a finger. "I know who you're talking about. And I'm willing to agree that she's not a bad pilot . . ."

"Wouldn't it be more accurate to say that she's an excellent pilot?"

"Maybe. But how's she going to behave in a crisis? Tell me that?"

"I can't," said Simpson. "But I can't tell you how any other pilot is going to react either."

"Women are more emotionally unstable than men. It's a fact of life. It's not their fault. It's the way they're made."

Simpson said, "No one's ever proved that men are constitutionally better able to handle an emergency than women."

Macleod said, "Okay, let's assume women are just as good under pressure. I don't agree with it, but I'm willing to *assume* it. There's still another problem. How the hell do you expect a man and a woman to work closely together in the intimate confines of a flight deck? Nature's going to take its course. It's inevitable. And if there's one thing you don't need in a cockpit, it's a couple of horny pilots more interested in jumping on each other's bones than in flying the goddam airplane!"

"Personally," said Simpson, "I think it's rather pleasant to have a female copilot. I like the way the shoulder harness brings out the curves."

"Aha!" Macleod jabbed at the air, triumphant. "That's exactly what I mean! Pilots should be paying attention to the airplane, not to a pair of tits in the cockpit!"

Simpson chuckled. "The world's changing, Mac. And you'd better get used to it." He picked up a stack of paper from his desk. "By the way, a crew scheduler just brought these in. You'll be taking the Stockholm flight on the twentieth."

"Fine," Macleod murmured with a shrug.

"Your flight engineer will be—let me see, Brad Steiner."

"Okay."

"And your first officer will be . . ." He snapped his fingers. "Well, what do you know—Karen Dempsey!"

Macleod glared. "But I just *had* her! The last trip, for God's sake—"

"I guess the computer doesn't care."

"Why me?" Macleod groaned.

"Just lucky, I guess," said Simpson. "Behave yourself and keep your mind on the flight, okay?"

The moment Macleod emerged from Simpson's office, he

saw her sitting there. And he knew she had heard some—or perhaps all—of their conversation through the open door.

She was visibly upset. "Good afternoon, Captain," she said, her voice taut. "I'll do my best not to distract you on the way to Stockholm."

9

IT WAS WONDERFUL to have the sky to oneself, to soar and roll, to cavort like some playful aerial puppy, carefree in the knowledge that no other aircraft could get in the way for the simple reason that no other aircraft could achieve such a stratospheric altitude. The XB-3A topped them all in so many ways.

But Mike Lockhart wasn't up here to play games. The object of this exercise, number 44 in the flight test program, was to investigate very-high-altitude stall tests. More data were needed to add to the mountain of figures in the project development reports.

He advised Flight Data Control through the microphone built into his helmet that he was initiating the first test, slowing the aircraft to what seemed a crawling pace but which was in excess of 300 knots.

"I'm extending flaps now. Five degrees. Now ten. Fifteen." Simultaneously he retrimmed the aircraft to compensate for the change an aircraft attitude created by the increased lift and drag of the flaps. "Twenty degrees of flap. Twenty-five. Okay, now the flaps are fully extended. Landing gear is retracted. Speed is two-seven-five," he added, although the engineers on the ground would be reading the same numbers from their automated data retrieval systems. "Okay, I'm now reducing power to idle and holding the nose in a twenty-degree, nose-high attitude."

The nose wanted to drop as the airspeed decreased further. But he maintained its attitude by steadily exerting back pressure on the control stick, trimming and retrimming. He watched the needle of the airspeed indicator continue to unwind.

"Two-five-five. She's getting a little sluggish. Two-five-oh; two-four-five; she's just about to let go. Down to two-forty and, yes, there she goes, just as you guys predicted. A nice, clean stall. Only a mild shudder with the right wing dropping slightly. No problems. Full recovery after losing only eleven hundred and sixty feet. Not bad for this altitude. Okay, the program says to conduct the next stall with the nose held twenty-five degrees above the horizon."

The XB-3A was so high that Mike could easily see the earth's curvature. Columbus was right.

Control stick aft once more; the shapely needle nose sniffing at the heavens. Directly overhead the sky was so dark he could see the stars. In the middle of the day. Power off; speed slipping away smoothly.

This time the Devastator fell out of the sky more abruptly, robbed of the speeding airflow over her wings. She showed her displeasure by tumbling into an incipient spin, an irritable reminder that this was a thoroughbred airplane, not to be treated casually or lightly.

Through his windshield, Mile could see the ground begin to gyrate.

"I guess you guys are getting this on your data-link recorders. I've released back pressure on the stick; full left rudder now; responding nicely; okay, everything's under control; adding power; raising the flaps."

Mike raised the electrical switch that controlled the flaps. But suddenly the airplane was no longer responsive to his command. She seemed to skid across the sky. Instinctively, his feet worked the rudder pedals. The aircraft rolled one way and yawed the other, insistently. He jammed the control stick to the left, his eyes rapidly scanning the instrument panel.

"I think I've got a problem," he announced with understatement.

"So we see," came the reply. "What's going on up there?"

"Well, it looks like an asymmetric flap problem. The right flap retracted normally but the left one won't budge. It's taking one helluva lot of airspeed to keep her from rolling over on her back." Mike was all business, somehow managing to keep the panic out of his voice. "Stand by. I'm going to extend the right flap to match the left. Gotta keep her on an even keel."

Damn. Nothing. No response. He cycled the flap-control switch several times. The electrohydraulic motor just whirred, an impotent hunk of metal.

"No luck," he reported. "I've checked the circuit breakers and gone through the emergency override procedures. Zip. The left flap is stuck down and right flap is stuck up."

"What are your intentions, Mike?"

"I'm not sure yet, but for starters, I'm taking her down to ten or twenty thousand feet where the air is thicker and I'll have better control. She's flying okay, but if I reduce airspeed very much, she rolls uncontrollably to the right."

Which wasn't news to anyone listening on the ground. They all knew that an airplane in that condition was about as stable as a bicycle with its front wheel jammed to one side. Even full left aileron wouldn't completely solve the problem; the roll control system had never been designed to cope with that kind of problem. But the combination of high airspeed, full left aileron and plenty of power did result in a passably controllable flying machine.

The question was: how to bring the thing back to earth at such a high airspeed without spreading titanium and aluminum pieces all over the real estate.

"I'm going to stick with her and land," he reported. "But I'll need one helluva long runway. Better call Edwards and tell them they're about to have an uninvited guest."

"Okay," came the reassuringly calm voice from Flight Data Control. "We'll call Edwards on the landline. See ya later, Mike. And good luck."

Mike reached toward the avionics console and changed to the UHF frequency for Edwards Approach Control. As he fought to maintain tenuous command over the willful aircraft, he heard the voice of the controller at Edwards Air Force Base. The Devastator was cleared for a north-to-south, straight-in approach to twelve-mile-long Rogers Lake. During the dry season, which was almost all year in southern California's Mojave Desert, this smooth, hardened-alkaline lake bed was the longest runway in the world. It was where America's first space shuttle landed in 1981. If there wasn't enough room to land at Edwards, then there wasn't enough anywhere.

The big unknown was how the XB-3A would behave near

the ground when he reduced the rate of descent and slipped off more airspeed moments before touchdown. He had to slow down; no way could he land at this speed and come to a halt, even though the runway was more than 60,000 feet long. But if he slowed too much, he'd lose control. At what airspeed? He could experiment at altitude to find out, but he had used too much fuel getting to Edwards. No time left for any more testing.

If he did get too slow, how would the Devastator react? Would she simply roll over without warning and plunge toward the desert? It was an unpleasant thought; if that did happen, he would be too low to correct the situation. The cameramen—who at this very moment were probably adjusting their focus toward the runway—would have a dramatic bit of footage for the early news: "Top-secret plane in fiery crash. Killed at the controls was . . ."

The altimeter kept unwinding; the airspeed was holding steady at the 400-knot mark. For the moment, the aircraft felt relatively solid, but only because of its velocity.

One thing was certain: the engineers could rewrite the structural data on flap strength. According to their figures, the errant left flap should long ago have been blown away by the devastating blast of the air. But no, it was still there, defiantly creating far too much lift for the left wing, necessitating extreme countermeasures, upsetting the whole delicate balance of the aircraft. Maybe he'd be in better shape if that damned flap did blow off. . . .

Altitude twelve thousand five hundred. Speed still holding. Ease up the nose a bit, slip off a fraction of the speed. Adjust the thrust levers, try to find the magic combination. Think. Anything left to try? What haven't I done?

"Lockhart Four-Delta-Delta," called Edwards Approach Control. "All traffic has been cleared from the area. The wind is holding steady at one-seven-zero degrees, seven knots. Present altimeter, three-zero-zero-three. You are cleared to land at your discretion. Emergency equipment standing by. No need to acknowledge."

JesusJesusJesus, the XB-3A was like a drunken tightrope walker, wobbling, sliding, swaying. She made him fight for control every inch of the way; she made him plumb the depths of his experience, trying to recall some morsel of advice, a word, anything that might help him negotiate these last miles to earth.

Please, baby, just behave a little longer, a few moments, that's all, not much to ask, just a few lousy minutes, four or five maybe, could be a little more, a little less, hard to know exactly when you've never made an approach at such a hellacious speed. . . .

But the aircraft became increasingly difficult to control as it neared the runway, and the airspeed was reduced. Too much speed and you'll never get her stopped in time; too little speed and she'll fall out of the sky. The airplane began to fight him with greater intensity, as if it sensed that it was running out of time in which to defeat the best efforts of the mere mortal in the cockpit.

He couldn't relax even for an instant; he had to keep adjusting, correcting, compensating, foiling her endless attempts to commit suicide, to fly wing over wing and plunge into the ground, to dissolve in fiery fragments. . . .

"Lockhart Four-Delta-Delta, we have you in sight."

The air traffic controller sounded as if he were talking to the captain of a commuter airliner.

Landing gear down. Still flying. A bit more buffeting.

The fire trucks and ambulances—the meat wagons—were lined up along the strip, like a mechanical audience waiting for the show, their red rotating beacons and white strobe lights flashing impatiently.

This won't be a gentle landing; no gradual reduction of power and speed to culminate in a gentle kissing of the wheels against the ground. Fly her all the way down, maintaining precious, irreplaceable airspeed until the tires were firmly planted. . . .

An official car of some sort had stopped beside the runway. Door wide open. A man stood, one leg still inside the car, the other on the ground.

Watching, mouth agape. He had a sandy moustache and wore a purple shirt. A hell of a color.

The man and his car vanished behind. The ground rocked in his windshield. Blurred by the awful, blazing speed. Fly her down. Down. Force the wheels to make contact. Yes, they might blow as soon as they touch. Yes, the landing gear

might collapse. Yes, the result would undoubtedly be a great
show for the television cameras. Would there be a fire?

But you've run out of choices, pal.

*Get her down. And hope. Cut the power. Put her on the
ground before she has time to realize that she's no longer
flying, before she gets playful and flips over on her back and
solves all your crummy little problems forever.*

The tires screamed when they hit the hurtling alkaline
surface. The aircraft tried to fly again, to bounce back into
the air. But he held her down, battling the shuddering control
column, listening to the agonizing noise of rubber being
tortured far beyond its failure point.

The incredible thing was how long the tires lasted.

They burst, one after the other, like a sux-gun salute to
herald his arrival. But by the time they burst the speed had
mercifully slackened. The XB-3A went wandering, skidding,
slithering, shuddering over the dry lake, narrowly missing an
ambulance and sending its crew diving for their lives, flop-
ping gracelessly on to one wing as the right main landing gear
leg folded.

But she came to rest within the confines of the dry lake.
And she was whole.

Mike pressed the canopy release switch. Fresh air from the
Antelope Valley flooded in. Never in the history of man had
fresh air tasted so sweet.

Lockhart had to clear his throat again and again; something
kept lodging there. When he spoke to Mike it was difficult to
keep his voice steady; he had to blink away the slight blue
that affected his vision.

"Why didn't you bail out?"

Mike shrugged and smiled. Obviously shaken, he was
sprawled on Lockhart's office sofa, still clothed in the same
kind of rumpled denims that he had worn under his jumpsuit
the day before. A son to be proud of; no man could ask for
more. Lockhart wanted to get up from his chair and embrace
Mike, to express his emotion through the raw pressure of his
arms. But for some reason he was unable to. He simply
reached across and squeezed Mike's shoulder.

"You *should* have bailed out."

Mike said, "You should have bailed out of that night

fighter back in 1942. But you got her down because you wanted to know why the rudder was fluttering. I wanted to know why the hell the flaps wouldn't work. Besides,'' Mike added, ''I'm afraid of parachutes.''

''That was professional flying at its best, Mike.''

''Thanks, Dad.''

''Even though I wish you hadn't taken the chance, I'm grateful that you brought her back.''

''If I hadn't, you might not have been able to find out what went wrong and correct the problem.''

It was the classic response of the experimental test pilot. God knows how many of them had lost their lives at it. Mike laughed nervously in the manner of someone still in mild shock. ''I should write a technical report on how to control a hypersonic airplane with one flap up and the other down. Great machine, but tough to fly in that configuration.''

''I want you to take a week's vacation.''

Mike shook his head. ''I don't need a vacation.''

''That's an order.''

Mike smiled. ''Okay, boss. Thanks.''

''Don't thank me,'' said Lockhart. ''I thank you. The whole company thanks you. You did a fantastic job.''

Mike's grin dissolved. ''You know, Dad, as soon as I was down I remembered that the government probably won't buy her. And then I wondered if it was worth risking my life to save her.''

Lockhart said, ''The air force would love to have this airplane, Mike. It's the politicians who are getting in the way, screaming about cost, scared that if we build the plane, the Soviets will come up with something even better. But the damned fools don't realize just what a huge technological advance this airplane represents. The Soviets won't be able to catch up with the Devastator. I tell you, this airplane could change the balance of power, Mike. It's that significant. That's why what you did means so much.''

''So what happens now?''

''I don't know,'' Lockhart admitted. ''But the fight isn't over, not yet. I'm convinced this is the most important project this company has ever developed. We must find a way to produce the Devastator. There's got to be a way. There simply must be.''

Mike said, "Seems to me they've already made up their minds."

Lockhart posed the question. "And what do you think might make them change their minds?"

Mike thought for a moment. "I guess they'd approve the airplane if we were on the brink of war."

"I agree," Lockhart said.

"So do we hope for war?" Mike asked rhetorically.

"Of course not, but isn't war inevitable? After all, Mike, in six thousand years of recorded history, there have only been two hundred years of peace."

"I suppose you're right. But if war does come, there wouldn't be enough time at that point to get the Devastator into production. What can we do now?"

"I just don't know," said Lockhart. "But something must be done before it's too late. Our country is being run by weaklings who are more interested in reelection than the national interest. They are a bunch of idealists blinded by their own visions. It's a catastrophe because this madness is happening at such a critical time. While the Soviets are building the most powerful military machine in history, America is becoming weaker, our armed forces neglected, our weapons becoming antiquated and more unreliable. If we don't turn this around, we'll be destroyed. You know as well as I do how unstable the international situation is. The weaker we are, the more those bastards in the Kremlin will pressure us. They were behind our humiliation in Vietnam, they outmaneuvered us in Poland and are undermining our interests all over the world. They view us as fat and complacent, afraid to take chances, desperate to avoid confrontation. It's the thirties all over again. The free world is weak and unprepared. Don't we ever learn? The only thing our adversaries understand and respect is strength. The only way to deal with them is through the proper use of power." He shook his head and apologized. "Sorry, Mike, I'm sounding off. Didn't mean to make a speech."

"It's okay, Dad," said Mike. "I know you're right. So what do we do?"

"I'm not sure, but we must do something," said Lockhart.

*   *   *

"Why didn't you tell me about Mike's accident?"

Dorothy flung the question as soon as he entered the house. The maid, Ruth, withdrew rapidly.

"It was an incident," Lockhart said, "not an accident. He had some trouble, but he got the airplane down. I was proud of him."

"You'll be even prouder of him when you kill him, you son of a bitch! Then you can point to his grave and say what a fine, upstanding son he was and how much you loved him! Why do I have to find out from the maid, for Christ's sake?"

Lockhart sighed. How did Ruth find out?

"It happened. It's over. I didn't think it advisable to, shall we say, burden you with the matter . . ."

"*Burden* me? What the hell do you mean by that?"

"I mean, Dorothy, that you've been drinking steadily for the past few days. It's been impossible to talk to you about anything . . ."

"Lying bastard!"

"Goddam it, it's the truth."

"You're vicious, Eric. Jesus, you're vicious." She stood, swaying slightly, pointing an accusing finger in his direction. "It appeals to you, doesn't it, to keep me in the dark about my own son, for crissake. I have to find out from my goddam *maid!* That stinks, Eric; it's just about as goddam low as you can get, to have my maid telling me that my son—my own flesh and blood—was nearly killed in one of your fucking airplanes!"

Repelled, he turned on his heels. "There's no point in continuing this conversation."

Her voice seemed to clutch at him like bony fingers. She screamed, "You stay here; I haven't finished with you, you son of a bitch!"

He walked quickly across the hall and started up the stairs. Her voice now assumed that scratchy, acerbic tone he knew so well. He was a goddam fascist, she shrilled—but there was a faint note of surprise in her tone as if the notion had only just occurred to her. She told him he had a super-race complex; people had to be as perfect as his airplanes on the production line, otherwise they'd be rejected by Quality Control. It was tiresome, confusing stuff, typical of her when she drank so much.

He closed the door of his study behind him, turning the key with a sigh of relief. She was quiet now; the only sound was the gentle heaving of the ocean. No doubt she had gone back to her Scotch. She would drink until she passed out; then Ruth would help her upstairs to bed.

He flopped into a chair, took off his tie and unbuttoned his collar. How long, he wondered, would it take Dorothy to drink herself into the grave? How long could a body take that kind of abuse? Hadn't the doctor warned her, telling her of the inevitable consequences of alcoholism? Dorothy's death would solve so many problems. A clean end to a disastrous marriage. He would get rid of this huge house and set about the creation of a new social life. A pleasant, warming thought. But temporary. Dorothy wasn't about to die. She would cling to him forever, secure in the knowledge that he hated the thought of divorce as much as he hated her. She knew him all too well. Divorce—even if Dorothy agreed—would mean an avalanche of publicity, of unsavory gossip, of months of office chatter about his private affairs. The thought was monstrous, physically nauseating. And so the marriage dragged on, year after grueling year.

Would Mike marry soon? He seemed fond of the blond girl. Lockhart shrugged; he couldn't remember her name. Pretty thing. Big eyes and breasts to match. No wonder Mike was attracted. Another wedding of the year; another Mrs. Lockhart. Another disastrous mistake? Would Mike be condemned to a fate like this? Was it The Curse of the Lockharts?

A sad smile touched his lips. It faded as his eyelids dropped. He was exhausted. He slept, dreaming that he was totally alone, friendless, powerless. He had an important message. But no one would listen. Desperately he ran from office to office, trying to make men pay attention. But it was as if he didn't exist. No one would acknowledge him. Cold eyes glared right through him; burly bodies brushed impatiently past him.

He awoke, glancing automatically at his watch. He fingered his eyes, rubbing away the sleepiness. He remembered the dream. It was familiar. He had dreamed it countless times. Still it disturbed him.

In a weird way, the dream now had a parallel in real life. Again he shook his head, rejecting the thought before it could capture his attention. It was essential to discipline the mind just as firmly as the body.

He crossed the room to his desk and sat down. He had some correspondence to deal with; but his attention kept wandering to the wall that his father had adorned with the history of his company.

Most of the pictures, the models, the memorabilia had been collected in the forties and earlier; Eric Lockhart himself had contributed no more than a few items. Somehow there was never time to think of such things. It was still his father's study; it always would be. Lockhart smiled sadly, remembering how important he had felt as a boy when his father invited him to sit in the leather armchair and put his feet up so that they could discuss some important subject, man to man. Willard Lockhart had possessed the gift of listening, always managing to seem intensely interested in what was being said to him. He was a man who endeared himself to everyone, without apparently making the slightest effort to do so. Eric Lockhart did not possess the gift. I didn't trouble him. He knew he was the better, tougher businessman, a product of M.I.T. and the Harvard Business School. Willard Lockhart had been an instinctive engineer; he lived in an age when a man's sense of proportion and design could carry him to the top of the aviation world.

What would Willard Lockhart have said about the XB-3A, about its incredible performance, its extraordinary capabilities? And what would he have said about his grandson nearly losing his life testing the machine, and about a government committee turning it down when it was needed so desperately?

He would think the world had gone mad. And he would be right.

Lockhart's gaze rested on the photos of his father talking to FDR. Big smilers both of them, professional charmers, both wagging cigarettes at each other as if they were conducting orchestras. There was his father with Rickenbacker. And Churchill. And Udet. And Betty Grable. It was the seat-of-the-pants era of aviation. There were pictures of the Lockhart aircraft used for long-distance flights in the twenties and thirties: Willard shaking hands with a smiling man and a couple of women in tight leather helmets and jodhpurs. Some were dead hours after the pictures were taken. World War Two:

Royal Air Force crews climbing aboard Lockhart aircraft in the early days; American airmen preparing to fly Lockhart ships to Japan and back. The first jets, now amusingly dated in appearance.

A small picture in a walnut frame caught his eye. It showed Willard Lockhart talking to the English actor, Leslie Howard. Again big smiles. Howard looked remarkably pleased with himself; perhaps he had just heard that he had won the part of Ashley in *Gone with the Wind*.

But the poor guy was destined to die a few years later in an airplane.

It happened in 1943. Howard had boarded a DC-3 in Lisbon, Portugal, bound for London. He never arrived. En route, a German fighter intercepted the airliner and shot it out of the sky. One theory for the outrage was that the Germans thought that Churchill was aboard the plane. They were wrong. But it was war. Mistakes happened. Tough luck and all that. Lockhart gazed at the picture, looking deep into the actor's eyes. Did Howard have any premonition of an early death? How long did the execution take? How many moments of sitting there, strapped in the seat while the cannon shells burst through the aircraft's fragile flanks? In the end, did the plane tumble, writhing as if in agony, wrapped in flames? Or did it explode in one merciful convulsion? Such an end was violent, but probably painless: an instant of blinding light and searing heat; then blackness. Alive one instant, in eternity the next. If a man could choose the manner of his own passing, he could do worse than to be blown to bits in the sky.

If Churchill had been on that DC-3, the whole thing would have been a brilliant move on the part of the Germans. It might have changed the course of the war, the shape of history itself: one cannon shell in one tiny corner of the sky; one shell out of God only knows how many millions. Think of the consequences, Lockhart mused. Then he tore his gaze from the old photo; he was wasting valuable time.

He dialed Virginia's number. She answered before the third ring, her voice bright with expectation. "I was hoping you'd call."

"I need to see you," he said.

"I'm right here," she said.

"I'll be there soon."

"You sound depressed. Problems?"

"Yes," he said. "The same."

"You'll solve them," she said.

"You think so?"

"I know so," she said.

The curious thing was how convincingly she said it, and how she could inculcate the thought that, maybe, yes, he could do something about it.

10

"JERRY FULLER GOT married," said her mother.

"How exciting," said Karen facetiously.

"A local girl," said her mother. "No one special. Jo Ann Mayberry, I think her name was. Maybe you knew her?"

"No, I don't think so."

"Well, she's Mrs. Jerry Fuller now."

"I guess she is."

"They went to Acapulco for their honeymoon. Stayed at Las Brisas. When they got back they moved into a lovely split-level apartment on Wilton Avenue. She's got her own car now, an Oldsmobile. He's got a company car, an Imperial. He's an area manager now."

"That's nice."

"He asks about you sometimes."

"Really?"

"Once he stopped his car when I was taking Toby for a walk. Pulled up right beside me. Asked me how I was. Said it was good to see me. Then he asked how you were getting along, said he'd read somewhere that you were a first officer now, said he hoped you were happy."

"I am, Mom. Very."

"He said whenever he flies on Trans American he always listens when they mention the names of the pilots; they do sometimes, you know."

"I know, Mom."

"He says he's hoping to be on one of your flights some day. I think he still cares for you, Karen. A lot of girls would have given their eyeteeth for someone as nice as Jerry Fuller."

"Mom, I was never that interested," said Karen.

"You didn't *try*. A girl has to make an *effort*."

"And pretend to be nuts about golfing or sailing or whatever the man likes? Well, I just happen to have my own interests."

"You only have one interest, just like your father. Airplanes."

"Correct."

"So Jerry married someone else . . ."

"Mother," Karen said firmly, "I'm glad Jerry's married. I hope he's happy. He wasn't my type."

Her mother sighed, a sigh that seemed to declare that she had done her utmost to bring up this daughter correctly, but something had gone wrong along the way, something she didn't understand and couldn't cope with. Karen felt like sighing too. The weekend had been a disaster. Fond as she was of her mother, she had to admit there were times when the two of them were totally incompatible, when they did nothing but peck at each other like bad-tempered hens.

"Jerry Fuller would have married you like a shot if you'd given him the slightest encouragement."

"But I already told you. I didn't want to marry Jerry Fuller. I never wanted to marry him. I found him boring and opinionated. All he ever talked about was the dog-food business."

"It's a very good business. You can make a lot of money."

"I'm sure that's true. But I don't care about dog food."

"He sent me a case of dog food after I saw him with Toby the other day."

"That was very nice of him."

"I think so. And he asked to be remembered to you. And I promised I would. It's my personal opinion that he still cares for you, even though he's married to this Jo Ann Whatever-her-name-is."

"Fuller, I presume."

"Pardon?"

"Jo Ann. Her name must be Fuller."

Her mother peered at her in that quizzical way of hers. "Of course it must be, dear. Whatever was I thinking about? They're legally married—although I strongly suspect Jerry still wishes he'd married you." She sighed again. "But things don't always work out the way we want them to work out. Is there someone else, dear?''

Karen shook her head. ''No one important.''

There was Marty, something to do with printing, but fickle; there was Herb, a sweet man, a fellow TAA pilot, but married and torn apart by guilt; there was Chuck, overpoweringly handsome, the thirty-seven-year-old actor still waiting for The Big Break; and there was Al, the orthodontist who was basically a nice guy but who loved his Mercedes 450SL with an almost unhealthy passion. Good company, all of them. But none mattered any more than had Jerry Fuller. In twenty-nine years there had been only one man, a newpaper reporter in Chicago, name of Ben. She was on probation with the airline when she met him. A funny, moody, brilliant guy, Ben; he had a Great Novel in the works. He had received an offer from a paper in Boston, too good to turn down. Would she please quit her flying job forthwith and follow him to Boston? *Please?* He said he'd shrivel up and die if he had to face Massachusetts without her. She told him she needed some time; she felt obligated to complete at least a year with the airline after their investment in her training. And when he had gone, she found to her faint surprise that she could live without him. Which was just as well, for when she went to Boston a few weeks later on a weekend visit, she found he had moved in with a redhead from Classified.

''When are you going to get over this flying thing?''

Her mother made it sound frivolous, like something an irresponsible teenager might do to while away the time. She hadn't the slightest idea of the effort, the dedication, the study that went into becoming a professional pilot.

Karen said, ''I'd like to make a career out of flying for Trans American. But I don't know if they feel the same way about me.''

She had expected some reaction from her mother. But all she got was a sniff. ''It's no life for a woman. You may think it's very glamorous and a lot of fun right now—''

''No, I wouldn't call it that.''

''—But there will come a time when you'll wish you'd settled down and had a family.'' She shook her head—and Karen sighed inwardly; she knew what was coming next. Sure enough: ''When you were born, I was so happy you were a girl. I'd prayed for a girl because I thought if I had a boy I'd have to go through what I went through with your father—worrying, waiting, scared to answer the phone—''

"Mother," said Karen, "he only had one accident in all those years of flying."

"One was enough, wasn't it? It killed him. A nice man, your father—a good, honest soul."

"I know," said Karen. "I remember." Her mother had a curious habit of talking about her late husband as if she were the only person who had ever known him.

"Why couldn't he have been interested in sailboats or baseball? No, it had to be airplanes. And airplanes killed him. I don't want them to kill you."

Karen reached out and touched her mother's arm. "They're not going to kill me, Mom. Flying airliners is as safe as riding around in a city bus."

That evening, on the way to the airport, she passed the scene of an accident: a city bus on its side in a ditch.

She felt uneasy as she sat down opposite Simpson. He was a little too friendly, his smile a fraction too wide. The word was he could be smiling graciously as he handed you your walking papers. He could explain the situation so well that there was nothing you could do but agree that you had to go.

He made a big thing of gathering up a dozen pieces of paper, then leafing through them, glancing at a word here, a figure there as if it were the first time he'd seen them.

"So," he said at last, placing the papers in the dead center of his desk. "So, how're things going?"

"On the ground they're a bit dull at the moment. In the air they're . . . shall we say, challenging."

"I see." The chief pilot examined his fingernails. He possessed long, surprisingly slender hands, the sort of hands that belonged on a concert pianist. He ran them through his iron-gray hair. Was he a little edgy? Uptight because he faced an unpleasant task, namely ridding the airline of an embarrassment by the name of Karen Dempsey? *Very sorry . . . but people who don't fit in just have to go, that's all there is to it. Nothing personal, you understand.*

He consulted his papers. "A little over a month since you

came here. You like it in Seattle after Chicago? Settled in okay?"

"Yes sir. Thank you."

A thoughtful look at the top sheet. "You've had six trips as a first officer. How do you like sitting in the right seat?"

It was, she told herself, important to be matter-of-fact, businesslike—*professional*. "I like it. Very much. But I'm not sure how much some of the other pilots—the men—like having me around. Even though you're very nice to me, Captain, I bet you wish I'd gotten married and settled down and had three or four kids and never gotten involved in aviation."

"You're very straightforward."

"It's the only way I know how to be. I also think I've been doing a pretty good job as a first officer. I don't pretend to know everything. I know I have a lot to learn. But I know I can learn. In time I'll be as good as any other copilot."

His eyes were gentle but they had a singularly penetrating quality. And he liked to let them linger, probing, searching. "You think the male pilots resent you?"

"A few. Others have been great, very helpful."

"Any idea why anyone would resent you?"

"Sure. It's because airline flying has always been an exclusively male preserve. The only females ever allowed on a flight deck were serving wenches, eager to obey their every command. I understand why men feel the way they do. But I'm not easily intimidated. I'm here until I quit or get fired."

Quietly, Simpson, said, "You can knock off that defiant female act, Karen. No one's going to fire you without a damn good reason. You're bright and capable. And you can do the job. I know some of the guys have given you a rough time. I also know that you and Captain Macleod haven't hit it off *too well*. But Mac, I mean Captain Macleod, has been having some problems lately. So, in view of all that's been happening, I thought you'd prefer to be taken off this flight and reassigned to another."

Karen almost said yes and thanks a million. But she didn't. Something stopped her. Perhaps, she thought, I'm as obstinate as Macleod. "I appreciate your concern," she said. "But I have an aversion to running away from things, including

Captain Macleod. If you don't mind, I'd prefer to take that flight, as scheduled.''

Simpson nodded, his fingers smoothing a crease in the top sheet of paper. ''I had a feeling you might say that.'' He scribbled something on the same sheet of paper. ''Okay, First Officer Dempsey, you're on.''

11

IT WAS STARTLING, totally unexpected, the way the idea crystallized at that particular time in that particular place, that oak-paneled temple of respectability, the board room. A meeting of the executive committee was in progress: a pageant of neat blue, black and gray suits, conservatively striped or polka-dotted ties; earnest, intent expressions in keeping with the significance of the decisions to be made; exhibit sheets before everyone, columns of figures to verify every contention; calm, eminently civilized voices shaping policies, people and events. It happened four times a year.

Burgess was addressing the meeting: Burgess, the plump and pedantic vice-president of Personnel; he seemed to swell as he spoke, as if he drew nourishment from the sound of his own stentorian tones. This was the high point of Burgess' year, this appearance before the executive committee. This was the day on which he presented his employment projection estimates—with the aid of countless charts, slides and graphs. The array grew larger each year. The man apparently believed that if one screen and one slide communicated efficiently, two screens and two slides communicated twice as efficiently; four of each were proportionately better. Burgess spoke without notes but his meticulously phrased sentences had the rhythm of a speech well rehearsed. No doubt he had been working on the presentation for weeks, practicing and polishing, adjusting an ''and'' here, a ''but'' there.

Burgess' mouth had an oddly mechanical movement, the lower section working vigorously on every vowel and consonant, while the upper section remained motionless. Like a ventriloquist's dummy, Lockhart noted inconsequentially, bored by the endless repetitions of the same tedious morsels of information.

For a moment the notion lay dormant.

Then the idle, unconnected thoughts gathered force.

Lockhart's spine tingled as if a mild electric shock had just snaked along its length. An idea had formed, struck him with an almost physical force. Involuntarily, he recoiled, catching his breath. He observed someone glance at him, apparently assuming that the chairman of the board had burped or had experienced a tiny cramp. The someone turned away, reassured by Lockhart's calm expression. But inside, Lockhart seethed with excitement; a veritable chain reaction of ideas had bounded through his brain. A single, random, foolish thought had set it off. Ideas had tumbled over one another. Ventriloquists. Charlie McCarthy. Edgar Bergen. The thirties. Radio. Movies. *Gone with the Wind*. Gable. Leigh. Howard. The war. Howard. The DC-3 disaster. Churchill. Howard. Walsh. Voices coming from across a room. Across an ocean. Looking in the wrong place . . .

And suddenly it was possible. *Simple*, given the electronic systems of the Devastator. The aircraft was capable of making its pilot a ventriloquist of awesome ability. It could be done. It had to be done. He wanted to dash out of the board room, return to his office, *do* something about it. But he sat calmly, his eyes on Burgess' ever-mobile mouth, absorbing not a single word of the presentation.

Good God Almighty, he possessed the answer that would change everything. Virginia had told him he would do it. She was right. She had been the catalyst; he had virtually given up all hope of solving the problem. But she had renewed his faith in himself. She *believed*.

Excitement mingled with a profound sense of relief. America could be saved; a single, daring act could do it, could change the destiny of the world, could compel two hundred and twenty million Americans to wake up and start seeing things as they really were. He, Eric Lockhart, was going to make it happen. In fact, *only* he could make it happen; *only* he had the means.

The thought seemed to glow within him; he could feel the warmth of it in his limbs and muscles. Half an hour before he had been helpless, like a man in a boat hurtling toward

violent rapids, watching disaster sweep nearer and nearer
without being able to do a damn thing about it. Now, an
awesome sense of power galvanized him.

It would work.

He examined the concept from every angle, searched for
pitfalls. What *could* go wrong? What were the dangers?

Perhaps the greatest danger was *not* to implement the plan.
And the biggest question of all was, would Mike go along
with it?

Without him, it was impossible. He could trust no one else.
So if Mike refused to have anything to do with it, there would
be no choice but to forget about it.

A chilling thought. A possibility? Yes, it had to be faced.

But Mike was an intelligent, perceptive individual. His son.
Surely he would see reason and comprehend the essential
rightness of the plan and the absolute necessity for making it
a reality. *Now*.

A fierce joy gripped him. He and Mike would be working
on this together: a father-and-son team. Together they would
perform a service of inestimable value to their country. And
only they would ever know about it.

His attention was distracted by a young man, one of Burgess'
aides. He placed a bound report on the desk before Lockhart.

"It's all summarized there, sir," he said, his tone quietly
deferential.

"I shall look forward to reading it," said Lockhart.

"Thank you for your attention, Eric," said Burgess, beaming with satisfaction.

"No," said Lockhart, "it is for me to thank you."

Mike was waiting outside the experimental hangar, a tall,
commanding figure, straight and lean. A born leader, Lockhart thought as he pulled up, reaching across the front seat to
open the passenger door.

"I hope I'm not interfering with your plans for the evening,
Mike."

His son shook his head. "Is something wrong? You said it
was very important. Something to do with Mother?"

"No, your mother's all right." Lockhart shrugged. "Or at
least as all right as we can expect." He slipped the gear-shift
lever into drive and turned toward the main gate, nodding to a

couple of employees on the way. "But there is something of great importance that I must discuss with you. I chose this somewhat unorthodox meeting place because what I have to say to you is top secret—and I feel there is far less chance of our conversation being overheard here than in the office."

Mike smiled. "Maybe the car's bugged, Dad."

"I doubt it. Security checks it every day."

Mike's eyes widened. "You're kidding."

"I assure you I'm not kidding, Mike. You know how susceptible we are to political and industrial espionage. And the dangers undoubtedly have increased since we began work on the XB-3A. There are a number of governments—and competitors—who would like to know more about the aircraft—and some who never want to see it produced."

Changing the subject abruptly, Lockhart continued. "Mike, I have devised a plan that will make the Senate Committee's decision totally irrelevant. I wanted to tell you about it because I desperately need your help to carry it out."

Mike replied quickly, "My help? Since when do you have to ask?"

Lockhart studied his son carefully and raised a cautioning hand. "What I'm about to propose may at first shock you. At first glance, it will seem to go against everything you've come to believe. It will require your total dedication and determination. I just ask that you take your time and consider very, very carefully what I'm about to suggest."

Mike was puzzled. What in the hell was his father talking about?

Lockhart continued, choosing every word with meticulous care. "Mike, we as individuals are unimportant. What is important is the future of America. You were willing to risk your life to bring back the Devastator. And wouldn't we both sacrifice our lives—if we had to—for the security of this country?"

"Of course, Dad. But what are you getting at?"

"Simply this, Mike. A sacrifice must be made for the greatest good of the greatest number. Now, here is what I propose. You know that Senator Walsh probably will be the next Republican nominee for the presidency."

"So I understand," Mike acknowledged.

"Walsh is our staunchest political ally. He is the embodiment of every real American's frustration with the weakness that possesses this country. As you know, he is leaving for Stockholm to begin a European fact-finding mission—''

Impatient, Mike interrupted. ''But I don't understand. What does Walsh's trip have to do with anything?''

Lockhart looked deeply into his son's eyes, paused, and said with calculated deliberation, ''Senator Walsh will never get there!''

12

HER INTENTION HAD been to arrive at the airport in plenty of time. But she had overdone it. She had far too much time. She could drive over to K's Deli, have a hot pastrami sandwich, return, and still have half an hour to kill. Stupid. She entered the crew mail room, the first stop during the preflight ritual. Her stomach lurched uncomfortably when she saw a captain reading the bulletin board. She thought it was Macleod. But no, it was a pleasant-looking man with a ginger moustache who asked how she was this fine day. Macleod wouldn't have asked such a question. Already she regretted not taking Simpson up on his offer. Damn stubborn streak. What was she trying to prove? She checked her mailbox; the neatly typed lable above it read: F/O DEMPSEY, K. Inside there was the usual junk: revisions to flight manuals, safety bulletins, next month's schedule change, a copy of the TAA publication *Update*, as well as a personal letter from the editor, one Gavell P. Jamieson, expressing his keen interest in doing an "in-depth" story on the first woman to become a first officer with TAA. He felt that a highly significant piece could be prepared on the subject, describing how she became interested in an aviation career, how she progressed through her flight training, how she had become accepted as part of the Trans American flight team, how she viewed life from the right seat of a Boeing 707.

She stuck the letter in her flight kit. Nice of him to think of her but it was a slightly nauseating prospect, answering a barrage of questions from Gavell P. Jamieson, then seeing pictures of herself in the magazine, knowing that everyone else in the company would also see them. An ego trip, but she shuddered at the prospect of focusing even more attention upon herself.

She had a cup of machine-brewed coffee in the crew lounge and consumed thirty minutes bestowing on her mail far more rapt attention than it deserved.

"Hi. You must be Karen Dempsey." The voice had an oddly flat tone.

She looked up. A uniformed man in his mid-thirties with a long, sad face that somehow brought to mind the image of a beagle pup.

"I'm Brad Steiner. I understand we're flying together."

"Nice to meet you," she said, shaking hands as Brad sat down beside her.

"Funny," he said. "I saw the name 'K. Dempsey' on the crew list but I didn't connect it with . . . ah, you."

"You thought it was Ken, or a Keith or a Kurt?"

"I guess so. Sorry," he added with a shrug that seemed to say, well, I goofed again.

She told him there was no need to apologize.

"I read about you when you upgraded to the right seat," he said, "but I didn't remember the name. You've done very well for yourself."

The congratulations must have been hard for him. His obvious age and the two solitary gold stripes on each sleeve told the story. Brad was one of the few flight engineers, or second officers, who probably would never make it to first officer. He had failed the flight test twice; now he was stuck at the bottom of the pilot's hierachy, sentenced to the same job for the rest of his career.

Why did Brad fail to make the grade? Karen wondered. Ability? Attitude?

"This is my last trip," he said, as if he had been listening in on Karen's thoughts. "Through with flying," he added with a phony smile. "Going into the printing business."

"Quite a switch," Karen commented.

"Better hours. Judy'll like that. My wife," he added, by way of explanation. "She never liked my flying, leaving her home alone with the kids to fend for herself. Couldn't get used to it, even after twelve, thirteen years."

"Will you stay in Seattle?"

He shook his head. "Des Moines. Family business. We've

sold the house; moving next month. Looking forward to it,"
he declared unconvincingly. "I'll miss flying in a way. But,
you know, there comes a time."

"Sure."

"Printing'll be a new challenge."

"Of course it will."

"Lot of new things to learn."

"Right."

A nice man, Karen decided. A shame that his career had
floundered.

They had more coffee and talked about movies and music.
Then, together, they made their way along the corridor to
Operations, a noisy, untidy place with dingy beige walls
almost totally covered by weather charts and operational
bulletins; teletype machines clattered incessantly; half a dozen
conversations were in progress as pilots asked about weather
advisories, airport conditions, jet stream paths, turbulence
forecasts, and notices to airmen.

The dispatcher, Fred Desrosiers, was a balding, middle-
aged man with a nervous tic in his left eye. He beamed as
Karen approached, his left eye half-winking. "Flight Nine-
Oh-Two, right?"

"That's it," she responded, to his evident pleasure. He
leafed through the various flight plans prepared by the
company's IBM computer, the tireless device that spent its
days and nights absorbing the essential facts of all Trans
American flights, the departure points and destinations, stirring in reams of data about the winds aloft, high-altitude
temperatures, projected payloads, adding a plethora of data
pertaining to aircraft performance, and in only a few seconds
concocting a scenario for each and every flight: calculating
the route that would require the minimum flight time and that
would, as a rule, cost the airline the least. The computer also
generated numerous columns of vital statistics: fuel consump-
tion, amount of fuel remaining on landing, the precise time
required to fly each leg of the trip, the various wind velocities
to be expected en route, the length of each leg, the ground-
speeds, flight times for each leg, cumulative times, the fuel to
be consumed each leg, the fuel remaining at the end of each
leg. . . .

Because of shifting weather patterns, the computer had

prepared three flight plans for the flight to Stockholm, one primary and two alternates, each with advantages and disadvantages.

"That's your minimum-time route," said Fred, tapping one of the computer flight plans with an authoritative finger. "It'll get you there the fastest."

Karen nodded. She studied the high-altitude prognostic charts with their gracefully undulating isobaric contours providing godlike views of the weather fronts and air masses that were moving across the Northern Hemisphere. The route would take them through a widespread area of high cloudiness with continuous light turbulence forecasted.

That was when Macleod finally arrived. Fred greeted him with friendly rudeness, typical of those who knew each other well. Did Mac really think he could find his way to Sweden at night?

"Sure," Macleod said, "as long as I don't have to follow one of your lousy flight plans."

Fred grinned delightedly. "Got three of 'em for you today, Mac. The little lady's been looking 'em over." He tapped one of the lengthy flight plans. "Told her this was the way to go. Minimum time."

Macleod grunted and looked at all three routes. Then he shifted his attention to the weather and pressure charts. He turned to Karen and, much to her surprise, asked, "Well? What do you think?"

Karen gulped. The moment of truth. Thank God, she'd had some time to study the flight plans. Had she overlooked anything? No time to wonder any longer.

"Captain, it seems to me we'd be better off to take Route Bravo. I know it's a little longer but I think it could actually save us some time and fuel in the long run."

Fred's tic speeded up. He wanted to know how she figured that.

"The minimum time route has us going through considerable cirrostratus cloud for about two hours," she said. "And according to the forecasted temperature at altitude, we'll probably have to use the anti-ice system for much of that period. That's going to reduce engine power, slow us down a little and increase our fuel burn. There isn't much in it but I think that by going Route Bravo, we'll pick up five or six minutes, save some fuel and give the passengers a smoother ride.''

Macleod scratched the tip of his obstinate chin as he peered at the data. Then slowly, almost reluctantly, he began to nod. He tapped the paper as if checking it for quality. "We'll take Bravo," he announced authoritatively.

Afterwards, Karen told herself that she certainly didn't expect a barrage of congratulations or even a thank-you from the great man for some astute reasoning. A simple acknowledgment would, however, have been appropriate. But there was nothing; Macleod turned and leafed through an ancient copy of *Playboy* that someone had left on a nearby table.

Karen turned also, feeling conspicuous. Thank God a bulletin board was nearby. She gazed at it intently, reading four safety bulletins telling of the latest rash of minor incidents: tails brushing runways during landing, bird problems at Zurich, a foreign airline captain acting on the takeoff instructions intended for another aircraft, a fire in the rear lavatory of a DC-10 caused by a passenger dropping a lighted cigarette in the paper-towel storage area. Then there was a telex from management reporting that fifty-eight pilots would be furloughed (the airline's euphemism for laid off) by mid-July. How marvelous it would be if one of them could be Macleod, she thought. But that was impossible. He possessed that most precious of all assets: seniority. He was safe as long as the airline stayed in business and his heart kept pumping. The junior pilots, those most recently hired, are the first to go.

Karen heard a woman greeting Macleod in tones of easy familiarity. Presumably Janet Spencer, the senior flight attendant on this evening's flight to Stockholm. Clearly they had known each other for years, and had probably flown together many times. Janet wasn't particularly attractive in a conventional sense, but she exuded a definite sensuality. Although only in her mid-thirties, she had that slightly weary look about the eyes that seems to be the inevitable consequence of so many years of running up and down aisles.

Macleod asked about someone named Mark; Janet said he had landed a job in a plant that made oversized cartons. When Macleod said good, Janet shrugged and said it probably wouldn't last.

Then, abruptly, Macleod nodded in Karen's direction.

"Karen Dempsey," he declared as if announcing a train. "First Officer. Janet Spencer. She'll be in charge of the cabin tonight."

"Nice to meet you," said Karen.

"Same here," said Janet. But there was little warmth in her smile. Some of the stewardesses seemed to resent a female pilot almost as much as some of the captains. Did the senior flight attendant dislike being replaced as the most important female on the crew?

"We might run into a little turbulence early in the flight," Macleod said. "Nothing much, though. Should be pretty smooth the rest of the way."

Particularly since we're taking Route Bravo, Karen thought, but didn't say.

"We've got a celebrity aboard," Janet announced. "David Walsh."

"The senator?"

"He's going to Europe on one of those fact-finding trips. I wouldn't mind telling him a few facts," Janet added with a grin. "He's cute. Kind of old, but still cute."

"I agree . . ." Karen began to say.

But Janet had moved away, still conversing with Macleod. There was intimacy in the way they talked. Had there once been anything between them? She shook her head. None of your business, so drop it.

Brad Steiner returned from his preflight ritual: a detailed visual inspection of the aircraft and its systems. "Everything's firmly attached," he announced, in the manner of a man who had made the same remark countless times. Then he snapped his fingers. "I just remembered. There was a man named Dempsey who ran a soaring school in the desert. Near El Mirage."

"My father."

"I took a couple of lessons there when I was in college. Lot of fun but I didn't have the dough to keep it up. Is he still running the place?"

"No, he died three years ago."

"Too bad."

Karen nodded, the memories pouring in again as if floodgates had been opened. The phone call; her mother's weirdly calm voice, flat, toneless, as if she were saying something she had rehearsed again and again. An accident; father critically injured; burned. In intensive care. He was dead before Karen could reach him. They buried him two days later. The man who had killed him was there, a slight, white-faced nobody, a student who had only recently soloed. Thoughtlessly, stupidly, he had allowed the glider to rise too rapidly during takeoff. It wouldn't have mattered if he had been in free flight. But the nylon cord was still attached to the tail of the Cub, the towplane, flown by Edgar Dempsey. Barely airborne, the Cub had been flipped into a deadly somersault. It was Edgar Dempsey's only accident in forty years of flying. And it wasn't even his fault. During the graveside service, Karen kept looking at the white-faced man. She wondered why she felt no hatred for him, no desire to strike him, to punish him for his unforgivable crime. Incredibly, she only felt compassion, pitying him for the agony he must have been experiencing. He could no more be hated than could a thunderstorm, a tornado, icing, fog, or an electronic component that had failed. He was a hazard, one of many willingly accepted by every pilot who ever climbed into a cockpit, because it was always going to happen to the other guy. . . .

"Have you flown with Mac before?" Brad asked, interrupting her stream of consciousness.

"Once."

"Hell of a nice guy to fly with, isn't he?"

"If you say so."

"Loves the seven-oh-seven. Gave me a lecture once when I said I wished the company would hurry up and retire these ancient birds. Said they should be kept in service for years to come. They were still young at heart. What d'you suppose he meant by that?"

"Maybe he thinks of himself that way," said Karen.

Fred called from behind his desk. "Karen. There's a guy here from the company newspaper. Wants to take your picture."

13

HE HAD A peculiar sense of being able to stand back and watch himself, the sober-faced man in the back seat of the limousine, his expensively well-dressed wife beside him. There was no conversation between the two. Neither acknowledged the presence of the other; both were apparently lost in their own thoughts as the imposing black Mercedes 600 swept them silently through the city. Dorothy had pulled herself together, as she always did when An Appearance was required. God knows how she did it; she must have felt like hell; twelve hours earlier she had been violently, unpleasantly drunk. But you'd never know it now.

It's not too late, a voice kept reminding him. There's still time to call it off. Even now. No one will ever know what you were planning. It can simply be forgotten.

But, the other voice responded, nothing has changed. It still must be done. You know the reasons; I don't have to repeat them. It's vital to the security of our nation. This time, certanly the end *does* justify the means.

The chauffeur announced that they would be arriving at Sea-Tac Airport in approximately five minutes. Lockhart glanced at his wife. She continued to gaze stonily out the window. She might have been a statue, something out of the Hollywood Wax Museum. A pity, a great pity she was accompanying David Walsh on Flight 902. . . .

He shook the thought away. It troubled him. He wondered why. He could be dispassionate about the deaths of more than a hundred people on Trans American's Flight 902. Yet the mere idea of disposing of a woman he loathed, and who loathed him, was curiously repugnant.

He smiled to himself.

A strange piece of machinery, the human psyche.

At precisely the same time, in Leningrad, a colonel in Soviet intelligence was complaining about the quality of state tailoring. Vassili Kalinokov's new tunic was baggy about the shoulders, yet the middle section looked as if it had been made for a dwarf.

But his aide, Morikilov, said that with all due respect he failed to see what the Comrade Colonel was complaining about. The tunic looked splendid, in his opinion.

Kalinokov pointed out the unseemly folds about the shoulders. "You call that very smart? It's disgraceful work! A tunic should flow with the movements of a man's body. It should create an image!"

What was the use? Morikilov's wooden eyes were incapable of seeing subtlety in anything. Why had the geniuses at headquarters sent such a specimen to him? What possible use was he in the Intelligence Service?

Morikilov telephoned the Tailoring Section. "Colonel Kalinokov is not satisfied with his tunic," he announced in the tone of a man who has been forced to convey the message and is not in any way responsible for its contents. He listened, nodded, then hung up.

"They inform me that the supervisor himself took your measurements and checked them," he reported.

"And?"

"That was all they told me, sir."

"You mean they're not going to do something about this?"

"They maintain that the tunic was manufactured according to the official specifications laid down in State Apparel Directive . . ."

"But the damned thing doesn't *fit!*"

"They suggest, sir, that it is a matter of opinion . . ." A diplomat, Morikilov, in his own crude way.

"Tell them I am not satisfied and I wish the tunic altered."

"If you say so, sir."

"I most certainly do."

Kalinokov sighed. Was it so much to ask for a tunic that actually fit? One that flattered his figure a little? Did the road to the Communist paradise have to be traveled in such ill-fitting garb?

In two weeks, Colonel Kalinokov would reach the age of fifty. The fact troubled him; soon he would no longer be considered the rising star, the brilliant young intelligence officer who had outwitted his counterparts in Washington, London, Paris and Beijing with such consummate ease. Soon they would be talking about him as the seasoned veteran or, even more distressingly, as the grand old man of the service. It was a chilling, intensely depressing prospect.

He had a slight headache. It was his own fault. Vanity prohibited him from wearing spectacles prescribed by the department optometrist. Now, more than half an hour's reading inevitably set the throbbing into motion. One day he would have to capitulate and wear the damned glasses. One day. But not today. Today his principal concern was his tunic.

On a desolate Canadian island far above the Arctic Circle, west of northern Greenland, an Eskimo hunter, Kulusuk by name, looked into the sky, puzzled and alarmed by an unusual noise.

What was it? An airplane? But it was too close to be one of the great machines that traversed the sky from time to time, leaving delicate white trails that slowly spread and dissolved. He had not been to this area for years, but the scarcity of walrus in the south had forced him unusually far north. Unfortunately, Kulusuk had no way of knowing that aircraft flying in and out of this remote base for Arctic testing had driven the walrus even farther north.

Suddenly a large aircraft emerged from behind a snow-covered hill, its landing gear extended. Mouth agape, the Eskimo watched as the aircraft descended. It vanished behind a slope but its rumblings could still be heard, echoing about the frozen wastes.

Excited, he secured his team of huskies and hurried forward; in a few minutes he was at the crest of the slope. Again his mouth dropped open in astonishment. The aircraft had landed and was rolling slowly to a halt at the end of a long strip of flattened snow and ice. Now, a second aircraft appeared in the sparking Arctic sky. It was smaller than the first. It roared over Kulusuk's head and sent up a shower of icy spray as it touched down.

David Walsh was intensely flattered that Eric and Dorothy Lockhart had journeyed to the airport to see him off. The very unexpectedness of the gesture made it that much more meaningful. What an enigmatic individual Eric was, so cold and self-contained, yet capable of unexpected warmth. It was, David Walsh decided, a particularly impressive performance considering how disappointed Eric must have been about the XB-3A.

"We couldn't let your twenty-fifth anniversary slip by without recognizing it in some small way," Lockhart was saying. "I understand Pamela's intending to join you for the big day."

Walsh nodded, gratified and surprised that Lockhart had taken the trouble to find out such trivial details. "She's flying to Paris on the fifteenth. We're meeting there."

"A romantic place to celebrate your silver anniversary," commented Dorothy. She looked striking this evening, causing heads to turn in her direction. Too bad she didn't always look this good.

"We brought you something to help you celebrate," said Lockhart, producing an immense bottle. "I'd like you to take this, David, and remember us on your anniversary."

Genuinely touched, Walsh could only stammer his thanks. This huge magnum was incredible, quite a marvelous gift . . . He read the label: Lafitte Rothschild, 1945.

Lockhart knew that Senator Walsh was a connoisseur of fine wines and would recognize that such a rare vintage probably was worth more than two thousand dollars.

Walsh shook Lockhart's hand. "I can't thank you enough, Eric. You know, perhaps we'll all have something to celebrate when I get back. This trip to Europe may do much to help our cause."

"I certainly hope so," Lockhart responded.

"The fight isn't lost yet," Walsh added.

Lockhart nodded. "That's exactly the way I feel."

*   *   *

"You surprise me," Dorothy admitted as the limousine pulled away from the terminal area. "How did you know it was the Walshes' anniversary? And why do you care?"

He shrugged elaborately. "Sometimes it's useful to know such things."

"Maybe it's because Senator Walsh might become President Walsh and you can use him the way you use everyone else. Including me."

"That's absurd."

"You exploit people, Eric. Otherwise they don't mean a damn to you." Opening the small mahogany bar built into the limousine, she said, "Pour me a drink, will you?"

From a window in the VIP lounge, David Walsh watched Lockhart's limousine until it disappeared into the evening traffic. He shook his head, still grateful for the unexpected sendoff by the Lockharts. An unpredictable man, Eric, but his heart was obviously in the right place.

He showed the bottle to Milt Bryden, the young aide accompanying him to Europe.

"Superb vino," Milt commented, examining the label with an eye of emphatic approval. "There's not much of this stuff left, anywhere, at any price. And a magnum! Lockhart must be impressed by you, Senator."

Much more than I knew, Walsh thought. "He's very considerate," he said aloud.

"I should have such friends," observed Milt, still studying the label. "Do you think it'll fit in your carry-on baggage, Senator? It's quite a handful. Probably too big."

Walsh nodded. Milt had a point. The magnum would take up almost all the space available in his carry-on bag. "I might be able to squeeze it in, but it's so damned heavy to carry around."

Milt snapped his fingers. "Surely you're not going to open it on the plane. So why don't we pack it in your luggage? Besides, it'll be safer there."

"But my luggage has already been checked."

"No problem," said Milt with a grin. "All I've got to do is tell them it's for Senator Walsh. They'll get it off the plane and I'll be able to pack the bottle, very carefully, of course. Back in a few minutes."

He pranced away with the elastic gait of an oversized leprechaun.

14

ALTHOUGH MACLEOD HAD never considered the flight deck of a 707 anything other than a place of work, the fact was that he had spent some of the most mentally stimulating and rewarding hours of his life there. This was where he was in his element, where everything made sense, where there was order and logic, where a man knew exactly what he was supposed to do and why. It was snug; the designers of the airplane had labored diligently to pack in a flight crew of three and still provide space for two jump seats (used by check pilots, deadheading pilots and FAA examiners) and a vast array of instruments, levers, switches, controls, warning lights and circuit-breaker panels. It was a place where intense activity could be followed by hours of having little to do but gaze out of a window and study the topography while the autopilot tirelessly maintained heading and altitude. A man's mind could wander at such times. There was space and a godlike view of the world to enrich his perspective. From seven miles above the ground, things tended to assume their correct proportions; you saw them for what they were rather than what they had come to mean. The mind had room to wander, to explore, to philosophize, to appreciate and admire; the pity of it was that, inevitably, there came a time when there had to be a return to earth.

Habit made Macleod enter the flight deck with a frown. He didn't assume the frown consciously; it was an expression of concentration, not irritation; some atavistic instinct told him that a man should be serious when he went to work, even though the work might be enjoyable.

His routine was always the same: stride into the cockpit,

hang up his jacket, stow his cap, and place his flight kit (or "brain bag") on the cockpit floor just to the left of his seat. He would then grab the captain's seat back with his left hand as he used his right foot to raise the position-release lever and slide the seat as far aft as it would go; this well-rehearsed procedure facilitated the task of squeezing into the seat and sitting down. Once seated, he would adjust the rudder pedals to suit the length of his legs. Then he would reach forward and snap out the "Boeing" nameplate from the center of the control wheel. The reason: pilots who flew the airplane occasionally left mementos of their sojourns in the form of obscene magazine photographs concealed inside the nameplate. (Other pilots were fond of inserting colorful magazine photographs—usually those exhibiting a large, erect male organ—inside the oxygen masks used by new flight attendants to demonstrate the emergency system to passengers.)

Automatically Macleod reached forward to remove the nameplate. Then he stopped, conscious that Karen was making her way forward to take the seat beside him.

The intruder.

Brisk and businesslike. And cool. Why the hell didn't she take up nursing or typing like other broads?

He pulled the shoulder harness straps over his upper body, then gathered the two lap straps and the crotch strap, clipping each of the five into the central buckle. He flexed his shoulders against the harness. Now he felt at one with the airplane, the central component, the brain with control over every aspect of its operation. Nothing happened without his approval. It was a good feeling, being in command; it meant that many people in authority had a great deal of confidence in him and were prepared to trust him with their multimillion-dollar airplanes and their precious passengers.

But God knows how long captains would be necessary. The scientists were seemingly devoted to making them obsolete. First they eliminated the radio operators, specialists who could send and receive Morse code with incredible speed. Then they eradicated navigators. The poor bastards with their charts and celestial tables and slide rules and sextants had vanished forever like some extinct species, replaced by computers, accelerometers and other electronic marvels, all of which, it had to be admitted, did a far more accurate job, far more rapidly and reliably. The whole business of finding one's way about the sky had been revolutionized; all you had to do was press the right buttons in the right sequence and the little black boxes would do all the work—indeed, do most of the flying. How long before unmanned airliners whisked their passengers around the world? After all, if an unmanned space-ship could be sent to Saturn and beyond, surely an unmanned airplane could be sent to Cincinnati. Macleod hoped they would wait until he was put out to pasture. Or was six feet under it.

To the rear, he could hear the passengers shuffling aboard like cattle, one hundred and twelve of them, everyone peering at seat numbers, stuffing their personal effects in overhead racks, dropping coats on the carefully styled hairdos of those already seated, settling down with sighs of relief, only to be moved by long-suffering flight attendants who had to explain that seat "A" was next to the window, not on the aisle. It was the same pantomime on every trip; it was as if an identical cast of passengers boarded time after time, doing the same things, like vaudevillians going through a well-practiced routine.

Macleod scanned the instrument panel as he tested the controls, left and right, fore and aft, ensuring that there was freedom of movement. People had been known to take off with jammed, locked or inoperative controls. Stupid, impatient people. They should never be allowed to fly airplanes. Would *she* ever do such a thing? Ridiculous question, he informed himself.

He further informed himself that it was time to settle down and begin to operate as a crew. The girl knew her stuff; according to Simpson she was better than most of the new copilots coming on the line; she had passed every test with ease. If she hadn't, she wouldn't be sitting there, so demure and attentive, waiting for his command.

Damn it all, why had he shot off his mouth in Simpson's office? All he had done was to make a bad situation even worse. What was going through her mind? Was there hatred behind those unblinking eyes? And why the hell couldn't he think of a few words—just the right words—to defuse the situation?

Behind her, Brad was preparing his dials and switches for

the engine-start procedure. He'd looked closely at her a few times. Couldn't blame the guy for that, of course. She was a nice-looking girl. And no patsy. Her reasons for selecting Route Bravo demonstrated that.

He glanced in her direction. It was all wrong, a pretty girl sitting there, wearing earphones, shoulder harness doing an admirable job of defining her curves. It should be a *guy* there, an ordinary, ugly, sweaty guy. A guy *belonged* in that seat. It was what nature had intended.

But there wasn't a damn thing he could do about it.

"Okay," he said, "let's have the before-starting-engines checklist."

"Yes, sir."

Would he ever in a million years get used to a female voice calling out the litany of the checklist?

"Gear lever and lights?"

His eyes shifted to the right. "Down and checked," he responded.

"Parking brake?"

"On."

"Flight instruments?"

"Checked."

"Altimeters and clocks?"

"Set and cross-checked."

"Radar and transponder?"

"Standby."

"Exterior lights?"

"Checked."

"Seat-belt, no-smoking signs?"

"On."

"Window heat?"

"Low."

"Emergency lights?"

"Armed . . ."

Captain and copilot intoned their arcane phrases, readying the big aircraft for flight, checking item after item, every system, every control. Then it was Brad Steiner's turn: battery, fuel quantity, boost pumps, crossfeed valves, hydraulic and engine oil quantity, circuit breakers, oxygen, flight recorder, DC and AC power . . .

"Before-starting-engines checklist is complete, Captain."

The female voice was never intended to utter phrases like that. "Thanks."

It must be tough for her, he told himself. She knows how I feel about women pilots. Simpson knows, too. So how come I seem to be getting her on every damn flight I take?

Simpson kept saying she was a damn good pilot. Hell of a lot better than a lot of men with a similar number of hours. Superb reactions. Fine judgment. Handled herself well during simulated emergencies.

But what about *real* emergencies?

With guys like Dan Simon or Bill Robinson, you had a feeling of confidence. You *knew* how they'd react if things started going wrong . . . like the time that engine fire developed over Burlington. Bill handled things perfectly, just as Macleod knew he would. You could rely on him. That was the point. You needed someone you could count on.

Who the hell knew what any woman would do at any given time during any given set of circumstances? Especially when she's getting her period—all biologically screwed up, out of balance. *Unpredictable, emotional,* that was the trouble with women, he thought.

Clearance Delivery accorded them a slot in the sky: "Trans Am Flight Niner-Zero-Two, you're cleared to Armanda-Stockholm, flight-planned route. After takeoff, turn left heading three-two-zero for radar vectors to Vancouver. Maintain one-zero thousand and squawk four-six-two-niner. Expect further clearance to flight level three-three-zero ten minutes after take-off, over."

Karen acknowledged the clearance, startling the air traffic controller who had expected a male voice to respond from Flight 902.

The ground crew reported: "All buttoned up down here, Cap'n."

Macleod nodded to Karen; she called ground control for permission to start engines. In so doing, she evidently startled yet another controller.

"Yes, ma'am . . . that is, Trans American Niner-Zero-Two . . . er, you're cleared to start engines. Expect Runway Three-Four-Right."

A ground cart provided the pressurized air needed to activate the pneumatic starter on each engine. These in turn forced the second-stage compressors to accelerate to thirty-five percent of their maximum rpm. At fifteen percent rpm, Macleod raised the start lever for the number-one engine. This opened a valve that allowed kerosene to flow into the burner section and simultaneously fired the igniter plugs. Now the number-one engine was sucking in air through its intake, compressing it, expanding it by the heat of combustion and then flinging it from the tailpipe in a lethal torrent.

Number-two engine next. Then four. Finally three. As per the official operating manual. Once the process of jet propulsion had been established, the ground cart could be disconnected.

Brad Steiner droned the after-start checklist: start levers, interconnect, brake and hydraulic pressures, flight recorder, beacon lights . . .

"After-start checklist complete," he reported.

Macleod scanned the panel once more. Everything was satisfactory. He nodded to Karen. "Let's go."

"Trans Am Niner-Zero-Two, ready to taxi with information Sierra, over."

"Trans Am Niner-Zero-Two, you're cleared to taxi to Runway Three-Four-Right. Current altimeter, two-niner-niner five."

Karen acknowledged in her precise way as Macleod nudged the thrust levers with his right hand. His left hand gripped the tiller that controlled nosewheel steering for maneuvering the airplane on the ground.

The 707 stirred herself, her great swept-back wings swaying as she began to roll. Macleod glanced at the weather. A dark, thick overcast. Rain. Fortunately they would be through it in a matter of minutes, soaring in dazzling sunlight while the poor bastards on the ground huddled under umbrellas.

The beginning of another journey. God knows how many times he had performed the preflight ritual, verifying that every complex system operated as it should.

They taxied past a row of jetliners—a TWA "Tristar," a United DC-10, an Air Canada DC-9, a Western 727—shapely noses nuzzling the terminal building like mechanical offspring seeking nourishment from the mother structure.

"Flaps fourteen."

Karen shifted the flap handle. Beneath the cabin floor

could be heard the gentle whirring of the hydraulic pump that shifted the massive flaps on the trailing edge of each wing, trundling them out and down, creating a drooping section for the wing, increasing its lifting power, helping it to prepare for the formidable task of hoisting 147,850 pounds of airplane and crew, 124,000 pounds of fuel, 8,200 pounds of cargo, 31,900 pounds of passengers and baggage—311,900 pounds in all—off the 11,899-foot-long runway and into the air.

"Let's have the taxi checklist."

Brad called out the items: flaps, aileron travel, probe heat, nacelle anti-ice, SCAT, yaw damper, takeoff data, EPR, airspeed bugs, stabilizer trim, fuel heat . . .

"Taxi checklist complete."

"Thanks, Brad."

Macleod braked near the threshold of the assigned runway. Automatically his eyes scanned the area, watching for aircraft on final approach, cars, trucks, joggers, anything or anyone that might suddenly decide to use the runway without bothering to inform the tower controller.

A Pan Am 747 swept past, its clusters of wheels reaching for the ground as if eager to smooth the transition from air to ground. A puff of smoke as the tires seared the concrete, spinning, absorbing the enormous, dynamic weight of the aircraft.

"Taxi into position and hold."

Macleod released the brakes. The 707 rolled forward, landing gear squeaking softly. Something needed more grease down there. . . .

The runway disappeared into a distant patch of ground fog; the Pan Am 747 was a dim shape in the distance, turning off the runway, leaving it solely for the use and pleasure of Trans American Flight 902, Captain F.J. Macleod in command.

Beside him, Karen shifted herself in her seat, preparing for the concentrated activity of takeoff. A crackling, indecipherable voice muttered something on the radio, then was cut off by the controller:

"Trans Am Niner-Zero-Two, you're cleared for takeoff. Wind check, three-zero-zero degrees at twenty-two knots."

Brakes off . . . power on.

"Niner-Zero-Two is rolling."

Awesome power drummed through the entire structure of

the 707, striving to be converted into motion. Four JT3D-3 engines, each rated at 18,000 pounds of thrust, each delivering more raw power than all the engines of a World War II B-29 "Superfortress." They heaved at the colossal weight, gulping fuel now at an extraordinary rate, nearly 1,000 pounds per minute.

Macleod steered by means of the tiller while Karen maintained a steady forward pressure on the control column, keeping the nosewheel firmly planted on the runway while the speed accumulated. Rapidly the white centerline stripes blurred into a single line. The idea was to keep the line disappearing into the dead center of the aircraft, cutting it into precisely equal halves. In practice it was not always that easy, especially with a crosswind. The big Boeing wandered slightly from side to side. She needed a firm but gentle hand. She had to be persuaded but never forced.

"Eighty knots!" Karen called. One of the first officer's jobs was to call the critical speeds as they mounted.

Dammit, that voice should be calling her kids, not takeoff speeds.

Now the airflow past the huge rudder and vertical fin was sufficient to make it effective. Macleod shifted his left hand from the tiller to the control wheel. The 707 was beginning to feel like an airplane. The great wings were forming the air as it swept over their curved surfaces, faster and faster; with speed came strength. Finely tapered, the wings seemed to shiver as if in anticipation of the adventure ahead.

"Vee-One," Karen announced. Crisply.

The point of no return. Too late now to abort the takeoff no matter what happened; there simply wasn't enough runway left.

Now the 707 was alive in his hands, urging him to defy the forces of nature.

Rotation speed: 142 knots. Gentle back pressure on the control column, a bit of left aileron to keep the wings level. The Boeing was pointed skyward at a fifteen-degree angle, poised for flight. The nosewheel was off the ground. But the main wheels, eight of them, still drummed along the runway, the airplane's weight shared equally by the tires and those majestically shaped, swept-back wings. But in seconds, the aerodynamic forces won over gravity. The trundling of the wheels ceased. The ground slipped away below.

Macleod was always thrilled by the surge of power, the miracle of lift. It still awed him. The exhilaration of takeoff was almost erotic. How the hell could anyone with an ounce of soul ever take such an experience for granted?

"Vee-Two!"

Minimum safe flying speed had been reached: 158 knots. Ten more knots to reach initial climb speed.

"Gear up."

Karen pulled on the lever and raised it, activating 3,000 pounds of hydraulic pressure to haul the landing gear up into the fuselage and wing roots; doors closed over the apertures, ensuring a smooth passage for the speeding air.

"Flaps up."

Macleod felt the aircraft shift predictably in his hands as the big trailing-edge flaps slid forward to become an integral part of the wing, changing its shape to suit it to high-speed flight.

He turned off the windshield wipers. They were needed during the takeoff. But now, enveloped by nimbo-stratus cloud, there was nothing to see. Just gray. Wispy muck flashing by. Air saturated with moisture. A steady dose of light turbulence.

Speed: 250 knots.

"Seattle Center, this is Trans Am Niner-Zero-Two, out of eleven for flight level three-three-zero, over."

"Roger, Trans Am Niner-Zero-Two, turn right to heading zero-five-zero. Report leaving one-seven thousand."

Macleod said, "Let's have the after-takeoff checklist."

"Okay," said Brad. "Rudder pump?"

"Off," Karen reported.

"Gear lever?"

"Off."

"Seat-belt, no-smoking sign?"

"Checked."

"Logo light?"

"Off."

"Landing lights?"

"Off."

"Ignition?"

"Off."

"After-takeoff checklist complete, sir." Brad sounded a bit more enthusiastic than usual. Trying to impress the lady pilot?

Three hundred knots exactly.

The sky was becoming brighter as the Boeing sliced through layers of cloud. Best to keep the seat-belt sign on until calmer air was reached. Okay to turn off the no-smoking sign though; the smokers were probably having a collective nicotine fit.

Eight hours and fifty-one minutes to Stockholm, according to the flight plan. En route, the four Pratt & Whitney engines would consume 99,200 pounds of fuel, almost 15,000 gallons. The 707 would average only one-third of a mile per gallon. On the other hand, it was hauling quite a load. When the airplane touched down 4,798 miles later, there would be 24,800 pounds of kerosene remaining in the four main fuel tanks.

So sayeth the computer; so it had to be true.

After passing over Vancouver, Canada, Flight 902 would head for Prince George, Peace River, and then pass to the southeast of Yellowknife and the Great Slave Lake. Continuing northeastward, the 707 would strike out across the frigid wasteland of the Northwest Territory, cross the Arctic Circle and then pass about halfway between the North Magnetic Pole and the northern reaches of Hudson Bay. At Clyde, a village on the east coast of Baffin Island, the flight would leave Canadian territory behind, heading over the icy waters of Baffin Bay to intercept the west coast of Greenland near Upernavik. It would then fly directly over the Greenland ice cap, cross the island's east coast near Myggbukta and pass closely abeam of desolate Jan Mayen Island in the Greenland Sea. Next solid land: Norway, crossing the coast at Vigra, flying over Oslo and finally reaching the Swedish border at Romskog. From there it was a two-hundred-mile flight, the last leg of the journey to Stockholm.

The flight plan instructed Macleod to cruise at 33,000 feet until he passed the radiobeacon at Clyde. He was then to climb to 37,000 feet for the rest of the trip. Average cruising speed would be Mach .80, which, in the parlance of earthlings, is eighty percent of the speed of sound, or 535 mph at 33,000 feet and 526 mph at 37,000 feet. Furthermore, the flight plan declared, the average outside air temperature would be $-60°$ F at 33,000 feet and $-74°$ F at 37,000 feet. It would be cold outside, but not unusually so. Assisting the flight would be a 32-knot tailwind at 33,000 feet and a 25-knot tailwind at 37,000 feet.

The computer knew it all.

15

SENATOR DAVID WALSH was tired. He had been up late the previous night, chairing a numbingly long committee meeting on fresh water supplies in the 1990s. He looked forward to sleeping most of the way to Europe. He found the seat-back control button and pushed it, keeping it down until he was semi-reclined. With his feet on the footrest attached to the front of his seat, he was almost as comfortable as if he were at home in his easy chair. He closed his eyes for a few blissful moments, letting his thoughts wander, to Europe where a hectic schedule awaited him, to Paris and the Plaza-Athenée Hotel where his wife Pamela would meet him in a little more than a week, to Washington where his best efforts had failed to win support for Lockhart's Devastator. But the battle wasn't lost, he told himself. Not yet. Perhaps NATO would buy the plane. . . .

He glanced up as Milt Bryden lowered his slim frame into the next seat. "I've been looking the situation over, Senator."

"I'm sure you have," Walsh said with a wry smile. Milt Bryden was a predator, constantly on the hunt for females.

"There are possibilities, Senator, very definite possibilities. Particularly the redhead. Name of Wendi. With an 'i.' Isn't that cute?"

"Very," said Walsh. "But you're not going to have much time over there. You'll only be in Stockholm for thirty-six hours."

Milt beamed. He was a wiry young man in his late twenties, with a crinkly smile and receding brown hair. "I'm hoping thirty-six hours'll be time enough, Senator. By the way, one of the stewardesses said that a lot of people know you're on board and would like to meet you."

"Not a chance," Walsh declared.

"I know you don't like that sort of thing on an airplane."

"Like it? I hate it!"

"I understand how you feel, Senator, but honestly, in this case it might be worthwhile. There's a P.R. guy from the airline. He's taking photographs. Says he'd love to do a piece about you for the company magazine; the wire services might even pick it up. This is an interesting flight; they've got a lady copilot flying this thing."

"There would be, with you on board."

Milt smiled modestly. "Mere coincidence, Senator, believe me. Anyway, she's the first girl to make it to first officer with Trans American and this is her first flight to Sweden. Nice to have the two of you chatting, maybe. Just a few minutes, that's all, Senator. The P.R. guy says he'll get Amelia Earhart, then he'll shoot the two of you together. You could be back in your seat in fifteen or twenty minutes, maybe less."

Walsh sighed. A persuasive bastard, Milt. He said, "What about the cabin crew? Won't they be serving dinner? I'd be in their way."

Bryden shook his head. "No problem. I talked to Janet."

"Janet?"

"Janet Spencer. I think she's the chief stewardess. Nice."

"I'm sure." Walsh grinned. He liked Milt, a bright and very ambitious young man who, although perpetually horny, was an efficient aide who could, when the situation demanded, present a solemn and quite dignified image to the world. "Okay. Let's get it over with. By the time we get back I'll be ready for a drink."

It was familiar stuff, glad-handing the citizenry: Hello, I'm-Senator-David-Walsh-and-I'm-pleased-to-meet-you. Nine hundred and ninety-nine times out of a thousand it was a pleasant encounter; you were greeted by a surprised smile of recognition and mumbles of pleasure at meeting someone of your stature. But not always. You could receive a punch in the nose from a disgruntled auto worker; dazzled females of anywhere between nine and ninety were liable to throw their arms around your neck. And then there was always an outside chance of some nut taking a shot at you. Or kidnapping you, like they did in that novel he had just read. In *The Vatican Target* a bunch of terrorists had actually hijacked an airplane carrying the Pope. The possibilities were endless.

The passengers aboard Flight 902 were friendly enough, however, seeing him as an added attraction, a welcome diversion on a long flight. They reached out to shake his hand. Some of them (two women and five men) said he deserved to be President and promised to vote for him, apparently believing he was already a candidate. Many asked for autographs; he obliged, scribbling his name (and best wishes to Chuck and Sue) on cocktail coasters, on tickets, on boarding passes. One elderly man wanted to discuss the entire Middle East situation; another wanted to know his stand on gay rights, pornography, abortion and the lousy mail service. A woman asked what he would have done if he'd been President when the "outlaws in Iran took our people hostage." He told her he would have taken "firm steps"; she nodded her approval. He withdrew before he had to expand on the subject. The trick was to get away gracefully, yet expeditiously. Agree, nod, exude empathy. It was part of the game; it was expected. Americans insisted on believing that their politicians were basically like themselves, crazy about baseball, hot dogs and television. Haughty, aristocratic politicians belonged in Europe and other backward places.

"How the hell are we going to avoid war with Russia?" a freckled, pudgy man with thin red hair wanted to know.

"We must be stronger than *all* adversaries."

"I'll buy that."

"Strength is the only language they understand."

"Right on," said the pudgy man. "And as soon as you've made us stronger than Russia you can get to work sending all the niggers back to Africa and the Jews back to wherever they belong."

Tight little grimace. No comment. Move on. Quickly. Ignoring the pudgy man and the fact that he is still babbling about welfare creeps, those stinking parasites sucking the life blood from those who work for a living. . . . Now broaden the smile for the silver-haired old lady who tells you how much you remind her of her nephew who is married to a niece of a former head of one of the largest insurance agencies in Santa Ana. . . .

"He's a dentist," she announced with obvious pride.

"Quite a switch after insurance," said David Walsh.

She frowned, shaking her head. "No, that was *her* uncle, not *him.*"

"Of course."

"You've got his eyes," she declared. "But the nose is wrong," she added, the frown returning. "Do you have any O'Keefes or Delaneys in your family?"

"I don't believe so, ma'am."

"Fosters?"

"Pardon?"

"Do you have any relatives named Foster?"

"Not that I'm aware of."

"I see," she said, her lips tightening; she appeared to have decided that he didn't deserve her vote after all.

Janet Spencer leaned over Macleod's seat in the familiar manner of someone who has spent much of her adult life working aboard airplanes.

"Mr. Flitch is asking to speak with you."

Macleod turned to her. "Who's he?"

"Public Relations. Here's his card."

Macleod glared at the card; it bore the red-and-silver logo of Trans American Airlines, beside which was the name: George M. Flitch, Public Relations Coordinator.

Now he remembered. Simpson had mentioned it. Asked that Flitch be given total cooperation although, needless to say, the ultimate decision rested entirely with him, as it did with every captain, et cetera, et cetera.

He said to Karen, "Flitch is on board to interview you."

"Oh?"

"Meant to tell you before takeoff. Forgot. Sorry."

"That's all right," she said. "I don't want to be interviewed anyway."

Brad said, "Bet they're not going to give you a hell of a lot of choice in the matter. You're news; news is publicity; publicity is free advertising; people will read what a wonderful airline Trans Am is, and they'll all run out to their friendly neighborhood travel agents and reserve seats with us. All because of you."

Janet said, "Captain, this Flitch character is wondering if

Karen would come back and have her picture taken with Senator Walsh.''

Karen shook her head. ''Oh God, do I have to?''

Christ, thought Macleod, what the hell is this, a flight deck or the Johnny Carson show?

''Can't he wait until after we land?''

''I'll ask him,'' said Janet and returned to the cabin.

She reappeared a few minutes later.

''He says he's got a problem and would really appreciate it if he could talk to you.''

Macleod sighed sufferingly. ''Okay, bring him up.''

Karen apologized again.

Macleod sighed again.

Flitch was a tall, rumpled man laden with notebook, camera and portable tape recorder. He smiled about the flight deck in friendly fashion, apologizing for butting in, like a man crashing a party. ''Sorry about this, Captain. Believe me, I didn't even want to go to Sweden. I was all set for a couple of hours of mixed doubles when they told me they needed the story and . . .''

''What story, for Christ's sake?''

''About First Officer Dempsey. The first woman to make it to the rank of first officer with TAA and the first one to fly overseas. It's news, Captain, and the company wants the world to know about it. And then, Senator Walsh being on the same flight, why, that makes it even better. Natural news, I call this kind of situation. We get a nice story for the company paper and great material for a press release. I figured I'd try and get the whole thing down before everyone has dinner and settles for the night. A few shots with the senator, then maybe a couple up here—if that's okay with you, of course. Then the interview.''

''You can interview her in Stockholm,'' Macleod said. ''Not while she's on duty in my airplane.''

Flitch sighed. ''Now that's what I had in mind too, Captain. But you see it's a question of deadlines. My orders are to do a piece on Ms. Dempsey, then an item on Senator Walsh, and file them as soon as we land and clear customs. The P.R. department finds Ms. Dempsey kind of interesting, Captain. Human interest . . .''

Macleod's neck tingled with irritation. He could hear the

bastards in management: And why, Captain, did you refuse to let Mr. Flitch complete his assignment? Surely it's obvious to you, Captain, in these days of financial pressure and increasing competition, that it's incumbent upon all members of the team to do everything possible to create just the right sort of image for Trans American, friendly people doing their jobs the best way they know how. . . .

"Just make it fast."

"You bet, Skipper," said Flitch.

Christ, but Macleod detested being called Skipper.

Karen turned to him and said, "Do I really have to do this, Captain? A guy from a newspaper already took my picture. I hate interviews; I never know what to say . . ."

"Do it," Macleod said. "It's for the good of the airline."

What the hell else could go wrong on this flight?

Fascinated, the Eskimo watched the parka-clad men working busily on the body and wings of the airplane, examining it in the intent way of hunters over a kill; they connected the smaller aircraft with the larger by means of a long, flexible tube.

A young man climbed alone into the smaller plane. The stairs swung up behind him, folding flush into the outer skin of the body.

At the front left window, the young man raised a thumb to the waiting ground crewmen.

A moment later the two engines whined into life. Behind the sleek aircraft, a shimmering curtain of frozen snow danced before the setting sun.

A wave from the pilot. The jet airplane began to move, engines roaring with power. The din echoed across the lonely, frigid wasteland as the aircraft gathered speed.

The Eskimo watched, astounded at the speed of the machine. It lifted off, thrust its nose skyward and hurtled away as if some giant arm had flung it with every ounce of strength. The sound of its engines rolled across the frozen slopes like the thunder of a thousand caribou.

It was after ten when he telephoned Virginia. "I'm sorry it's so late. Did I wake you?"

She replied matter-of-factly, "No, the three guys in bed with me won't leave me alone."

Lockhart managed a quick chuckle. "For a moment I thought you were serious."

"I figured you might," she said with a giggle that was almost girlish.

Lockhart sighed. An unpredictable personality, Virginia. Formal, then crude; cool, then playful.

"Had a pleasant evening?" he asked.

"Quiet," she said. "You?"

"Boring. A business dinner. Before that I was at the airport, seeing off David Walsh on his flight to Stockholm."

"I saw him on TV," she said. "He looks, ah . . . very presidential."

"He is," Lockhart told her. "Quite charming and moderately amusing when he's in the mood. I'll introduce you to him some day," he said. Mention of Walsh had generated a tiny thrill, not unpleasant, that sped through his guts. "He'll be flying all over Europe," Lockhart added, noting with satisfaction how calm his voice was. "One of those fact-finding tours that presidential hopefuls always seem to take."

It was a little test: to state the fact without being forced into it. No apparent change in tone. No fumbling with the words. No doubt.

He had done what had to be done. He had the courage and the will. Historians might look back upon this period and see it as a turning point, the time when America finally faced the realities of the world in the last part of the twentieth century. No one would ever know that he, Eric Lockhart, was the catalyst, the unsung hero who made it all happen, the man who literally changed the course of history. No one except Mike. Even Mike's crew in the Arctic were unaware of his true mission, believing it was all simply part of a month-long testing program of electronic systems in sub-zero conditions.

But it was enough that he and Mike would know.

"Tired?" she asked.

"No," he said.

"It's late, but if you'd like to come over, I'd be happy . . ."

She had a way of letting the end of a sentence drift away. It was curiously exciting. Fantastic how she could stir him, even over the phone. With her he felt young again; it was all so fresh and thrilling, as if he had been reborn.

"I'll be right over."

"Please hurry."

He hung up, smiling to himself. Dorothy had done her duty at the dinner, drinking only Perrier, making polite conversation. Upon arrival at the house she had drowned half a dozen glasses of Chivas on the rocks; now she was in bed; she wouldn't move until late morning.

He changed quickly from his dinner jacket into a sports coat and slacks. A rapid clean-up with his electric razor. An even more rapid brushing of his hair. Gray, almost white now, but still thick, thank God.

He went downstairs. The evening paper lay on the hall table. As he slipped on his raincoat he glanced at it. A picture caught his eye. A pretty girl in uniform. The hair style reminded him of Julie Andrews. TAA's first female copilot, the caption stated.

Flying to Stockholm. Same flight as Senator David Walsh.

He winced as if struck. He'd never for one moment thought there would be a woman in the crew. . . . He shook his head. It was ridiculous, utterly illogical to agonize over a woman just because she happened to be on the flight crew. No doubt there were scores of women on that flight—flight attendants as well as passengers. The difference was simply that they were anonymous; she wasn't. She had a face and a name.

Karen Dempsey.

He kept gazing at the picture in the paper; for some reason it seemed physically difficult to drag his eyes away from it.

A shame about her . . . a dreadful shame.

But there was no other way. She was one of the involuntary soldiers. He wished that in some way she might understand.

Karen shook hands with the senator. She had seen him many times on television and in the papers. He had a relaxed, easy style that seemed curiously out of character with his hawkish philosophy.

"Very sorry to get you out of the cockpit, Miss Dempsey, but they seem to want to take our picture together. I hope you don't mind."

"No," she said. "It's a pleasure." Wow, she thought, this man could be *President* next year!

"I've never met a lady airline pilot before," he said as

he moved closer to her in obedience to George Flitch's gesticulations.

"I've never met a senator," she replied.

He grinned. "Do the male pilots give you a rough time?"

"No," she said, "they've all been very nice to me."

"Do you think many women will follow in your footsteps?"

"I hope so."

"Women make good pilots, don't they?"

"Some do. Some don't. The thing is, women have to be as professional about the business as men are. Too many like to be charming amateurs—and there's no place for that sort of attitude in an airline cockpit."

"What about marriage and children?"

"What about them?"

"Don't you feel that you're missing something, not being at home looking after kids and a husband?"

"At times. But in life you have to make choices. A long time ago I found out that I loved to fly more than anything else I had ever done. I still do. So I've built my life around it."

Walsh nodded approvingly. "You've really got it all together."

"I certainly hope so," Karen told him.

Flitch snapped half a dozen shots; then Walsh was shaking her hand again and wishing her every success.

"You too, Senator," she said.

He thanked her. She went back to the flight deck and apologized to Macleod. "Sorry. I really didn't want to do that."

Macleod shrugged. "It's okay. No sweat." He cracked half a smile. "We all have to do our thing for Trans Am in our own little ways."

===16===

MIKE LOCKHART PEERED into the distance. The sky was assuming a soft bronze tone as the eerie neither-day-nor-night Arctic twilight took over. Below, the ground was sheathed in soft shadow. There were no lights to be seen, no signs of human habitation.

A frigid wilderness.

He glanced at the instrument panel of the Grumman G-III business jet in the casual, instinctive manner common to all professional aviators, scanning the gauges yet hardly conscious of what information each conveyed. But if one needle had indicated a problem it would have registered on his mind like a flashing red light.

Nothing to do for a while. Sit back and let the plane fly him to the destination—he winced—the intercept point. Somewhere in the distance, in that mingling, thickening of shadows that vaguely defined the end of solid ground and beginning of sky, was the target. It was flying on a converging course at an altitude of 37,000 feet.

He pictured the passengers aboard the jetliner. Rows of them. Men, women, children; the young, the old. No! He shook his head. He had to banish the image. It could weaken his resolve, as it had done God knows how many times already, filling him with the poison of self-doubt.

Why him? Why was he the one out of God knows how many millions to be saddled with this terrible, ugly task? Why wasn't there someone else to do it? And, worst question of all, did it really *have* to be done?

He had discussed it all with his father, in endless, agoniz-

ing sessions. There had to be another way. There had to be a
better alternative than to kill innocent people.

There had to be. But the horrible reality had to be faced.
There was no other way.

"No one is forcing us to take this initiative," his father had
declared, his strong hands shaping the air before him. "We
can let it slip by. No one will blame us. Nothing will happen
that isn't already happening. We will simply watch as our
country's power and prestige continue to erode. But we—you
and I—will know there was a time when we could have
changed the course of history."

He was right, of course. He always was. An extraordinary
man, his father, a genius who possessed the ability to perceive reality instead of being influenced by the distortions
created by politicians and the media.

But, right or wrong, it was a hideous thing to do.

Several times in the last few days, Mike had been tempted
to make an anonymous call and warn David Walsh not to
board Flight 902 because of some terrorist plot to assassinate
him. Once he had even started to dial Walsh's private number
before an inner voice commanded him to stop.

It was the coward's way out. He was ashamed. Yet he kept
asking himself: why did Walsh choose this particular time to
fly to Europe, precisely when the long-planned Arctic tests of
the XB-3A's electronic systems were taking place, precisely
when the U.S. and Soviet governments were embroiled in
bargaining over the Mutual Arms Reduction Treaty?

It all fit together like some giant cosmic puzzle. There
seemed to be a frightening inevitability about it all. Yet, as
his father had said, it all came down to one question: Did they
believe in the cause strongly enough to justify this action?
Yes, of course, of course, of course . . . What were the lives
of a hundred when the destiny of hundreds of millions was at
stake?

He rubbed his eyes. He was tired. He had slept fitfully, in
spite of the sleeping pills. He hated himself for what he was
about to do, yet he knew he would hate himself far more
intensely if he *didn't* do it.

Why did being a Lockhart have to entail such awesome
responsibilities?

He wondered how he would live with himself when it was

all over. His father had assured him that he would learn to cope with it. "When you know it is necessary you can handle the situation. You remember what the alternatives are and the sense of proportion returns."

"But," he had asked, "suppose we do it . . . and it doesn't accomplish what we expect? Think of all those wasted lives."

His father had pondered the question for a long, painful moment. "Then we will have to comfort each other as best we can, Mike, knowing that at least we tried."

In the third row of the first-class cabin sixty-four-year-old Harriet Lawson glowered at Flitch. In her opinion, the man was a cretin, a disgrace to his profession. The damn fool was only interested in that politician. Didn't he realize there might be someone *else* noteworthy on board? It was infuriating! And humiliating! She shook with indignation, a curiously poodlelike shake that set her ample jowls ashivering. Her hair was jet black, not a trace of gray to be seen; her features were handsome but their definition had been softened by the years.

Her eyes were still bright blue. Baby blue.

She glanced up as a stewardess breezed by, professional smile plastered on her thin lips. Not even a glimmer of recognition in those dreary eyes. Stupid bitch. For Christ's sake, there was a copy of the book on the empty seat next to her, the famous still from the movie, *Marcie McGuire*, on the cover. But did it register? Like hell. What did you have to do? Stand up on the goddam seat and point to the cover of the book and identify yourself? On the trip to London a few years ago, she'd no sooner stepped inside the damned airplane than they'd been fawning all over her, telling her how marvelous it was to have her on board and how everyone had enjoyed all her movies and how they still were great, after countless reruns on television.

This time? Nothing. Had she changed that much in a few miserable years?

She glanced down at the book as if it were some despicable insect. It had been a flop, a total disaster. All that work: endless hours in front of tape recorders, conferences with that egocentric bastard of an author, wanting equal billing just because he put the lousy words together. Proofs. Blurbs. Promotions. Cocktail parties. Autographing sessions. Appearances in book stores. Interviews. For naught. All very disappointing, according to the publisher; unfortunate timing; Hollywood kiss-and-tell books had peaked, he said. The book had bombed.

The Swedish version looked as if it was going to be the only foreign-language edition. Hence this trip. The name Harriet Lawson was still big in Sweden, they said.

But they were the same people who had said everyone and his brother were going to be running out to buy the book in the States. The so-called experts. It was sickening, the way the public forgets; it was as if your name got wiped off some lousy blackboard and you ceased to exist.

Once in Brentano's Book Store in Beverly Hills, she had seen a girl—woman, really, at least forty, old enough to know better—take the book off the shelf, look at it and *shrug*, clearly indicating that neither the name nor the face meant anything to her. Where did she spend her childhood, in Tibet, for Christ's sake?

The coach-class section began at row six. Seats 9A, B and C were occupied by the Parker family: Clifford, thirty-four, a mailman, his wife Joanne, thirty-one, and their eleven-year-old son, Neil. The flight to Stockholm was the first leg of a two-week European tour for the Parkers—all expenses paid, thanks to Neil. He had won first prize in a nationwide contest for sixth-graders, having written a two-thousand-word essay on the subject "The Future I Want to See for America." A brilliant boy; everyone said so. His future was undoubtedly bright and his potential unlimited. Learning came so easily to him; his mind was a steel trap and his memory was photographic—at least his mother said so. He was a pale little fellow with soft green eyes and long sandy hair. People kept asking him whether he intended to go into medicine or law, teaching or writing. He usually shrugged and tried to change the subject. But now, sitting in a jet bound for Europe, he had just about made up his mind. The unexpected appearance of Senator Walsh had given him a new idea. It was perfect.

Seat 14C was occupied by Sam Coglin, the pudgy man who had expressed such virulent views about minorities. He was still agitated. That damn senator hadn't stopped to listen to the real facts; he'd slid away with a condescending smile on his lips. No one had the guts to face reality. The forces of the devil were at work, that was the truth of the matter. Like many bigots, Mr. Coglin believed fervently that God was his ally, a wrathful super-being who watched earthly goings-on with the suspicious eyes of a custom officer. Mr. Coglin was traveling to Sweden on business. He sold children's clothing.

Four rows back, in Seat 18A, sat one of the men so hated by Mr. Coglin. Name of William Jarvis. A slim black man in his late thirties, Jarvis was neatly but casually dressed in a leather jacket and open-necked shirt. He was a musician, a pianist, and he was on his way to Stockholm to play in a jazz concert, after which he would perform for three weeks in a club in Copenhagen; then there would be a series of engagements in Munich, Hamburg and Bonn. He was looking forward to the European gigs; it would be refreshing, working with a lot of new people; some would be fantastic, some would be a drag. But one thing was for sure: the fans would be beautiful people, well-informed, respectful, eager to listen. Too bad Phil couldn't come along this time. But Phil was a teacher and it was tough for him to get away so close to final exams. Phil was William Jarvis' lover; Phil was white, and Jewish.

The Lees, in 21A and B, were honeymooners. Both were giggling secretly; he had just described in graphic detail what he planned to do their first night in Stockholm. She said she was game if he was. Melvin Lee was eighty-two; Tina Lee was seventy-nine.

In 24F, a young Swedish man named Carl Neillsen wished the plane would crash. What seared through him like a red-hot poker was that, after everything that had been said, everything they had done, she had decided to stay with her husband. She had shrugged—*shrugged*, for God's sake—she said that she just couldn't face all the upheaval, the pain, the trauma of a breakup. She was sorry, really sorry. Shocked, he had reminded her that he had already broken with Marie. She kept nodding, agreeing that it was awful, but not changing her mind. She said she would always have the fondest memories of him. Tears misted his eyes when he thought of her. She had wormed her way into his life so completely that now it seemed totally worthless without her. Thank God there had been the sales trip to America. But now he had to return to Sweden. And nothing.

Mrs. Henry Warren, seat 28C, was still recapping her brief conversation with David Walsh. Such a nice-looking man, the senator, although, in her opinion, a little slow on the uptake. But the fact remained that he could become the President and it certainly wasn't every day that one actually conversed with someone who was likely to be President. It was very definitely something to store away and drop in at strategically useful opportunities: "As I said to David Walsh—that was when he was just a senator, you know . . ." She nodded to herself; a very worthwhile encounter. It was a pleasant little opener for her Big Trip. Frankly, she wished she could go somewhere other than Sweden. What on earth made Joanie marry a Swede? And what sort of place to live was Kristineham? And would she find anyone who could speak English?

Flight 902 carried one hundred twelve passengers, sixty-three of whom were business travelers: sales representatives, accountants, a metallurgist, an antique dealer, a literary agent, a company vice-president (who had been booked first-class on the flight but who had quietly converted the ticket to coach-class before departure and had pocketed the difference in fare). Five young women and one man were TAA flight attendants "deadheading" to Stockholm on their way to Paris, where they would join a TAA Boeing 747 and work the trip to New York. (When men were first hired as flight attendants, some narrowminded employees referred to them as "ball-bearing stewardesses.") The youngest person on board was Neil Parker, the oldest Melvin Lee. Eighty-four passengers were Americans; sixteen were Swedish, two British, three Canadian, two Norwegian, four Turkish and one South African.

"Do you have to go?" Virginia asked.

"No," said Lockhart, "not yet. Why do you ask?"

"You keep glancing at your watch."

"Do I? Sorry. I wasn't aware of it."

"Only half of you is with me tonight." She grinned in a wicked way. "Thank God it's the right half. See, this half is standing up and paying attention to me even if the rest of you isn't!"

*   *   *

It's still not too late, he told himself. There's still time to call it off. Abandon the mission; turn around and head back. Make up some excuse. Invent a problem. Say there was a malfunction, some kind of system failure. Nothing happened when I pressed the button.

Deep inside he hoped for a way out. A real reason to abort this flight: an actual engine failure, a cracked windshield . . . Anything. But no, everything was working perfectly.

To his left, a small dot glowed on the radar screen.

The target! Right on schedule!

Trans American Flight 902, a jet-propelled lamb to the slaughter.

He peered into the distance. The 707 was dead ahead, somewhere in that layer of cirrostratus cloud that diffused the Arctic light. He studied the radar screen. The Grumman Gulfstream III was converging steadily with the target. In a few minutes, he might even establish visual contact with the Boeing 707. Instinctively, his eyes scanned the instrument panel; then he glanced at the aeronautical chart spread out on the empty co-pilot's seat beside him. A licking of dry lips. His hands began to perspire; he wiped them, one at a time, on his pants leg.

He thought of Wanda. He dreaded the thought of seeing her for the first time after this mission. She knew David Walsh, had met him at the Lockhart house, admired him, hoped fervently that he would win the presidential nomination.

No, he mustn't think of Wanda. It was distracting. Must not think of anything or anyone except what had to be done. And he was the one that fate had chosen. . . .

There!

The 707 seemed to be suspended in the sky, a tiny, motionless silhouette . . . full of life and activity.

If only he had a missile, the surgical procedure of destruction would be more acceptable, more like a military sortie. But aircraft manufacturers could not get their hands on such lethal hardware.

He reached forward and uncovered a guarded button on the instrument panel.

Six-point-eight nautical miles . . .

The jetliner seemed to swell as the distance shrank.

Five-point-zero nautical miles.

Oh God, forgive me, Mike screamed.

He depressed the red button.

────17────

A MAN COULD go berserk staring at radar screens. Particularly if he was stationed at a place like Resolute Island, a joint U.S.-Canadian communications base only miles from the Magnetic North Pole. Resolute Island, a rocky, ice-and-snow-covered place of frozen desolation.

It was Airman Second Class Herbie Mannerman's contention that the U.S. Air Force had it in for him. A grudge. Some long-forgotten remark to some equally long-forgotten officer. Probably someone in Records. There were assholes like that. Sadistic. And the trouble was, you could never track them down. You had no idea whom you were even looking for. Bastards. They had all the advantages. They controlled his file. And his life. It was obvious. In the normal course of events he would have been reassigned by now, transferred to someplace like England or Germany, somewhere with girls and bars and lots of action, where a guy could enjoy life. Sometimes it seemed as if he had spent his entire life on this crappy island staring at this crappy radar screen.

Hoagland came in. Ugly as ever. And nasty. It pleased him, gave him some sort of peculiar, sadistic pleasure to harp on the miseries of Arctic duty.

"I've been reading a report."

"Bullshit," said Airman Mannerman. "You can't read."

"It says that duty in a place like this can ruin a man for life. Can even make him impotent."

"Fuck off."

Hoagland sniffed. He sniffed a lot. "Every experience in life leaves its mark. Some small. Some big. Guys who've been in prisoner-of-war camps are never the same again, they

126

say. They're affected," he declared with the doleful tone of a man announcing the arrival of a plague. "We'll never be the same again. They've cut us off from our fellow man. And, a hell of a lot more important, our fellow women . . ."

"Knock it off," said Mannerman.

"They say a guy hung himself a couple of years ago. Couldn't take it any more. Didn't see the sun all winter. Too much ice and snow and wind. Too many men. Got depressed as hell. Hanging was the only way out. The government didn't give a shit. Why should it? He was just an enlisted man."

Airman Herbie Mannerman peered at the blip appearing on the left side of his radar screen. He consulted the flight list on his clipboard. That must be Trans Am 902, Seattle to Stockholm. Right on schedule. They've probably had their dinner by now. Still digesting it, maybe slurping down a bourbon or two with their coffee, eyeing the stewardesses; maybe some smooth son of a bitch has already made a date for Stockholm. No wonder airline people call them *lay*overs. . . .

"You know, Herbie," said Hoagland, "there's probably fifty females on that flight. Let's say half of them are too young or too old. It doesn't matter. That still leaves twenty-five warm, loving female bodies, fifty delicious tits . . ."

"Jesus," said Airman Herbie Mannerman. He frowned at the radar screen and gripped the edges of the set with both hands as if he were about to shake it.

"What's up?"

"It's gone."

"What's gone?"

"Flight Nine-Oh-Two."

"Huh?"

"Goddam target's vanished. It was there a second ago. Now it's gone."

"C'mon," Hoagland said disbelievingly. He flopped his lengthy frame across Mannerman's desk.

The target reappeared.

"There. There it is big as life. What the hell are you talking about?"

"It . . . it did disappear. I'm not kidding."

Hoagland shrugged. "You're full of shit. Or maybe your

vision is starting to go. That's another problem with spending too much time up here. You start seeing things. Or not seeing them . . .''

In a Soviet radar installation north of Murmansk, an electronics technician named Isokov was monitoring radar data from a network of surveillance satellites. He was as puzzled as his American counterpart. An apparently normal radar image had vanished without warning from his screen.

"It was one of the regular flights the Americans fly from their Pacific Coast to Stockholm," he reported to Lieutenant Antonzak.

"And then?"

"The target reappeared, sir."

"*Reappeared?*" Lieutenant Antonzak's voice was scornfully incredulous, as always. "How long was it off the screen?"

"Approximately thirty, perhaps forty seçonds, sir."

"A technical problem."

"This is what I think, sir."

Lieutenant Antonzak duly recorded the incident in his daily report. A total waste of time, in his opinion. But orders were orders. It was all very well, thought Antonzak, to record all these facts and dates and times and positions, but of what use were they? The temporary loss of a radar target was undoubtedly due to a sunspot or a flock of Arctic terns, or possibly an incompetent radar operator. Or maybe it was the weather. The intense cold could do strange things to electronics. And to people. But presumably some dutiful bureaucrat was making a comfortable career out of collecting all these facts, recording them, analyzing them, programming them on some computer . . . then probably forgetting all about them. There were, in Lieutenant Antonzak's opinion, far too many people creating such jobs for themselves. But Lieutenant Antonzak kept such opinions to himself. It was safer.

MACLEOD HAD JUST yawned.

Karen was thinking, inconsequentially, about a young man named Brian. At the municipal swimming pool, some fifteen years ago, he had undone the bra strap of her bathing suit just as she had started on her journey down the slide. She had entered the water clutching her budding breasts with cupped hands as if trying to fasten them to her chest.

Brad Steiner had just observed a very slow, insignificant leak in the auxiliary hydraulic system, something to be checked after the landing. He recorded the leak in the airplane log.

Senator David Walsh was dozing, dreaming of riding a motorcycle, streaking along at breakneck speed, hurtling past wide-eyed pedestrians along Pennsylvania Avenue, Washington, D.C.

His aide, Milt Bryden, had just sat down. He had been talking to Janet Spencer, asking about Stockholm—asking how she enjoyed being a stewardess. He noted with interest the subtle change in tone when she mentioned her husband. Milt was a student of tones. It was his guess that Janet Spencer and her husband had problems. And marital problems usually meant opportunity.

George Flitch was scribbling the lead to his story about Karen, trying to paint a prose picture of a lady who was both feminine and a highly proficient airman . . . or was it airperson?

Carl Neillsen had dozed, but he had awakened a few minutes later, abruptly, his peace shattered by the vision of *her* and her damned husband, in bed, limbs entwined, reveling in each other.

Harriet Lawson had just flipped her paperback onto the

empty seat next to her, having condemned it as unreadable. Her daughter Shirley had recommended the book. Just the thing for a long plane ride, she had said. What the hell did she know? Shirley's taste in books was clearly just as lousy as her taste in husbands.

The Parker family talked about Europe. Neil had just explained to his parents about Sweden being a constitutional monarchy. The king was only a figurehead and real executive power was vested in the prime minister, the leader of the majority party. He told them that the parliament was known as the *Riksdag*. "It's bicameral," he added. Then he told them what that meant.

Sam Coglin was enjoying a prolonged sexual fantasy about the cute stewardess named Wendi. Hide-and-seek. In the nude.

Melvin Lee had dozed off; Tina Lee, in the window seat, gazed at the *nothingness* outside. How did the pilot find his way about the sky? This was Tina's first time in an airplane.

William Jarvis was writing a letter to Phil, trying to convey his ambivalent feelings about the trip: on the one hand, an experience, a blast, a thrill; on the other, an emotional strain being away from him for even a few weeks.

Janet Spencer had just decided to accept Milt Bryden's invitation to meet in Stockholm. Why not? She shrugged. It was a question she seemed to be constantly asking herself these days.

Mrs. Henry Warren in seat 28C had just popped a Valium into her mouth. She closed her eyes.

That was when it went off.

They felt it as much as heard it. The very air about them seemed to recoil in shock. It was as if a giant's hand had reached out and swatted the 707 as it passed. The structure squealed in pain, absorbing the horrendous shock, passing the stresses from component to component, trying desperately to tame them before they tore the aircraft apart.

Someone screamed.

Mrs. Henry Warren's ears began to hurt.

For a confused instant Macleod thought he had fallen asleep. He was dreaming. That had to be the explanation.

But it wasn't.

Even as he reached for the controls, the 707 lurched, swinging violently to the right. Simultaneously the loud-yet-muffled boom burst into the cockpit, invisible yet intensely physical, a single, shattering blow coming through the floor, the seats, the controls, stretching, twisting, bending, a moment of traumatic stresses.

Macleod grabbed the wheel and disconnected the autopilot.

The aircraft responded, thank God. For the moment things were stable. But the controls felt peculiar: unbalanced.

"Jesus," said Brad in an oddly mild tone.

Startled, Karen turned instinctively to look out her side window. No visible problem.

"What the hell was that?" As he asked the question, Macleod's eyes flashed over the instrument panel. The only immediate sign of trouble was the trembling, the shivering of the airplane as if it were afraid of what was about to happen.

There was another sign: reduction of cabin pressure.

Macleod's ears popped. His intestines began to ache and his collarbone hurt where he broke it playing football twenty years before. He threw a glance toward Brad. "What's going on back there?"

Frowning at his panel, Brad shook his head. "Dunno. All I know is that I can't hold the pressure." He had closed the outflow valves, but the precious air was escaping in horrific quantities.

Macleod ordered the crew to put on their oxygen masks and use the interphones for further conversation. He nodded at Karen. "Cabin-pressure-loss checklist." His words passed from the microphone in his oxygen mask and through the cockpit speakers.

"Okay, Captain." She reached for the emergency checklist as she donned the oxygen mask, tugging it over her head as she had practiced so many times during emergency training in the simulator.

"Damned airspeed's dropping," Macleod observed. He advanced the throttles, but it did little good. At 37,000 feet there wasn't much power in reserve.

Karen's voice was calm and curiously reassuring as she went through the checklist items: air sources, equipment cooling, cabin air thrust valve, manual pressure control, pack area, wing ducts, oxygen regulator, passenger oxygen . . .

Nothing. The air pressure was still decreasing.

Was the problem due to structural damage? Probably. Obviously not a wing. The plane was still flying. Barely. What now? Descend rapidly to where the air was rich enough in oxygen to sustain consciousness? But might not a high-speed descent further damage the aircraft, whatever the hell that damage might be? And wouldn't descending to such a low altitude severely limit how far the 707 could be flown? Absolutely. My God, think of all the fuel we'd burn down low.

Why the Christ couldn't Brad restore the goddam cabin pressure? What kind of a damned flight engineer was he anyway?

Knock it off. Unfair. And a waste of time. No choice but to descend. The passenger's oxygen supply won't last forever. Okay. Decision made.

Besides, he simply couldn't maintain altitude any longer. The 707 was sagging, wallowing. It was as if he were flying with the flaps and landing gear extended. And there was that buffeting to contend with. The Boeing felt as though it had been hit by flak. It had to be some sort of structural failure. *Had* to be. Which made it awfully dangerous to undertake a by-the-book, high-speed descent with throttles closed, speed brakes up, landing gear extended and the nose pointed sharply downward. The strain of such a maneuver could further weaken the structure. The airplane might come apart in midair. . . .

"We'll take her down. But gently."

Nods. No arguments. No recommendations for an alternate plan.

Gingerly he retarded the throttles and edged the nose earthward. So far so good. Everything holding together. But something strange had happened; it would be helpful to know what it was.

He was conscious of Karen talking to Janet Spencer on the interphone—*talking*, not yelling; good girl; keeping her cool. Saying, yes, there sure as hell was a problem. No one was precisely sure what it was, but everything was under control and she should keep the passengers calm. Keep them on oxygen and in their seats until you hear from the captain.

He turned to her. "Call Sondestrom Radio. Two-eight-six-eight kiloHertz. Tell 'em we've got a problem. And get their latest weather. Looks like we're going to have to divert and land there. Stockholm is out of the question."

He heard her calling: "Sondestrom Radio. Sondestrom Radio. This is Trans American Flight Niner-Zero-Two, over?"

He listened to the speakers on the left and right sides of the cockpit ceiling, willing the helpful voices to respond. But there was no reply. Why the hell not? Weren't those damn bastards in Greenland listening? They were *supposed* to be listening; it was their goddam *job* to listen . . . and respond.

Karen tried again: "Sondestrom Radio. Sondestrom Radio. This is Trans American Flight Niner-Zero-Two. Do you read?"

Silence.

"Anyone . . . *any*one guarding this frequency, this is Trans Am Flight Nine-Oh-Two, calling in the blind. Do you read?"

Nothing.

He saw her changing frequencies, transmitting on one and then another. No response on the emergency frequency either. Nothing. What the hell was going on out there? Was everyone asleep? Jesus Christ, didn't anyone *care?*

Calm down, he instructed himself. Ridiculous to get mad about something you can't control. Concentrate on *here* and *now*. He had to clutch the wheel tightly to fight the aircraft's shudderings.

Then Brad's voice, harsh with urgency: "Captain, Jesus, we've got an electrical fire!"

Christ-oh-Christ, not *that*. The word fire had the power to numb any pilot with terror, instantly creating ghastly images of exploding fuel tanks and charred bodies, flaming fragments of airplanes and occupants tumbling, smearing the clean blue sky.

Brad was kneeling on the floor, a carbon-dioxide fire extinguisher in hand, directing it down through the grilled hatch leading to the electrical compartment immediately beneath the flight deck. Smoke spewed up through the opening, heavy-looking stuff with that pungent stink typical of electrical fires.

No time to waste. Macleod snapped, "Brad, open the main generator relays. You—" he nodded at Karen—"get to work on that fire. And put on your smoke goggles, both of you."

Brad scrambled for his panel. Karen flung her shoulder harness back and pulled herself out of her seat. Grabbing the extinguisher, she quickly went to work on the fire.

Macleod coughed as the stinking smoke affected his throat, despite the oxygen mask. He tugged the yellow plastic smoke goggles into position.

Opening the generator relays would shut off most of the airplane's electrical power. This should starve the fire, allowing the problem to fizzle out. So goes the theory. The only electrical power remaining would be that essential to aircraft operation.

He turned to Brad. "Let's have the electrical-fire checklist."

They ran through the items as the aircraft continued to shudder and vibrate during its descent: oxygen masks . . . oxygen regulators . . . crossfeed valves . . . air source switches . . . rudder power switch . . . background lights . . . bus tie relays . . . field relays . . . Yes, they were doing everything possible to tame the conflagration, following the book to the goddam letter.

And still descending. And still accomplishing little more than pleading with the 707 to please not fall apart at the seams.

The smoke seemed to be clearing now, sucked out to the rear of the flight deck.

Macleod shook his head in dazed wonder. He'd had more problems in the last few minutes than during his entire fifteen years with the airline. But the aircraft was still flying, holding together despite some sort of structural failure; the fire was down to a few sparks and spurts in the electrical compartment; the passengers were okay as far as he was aware. What next?

He glanced at the altimeter. The 707 was down to almost 12,000 feet now. Time to push the throttles forward and stop the descent. The passengers and crew could breathe at this altitude without help from the oxygen system. He started to pull off his mask. The cool air felt good on his face after the mask's clinging.

Karen had returned to her seat beside him. She was buckling herself in when, suddenly, shockingly, she pointed. "Captain, look! Number four."

His gaze flashed to the instrument panel, to the row of gauges for the right outboard engine. More goddam problems! The exhaust gas temperature was going through the roof.

Macleod reached for the throttle. Got to reduce power before the number-four engine blows itself to bits . . . But even as his hand closed on the lever, the 707 staggered again. A shuddering, bloodchilling explosion reverberated through the entire airframe as the number-four engine disintegrated.

He braced himself, instinctively preparing for the horror of the machine falling apart around him.

Incredibly, it still flew. Still maintaining a form of balance in the now turbulent air. But shivering, pulsating. Was it her death rattle? Was she about to roll over and die?

He turned to Karen, voice calmer than expected, bearing in mind jangled nerves and shuddering innards. "Engine-failure checklist."

The checklist was already in her hand. Face pale, marked by the outline of her oxygen mask. Her voice was unusually calm, as if she had been expecting this kind of lunacy.

"Throttle closed?"

"It's closed."

"Essential power?"

"Checked."

"Start lever off?"

"It's off."

"Engine fuel valve closed?"

"Closed."

"Electrical power."

"Okay, it's checked."

When they were through, Karen announced, "Engine-failure checklist complete, Captain."

She *had* to be more frightened than she showed. *Had* to be.

Macleod acknowledged. More obedient following of the manual; one hell of a gigantic waste of time if the airplane refused to fly any more. And that might happen at any time. Every quiver told him so. He couldn't maintain altitude any more. Speed was the critical factor. It created the airplane's lift; it provided control; without enough speed the 707 would become a large, beautifully proportioned brick, full of inflammable fuel and fragile human beings.

He had to concentrate on flying the 707 evey inch of the way; if he allowed the airspeed to slip even slightly below 180 knots, the airplane would become uncontrollable and fall out of the sky, so much junk metal. Correcting, recorrecting; endlessly manipulating the controls; maximum power from the three remaining engines. Nothing helped. The jet simply didn't want to fly any more. She wanted to die.

Janet entered the cockpit and conferred with Brad. When she had gone, Brad said, "Captain, I think our problem is down below. The flight attendants report a loud air noise beneath the floor in the forward cabin. Sounds as though something might have gone off in the baggage compartment."

"A bomb?"

"Beats me. I guess it's possible. Number-four engine is gone. Badly twisted and hanging in its mount—at least, what's left of it. It's creating one helluva lot of drag. And I wouldn't be surprised if even more drag was being created by damage that we can't see. It would certainly help to explain why we're having so much trouble remaining airborne."

Macleod nodded. And still *more* drag was being created by the rudder deflection necessary to keep the 707 pointed in the right direction, itself an inevitable result of having two engines operating on one side, a solitary engine on the other.

He glanced at the altimeter. Ten thousand, two hundred feet. Christ, they were steadily flying themselves toward the ocean! Every time he tried to preserve altitude, the speed fell alarmingly. He had no choice; he had to keep the nose down to maintain the speed needed to keep the airplane flying. If he continued to keep the nose down he would wind up taking a very cold swim. It was an impossible balancing act. But one solution to the problem might be to lighten the aircraft. If he dumped sufficient fuel, would the aircraft be able to maintain altitude?

Perhaps. Definitely worth a try. The trick was to unload to that delicate point where the 707 might stay in the air, but remembering to leave enough fuel to reach Sondestrom Air Base on the west coast of Greenland.

Great idea. Except for the inconvenient fact that fuel dumping would require closing the main generator relays and repowering the electrical system. And this was simply pleading for another fire in the "Lower 41," the electrical compartment beneath the flight deck.

It was a risk he had to take.

"Brad, I want you to repower the electrical system and prepare to dump fuel."

"Yes, sir."

He glanced at Karen. "Plot a course to Sondestrom. Try to figure out how much time and fuel it'll take to get there. And get Janet Spencer up here, right away."

They were flying through thick cloud, endless gray that swept past the cockpit windows, freezing in tiny patches on windows and wings.

Jesus, why can't I think of something brilliant, something that will get us out of this mess? That's my job, isn't it?

"Yes, Captain?" Janet stood beside him, white-faced and almost out of breath, her usually impeccable hair falling across her forehead in untidy ringlets.

"I want you to prepare the passengers for a possible ditching . . ."

"Christ . . . yes, okay, Captain." Poor kid, she was trying like hell to be calm and professional; but she was quaking inside. Who wasn't? Training could never prepare you for something like this.

"It probably won't come to that," he told her. "But it may. So I'm counting on you to keep everyone as calm as you can. I know it's tough, but we'll pull through this all right. Understand?"

She nodded, jerkily, mechanically. Yes, she understood.

"Good girl."

Janet went aft to tell her passengers what the *Emergency Procedures Handbook* told her to tell them: that there might be a water landing, that the crew was capable and trained to handle the situation, please remain calm; to put on coats; to remove life jackets from under the seats; to remove the jacket from the plastic pouch and put it on according to instructions; to fasten seat belts tightly and place seat backs in an upright position, stowing and locking tray tables. Then tell them to remove shoes, placing them in seat pockets; to remove sharp objects such as pens, tie clasps, hairclips, and put them in the seat pockets alongside the shoes; to remove eyeglasses and dentures and put them in pockets; to remove ties and scarves and loosen collars. And to remember, before touchdown, to clasp hands over heads, bending over as far as possible with feet flat on the floor. And remind them of the location of the emergency exits and life rafts. Urge them to review the safety instruction card: "And after touchdown, remain in your seats until the life rafts have been removed from the overhead compartments. This will expedite the removal and launching of the life rafts . . .''

Were there any passengers who seriously believed it was possible to survive landing a Boeing 707 in the Arctic Ocean? Was anyone naive enough to believe there would be time to deploy the rafts and get everyone aboard *before* the 707 submerged?

Macleod felt an odd, lunatic twinge of relief that it was Janet's and not his job to say these things to more than one hundred paying customers.

Brad Steiner's voice: "Captain, I can't get any of the generators back on line. The goddam relays keep tripping open."

Jesus Jesus Jesus. "Keep trying!"

Now the 707 had descended to beneath the overcast. Below, the Arctic waters stirred in frigid splendor, the black surface polka-dotted with innumerable ice floes and icebergs. A seascape of black and white. Forward visibility was about three miles, Macleod estimated.

A half-turn toward the flight engineer at his panel.

"Any luck with those relays?"

Brad shook his head. Pale face; eyes big and scared. "The relays won't stay closed, not even one. They . . . *won't*," he shouted as if frustrated by a group of recalcitrant kids.

Karen had the course and fuel data for Sondestrom. But it was all academic now. They would never reach Sondestrom at this rate.

"If we can't dump fuel, we can't maintain altitude."

"So we ditch?"

"Do we have a choice?"

Karen shook her head and reached for more checklists. If her innards were churning with fear, she was doing one hell of a good job of hiding it. Macleod gazed over the cold waters, mentally considering all the steps necessary to land a jetliner on the water without smashing it to pieces. First, said the book, it was vital to establish a heading parallel to the swell of the ocean. Then estimate the wind velocity and direction by observing the breaking action of the waves. Then dump fuel—only he couldn't. Suggested rate of descent: 200 feet per minute or less. Flaps fully extended. Landing gear up. Then touch down on the face of a swell, the book informed him, just downslope of the crest . . . He kept recalling in vivid detail a report he had read about a ditching: The appalling impact resulted in a violent deceleration for about one second. A healthy person could withstand such a shock. But in this case the seats couldn't. So most of them broke loose when the aircraft hit the water, taking their occupants on horrifying, bone-snapping, body-crunching tumbles about the cabin. To make the situation even worse, a life raft inflated while still inside the aircraft, blocking an exit, and the galley bins spilled packed lunches, bottles, knives. . . .

"Shoulder harnesses and seat belts secure . . . landing gear up . . . emergency exit lights on . . ."

Karen announced that the ditching checklist was complete.

Relentlessly the altimeter needle kept unwinding as the 707 wobbled and staggered through the air, constantly on the brink of becoming uncontrollable, wanting to quit flying. Macleod still coaxed her, trying to get the most out of the least, persuading her to stay in the air a few minutes longer, than just a few minutes more. . . .

"Tell the girls we'll be in the water in three or four minutes . . . get the passengers in their ditching positions."

Nods. Then the sound of a voice amplified by the public-address system; a brave voice of a brave young girl who was surely close to wetting her pants with fright but who had the responsibility to present a calm and confident facade to her passengers.

The sea was closer now, close enough to study the swells and to estimate the strength and direction of the wind.

The time for decision was rapidly approaching. Make up your mind just where and how you're going to put her down. And get it right the first time because you sure as hell won't be able to go around and try again. . . .

"Captain, look!"

He flung a glance in Karen's direction. She was pointing. God! There, to the right, a couple of miles away, floated the largest ice floe he had ever seen. It must have been at least two miles long. And it looked reasonably flat. A nightmare of a place to land. But one hell of a lot more inviting than frigid ocean.

He nodded. No time to consider alternatives. It was now or never.

19

HE TURNED THE aircraft, cautiously, unsure how a change in altitude might affect her already tenuous hold on stability, only too aware of how rapidly she might give up the game and plummet into that God-awful water. . . .

The ice floe wobbled into line.

Jesus, there was thick fog ahead, clinging to the ice floe. So it was impossible to know how long the thing really was; the far end disappeared into the frozen curtain of fog. Maybe it ended *there* . . . maybe it wasn't long enough. . . .

But better ice than water.

The frightening thing was, an emergency landing area could look smooth as silk from five hundred feet up. Closer down you might find broken and ragged ridges far more dangerous than water.

So, the little voice inside told him, if it's a rough surface, you'll most likely kill everyone in the next fifteen or twenty seconds. But if it is reasonably smooth you might—just might—make it down safely. But have you ever heard of anyone doing this? And living to tell the tale?

Was his sanity finally snapping? How the hell could anyone in his right mind have a long-winded conversation with himself in the last minutes of the most important, most dangerous landing of his career? As he wrestled with the weary, dying aircraft, he seemed to be two individuals—the one concentrating, using every morsel of skill, every speck of knowledge he had ever absorbed, the other pontificating like some orotund professor on the problems of the approaching collision between the landing gear and the untried surface.

From the corner of his eye he saw Karen, her left hand edging toward the flap handle, ready for his command.

One hole or soft spot in that enormous surface of ice would be enough to tear the landing gear right off the bottom of the aircraft. Then what? Would the 707 go spinning off the ice and into the ocean? Or would she fall on a wing, rupturing a fuel tank, spilling volatile kerosene all over the place? Or would her nose dig into a hole and flip the big Boeing on her back?

None was an enticing possibility.

Speed slacking; control becoming spongy and surly. At any instant the 707 would refuse to play this impossible game any longer; she would simply fall out of the sky.

Which might solve all of your problems, declared the little voice.

Christ knows what was going to happen just before touchdown, when even more speed might slip away.

You're going to find out, said the little voice.

He could see dry snow being whipped across the surface of the ice. A strong crosswind. Twenty or thirty knots, probably. And coming in at about thirty degrees. It would be crazy to try a conventional crosswind landing by lowering a wing and sideslipping. Liable to kill everyone. Better to land on the slick stuff while drifting and with the wings level. *If* we get to the ice, said the voice, which now seemed to be located somewhere immediately below his epiglottis.

Coming in fast. Too fast. But speed was vital. Even now.

The ice floe grew, fattened in his vision, rapidly filling the entire front window. A glimpse of the jagged edges, the ice sharp and clean as if it had just broken away from another floe.

"Gear down . . . full flaps."

Now the frigid surface swept below, a blurring image, a strip of unknown length or texture, a runway in the middle of nowhere.

Please God.

Incongruously, a fragment of a memory sped across his consciousness: his first solo landing, an Aeronca Champ, a hazy June day, a friendly grass strip in New Jersey.

Power off!

The engine noise died; for a moment he seemed to hear the sound of the wind. The structure creaked.

Then came the impact. The shock flashed through the control column, through the floor of the cockpit, through the landing gear, through every rib, rivet and spar.

Spoilers!

He stomped on the brake pedals.

Reverse One, Two and Three!

A momentary conviction that the 707 was burrowing its speeding way into the ice, digging a grave for every occupant . . . No! She was skidding, slithering, making an unbelievable din . . . every drummer in the world creating the most God-awful cacophony! Everything shaking, vibrating, threatening to fall apart around him. And all he could do was watch and hope and keep his feet on the brake pedals and keep trying to maintain some directional control by varying the reverse power of the three operative engines and frantically working the rudder and nosewheel steering. God knows whether any of it was helping.

The cabin reverberated with bangs: shuddering, crunching, squashing bangs. Did that one break her back? Was she disintegrating as she skated and bounced on the treacherous surface, leaving her tail section and half the passengers behind on the inhospitable ice?

The surface of the floe seemed to swing right and left across his window. Another silly, pointless memory: standing in a penny arcade in front of the machine: Test Your Driving Skill: the winding road unrolling at insane speed as he frantically tried to keep the toy car between the lines. Every time he wandered off the road, rude lights flashed and a horn blared.

Was the landing gear still hanging on? If so, how? Or was the 707 sliding along on her belly? Who could tell? It didn't matter; the idea was simply to remain fastened in your seat and to absorb the next awful shock. . . .

But the speed was slackening.

How much more ice was left? Impossible to tell. The fog swept by in ugly patches. He caught a glimpse of the ocean, looming out of the fog on the left, gray waters slopping heavily over the edge of the floe just beyond the 707's wing. . . .

Christ, end of runway!

He visualized the 707 tumbling helplessly into the water, passengers struggling to escape as the cabin filled with icy, merciless water. . . . Reducing the reverse thrust produced by the engines on the left wing, he pulled hard on the reverse thrust lever for the one engine on the right wing. Full power!

It took an awful moment for the number-three engine to spool up. Then it surged! The jet swung wildly as the solitary engine cut in, pulling on the right side, helping to drag the still-moving airplane away from the water.

She went skidding and thumping across the craggy, uneven ice surface, groaning, crying, complaining. But obeying. Reverse thrust reduced, its job done. They were down to walking speed.

The wind was almost as loud as the noise of the landing gear battling with the ice. With a last, crunching groan, the 707 came to a halt.

The three members of the flight crew exchanged disbelieving glances, dazed by the cataclysmic events, still hardly able to accept the evidence of their senses.

Brad broke the brief, poignant silence. "Captain, you're really going to have to do something about your landings."

Macleod grinned shakily. "I'll try and do better next time."

"Unreal," Karen commented. Then she smiled and shook her head at the inadequacy of the word.

Macleod nodded, shrugging. What can you say when you don't know whether it was your skill or just plain dumb luck that got you down in one piece?

The cockpit door burst open.

Janet was half-laughing with relief.

"I thought we were ditching . . . and then there were those loud noises; I'd heard it made a lot of noise when you ditched . . . and then we weren't in the water after all . . ."

"Disappointed?"

"You gotta be kidding."

"Is everyone all right?"

The question seemed to calm her. She nodded. "I think so. But kind of dazed."

"So are we."

"We're on . . . *ice?*"

"Right," said Brad. "As in a glass of Scotch."

Macleod glanced at the hatch on the floor behind his seat. The fire in the electrical compartment seemed to be completely out. So there was no apparent need to evacuate the aircraft. Which was just as well, he told himself as he glanced through his window. A grim panorama: ice and fog, with the Arctic Ocean lapping only feet away like a hungry monster eager to devour the 707 and its occupants.

The passengers were bewildered and confused, some in shock. They looked across the aisle at one another as if suddenly interested in who shared this incredible experience with them. The cabin was a mess: overhead compartments had burst open, regurgitating their contents, depositing coats, hats, umbrellas and cameras on the passengers below; galley doors had popped open and had deposited frozen meals and canned soft drinks along the aisle in multicolored confusion.

But everyone was *alive*.

One of the passengers regretted the fact, bitterly. Carl Neillsen, thirty-one, the Swede, had been prepared for death, had welcomed it. But he had been cheated again.

The scene kept repeating, like a piece of movie film in a continuous loop. Again and again the 707 staggered from the explosion, streaming smoke, disappearing into the clouds below and diving toward its Arctic grave. As soon as the scene ended, it reappeared to start the sequence again.

Mike Lockhart tried to blink the vision away, squeezing his eyes shut for long moments. But the 707 kept falling, vanishing.

He had done it. He had accomplished his mission, performed the act that would solve everything. Now, he told himself, the world is safer. Somehow.

No problem. Press a button. Change history.

He had expected to see the jetliner disintegrate in one convulsive explosion. But it didn't happen that way. The 707 had remained essentially intact as it went down. But it was burning, no doubt about that. Did it dive straight into the ocean? Or did it come apart before it hit? What difference did it make? It must have seemed like an eternity for those aboard that doomed airplane. If only they could have died more quickly.

But why did he see it happening over and over again? It was crazy, a trick of a sleep-starved mind.

Concentrate, for God's sake. There was still much to do. He had to continue along the precise route of Trans American Flight 902. He had to give the same enroute position reports expected by air traffic controllers along the way to Stockholm. He must not allow anyone to suspect that he, Mike Lockhart, was not in fact Flight 902. The world would not know that the real Flight 902 no longer existed.

He studied the aeronautical charts. But all he saw was the 707, descending yet again, streaming smoke, vanishing into that somber cloud to its inevitable fate.

20

THE PASSENGER CABIN was like a lunatic asylum. People milled about, climbing over seats, peering out of windows; they talked and shouted to one another, laughing, shaking hands as they dragged off life vests, their voices high-pitched with excitement and relief of the moment. Except for a few minor bruises and abrasions, everyone was apparently okay after the bone-rattling landing—okay but sloppy. Collars and jackets were unfastened; feet were minus shoes: mouths were minus dentures. One visibly nervous, elderly man began playing solitaire.

As Macleod entered the cabin from the flight deck, a middle-aged woman in first class caught his arm.

"What happened? Are we safe? Are we going to be all right?"

"Yes, we'll be all right. We landed on a very large, thick sheet of ice."

"For God's sake," she murmured. She looked up at him. "Do you recognize me?"

"No, I don't think so."

She sighed. "It figures."

Senator Walsh wrapped a comradely arm around Macleod's shoulders. "One hell of a job, Captain. I know a little about flying and there aren't many pilots who could have pulled off that landing."

Macleod nodded his thanks. "I just hope they don't want me to do it again to show how it's done."

The senator grinned. "Where are we?"

"In the middle of Baffin Bay. Somewhere between Canada

and Greenland. Now, if you'll excuse me, Senator, I think I'd better say a few words to the passengers."

"Of course. Anything I can do?"

"Not right now. But I may need your help later."

"Fine."

Macleod raised the powered megaphone to his lips. "Ladies and gentlemen, may I have your attention, please!"

To his surprise they silenced instantly: wide-eyed faces turning to him in concert, some with smiles still on their lips as if they had been stopped in the middle of a game.

"First of all, is everyone all right? Is anyone hurt? Does anyone need immediate assistance? Please speak up so we can get a flight attendant to you."

A silver-haired lady spoke up. "I cut my leg somehow. It's bleeding."

"Okay. We'll look after you. Anyone else? And is there a doctor on board?"

No answer. Apparently not. In the movies, there was always a doctor on board.

A burly man said he had lost his glasses in the confusion and the preparation for ditching.

"We'll try to help you find them, sir. Anyone else. Hurt? Cut?"

"I'm scared," said a voice.

Laughter, more than the remark deserved.

"Sure, you're scared. I don't blame you. This doesn't happen every day." Jesus, how his heart was thumping. It would be one hell of a time to have a cardiac arrest. "I want to thank you, ladies and gentlemen, for the way you're conducting yourselves during what is a frightening ordeal. And to be honest with you, we still don't know why we're down here and not up there. Something obviously happened. We're checking things out and I'm sure we'll soon discover the cause of our problem. There seems to have been an explosion of some sort. But I'm sure you're all aware of that. I just don't know what caused it."

"Was it a bomb?" A pudgy man with thinning red hair asked the question. "It could've been a bomb, couldn't it?"

"Yes, that's a possibility."

"Well, what the hell else could it have been?" Aggressive,

overbearing, the kind who was always right, an opinionated, self-righteous s.o.b.

"We don't know yet," said Macleod. "That's what I was just saying."

A black man a couple of rows farther back stuck up his hand. "How long do you think we'll be here, Captain?"

"I can't answer that. But with a little luck, we could be out of here in a matter of hours. I'm certain that a search-and-rescue operation is already being organized."

"Have they told you that?" an elderly man asked.

"No, sir."

"Why not?" demanded the pudgy one.

"We can't communicate by radio," Macleod said. The announcement was evidently a shock; the rows of faces suddenly looked alarmed; dozens of mouths dropped partially open; brows furrowed. "The explosion caused a fire in the main electrical compartment. It knocked out all of our radios. But you must understand, that doesn't mean that no one knows about our problem. You see, while en route we make periodic position reports to advise the air traffic controllers of our progress. If we fail to report and can no longer be contacted, they know we've got some sort of problem. And they start looking for us."

"But how do they know we're *here*, on this spot?" A young man with a foreign accent asked the question.

"Because they know the route we were flying. They know where we should be at any given time. On top of that, we can use the battery-operated radios from the life rafts to communicate with the search-and-rescue aircraft. You may have noticed the flight engineer has unpacked the rafts to get at the survival equipment. This includes portable transceivers, which means we can transmit and receive." It all sounded so simple. But it wasn't.

A hand shot up. "How much range do those radios have?"

"About fifty miles, I'd guess."

"So you just use them if you hear a plane or a ship, right?"

"Yes, sir."

"So until we hear a plane or a ship, there isn't a hell of a lot we can do. Isn't that right?"

"That's essentially correct." Goddam know-it-all.

"There's a draft over here," a middle-aged man complained.

"We'll try to do something about that, but I can't guarantee anything. The problem is that we don't have any stairs to get down to the ground—or, rather, the ice. So we have to use an emergency evacuation slide. The problem is, once the slide is deployed, we can't close the door all the way. For the time being, may I suggest that you move away from the door."

"Why the hell don't you carry ladders, for crissake?" The pudgy man with the red hair again.

"Because TAA has an excellent record of landing where we intend to land, that is, on an airport with the proper facilities for handling passengers and baggage. We've gone a long time without landing on an ice floe."

They chuckled good-humoredly, most of them, still reveling in the euphoria of finding themselves alive and in one piece.

A man in a business suit wanted to know how big the ice floe was. "Big enough to land a 707 on," said Macleod. "I can guarantee that. Beyond that I don't know. But we'll find out. We'll keep you advised of everything we learn."

"Can't we get some heat in here?" The voice came from midway down the cabin. There was a faint tone of indignation, as if the owner couldn't believe that the airline would be so thoughtless as to let its passengers get chilled feet.

"I'm not sure we can do much about that right now," said Macleod.

"*What?*" Disbelieving tone.

"You see," he explained, "the airplane has been substantially damaged. We don't know the extent of it yet. We don't know which systems we can operate and which ones we can't operate. But we'll find out. And, believe me, as soon as we think it is safe to start an engine to provide heat, we'll do it. The important thing for the moment is that we're reasonably safe and sheltered from the elements. We have plenty of food on board and no one is seriously injured. That's what counts. And we're going to get out of here as soon as possible. Now, the next few hours may not be the most comfortable ones you've ever spent in an airplane, but we'll get through them just fine. For the time being, it would be best for everyone to stay on board the aircraft. It's extremely cold out there. Besides, there isn't much to see except a lot of ice and fog.''

"How long is the fog going to last?"

"I really have no way of knowing."

"What's your *best* estimate of when we're going to get off this hunk of ice, Captain?" A burly, bald man asked the question.

"I'm in no position to make promises, sir. Naturally it's going to take time for them to find us. And then it's going to take a little longer to effect a rescue. It could be as little as three or four hours. Or it might take longer. It all depends on how quickly things come together."

As he spoke he heard the wind pressing insistently on the aluminum fuselage that separated them from the harsh elements. Why didn't the wind blow all the damned fog away? An old man in seat 24E started thumping his feet against the floor, trying to keep them warm. The flight attendants began passing out blankets.

Macleod raised the megaphone to his lips. "Without electrical power to operate the ovens, we can't cook any food right now. But we can serve drinks. So I'm going to have the cabin crew serve some beverages. We'll have to impose a limit of one drink per person to conserve our supplies. Right now, I'm going outside to join the first officer and the flight engineer, who are trying to find out what happened to our airplane. Thank you very much for your attention. The cabin attendants will be serving beverages in a few minutes."

He made his way to the exit after placing a blanket over his head and shoulders. A blast of frigid air enveloped him.

And there was a distant sound. A metallic sound, like the cooling of metal when engines are shut down. But it wasn't the engines. It was the ice. Cracking. Breaking up.

21

NOW IT WAS easy to see what had happened. There was a cavernous, ragged hole in the lower right side of the 707, ripped out by an explosion in the forward baggage compartment. The cargo door was a large, pathetic, twisted slab of metal jutting out at an absurd angle. Macleod studied the remains of the number-four engine. It was severely twisted in its mount and pointed sharply downward. God only knows why it had clung so tenaciously to the underwing pylon. Hanging by a thread. Probably blew apart after ingesting shrapnel from the explosion. He shook his head in wonder. Certainly there was no mystery about why the airplane had behaved and performed so poorly. Even three healthy engines couldn't provide enough power to overcome all that air resistance. And to top off the list of aerodynamic problems, it looked as if the cargo door, sticking out awkwardly into the airstream, probably had spoiled much of the lift normally developed by the inboard section of the right wing. What a mess.

In short, it was a miracle that the 707 had stayed in the air as long as it did.

"One hell of a bomb," said Brad, pointing. Much of the cargo had been blown overboard during the explosion. What remained inside was a crush of shredded and burned baggage, bits of clothing, toiletries, golf clubs. . . .

"I think I can explain our electrical difficulties," Brad added. "Looks like the blast overheated some of the circuits feeding into the electrical compartment forward of the baggage area. Something got shorted out."

"I think we were lucky," said Karen.

"Lucky?"

151

"Let's assume the bomb was in one of the bags. If that bag had been stowed at the top of the baggage compartment, the bomb would have blown through the floor of the passenger cabin. God knows how many people would have been killed. And no telling what would have happened to the airplane. Might've even broken its back. So it looks as though we were somewhat shielded by the baggage on top."

Macleod nodded. She was undoubtedly right. The bottom, outboard side of the cargo bay had simply been blown out, directing much of the energy into the outside air.

"But who the hell would want to blow us up?" Brad wanted to know; he sounded aggrieved, as if challenging an unfair parking ticket.

"Beats me," muttered Macleod. He looked around him. God, what a sight. The fog had gotten thicker, a dense, dark, freezing curtain. You could no longer see the ocean. But you could hear it, lapping hungrily at the edge of the ice floe. And you could hear the ice itself, groaning, stretching, creaking, like some living thing in constant pain. Every sound evoked images of the whole damn thing breaking up, depositing the Boeing and its occupants into the freezing water. What the hell was the use of working so hard to get down, landing the 707 like none had ever been landed before, if the end result was to be just the same? Why didn't he ditch or dive straight in and mark finis to the whole thing as rapidly as possible?

No, he chastised himself, don't think like that. Be positive. Now, if the ice did crack, would there be enough time to evacuate everyone? The life rafts were already in position outside the airplane, inflated and waiting. But how long would it take to get everyone out of the airplane and into the rafts? Old people, sick people, scared people. Did everyone know precisely what to do? Probably not. He made a mental note to discuss the matter with Janet Spencer when they got back into the airplane. Organize the cabin crew for the worst and hope it doesn't happen. Hope fervently.

The cold shrouded him like a blanket imbedded with millions of freezing needles that jabbed him, relentless, merciless tormentors.

"Keep your gloves on," he told Brad. The engineer nodded unhappily.

Karen and Macleod climbed back into the aircraft, pulling

themselves up the evacuation slide. It was a struggle; both were puffing as they dragged themselves into the cabin. The complaints began immediately.

"Can't we have some heat in here?"

"We need some light. It's almost dark."

"How about some hot drinks?"

He had to control the anger that surged within him. Didn't these idiots understand the danger of starting an engine without first checking the damage? Didn't they understand that it could lead to fire? To an explosion? Didn't they appreciate that the poor bastard of an engineer was at this very moment manipulating the valve on the compressed air cylinder in the right wheel well? No, probably not.

"Everything's all right," he told them. "We've checked and there's no reason not to start an engine. We'll have plenty of heat in a few minutes. I'm not sure about the lights though. Our electrical system may have been damaged."

That satisfied them for the moment. He had to push his way through them to reach the flight deck. They stood in the aisle, stamping their feet to keep warm, talking, bitching, asking ridiculous questions that no one could answer.

He slammed the flight deck door; the jabber of the passengers sounded like something at a zoo. The seat felt cold and clammy at his back. He picked up his microphone and began speaking through the powered interphone system. "All set?"

"Ready down here!" Brad called from below.

"Okay, Brad, we're ready up here. Open the valve."

He turned to Karen. "Okay, let's see if it'll work."

He flipped the start-selector switch to "high pressure." Then he raised the start lever to idle, opening the fuel valve and arming the ignition. Next, he depressed the starter switch for the number-three engine, permitting high-pressure air to flow from the compressed air cylinder in the right wheel well to the engine starter.

"Please, baby," he whispered.

There was only so much air in the cylinder; once it was gone there was no way to replenish the supply. There were only two cylinders in the wheel well.

Anxiously he watched the tachometer in the center of the main instrument panel. The needle moved, indicating that the engine had begun to spin. Seconds later, the exhaust-gas temperature gauge showed that ignition of the fuel had occurred. The rpm of the engine continued to increase. Macleod felt the tremor run through the structure of the airplane. Number three was alive! And the lights flooded the cockpit. Karen had been able to get number-three generator on the line.

He heaved a gigantic sigh of relief, even though the aircraft radios were still inoperative.

Everything working well. A goddam miracle. God knows, he wouldn't have been surprised if the engine had refused to budge. It was possible, even likely, that the plumbing carrying the compressed air from the cylinder to the engine starter would have been damaged by the explosion.

"Let's have some heat," he said to Karen.

"You bet," she responded.

Macleod relaxed. At least everyone could be reasonably comfortable for a while. There was plenty of fuel in the tanks. With any luck the fog should have cleared and the search-and-rescue guys would be able to do their thing. . . .

"I think we deserve a couple of Scotches on the rocks," he said. As he looked at the frost-covered windshield, he mused, "On second thought, hold the rocks."

Karen grinned, nodding, agreeing.

The tension evaporated. He relaxed. Thank God it worked. The thought of sitting in a metal shell on a bed of Arctic ice without heat or light was terrifying. Soon the cabin would be snug; then the girls could serve some hot food. A few hours' sleep for everyone, then it would be another day . . . the day of rescue, please.

"Are you all right?" he asked Karen.

She nodded. "I think so."

"I bet you never expected anything like this when you signed up with the airline."

"You can say that again." She smiled. "You know, you're going to be famous."

"Famous?"

"The first pilot ever to land a Boeing 707 on an ice floe."

He shrugged. "If you hadn't spotted the ice, I'd have ditched. So I guess that makes us a pretty good team."

"I'll buy that," she grinned.

Now he wanted to say the right thing, the appropriate words to bridge the chasm between them. God, it was tough to get started; the first words would set the course for what was to follow. Awkwardly he said, "I know we got off to kind of a rocky start. It was my fault," he added before permitting himself time to reconsider. "I've had some personal problems. Soured my disposition. I'm really sorry that I treated you so poorly."

There. It was said. Done.

She nodded, smiling. "Thanks, Captain."

"You're welcome. And you can knock off that 'captain' stuff; everyone calls me Mac."

"I think I know how you must have felt, Cap . . . I mean, Mac."

"You do?"

"Yes," she said. "I heard that you were having problems."

"I see." Airline rumors. Everyone knew who was sleeping with whom. "And what did you hear?"

"About your divorce. Sounded like you were given a pretty rough time."

"Rough? It was criminal."

"I'm sorry."

"Me too. Have you ever been married?"

She shook her head. "I almost was, once. But it just didn't work out."

"Career get in the way?"

"Something like that."

"It happens . . ."

Brad came in, a shivering hulk of frigid air.

"Nice work," said Macleod.

Brad sat down. "Thank God it started." He glanced at the engineer's panel and nodded to himself.

"Everything okay?" Macleod asked.

"Looks all right back here," Brad replied. "Don't ask me why. I can't understand why anything still works."

"They build these babies tough," said Macleod. He stood up. "I'd better go back and check on the passengers again. Any idea how long our fuel will last?"

Brad consulted his gauges. "With only one engine idling, probably a couple of days. I'll compute something more accurate in a few minutes."

"Okay." Macleod glanced briefly at Karen, according her

a tiny nod. She responded in kind. Brad glanced at her, then at Macleod. Macleod put on his hat and went aft.

The passenger cabin was as noisy as ever, but now it was a cheerful, good-natured noise. The rapidly rising cabin temperature and the prospect of something warm to eat were working wonders.

He asked Janet Spencer how she and the other girls were coping.

"We're okay, Captain. Thanks. But I'm sure glad you got that engine going. Before then it was bitch, bitch, bitch."

"How long before you feed them?"

"We can start in about fifteen minutes."

"Good girl." After a pause, he added, "Janet, don't give them too much to eat or drink. We should conserve our supplies, just in case. It's nothing to worry about, though. They'll get us out of here before you know it."

"I certainly hope so," she said.

He moved down the aisle, beaming in his best avuncular manner at the passengers. How were they? Everything under control? Getting warm enough now? Looking forward to a meal? They all asked the same questions. How long would they be stuck here? Would they be rescued by helicopters or ships? Were the rescue teams already on their way? Did relatives and friends know that the plane was down safely without anyone being hurt? Where would the rescue teams take them? How would they then make connections to Stockholm? How soon could they get back to the States? Was it possible to send a message? Could Uncle Red be told not to go to the airport to meet the plane? Would the airline compensate for the loss of baggage and belongings?

"We're going to be here for a while," he told them. "It's foggy outside. There's no way a rescue team could find this ice floe let alone get us out of here. You've got to accept that we're stuck here until the fog clears. But we'll get out of here in good shape. I promise. And Trans American always delivers on its promises."

"You should be in politics," said David Walsh as Macleod made his way forward. "You have a way with words."

"I just tell people the truth," said Macleod.

Walsh smiled. "Ah, well, then perhaps you shouldn't be in politics after all. Is there anything I can do?"

"Appreciate your offer, Senator. But right now everything's under control. I think."

"Any further thoughts on the explosion?"

- Macleod shook his head. "It was a powerful son of a bitch, that's all I can tell you. It blew out a large chunk of the belly. We were lucky to get the airplane down in one piece."

Walsh smiled. "And I think we were lucky to have had you at the controls, Captain."

Macleod shrugged his thanks.

Bryden, the senator's aide, asked, "Do you think there was a bomb in someone's baggage, Captain?"

"That's what it looks like."

"Any thoughts on who might have planted it?"

"Not a one," said Macleod.

"It could have been one of those insurance schemes," mused Bryden. "Take out a few hundred thou on someone and then stick a bomb in his luggage."

"It's a possibility," Macleod admitted. "Crackpots have done that sort of thing before. If that's what it was, the device may have been timed to go off while we were over the Arctic Ocean."

"So there was a hell of a good chance that all of the evidence would go straight to the bottom," declared Bryden. He turned to Walsh. "Certainly sounds logical, doesn't it, Senator?"

"Sure does, Milt, what other explanation could there be?"

The Grumman Gulfstream III was cruising at 37,000 feet over the Greenland Sea, north-northwest of Jan Mayen Island. Mike Lockhart noted from the inertial navigation system that it was time to transmit another position report.

"Sondestrom Control, this is Trans American Niner-Zero-Two on five-seven-two-four, over."

The reply was almost immediate. The air traffic controller had been expecting the call. "Roger, Niner-Zero-Two, this is Sondestrom. Go ahead."

"Okay, Sondestrom. Trans American Niner-Zero-Two was overhead seven-five degrees north, one-five degrees west at two-seven maintaining flight level three-seven-zero, over."

"Roger, Trans Am Niner-Zero-Two, I copied your position

at two-seven past the hour. Contact Bodo Oceanic Control on two-eight-six-eight. And good morning to you, sir.''

"I'm starving,'' complained Brad Steiner.

Karen nodded. She was hungry too.

"It's terror,'' said Brad. "It gives you an appetite. Any idea what they've got? Steak? Chicken?''

"With our luck, it'll be chicken.''

"I'm going to miss that plastic chicken after I quit,'' said Brad. "They've got a celluloid farm where they breed chickens for airline meals. They feed them plastic grain . . .''

"Be quiet!'' Karen snapped.

"What?''

Karen held up her hand. She had become aware of something. Something frightening. Quickly she turned and slid open the cockpit window by her right shoulder. The icy air and the screaming whine of number-three engine embraced her as she leaned out, staring into the sullen mist.

It was so damned hard to see anything . . . so tough to penetrate that lousy, freezing fog . . . eyes aching with the effort.

But she had seen something. It was there. She was sure of it. For a moment the mist parted sufficiently for her to see it again.

She turned. Brad was staring at her, astonishment stamped on his features.

Macleod was still back with the passengers. No time to call him.

Now!

She reached for the thrust levers. Her fingers found number three and then moved forward to close on the reverse thrust lever. She hauled it rearward. And prayed.

The aircraft shuddered as the jet exhaust abruptly changed direction. An instant later Macleod stormed into the cockpit.

"What the hell are you doing?''

"We're moving, Captain.''

"What?''

She pointed. "We're sliding toward the edge of the ice floe.''

"Jesus!'' Macleod jumped into his seat and spent hopeless seconds attempting to steer the 707 away from the edge of the ice. It was an impossible task with power emanating from only one side and the wind slowly pivoting the airplane like a giant weather vane. The water came ever closer, threatening.

There was no choice. Macleod shut down the number-three engine. As it whined into silence he glanced at Karen. "Nice work."

"Thanks."

"Shit," muttered Brad.

Janet burst into the cockpit. "Captain, the lights and power . . ."

"I know. We had to shut down the engine."

"Shut it down? But . . ."

"It was pulling us toward the edge of the ice. Another few minutes and we might have been in the goddam ocean."

"But if there's no engine, there's no heat . . ."

"I'm well aware of that," Macleod said. "But there's nothing I can do about it. We wouldn't last more than a few minutes in that water. I'll talk to the passengers. Get me a megaphone, will you?"

He explained it to the shadowy figures in the dim cabin. He said he was sorry. But there was nothing he could do about it. No, the aircraft couldn't be wedged with cushions and life jackets; such items couldn't restrain such a powerful jet engine on such a slippery surface. The cabin crew would still be serving some food. Unfortunately, there hadn't been time to cook all of the meals. There was nothing to do except make themselves as comfortable and warm as possible, wrapping themselves in blankets, huddling together when possible and trying to get some sleep. Sorry, he said again. Really sorry.

He went back to the cockpit, where Karen and Brad were shivering in coats and blankets. Already the place was like a meat locker. How long before everyone froze solid? When the rescue team finally arrived would they find one hundred nineteen statues staring at eternity?

No, he told himself. Don't think like that. It doesn't do any good. But how could you make yourself stop wondering? Where would they be twenty-four hours from now? One lousy day. In the normal course of events it was nothing, an interval, meals and some sleep, a single revolution in a man's life. But now a day seemed like a lifetime. Incredible the way things happen. Everything in life becomes totally irrelevant when confronted with a desperate need for survival.

Odd how your mind keeps on playing your life like some old movie: the house in New Brunswick, Dad's Hudson, Mom's fruit cake, boredom, longing, playing tag, baseball, hockey, being horny for days, weeks on end, dirty pictures from Eddy Tripp's father's secret collection, pursuing the *action*, feeling the frustration of desire, imagining what it was like to participate, coming to the startling conclusion that most of what the Sunday-school teacher said was bullshit, wondering if ninety-nine percent of what was said by almost everyone wasn't the same thing . . . longing to fly as much as to get into Marsha Frank's pants, aching to learn the mysteries of every little thing . . . finding out, making mistakes, learning bit by painful bit . . . reaching goals, sexual as well as intellectual, discovering that bullshit—not the atom—was the basic building block of the universe, that there are rewards nevertheless; flying, working, earning . . . instructing, charter-flying, then the big time, the letter from Trans American . . . being there at the right time, advancing rapidly because of a booming airline business . . . all dreams realized and then everything disintegrating with Angie. The nagging. The jabbing. The insults. The pettiness and the important things . . . and it was impossible to distinguish between them.

And it all added up to this. Here, Macleod told himself, is where it could all end. Hell of a good chance of it happening that way. If the ice cracked apart; if the fog persisted; if, if, if.

He regarded the likelihood of death without fear, but with a sense of regret of leaving too many things undone. Hell of a shame for it to end like this, now, in this icy armpit of the world. Like all pilots, he had recognized the possibility of death in a flaming crash against the side of a mountain or at the end of a runway. Things could go wrong with airplanes; things could go wrong with radar; traffic controllers could screw up and send two airplanes into the same piece of sky at the same time. Such things happened. Occupational hazards.

But somehow being frozen to death didn't seem to qualify as part of the bargain.

But there was a positive side to it all. If he died he would never have to pay Angie another dime. He smiled to himself, and the thought warmed him a little.

Harriet Lawson stared, appalled. She turned and strutted indignantly into the cabin. She grabbed a flight attendant by the arm.

"The goddam toilets. They're . . . *full!*"

The girl nodded matter-of-factly. "No electrical power," she said. "So they won't flush. And now they're frozen. Solid. Sorry."

"What the hell am I supposed to do?"

The girl shrugged. "Use one. And hold your breath, ma'am. That's all I can suggest."

It was on the tip of Harriet Lawson's tongue to ask the girl just who in the hell she thought she was talking to. But what was the use? She was so incredibly young. God, "Sesame Street" was a classic to these kids. If Harriet Lawson had said, "I used to be in the movies," the girl would have shrugged again and muttered, "Is that so?" There was a time when it was impossible to walk across the street without people pestering her for autographs. Now, no one cared. For the first time in years she was on the brink of tears.

In 14C, Sam Coglin wondered about the prospects of suing Trans American. The stupid bastards should have inspected the baggage before it was loaded on the plane. It was their duty. And they failed. What was the failure worth? A million per passenger?

In Row 21, Melvin and Tina Lee giggled over a crude joke he had just told about three parakeets and a male prostitute.

Senator David Walsh closed his eyes and tried to forget about the cold that edged its unpleasant way up his legs. Strange, how your life can suddenly be exposed to such unexpected jeopardy. A few hours ago everything had seemed so secure. His political career was proceeding according to plan. An increasing number of pollsters kept telling him he was going to make it all the way to the White House. He smiled wryly to himself; if enough people tell you something you'll start to believe it. The unbelievable starts to become the improbable, which in turn becomes the possible. "Not inconceivable" was the phrase that lately kept recurring in his mind like an echo of a half-forgotten song. He had to keep reminding himself of the odds, of the countless things that could go wrong along the way. The only certainty about politics was its uncertainty. Who had told him that? What did it matter now, anyway? Life had been reduced to elemental proportions. Only survival mattered. All the rest was speculation. Besides, it could all end right here.

Macleod listened to the creaking of the ice. Every sound sent a shiver of trepidation along his spine. Would the ice rupture immediately beneath the aircraft, creating a chasm? The 707 would tumble in. There'd be no time for any sort of orderly evacuation. It would be instant chaos and panic. Every man for himself. How long would the aircraft float? He shrugged to himself. Unanswerable questions. So why ask them? He could think of no way to prepare for the possibility other than to camp the passengers and crew outside on the ice. No way.

He listened to the intense persistence of the wind. Was it getting stronger? It seemed like it. A north wind. The temperature outside was about ten degrees below zero, Fahrenheit. What was the wind chill factor? Minus forty? Minus sixty? He didn't know.

A strong north wind. Did that mean the ice floe was being blown toward the south, toward warmer waters? Such a movement would only accelerate the breakup of the ice.

22

THE MESSAGE CAME in on the primary HF frequency, suddenly, shockingly.

"Mayday, Mayday, This is Trans American Flight Niner-Zero-Two. Coordinates: one degree, seven minutes west; six-five degrees, three-four minutes north. We are being fired on by Soviet MiG-23s. I say again: Soviet MiG-23 fighters are attacking us. My God, we've been hit. The bastards are trying to shoot us down! . . . Do you read? . . . someone . . . anyone. This is Trans American Niner-Zero-Two . . . Mayday, May . . ."

Silence. The transmission ended in the middle of a word.

The air traffic controllers at Bodo, Norway, gazed at one another, momentarily stunned by the impact of what they had just heard.

"No, it can't be . . . it *can't!* God, if only our radar extended that far out to sea."

"Play the tape back. There has to be a mistake."

"Mistake? What mistake, for Christ's sake?"

"Get Oslo on the line."

"Play the tape back! I've got to double-check those coordinates."

"Did you get a fix on the transmission?"

"It's absurd . . . even the crazy Russians wouldn't shoot down a civilian American airplane."

"Maybe they weren't Russians."

"The pilot said 'Soviet.' "

"No, he only said 'Soviet MiGs.' They sell those planes all over the world, don't they?"

* * *

163

Soviet airmen aboard a Tupolev "Bear" reconnaissance aircraft over the Norwegian Sea were as puzzled and alarmed as the Norwegian controllers. It was madness, unthinkable; the sort of lunatic act that could trigger war. . . .

They lost no time in relaying to Moscow what they had heard.

But they took no action.

The first American to hear the news was Captain Victor Brewster, Operations Duty Officer at NATO Military Headquarters, West Germany. Captain Brewster had been drafting a letter to his wife in Columbus, Ohio. It was a difficult letter to write. Explaining about Ilse. About how he hadn't wanted things to happen this way. But they had. And facts had to be faced. He hoped she might understand. . . .

Somehow the letter wasn't coming together the way he had planned.

The telephone rang, and he pushed his letter aside.

"You mean, they actually shot down an American airliner?"

The voice said no, that was not exactly what was meant; the message received at Bodo had indicated that Soviet MiGs were firing on the jet but there was no confirmation at this moment that the jet was actually down.

Captain Brewster fumbled for a pencil and paper, his mind a whirl.

"What flight? Trans Am Nine-Oh-Two? Seattle to Stockholm? Yeah, I got it. But you gotta be kidding . . . Russian jets? This can't be for real . . ." But perhaps it could. Perhaps every fact he was frantically scribbling would be recorded in history books. If there *would be* any history books.

In Leningrad, an irritable and uncharacteristically disheveled Colonel Vassili Kalinokov entered the conference room. He had been about to get out of bed when the call came. Not a moment to spare, the message declared. He had thrown on his ill-fitting uniform and rushed immediately to the office. A top-level meeting was being held. An emergency. Code Orange.

Fortunately, the Communications Center was only a seven-minute ride from Kalinokov's apartment. It occupied an isolated wing of the Ilia Mourometz Museum, one of the few nineteenth-century structures to have survived the German siege of Leningrad during World War II.

Eleven representatives of the Military Preparedness Sub-Committee of the Politburo's Central Committee sat themselves around the long table. And listened. And pondered the significance of the reports being presented. Most of them were old enough to have lived through the horrors of World War II, the Great Patriotic War. Was this the start of another, even more devastating conflict?

Kalinokov said, "Comrades, if this American jet is indeed down, must we not ask ourselves if there is any truth in that claim that our MiGs shot it down?"

"Of course there is no truth in it," declared the director. "I have it on the highest authority."

"But is it possible that some independent action was initiated without approval from Defense Command?"

"No."

"Are we certain?"

"As far as we know, none of our fighters was anywhere near the area."

"Has there been any reaction from Washington?"

"Not yet, but we're awaiting the inevitable."

"Did satellite radar reveal anything about the incident?"

"Nothing."

"But the American aircraft was tracked earlier, was it not?"

"Yes."

"And it suddenly disappeared?"

"Correct. It seems certain that the aircraft is down."

"How many other aircraft were detected in the area by radar when the attack was reported?"

"That's what is so confusing. There were *no* other aircraft observed anywhere near the Boeing airplane."

There was a long silence.

"Has news of the incident been released?"

"We won't release it until the appropriate time. But I have no doubt that every radio and television station in the United States is broadcasting nothing else."

The newscaster's voice was tense and reflected the predictable urgency.

"There is a report, as yet unconfirmed, that Soviet jet

fighters have shot down a Trans American Airlines Boeing seven-oh-seven northwest of Norway. The airplane, Trans American Flight Nine-Oh-Two, was en route from Seattle to Stockholm. It is further reported that one of the passengers was Senator David Walsh, the Republican presidential hopeful. The airline states that there were one hundred and twelve passengers and a crew of seven on board. As yet there is no confirmation of the incident either from Washington or Moscow. I repeat, we have an unconfirmed report that Trans American Flight Nine-Oh-Two bound from Seattle to Stockholm has been shot down by Soviet MiG fighters . . .''

Within moments the telephone lines into the White House were jammed with calls. Didn't the shooting down of an airliner constitute an act of war? Was the plane in Soviet airspace? What was the President going to do? Would there be an emergency session of Congress? Most of the callers demanded action, from diplomatic retaliation to dropping the ''big one'' on Moscow.

Supermarkets noted an immediate increase in business; citizens loaded their cars with canned goods. Long lines quickly formed at gas stations as Americans by the millions filled up while there was still gas to be had.

The Soviet president wasted no words.

''We did not attack your airliner, Mr. President. Furthermore, we do not have any knowledge of this incident. I have no doubt that a transmission was made about Soviet MiG fighters. But I can tell you without qualification, Mr. President, that if the American pilot saw MiG fighters, they were not *Soviet* MiG fighters.''

Quickly, the interpreter translated the message.

The American President replied coldly, ''I acknowledge your denial, Mr. President. However, the fact is that the emergency transmission said quite specifically that the attacking fighters were Soviet MiGs. Undoubtedly, the pilot recognized the markings of the Red Air Force.''

''I am aware of that. But I insist that they were *not*.''

''Then whose aircraft were they?''

''That I cannot answer.'' The intake of breath could be heard over the telephone line. The Soviet president was said to have asthmatic problems. ''I must repeat categorically, Mr.

President, that the Soviet Union had nothing whatever to do with this unfortunate incident.''

The President sighed inwardly. Damn it. It was hard to talk to a man through an interpreter. You had to listen to him speaking in his native tongue, try to read the tone, the inflections and the pauses, the hesitation, the groping for just the right word. Then you heard it all over again, the interpreter's version.

The American said, ''Mr. President, is it not entirely possible that some of your pilots took this action spontaneously and without approval?''

''No, Mr. President, that is not possible!''

''How can you be so certain? What compounds the crime is that the flight carried Senator Walsh. He was, of course, internationally recognized for his views on increasing American military power. And it was widely known, Mr. President, that Senator Walsh was aboard that flight.''

''I know of Walsh. He was a virulent anticommunist.''

''Perhaps that is the motive for this crime.''

''That is a vicious insinuation,'' retorted the Soviet president. ''Are you challenging my word . . . my integrity?''

''The fact remains that the airliner is down.''

''We know that, Mr. President, but we did not shoot it down.''

Did the Russian protest too much? Who wouldn't, given such a crisis? He was probably lying. But was their downing of the 707 intentional or accidental? Upon the answer to that question might hinge the fate of the world. Wars had been triggered by lesser events.

In Washington, a man emerged from the Soviet Embassy— and was attacked by a score of club-swinging demonstrators. Police rushed to intervene, but before they could disentangle the struggling bodies, the victim had suffered a broken arm and several ribs, and the loss of two teeth, plus severe cuts and bruises. As they carried him away he finally made them understand that he was not a Russian but a reporter from the London *Daily Express*, trying to get the Soviet side of the story. . . .

In Los Angeles, members of the Ballets Russes locked themselves in their rooms at the Bonaventure Hotel, terrified to emerge because of the angry crowd in the lobby and outside. Even on the twelfth floor they could hear the chant: "Russky ballet, out of L.A. . . . Russky ballet, out of L.A."

In a Kenosha, Wisconsin, supermarket two women simultaneously came across the last remaining six-pack of Tab. Each claimed to have seen the six-pack first. Both clutched it; both refused to let go. They screamed at each other, their faces turning red with anger and hatred. Suddenly one woman let go of the six-pack. She pulled a .25-caliber automatic pistol from her purse. She fired directly into the face of the other woman, hitting her just above the right eye, killing her instantly. Horrified onlookers saw the assailant pocket her gun, grab the soda and hurry away to the checkout counter, where terrified cashiers let her go straight through.

The two Lockharts, father and son, were in the ten-acre orchard that adjoined the big house. The trees were bright with blossoms that, for Mike, somehow made the horrible events seem momentarily unreal.

"There were no problems," Mike reported, his voice curiously monotone, as if the event might have been of only passing interest to him. "I intercepted as planned. And detonated the device by radio."

"The airplane exploded?"

"No, but it went down trailing smoke."

"I can't understand that, Mike. If Walsh had it with him, the explosion should have blasted the center fuel tank underneath and behind the first-class cabin and torn that plane apart."

"Maybe he didn't have it with him in the cabin."

"Perhaps. Did you see the seven-oh-seven crash?"

"No, it disappeared in cloud. Heavy stuff. I listened for an emergency transmission. But there was none, no message of any kind. They must have gone straight in." He rubbed his forehead as if he were suffering from a violent headache. "The only deviation from plan resulted from the airplane not blowing up immediately."

"What do you mean?"

"The anti-radar system from the XB-3A was working perfectly. There is no way that any radar system could have detected me as I approached the Boeing."

"So?"

"The problem occurred when I tried to determine when the seven-oh-seven would no longer be visible to radar. I didn't know exactly when to turn off the anti-radar device and become visible myself. So ground radar may have detected two aircraft for a few seconds or none at all."

"I wouldn't worry about that, Mike. Even if the radar operators were alert enough to notice, they'd probably consider it a temporary glitch. Happens all the time. You know, it's a good thing that the Devastator is sitting in the hangar. The way we've been wreaking havoc with radar systems around the country, even a temporary radar problem could throw suspicion our way. So forget it. What happened next?"

"Everything else went exactly according to our plan. I followed the airliner's flight plan to the point where the MiGs were supposed to attack. I transmitted the Mayday message, turned on the anti-radar system and returned to base."

The elder Lockhart said quietly, "You performed a magnificent service for your country, Mike."

"Did I?" Mike was pale with fatigue, his eyes dark-rimmed, his shoulders uncharacteristically hunched as if the weight on them had suddenly become too burdensome. "I keep seeing them."

"Them?"

"All the people on that plane. There were human beings in there; there were women and little children in there. It wasn't just a hunk of metal."

"I know that, Mike."

"Now I wonder if I'll ever be able to sleep again. Isn't that a hell of a thing to worry about? Maybe I'm going nuts."

"Come on, Mike. You're stronger than that. You had to do what you did. We never told ourselves it was going to be easy."

"But it *was* easy, easy as hell. Just follow the numbers. Press a button. The job's done."

"It had to be done."

Mike nodded rapidly, almost mechanically. "I know that. We talked it all out. I understand it intellectually. But I've just killed a hell of a lot of people. And they won't leave me alone."

Lockhart gripped his son's arm. "Time will take care of

that, Mike. The truth is, men who shape history often are not permitted the luxury of conscience. This is not a moral issue. Sometimes, as in war, it is necessary to kill. Even the law says that if homicide is justifiable, it is *legal* to kill. Senator Walsh was a great man. I though a great deal of him and considered him a close friend. I wish he were still alive. But we did what we had to do. For the national interest, Mike, for two hundred and twenty *million* Americans. Think of them, not the few who were on that plane.''

Mike sighed. ''But for crissakes, Dad, this could lead to war, couldn't it?''

''I seriously doubt it,'' said his father. ''And that's the point. Neither Russia nor the United States will go to war over this. Of that I am convinced.''

''How can you be so sure?''

''Because I know the manner of men with whom we're dealing. Wars don't start over this kind of thing, not these days. The important thing is, we are changing the thinking of a nation. We are waking this country up. For the first time in a long while, Americans are really angry. And they're united. And most important, they are focusing that anger where it should be. At Moscow. Do you realize what we have accomplished?''

Mike said, ''There was a girl on the crew of that jet, the first officer, Karen Dempsey. It must have been a big trip for her, the first female copilot to make an international flight for Trans American Airlines.''

''I know, Mike. I too was sorry about that.''

''I saw her picture. She was a good-looking girl . . . and now she's just pieces of flesh for the fish to feed on.''

''That kind of thinking doesn't accomplish anything, Mike.''

''But I don't think I like what I *have* accomplished, for Christ's sake!'' Mike's voice flared, crackling with sudden anger. He apologized at once. ''I'm sorry, Dad.''

''It's all right, Mike. I understand. It's tragic that the girl had to die. No one is sorrier than I am. But what counts is that her death had purpose. It *mattered*. You do see that, don't you?''

Mike nodded. ''Yes, it mattered.'' He seemed to be

repeating the word to himself as he walked slowly beside his father.

"The real tragedy," said Lockhart, "would have been if the mission had failed. But it didn't. I only wish everyone could know what you've done."

23

COLONEL VASSILI KALINOKOV sipped his clear tea as he smoked a cigarette, a traditional Russian Papyross. Some said the long cardboard tube helped to filter the smoke, making smoking safer; others declared just as convincingly that the device intensified its harmful qualities. You believed whom you wanted to believe.

Kalinokov was still hungry; his breakfast of dry biscuits and a paper-thin layer of honey hadn't been enough to satisfy a kitten. Long before noon he would be ravenous, his stomach growling and gurgling like the plumbing in his apartment on Red Star Prospekt. Damn his waistline! Instinctively he sucked in his stomach. As he did so, he glanced at his reflection in the window beside him. The shadowy outline displeased him. It was positively lumpish. He pulled back his shoulders. A little better. God, what a hopeless business it was, trying to fight age. All you could hope to do was to postpone the inevitable defeat. Why did nature take such a fiendish delight in robbing a man as he got older? Why steal his hair? Why thicken and distort him? Why dim his eyes so that he was forced to wear spectacles?

The ghastly process would not perhaps have offended him so deeply had he been married and settled down with a couple of children. But Vassili Kalinokov had always evaded permanent relationships with women. He liked them; indeed, he grew fonder of them as the years rolled by. Having tasted most of life's pleasures, he knew that none could compare with the joy of a fresh, new affair: the jousting, the discovery, the giving, the taking. Every relationship was like being born again. Why deny himself this pleasure by marrying? (He enjoyed quoting the American journalist, Ambrose Bierce, who claimed that love is temporary insanity curable only by marriage.) Unfortunately, it was becoming more difficult to initiate relationships. The fact had to be faced: young women simply didn't regard him the way they used to. They saw him not as an interesting animal of the opposite sex, but as a senior officer of middle age. A man worthy of respect. A man old enough to have a daughter in her twenties—or possibly in her early thirties. In the old days, he had only to chat for a few minutes. They all got the idea. Nowadays it was necessary to spend valuable time and risk a derisive, giggling rejection, before being able to establish that first vital bridgehead. And rejections hurt more deeply than they used to.

Kalinokov ground out his cigarette in the ashtray, an attractive Eskimo sandstone carving. He had picked it up during his tour of duty with the embassy in Ottawa, a frustrating period during which he had attempted, with little success, to exacerbate the stresses between Quebec and the rest of Canada. Now there was this new crisis, an infinitely more dangerous affair. This damned jetliner. There seemed little doubt that it had been shot down. But by whom? And for what reason? Those were the questions everyone was asking—everyone in the department, that is, for the general public still had not been informed of the incident. For them it was just a delightfully warm day in early June, a day of blossoming flowers and gentle breezes, a day for opening windows and breathing deeply of the mild spring air.

Not a day for pondering aeronautical riddles.

Kalinokov's office was comfortable enough; he had softened the harsh lines of the bare walls with a couch (he insisted on thirty minutes of sleep after lunch—or what passed for lunch these days) and half a dozen framed copies of Pevsner sketches, startling little things even though they were pre-Revolution. It was hardly the sort of wall decoration that would earn points with the Central Committee. But no one complained. Kalinokov was generally considered an odd man out, a specialist, an eccentric who could be excused his idiosyncrasies because he was very good at his job and would be extremely hard to replace.

His assistant, Georgi Morikilov, brought in a report from a

reconnaisance flight that had flown out over the Norwegian Sea to search the area where the American jetliner crashed. "They saw nothing, sir," Morikilov declared in his forthright way. Morikilov possessed a face that reminded one of a not particularly intelligent bloodhound. But he was ploddingly reliable and always utterly obedient. One could depend on Morikilov to do what he was told—but if one was smart, it was advisable never to say anything even faintly seditious in his presence. Loyalty had its limits.

"Nothing?"

"Not even a trace of wreckage, sir."

"Hardly conclusive," Kalinokov reflected. A jetliner could, after all, go straight to the bottom of the ocean, leaving not a fragment floating on the surface.

"Quite true, sir," said Morikilov.

Kalinokov fingered the flesh beneath his chin. Was it a shade flabbier than it had been yesterday? Were there exercises he should be doing to delay further deterioration? "Let's sum up the known facts," he said. Morikilov nodded, attentive as always. "Number one, we know that no Soviet aircraft were in the vicinity when the seven-oh-seven went down. Number two, our satellite radar did not detect *any* other aircraft anywhere near the Boeing jet when the distress call was made. Third: we are told by our search aircraft that there is nothing to be found on the surface of the ocean. But, four, a Boeing seven-oh-seven of Trans American Airlines is indeed missing. So, my dear Georgi, we must ask ourselves, what really happened? And why would a pilot accuse Soviet MiG interceptors of attacking his aircraft when none was there? Was our radar at fault? Is Moscow withholding something from its own intelligence service? Maybe the whole cursed thing is a hoax. But who would perpetrate such a hoax? And how? And why? Perhaps the Americans are behind the whole thing."

"Yes, sir," muttered Morikilov. "A distinct possibility."

"The distress call specifically mentioned 'MiG-23 fighters.' *Soviet* MiG-23 fighters. Not East German, not Hungarian, not Polish. *Soviet.* An error in identification? A deliberate lie? A vision—an Arctic mirage? Any suggestions, Comrade?"

"None, sir."

"Evidently, the jetliner did take off from Seattle, Washington. Evidently, it did not arrive in Stockholm."

"Yes, sir."

"So now we must ask why it did not arrive in Sweden."

"I don't know, sir."

"Maybe this is a puzzle that defies solution."

"Do you really believe that, sir?"

"Not really, Morikilov."

"There's another element," said Kalinokov.

"What is that, sir?"

"When Flight Nine-Oh-Two was over Canadian territory, it vanished briefly from our satellite radar screens."

A brisk, businesslike nod. "Yes, that is entirely correct, sir." One thing about Morikilov, he seldom disagreed.

"Splendid," said Kalinokov. "I wonder why it disappeared. Was it due to some minor temporary failure of our radar system? On the face of it, that would be a likely explanation, wouldn't you say?"

"I would indeed, sir."

"Yet our radar technicians have examined the system and say they can offer no explanation, except to make vague references to sunspots and flocks of Arctic birds. So if we accept their word for it, we have a radar system that seemed to fail for a matter of twenty or thirty seconds. And it just so happens the target at the time was the same airplane that later vanished completely. Curious, yes?"

"Most curious, sir."

"Do you wonder about it, Morikilov?"

"I certainly do, sir."

"And have you arrived at any conclusions?"

"In my opinion the Americans are lying." Morikilov always thought the Americans were lying.

Kalinokov said, "You may be correct. But I think we must ask ourselves what the Americans would accomplish by lying, other than stirring up more anti-Soviet hatred. I must confess that the answer eludes me."

"Whatever it is, sir. I am sure that it is not in the best interests of the Soviet Union."

Kalinokov smiled to himself, recalling that he had employed the very same phrase at a Division Committee meeting ten days before. A stout fellow, Morikilov, but not to be counted among the world's most original thinkers. "Did you

know that Senator David Walsh was one of the passengers
aboard the airliner?''

Morikilov nodded. ''He hated the Soviet Union.''

''I knew him,'' said Kalinokov. ''I first met him at a party
in Ottawa. Before he became a senator.''

Morikilov frowned; his cropped head jerked back a fraction
as if he feared that his commanding officer had developed a
highly contagious condition. ''Was he hostile, sir?''

''No, not at all. We talked about skiing. He had a place in
the Rocky Mountains outside Denver. He invited me for a
weekend.''

''Did you go, sir?''

''Certainly.''

Morikilov's eyes widened. ''And was there . . . any *purpose*
in his invitation?''

Kalinokov shook his head. ''Nothing more than a pleasant
weekend of skiing,'' he said. And a raven-haired beauty
named Michelle. God, he had damned nearly defected because of her. It was a gut-wrenching decision, to come back,
to leave her. And, he reflected, the only reason he was here
and not in Canada or the United States was that he never
completely trusted her. Was she there simply to lure him into
the enemy camp? Was her passion counterfeit? It certainly
hadn't seemed that way. The question had haunted him for
years.

''You risked a great deal, sir. Walsh might have destroyed
your career.''

''There was little danger of that, I assure you. I got to
know Walsh quite well after he became senator. In private he
was very pleasant; in fact we rarely discussed politics. There
is often remarkably little connection between the public
perception of American politicians and the men themselves.
The whole thing is based on winning votes. The result is that a
man who hates blacks will present himself as a friend of the
Negro—particularly if there is a large number of black votes
to be won. In the same way, a man may declare himself an
advocate for a stronger, more militant America simply because it is a politically expedient thing to do. Some years ago
there was a senator named McCarthy. He made a reputation
for himself by accusing everyone from schoolteachers to screen-
writers of being Communists. God knows whether he was

sincere in his beliefs. It didn't matter. The time was right for such an attitude; Americans by the millions supported the senator; he achieved considerable power.''

"An extraordinary system," murmured Morikilov.

"Quite extraordinary," Kalinokov agreed. "But in the case of Senator David Walsh, I am convinced that his political philosophy was genuine." He sat back and gazed up at the high ceiling. The regulation gray paint did not conceal the cherubs and floral arrangements that had been worked into the cornice when the place was built, back in pre-Revolutionary days. The building had once belonged to a count, a thoroughly dissolute fellow, according to the whispers. It was said that he and his friends entertained a dozen or more stark naked females, eating, drinking and ravishing until they could eat, drink and ravish no longer. The count died at thirty-nine. Death by debauchery. A damn sight better than dying by dull degrees, boring yourself into eternity. It was Kalinokov's private opinion that he would have made a splendidly outrageous aristocrat.

Walsh. Senator David Walsh. Tiresome to drag oneself back to the harsh realities of the moment. Was Walsh perhaps the key to the puzzle? But why would anyone want to kill him? Could it be a political assassination or did his death have nothing to do with politics? Jealousy? Revenge? Had he been discovered sleeping with someone else's wife?

Were the Chinese involved? God knows, they never objected to fomenting trouble between the United States and the Soviet Union. But again, the technicalities seemed formidable indeed.

He shook his head, frustrated. Now he had to place the various facts in fertile soil and allow them to germinate. . . .

The general called before Kalinokov had time for a second cup of tea.

"What progress?"

"None, sir."

"Why not?"

"I am doing the best I can with what is available."

"You must understand that this situation is rapidly deteriorating. All because of an incident in which we weren't involved. I must have answers soon."

"Are you absolutely sure we weren't involved, sir?"

"Damn it, of course I'm sure," said the general in his dogmatic way. "The situation is critical, Kalinokov. It's vital that we find out what happened. The Americans are blaming us for everything. Our position is becoming untenable. I want answers. Do I make myself clear?"

"Very, sir."

"Good," said the general. And hung up. He rarely wasted words.

Kalinokov found himself staring at the telephone as if expecting it to tell him more. Damn the general! Maybe he was part of a conspiracy behind the whole thing? No; it was inconceivable. Or was it? Stranger things had happened.

His mind dwelled on the satellite radar system. It normally was so reliable. But it had failed to indicate any evidence of other aircraft near the 707. Was someone ordering the radar operators to remain silent? To conceal the fact that our interceptors really did shoot down the 707? Perhaps this whole mess was caused by a radar operator falling asleep on the job. Malfunction due to sloppy maintenance? Failure to report this because of fear of the consequences? Anything was possible. Did the captain of the 707 *imagine* the fighters? Was he under the influence of drugs? Was he mentally deranged? Was he lying?

Kalinokov shrugged. His stomach growled. The hunger pangs were starting early today. Like everything else.

24

THEY STIRRED BENEATH their blankets, the three of them, like animals waking within cocoons.

Their sleep was interrupted by the passengers. The shouting and yelling had begun at the airplane's rear door, where one of them had been taking his turn standing guard. It quickly spread throughout the entire cabin, becoming louder and more frenzied as it did so: "It's an airplane . . . there's a plane . . ."

Wide awake now, Macleod and Karen opened their sliding side windows. Brad closed the cockpit door to muffle the noise from the cabin. They strained to hear the airplane.

"It *is* a plane," hissed Macleod. "A propeller-driven plane."

"But *high*," Karen murmured, frowning.

Macleod nodded. She was right; nevertheless the sound represented the first sign of interest from the outside world. He dragged himself out of his seat. His blood seemed to be congealing in his veins. His limbs ached with the cold; there was a frightening brittleness about his bones; it felt as if any sudden movement would snap them into splinters.

"Got the flares?" he asked Brad.

The flight engineer nodded.

"Okay," said Macleod. "Fire one. I'm going outside to transmit with one of the emergency radios."

He should have stationed one of the cabin crew by the door, he thought; a qualified person who could hurry out at the first sound of any aircraft and begin broadcasting immediately. Stupid of him not to have thought of it before.

He hurried aft, through the crowded, chaotic passenger cabin, ignoring passenger after passenger who asked him about the airplane that was said to be overhead. Was this the search-and-rescue team at last? How long would they take to get everyone off this godforsaken ice cube? Didn't they realize how *cold* it was down here?

The mist enfolded him as he slithered down the slide to the ground. According to the time it was daylight but the thick fog almost masked the fact. Even if the search plane was directly overhead, how could the crew possibly see them through this crap? And where the hell was the aircraft noise coming from? There? There? The goddam fog seemed to numb your senses.

Brad fired a second flare from the cockpit window. It cut a bright orange path through the fog, then vanished, leaving only a hint of a trail, specks of pink dust that soon were gone.

No change in engine sound from above. No sudden banking and diving to signify sighting the flare or receiving the transmission. Nothing. Just a maddening, self-satisfied drone that painted a picture of well-fed pilots dozing contentedly while their automatic pilot did all the work, not giving a damn about the poor bastards down on the ice. . . .

The transmitters from the life rafts were supposed to send a strong signal at least fifty miles. So why the hell wasn't there any reply from above? Weren't they listening to the emergency frequency? What the hell was the matter with them up there, for Christ's sake? Hadn't they heard that Flight 902 had gone down? Didn't they give a damn?

Macleod had to suppress a fierce desire to shake his fist at the now-fading sound. Bastards! By God, when he got out of this lousy predicament he'd move heaven and earth to find out who the sons of bitches were who flew over this spot, at this time, on this day without sparing a thought for Trans Am 902. Criminal negligence, that's what it was.

He listened glumly as the last echoes dissolved into silence. Then with a sigh he switched off the transceiver. No point in wasting the battery. In this numbing cold, there was no telling how long the batteries would last. Probably not very long.

He stood up, his bones creaking. In the freezing half-light, the 707 looked like some prehistoric bird frozen for all eternity. The fuselage and wings were caked with ice; the entire structure seemed to be sagging under the weight of the stuff.

One of the passengers came slithering down the evacuation slide—the pudgy, middle-aged man with thinning red hair.

"You're better off inside," Macleod told him.

"Your radio didn't work, huh?"

"It works all right," Macleod told him. "But for some reason the aircraft didn't respond. I don't know why. Maybe they weren't listening to the emergency frequency."

"Why wouldn't they be listening to the emergency frequency?" The man had an abrasive, insistent tone.

Macleod said that he couldn't answer that question.

The man said, "You told us the whole world knows we're down here. You said every plane and ship would be on the lookout for us."

"Yes," said Macleod, "I did say that."

"Well, is it true or isn't it?"

"Of course it's true."

"Then why the hell didn't that plane come down and look for us? Why didn't they answer you on the radio? Seems to me that airplane was just flying along as happy as can be, not giving a good goddam about us."

"I can't explain it," said Macleod, fighting the irritation rising within him.

"Seems to me a whole lot of things need explaining," said the man, his breath condensing in aggressive little clouds. "Aren't you going to start the motors again?"

Macleod pointed. "If you'd shut your mouth and open your eyes, you'd see how close we are to the edge of the ice. If we start the engine, we'll start sliding again. The brakes won't hold on this ice. You want to end up in the ocean?"

"Don't get smart with me," snapped the man. "You think you're big shit, you goddam airline pilots. You're just glorified bus drivers, that's all you are. You're not God almighty, you know. You're just a fucking mortal, buddy. And I'm not too goddam impressed at the way you've been handling things, let me tell you. I'm going to be taking it up with your company when we get out of here. I know some pretty important people at TAA . . ."

That was when it happened.

The crack was sharp and extremely loud, like a powerful rifle shot at close range. It was quickly followed by more cracks. The ice shifted, seeming to squirm and shrink beneath their feet. The red-headed man had to reach out and grasp part of a wheel-well door to maintain his balance.

Macleod fell to his hands and knees. He stared, horrified.

The ice floe fractured. The part bearing the 707 wallowed to one side as it came free. Then, as if it were on a spring, the ice and the great aircraft wallowed the other way.

Half a dozen passengers came scrambling down the escape slide and into a raft, white-faced, scared to death.

"What happened?"

"Are we sinking?"

Macleod stood and tried to calm them.

"No, I think it's okay. The ice flow broke. The part we're on has snapped away from the main body of the floe. We're okay, though. We're still floating. No problem."

But the ice now had a strangely unsubstantial feel beneath his feet. It moved, swayed and rolled ever so gently with the movement of the sea below. How long before there were more breaks? How long before there was insufficient ice to support the weight of the 707 and its passengers?

Ridiculous questions. Ridiculous, because there were no answers.

He stared into the fog to catch a last glimpse of the main ice floe, its edge bright and clean where the break had occurred.

"My God. Help me! Help me!"

Macleod turned. The red-headed man looked as if he were trying to pull the aircraft along with his hands. His face was pale with fright and pain.

Then Macleod saw the reason: the belligerent bastard was stuck to a wheel-well door, the flesh of his hands frozen solid to the metal surface.

"Don't pull!" Macleod yelled. "You'll tear the skin off your hands!"

The man's mouth dropped open. His beady eyes were wide with terror. "What the fuck am I supposed to do, for crissake?"

"Hold it. Just stay there," Macleod ordered him.

"What?"

Macleod turned. There were three men on the ice. He beckoned to them.

"Can you guys take a leak? And I mean right now?"

An instant of bewilderment, followed by an explanation

from Macleod and then nods of agreement. They unzipped their pants.

Macleod pointed to the red-headed man's hands.

"There. Aim at his fingers and palms."

Within moments Sam Coglin's warm, dripping hands came free. He clutched them to his plump chest, moaning, his eyes rolling.

Macloed examined the hands. They were a little raw but would be all right as long as he nursed them for a while. They heaved and pushed Mr. Coglin back up the slide and into the aircraft, where Janet Spencer set about the task of cleaning and protecting the tender skin. Fifteen minutes later, his hands treated and bandaged, Sam Coglin sought out Macleod.

"How are your hands, Mr. Coglin?"

"Think you're pretty fucking smart, don't you?" the red-haired man snapped.

Macleod blinked, surprised. "I'm sorry, Mr. Coglin. I know it wasn't a very pleasant way to get you free but without any other hot liquids available, I couldn't think of any other way to do it."

"It was humiliating!"

"But it was better than tearing off your skin, wasn't it?"

"You know what I mean," Coglin growled.

"I'm not sure I do, sir," Macleod said, puzzled.

"You'll live to regret this." And with that, Sam Coglin stalked away to his seat.

"I kind of think I'm the reason he's so angry," said a voice.

Macleod turned. A black man sat alone, huddled in a blanket.

"You, sir?"

The man grinned. "I was one of the hot water suppliers. Or didn't you notice?"

"Not really," Macleod confessed.

The man's grin widened. "Well, I know *he* did. That guy would rather have lost his hands than have a black man do that to him. I know his type. Do me a favor, will you?"

"Sure."

"Tell him that I'm also gay. And that I've got a Jewish lover back home."

But there was no need for Macleod to tell Mr. Coglin. He had overheard William Jarvis. And got the message.

*   *   *

Karen examined the landing gear, the tires scarred from the landing and sheathed in frost. Was there some way to anchor them in the ice, so that an engine might be started without the 707 slipping away out of control? Dig holes? Yes, that would work, but they would have to be deep holes; if not, the wheels would roll out as soon as the engine was started. It would be necessary to shut down the engine again. And then they wouldn't have another chance; the second and only remaining cylinder of compressed air required for starting would have been used up. Besides, the ice was like concrete; heavy power tools would be needed even to make a dent in the stuff. And the nearest power tools were probably in Greenland or Canada.

There had to be a way. There was always a way, her father used to say; it was just a matter of finding it. She shivered. Was her father watching her at this moment?

Instinctively, she looked up. Any bright ideas, Dad?

But the fog was uncommunicative.

"Captain Macleod and his crew are doing everything possible." Senator Walsh was weary of repeating the phrase. A number of passengers had come forward to the first-class section. Bitching. God only knows what they expected of him. The dump-it-in-the-politician's-lap attitude seemed to prevail even on ice floes in the Arctic.

He turned, aware of another person at his side. It was a boy, short and serious-looking, cocooned in two red airline blankets.

"Would it be all right if I talked with you, Senator?"

Walsh masked a tiny sigh and nodded. "Sure, son, sit down."

The boy did so and introduced himself in a quaintly formal way as Neil Parker of 128 Worthington Drive, Seattle.

"Very pleased to meet you, Neil."

"Same here, Senator."

They shook hands. The boy pulled his blankets tightly around his small body.

"I recently made an important decision," he said.

"Really?"

"Yes. I'm going to be President of the United States."

"That's a great idea."

"I think so," said the boy. "I've given it a lot of thought. By the way, my dad says you might be the next President."

"It's not . . . inconceivable," Walsh murmured.

"Do you enjoy being a candidate?"

"Enjoy it?" Walsh smiled. "Yes, I guess you could say I do. Why do you want to be President, Neil?"

"Because there's a lot of things I'd like to change."

"What do you have in mind?" asked Walsh.

"Well, Senator, what really bothers me is that the country seems so divided with strikes and demonstrations and stuff like that. In the end a whole lot of really important things never get done because we can't agree. In Russia they tell people to do things and they do it. It's a question of efficiency," he added after some thought. "I think our way is much nicer but what bothers me is whether it can go on like this."

"A good point," Walsh commented. He motioned toward the window. "Try to think of our democratic system as an airplane wing. It has to bend as it takes the loads. It gives, then it flexes and returns to normal. If it were too rigid it would break."

"So you think the Soviets are too rigid."

"In many ways, yes."

"Interesting thought," Neil commented.

"Thanks," said Walsh. "Remember, many great men— Abe Lincoln and Franklin Delano Roosevelt among them— have recognized that in many ways the democratic system is full of flaws but history has proven that it is the best form of government ever developed. It does provide the greatest good for the greatest number."

They talked more about democracy, its beginnings in Greece, Plato and Aristotle. And then feudalism, communism and fascism. The boy was remarkably well read and possessed sensible opinions on everything from organized labor to nuclear power. He finally stood up and thanked Walsh for taking the time to talk to him.

"It was my pleasure," Walsh assured him.

"I really hope you get to be President, sir."

"Thanks, Neil. I hope you make it too."

* * *

"The sensible thing," said Milt Bryden, "would be for us to share our blankets. Then we'd both be under two blankets instead of each of us being under only one. Didn't they teach you about taking advantage of body heat at stewardess school?"

Wendi shook her head; her blond curls bobbed prettily; the cold had made her cheeks even rosier than before. "No, but they told us about horny male passengers and how to handle them."

"Terrific," declared Milt. "So handle me."

Carl Neillsen stood beneath the huge tail of the Boeing 707, watching as the lady copilot studied the landing gear. What was she looking for? Could he help? No, she turned around now, making her way back to the slide, still glancing back at the wheels, deep in thought. Carl hunched himself down into his shoulder, striving to reduce his bulk against the biting cold. The fog swirled about him, brushing his forehead and cheeks with icy fingers. He walked a few yards, carefully, conscious of the uncertainty of his feet on the slippery surface. He stopped and looked back. The tail was now the only part of the aircraft he could see through the fog; it seemed to hover, a strange flying machine in motionless flight. Odd how the fog deadened sound, blunting it, absorbing it. He walked a little farther and stopped again. Now the tail was only faintly discernible. He turned and plodded away from the aircraft, that metal tube packed with people. He felt as if he were alone in another world. And, curiously, it was a comforting feeling. He seemed to have left the nagging, hurting problem behind. Solitude was a balm. No matter that the frigid air stung his lungs as he breathed; no matter that his feet had lost all feeling; no matter that the fog was freezing on his eyelashes, caking them with tiny needles of ice; no matter that his chapped lips had begun to crack. It was good to get away from humanity, to think rationally about her and tell her to go to hell, to say he didn't need her, to inform her that his life didn't revolve around her, that the wound would heal— damn it, the healing had already started. . . . Introspective by nature, Neillsen wondered at the sudden shifting of his emotions. Was this a reaction to the miraculous landing on the ice? Or was it the result of intense relief at finding himself alive when he had thought he was going to die? Would the euphoria soon dissolve? He shrugged. Time would tell. In the meantime, he found pleasure in a feeling that he had not experienced for some time: a feeling that it was moderately pleasant to be alive.

He stopped. Turned. The aircraft had vanished. He could hear the ocean lapping near him. But the fog played tricks: first the ocean was to his left, then behind him, then in front of him.

He walked for a few moments. And stopped. No sign of the aircraft. Still the water slapped against the icy shore. Somewhere to the left, or right, or behind or in front. . . .

"Hullo!" he shouted.

His voice rolled dully in the icy mist, seeming to surround him before rumbling away somewhere behind.

"Hullo! Can anyone hear me?"

Carl Neillsen smiled. He realized he had been calling in Swedish.

Anyway, it didn't matter if anyone heard him or not. He remembered that the aircraft had stopped very close to the water's edge. Therefore, if he found the nearest water—and it certainly wasn't far away; he could hear it—then all he had to do was follow it until he found the 707.

Simple.

25

THE PRESIDENT HAD been up most of the night. His eyes were heavy and sticky with fatigue; it felt as if someone were hammering on the inside of his temples with a sharp instrument. He was becoming increasingly agitated, on the brink of losing his temper.

When the Soviet president came on the line, the American had the utmost difficulty in restraining himself from shouting, giving vent to his anger and frustration.

The Russian declared that he had nothing to add to his remarks of the previous telephone conversation; much investigative work had been undertaken by Soviet intelligence but nothing had been uncovered that shed any light on the crisis.

"Do you have any more news, Mr. President?" asked his Soviet counterpart.

"I must tell you that there is no evidence to contradict the emergency broadcast stating that your MiGs shot down our aircraft."

The Russian said, "Mr. President, again I assure you unequivocally that you are mistaken. We deny the charge."

"You also denied having shot down the Korean Airlines flight near Murmansk in 1977."

Long agonizing moments dragged on while the translator did his work; then the Soviet leader responded, righteously indignant as expected. "We simply denied any knowledge of that incident because the facts were not immediately known to us. Besides, the two incidents cannot be compared. The Korean aircraft was in Soviet airspace and the pilot refused to obey or even acknowledge our instructions. He was flying near a top-security area. We were naturally concerned that the aircraft might not have been an airliner at all, but a reconnaissance aircraft in disguise. Nevertheless we continued to warn the pilot. We resorted to an attack only when all other options were closed to us. The Koreans had no one but themselves to blame."

"And who, do you think, is to blame for *this* crisis?"

"I have no way of knowing, Mr. President. I give you my word, however, that the Soviet Union was not involved in any way."

"Are you trying to claim that the fighter aircraft belonged to another power, and were disguised with Soviet markings?"

It was a complete shot in the dark, a probing of the man, a testing of his reactions. Too vehement a protest might have provided a clue, to something, God knows what. The Soviet leader said he thought the notion fanciful in the extreme. Besides, the practical difficulties were surely insurmountable.

"I understand your deep concern over this matter; we too are deeply concerned," the Russian continued. "But I must reiterate that no Soviet personnel or equipment—civilian or military—had any involvement with the tragedy; and in all candor I must tell you that I see little point in continuing to debate the issue when you obviously are disinclined to believe anything we have to say."

"Would you believe us if one of your Aeroflot pilots reported being attacked by American F-14s and then disappeared into the ocean?"

"You ask hypothetical questions, Mr. President."

Jesus Christ, it was hard not to explode, to let fly in his damned carved-in-granite face, to let emotion take over. But he had to think of tomorrow, of the implications of any rash or emotional behavior.

He said, "There's nothing hypothetical about the one hundred and nineteen men, women and children on board that airplane. I feel I must tell you that I am still waiting to be convinced that the Soviet Union is not responsible for this atrocity."

The translator seemed to labor uncertainly over the words, perhaps striving to capture the precise meaning of what the American had to say.

The Soviet leader responded at last: "Your attitude can hardly be considered constructive, Mr. President. Frankly, I find it disappointing that you take this position; it seems that you are more anxious to find a scapegoat than to discover the truth. We in the Soviet Union, however, are not concealing anything. We will do everything within our power to unravel this mystery, but in the meantime I have nothing to add to what I have already said: we are not responsible.''

The President hung up, conscious as always on such occasions of having not made any significant progress with the Russian. What a way to conduct a conversation that might be recorded in history books as one of the most meaningful of the twentieth century. Was the Russian really telling the truth? The American interpreter seemed to feel that the Russian sounded sincere in his remarks. Righteously angry, as if confronted by unjust accusations. Either the man was a superlative actor or he was telling the truth. But how could you tell? The bastard was known to do anything, say anything, to gain a point. The truth was a totally flexible commodity as far as he was concerned. He had proved it at conference after conference, vehemently rejecting anything that stood in the way of Soviet interests.

But maybe this time he was telling the truth, the whole truth and nothing but. Or maybe he simply didn't know what his military had actually done. Maybe he was trying to keep the lid on a terrible miscalculation, doing everything in his power to keep the facts from leaking out. Maybe, maybe, maybe.

He would run the tape for the National Security Council. It was essential to get their input. In spite of countless contingency plans and the incredible network of communications and computers, great decisions often resulted from either believing or not believing another human being.

He sighed and wondered whether he should rest for a couple of hours. It might freshen him up, help him to handle the load. But how could anyone sleep at such a time—in spite of the fact that sleep might be just what one needed?

Every President seemed destined to grapple with some crisis of awesome significance. Ike had the U-2 spyplane. Kennedy had the Cuban missile crisis. Johnson . . . Vietnam. Nixon . . . Watergate. Carter . . . Iran. Reagan . . . the economy. But this time there was an important difference. The American people seemed at last to have become united in their reaction to this; they hadn't been galvanized like this since World War II. Would they actually support a war over this? Most of the signs indicated precisely that. No more insults; no more retreat; no more appeasement. Their seemingly inexhaustible patience had at last worn out. Was this to be the Sarajevo of the eighties? The spark that could set the world aflame?

It was easy to be wise about great events when you knew what happened and why. Yes, in retrospect, Patton should have taken Berlin; MacArthur should have crossed the Yalu River; the United States should have achieved victory in Vietnam. But now an entirely different set of pressures was at work. Future historians might look back and declare that the President was foolish and ill-advised, or possessed extraordinary intelligence and great perception. Depending on how it all turned out.

Was Senator Walsh the pawn in all of this? But what purpose could his death possibly serve?

The President shook his head, baffled. Sometimes he wished he had followed his father's advice and gone into the chainlink fence business.

He had explained it all to them: how the ice floe had cracked, how the 707 was now sitting on a smaller slab of ice—a huge piece by normal standards, he added, but still smaller than the one on which they landed—how they still didn't dare start an engine for fear of sliding off the ice and into the ocean, how the emergency transceivers were ready at a moment's notice to broadcast to passing aircraft, how the life rafts were being kept inflated and deployed on the ice, tied with long cords to the aircraft. . . . But still they had questions, complaints, suggestions. Some passengers were infinitely patient, grateful just to be alive; others complained constantly, bitching about every inconvenience and discomfort.

The cabin crew fashioned aluminum saucers and suspended them from the cabin ceiling; then they put Sterno cans from the survival kits in them. The result was a modicum of heat. Someone added marijuana to one of the cans, hoping to overcome the stench from the unflushable toilets.

A hand caught her sleeve. "Are you a stewardess?"

Karen shook her head. "No, I'm one of the pilots, the first officer."

The old man nodded. "First officer, huh? What's that mean?"

"It means I'm the copilot," Karen told him.

"Is that so? Yep, seems to me I did hear we had a lady pilot on this trip. So you're her."

"That's right, sir."

"A pretty important job for a young girl. No offense, mind you. I'm not suggesting you can't handle it, nothing like that. I've never been one to put down ladies and what they can do. Isn't that right, dear?" he asked his wife.

"I wouldn't put up with it if you did," said the elderly lady at his side.

He chuckled. "Always got something to say for herself. I'm Mel Lee," he said. "This is my wife, Tina. We're newlyweds, on our honeymoon."

"Congratulations. I'm sorry we can't make it a more comfortable wedding night for you."

"I don't imagine it was your fault, so there's nothing for you to be sorry about. Anyway, it's pretty exciting." He inclined his head as if to impart something confidential. "Tina here had thought we might have kind of a dull honeymoon since neither of us is exactly in the first bloom of youth."

The old lady flushed. "I never said that, dear!"

Her husband chuckled, eyes sparkling. "I told her there'd be lots of action and she didn't believe me!" He slapped his knee, reveling in his own repartee. Then he turned to Karen. "But we'd sure love something hot to drink, miss."

"Yes, I know. So would everyone else, but we can't start an engine. So that means we don't have any electrical power for the galley."

"The engines are busted?"

"No, sir. You see, it's this icy surface. As soon as we start up we start to slide, even with the throttle pulled back all the way. The brakes won't stop it either, not on this ice. We're very close to the edge, so we're afraid that the aircraft will slide into the ocean."

"Seems like we've got a real problem, young lady."

"Yes sir."

"You got to anchor the wheels somehow," he said professionally.

"That's what we'd like to do, sir."

Mr. Lee scratched his white head. "I used to like to go ice-fishing when I lived in Cleveland. Up to Lake Erie. I remember once I drove like hell to get there. Eighty, ninety all the way. Always used to drive like that when I was young. I was pretty damn fast in lots of ways," he added with a wink at Tina. "So anyway, the tires got kind of hot. The moment they got parked on the ice, they melted it a bit, see, then it froze up again. And I was stuck fast; couldn't move . . ."

Karen stared at him. "That's very interesting, Mr. Lee."

"Yeah?"

Karen took his hand. It was cold. She said to Mrs. Lee, "You married a very smart man."

She shrugged. "My mother always told me, 'If he hasn't got good looks or money, make sure he's got brains.' "

Karen made her way forward. Thinking. Was it feasible? Was it possible? She searched her memory. She had never heard of anyone doing it before. But no one had ever landed a 707 on an ice floe before. It might just work. There were dangers, of course, but there were worse dangers in doing nothing and waiting to be frozen to death.

Macleod and Brad were in the cockpit, huddled in blankets, faces barely visible through the folds. Macleod sat in his characteristically hunched way. There was no conversation, just a kind of gloom and depression that set in with the cold.

She sat down in the right seat. The windows had frosted. It didn't matter; there was nothing to see. She turned to him. "Mac?"

"Yeah?"

"I have a crazy idea." No response. She went on. "I was thinking. If we could somehow anchor the wheels in the ice, we'd be able to start an engine again without worrying about sliding into the water."

Macleod glanced at her. "And how do you propose to do that?"

"This may sound a little ridiculous," she admitted. "But wouldn't it be possible to start small fires around the tires?"

He raised an eyebrow. "What? Fires? This is no time for jokes, Karen."

"But then the ice would melt and . . ."

The other eyebrow was elevated. "And then the tires would sink in and the ice would freeze up again . . ."

". . . and the tires would be *anchored!*"

His head emerged from the blanket. He grinned. "By God, you could be right! Might be worth a try. It's a hell of an idea!"

"It wasn't really my idea, Mac. Mr. Lee suggested it."

"Mr. Lee? Who's he?"

"A passenger. An old man."

"And very clever," murmured Macleod as he climbed out of his seat, nodding thoughtfully to himself. "It could work, you know. It really could."

"That's what I was thinking."

Brad Steiner extended a restraining hand. "Wait a minute, guys. We've got more than seventy thousand pounds of fuel in the wing tanks. You go lighting fires under there and you're liable to blow us all over the Arctic."

"Not if we're careful," said Macleod. "Seems to me we can keep the fires fairly small and not allow the flames to reach the wings."

"What about the passengers?" asked Karen.

Macleod shrugged. "Probably be a good idea to get them all out. Just in case."

Brad's voice cracked with alarm. "Hey, just think about it for a minute, will you? More than seventy thousand pounds of fuel and you're talking about lighting bonfires. It's insane. We'll finish what the mad bomber started."

"It's even more insane to sit here and freeze our butts off doing nothing," Macleod retorted. "Look, I never thought we'd be here this long. I figured they'd have found us by now in spite of this lousy fog and they'd be arranging to get us out of here. But they haven't done a goddam thing. I don't know why. I just don't know. But I do know that if we can get one of the engines going, we can have heat and light and some hot food. Sure, there's a risk. Things could go wrong. But I think it's worth the chance."

"And you're the captain," added Brad, tight-lipped.

It was a tedious business evacuating the aircraft, lining up the shivering passengers at the main rear door, persuading them to take their shoes off to prevent ripping the inflatable slide on which they would slither to ground level, explaining to them that, yes, it was an inconvenience and, yes, they would be much colder outside than they were inside but in the end it would mean that they would be warm and well fed because, if all went well, there would be power. But why, passenger after passenger asked, was it necessary for everyone to go outside? An essential safety precaution, the crew members said; and down went the passengers, sliding, rolling, tumbling to the bottom of the evacuation slide.

In the middle of the evacuation, a loud rumbling crack shocked the shivering passengers. Another crack! Another audible declaration that their landing field was impermanent. Someone uttered a short, involuntary shriek. Someone else emitted a nervous giggle.

Brad protested, "Captain, this stuff's breaking up fast enough already. Lighting fires is liable to weaken it right under where the plan is parked."

Macleod shook his head. "No way. Do you have any idea how thick this stuff is? Ninety percent of the ice is underwater."

"What if you're wrong?" asked Brad.

"If I am," said Macleod, "I'll tell everyone you warned me against doing it. I'll tell everyone you were right, okay? Now let's get to work. I want you to partially deflate the tires so they don't explode when we light the fires."

The cabin crew had collected torn bits of clothing from the remains of the baggage compartment: pathetic little bundles of bright blues and reds, checks and stripes, all that remained of sport shirts and blouses, underwear and scarves, once so carefully packed into suitcases, now jammed against the tires of the left main landing gear. The now deflated tires were white with frost, the threads packed with ice.

The passengers stood in a huge semicircle eighty feet from the aircraft, looking curiously monklike wrapped in their blankets as they watched the proceedings. A witness appearing on the scene without warning might have taken it for some arcane religious ceremony, a sacrifice to the gods of the Arctic.

Macleod took a deep breath of the frigid air. "Everybody ready?"

Brad looked, nodded unhappily and climbed up onto the wooden crate that they had removed from the rear cargo compartment and which now served as a ladder. Standing on the crate he could reach up to the underside of the left wing where the fuel drain valve was located.

"Okay?" Macleod called.

"Yeah," was the reluctant response.

"Be careful of that stuff," Macleod told him. In this temperature there was an acute danger of frostbite if the cold-soaked kerosene happened to splash on bare skin.

Brad reached up with a screwdriver to probe the valve. He placed it in position. And pushed. Fuel streamed out in a steady flow. In a moment it had filled the pan. Brad released the valve and passed the pan to waiting hands.

"Nice work," Macleod commented.

Brad didn't respond.

Macleod armed himself with a fire extinguisher from the cabin while Karen poured the fuel onto the packed material.

She lit a match and applied it. Nothing happened.

"We need more fuel."

"*More?*"

"Yes. A lot more."

Macleod nodded. "Okay," he called to Brad. "Another panful."

Brad shrugged, absolving himself of all blame. He opened the drain valve again and retrieved more kerosene.

They poured it over the tattered bits of clothing packed around the left main tires.

It caught fire, flared frighteningly for a moment. And then died. The ice wasn't even damp.

"We're still going to need more fuel," said Karen. "And it might not be a bad idea to use some sheet metal to reflect the heat down toward the ice once we get the fire going. It'll speed up the melting process. I hope," she added quietly.

They tackled the huge engine pods with their screwdrivers, removing sections of the curved sheet-metal cowling, each of which had to be held in position near the tires.

The passengers wanted to know how much longer they would have to stand there in the freezing cold; not too long, the red-nosed flight attendants assured them as they stamped and pounded themselves to fight the numbing cold. Soon an engine would be running and there would be heat and light.

But it took time. Time to remove the engine cowling. Time

to recover more fuel from the wing. Time to rearrange the materials around the tires. Time to get the fire going . . .

But it was finally working. The tires of the left main landing gear were partially submerged in the now slushy ice.

"Get more stuff to burn," Macleod told Janet Spencer. "We need lots of it. And more fuel," he added to Brad.

It took almost an hour to get the wheels on the left side of the airplane sufficiently embedded. The ice quickly refroze. It looked as solid as concrete.

They moved operations to the right landing gear. This time the work went a little more easily. They were learning the tricks of the trade. But at one point the flames got out of hand, flaring above the hand-held metal shields, licking at the underside of the wing: thin aluminum skin above which reposed almost seventy thousand pounds of volatile kerosene. Cabin-crew members attacked the fire with extinguishers. They doused the blaze. Everyone breathed again.

By the time they got to the two nosewheel tires, they had become experienced. In less than twenty minutes, the bottoms of the tires were vanishing beneath the rapidly refreezing ice.

Macleod nodded to the others.

"Nice work. Let's get the passengers aboard. Then we'll see about starting number three again. Check the cylinder, will you?" he said to Brad.

The flight engineer nodded curtly and made his way to the right wheel well.

Macleod and Karen glanced at each other, both conscious of the awful possibility that this tedious, nerve-tingling procedure could prove to have been a total waste of time. The remaining cylinder of compressed air might be low on pressure. It might be defective. Whatever the reason, if this one failed there could be no power because there were no other cylinders available.

Macleod said, "Look, even if the damn thing doesn't work, it was one hell of a good idea."

Karen smiled between her shivers. "Thanks, Mac."

A shriek startled them. Through the clusters of passengers ran a woman, arms outstretched. She slipped on the ice and tumbled; someone helped her up.

"My son!" she gasped at Macleod. "He's lost!"

"Lost?"

"He wandered away from the airplane. I called but he didn't answer. He's lost in the fog!"

A man hurried forward, panting, his breath condensing in icy puffs. "His name is Neil. Neil Parker. He's eleven. We're his parents," he added unnecessarily.

Macleod tried to calm them. "Don't worry. We'll find him. He couldn't have gone very far."

They found the boy twelve minutes later, a few hundred feet from the aircraft. He was kneeling at the edge of the floe, clutching the hand of a fair-haired young man who was in the water, ice encasing most of his face. They had to pry Neil's hand free.

"He's dead, isn't he?" Neil asked when Macleod had examined the Swede.

Macleod nodded. "Yes. There's nothing we can do for him."

"I thought so," said the boy. "I tried to pull him out. I pulled as hard as I could but he was too heavy."

"I know," Macleod said sadly. The first casualty.

26

HE KNEW VIRGINIA would be watching at this moment, captivated, deriving a semisexual pleasure from the fact that he was there on the television screen, commanding the attention of millions of people, all eager to hear what he had to say about what was already being called the most serious crisis of recent times.

No doubt she was sitting on her living-room floor, on the brown and white Thai-silk cushions, legs pulled up against her chest, chin resting on her knees, eyes glued to the set. Knowing her as he did, he felt sure she was aglow with excitement, probably nipping at a fingernail as she watched. In contrast, he was utterly calm, almost bored by the probing, incisive questions of the CBS interviewer, Mike Wallace. The questions were really simple; the only challenge was how to phrase the responses and how to make points effectively. But it certainly wasn't difficult; he knew the subject so intimately that the answers seemed to be just lying there, waiting to be used.

"What was your reaction, Mr. Lockhart, when you heard that it had been decided to take the whole question of the XB-3A out of committee for consideration by the full Senate?"

"I was pleased, of course. The Western powers desperately need this weapons system, now more than ever before. We are at a crossroads. We either take the path of strength and security or the path of weakness and defeat. It is my fervent hope that we choose the former. If so, Senator Walsh and the other Americans aboard that flight will not have died in vain. The tragedy is that it had to take the deaths of all those innocent people to alert the public to the imminent threat that confronts them." He knew precisely what he was going to say but he purposely took his time, measuring his words to achieve the desired effect. "There is an idealism that pervades our society, an almost fatal idealism. It's a philosophy that contends that all matters between adversaries are negotiable. However, I am a realist, not an idealist. I view the world as it is, not as it ought to be. It is the idealist who will accommodate and appease the Soviets even in light of this latest criminality. Senator David Walsh would have agreed with that. The world is not filled with reasonable men. Those who rule in the Kremlin are committed to world domination. That is why they despise and fear Americans like Senator Walsh. They knew that if he became the next President of the United States, the balance of power would start to shift."

"Are you implying that the Soviet Union would risk war to eliminate Senator Walsh?"

Lockhart looked directly into the camera, not at the interviewer. "I am implying that the Communist mentality is entirely predictable. They will, as Lenin said, use any trick, artifice, guise or deceit to advance the cause of communism. If an individual, a nation or even one of their own satellites threatens their self-interest, they will use whatever means are necessary to accomplish their goals. That is what I am saying."

"If all of this is true, how do you think Moscow expected to get away with shooting down an American airliner?"

Lockhard shrugged. "I seriously doubt that they ever expected to be incriminated in this vicious attack. My guess is that they expected the airplane to blow up instantly and not give the pilot an opportunity to broadcast what was happening. Do bear in mind, however, that what I said about their eliminating Senator Walsh is only speculation. But I do know that Walsh's words had as much impact in Moscow as they did in Washington."

"Simply put, Mr. Lockhart, it seems that you are suggesting that one of the most powerful nations in the world is guilty of premeditated murder. Is that an accurate assessment of your position?"

Lockhart no longer measured his words. They spewed forth as from a machine gun, with emotion and conviction. "The history of civilization is the story of such violence. Governments have murdered thousands, millions of people in acts of genocide. Do you really think they would let one man stand in their way? Julius Caesar was murdered by his own Senate. The assassination of one archduke triggered a world war. The reality is that governments have purged their own and murdered their adversaries. To the Soviet Union, Senator David Walsh was just another obstacle to eliminate in their quest for global domination.''

"Do you expect that the earlier decision to cancel the XB-3A project will be reversed because of this incident?''

"It certainly looks that way. I think the tide is turning. Obviously I believe it should be reversed. The Free World desperately needs the Devastator.''

"But why this particular weapon, Mr. Lockhart?''

"I'm sure you understand that I can't answer that question completely. It's a matter of security. All I can say is that it is the most advanced weapons system ever developed; it is not just another airplane. The Devastator embodies numerous features that make it invulnerable to any current defense. It will make us far more powerful than we are today.''

"If the Congress decides to go ahead with the XB-3A, the economic impact will be enormous—especially, of course, for your own company. It would mean huge profits for Lockhart Aerospace.''

"I don't think economic considerations are of any significance when national security is at stake. But remember, a favorable decision would mean tens of thousands of jobs, not only for Lockhart but also for hundreds of subcontractors all across the country.''

"Isn't it true that David Walsh was a personal friend of yours?''

"Yes.'' Lockhart nodded somberly, taking his time, working his mouth as if trying to control his emotion. "I knew him for many years.''

"And you shared his political views?''

"Many of them. But our relationship transcended politics. David and I first became friends because of our mutual interest in aviation. He was a fighter pilot in Korea. He flew Mustangs and Sabre Jets. Later he worked for my father, before he decided to go into law. When he became a senator, we saw each other infrequently . . . although we sometimes managed an occasional set of tennis, at which he consistently beat me, I should add.''

God, she was exciting, now passive, now aggressive; she took him on a fantastic journey, a flight into a whirlwind of passion. Only the senses mattered. Only feeling made sense. The day, the time, the moment seemed to become disconnected, to hang in suspension while the intensity raged.

When at last they were spent they lay in utter relaxation, limbs flung across the bed as if they had served their purpose and could now be discarded. The soft breeze from the open window played on their bodies, a delicate finger of air that moved with marvelous grace as it cooled and caressed them.

She was the first to stir. She raised herself on one elbow and smiled down at him.

''I've never known anyone so passionate, Eric.''

''I may never move again.''

''That's okay with me.''

''There's nowhere I want to go.''

''So don't go.''

He reached up, took her face in both hands and drew her down to kiss her gently, slowly.

''You make me forget everything.''

''I'm glad.''

''I just wish it could be . . . different.''

''I told you. I'm very happy the way things are.''

''But you deserve more. And I'm going to make sure you get it.''

She chuckled in her girlish, wholehearted way. ''I always thought men made promises before they got laid, not after.'' She noted the tiny frown that creased his brow. ''Ah, my love, you don't like me saying things like that, do you? Not ladylike, right? But I'm a very earthy person.'' Smiling, she began to massage him, working his flesh with her long-fingered hands.

''God, I love the way you do that,'' he said. ''I just don't know how you can be so fragile one moment and so strong the next. Gentle, then wild. I never know what to expect from you.''

''Good. That's the way it should be. You know, when I

saw you on television tonight, I wanted to run out into the street and shout, 'Hey, that's *my* man! The man I adore! The man I love to fuck! The man who loves to fuck *me!*' The whole country was watching you. God knows how many millions of people. And I was the only one who really knew you. Can you imagine how that made me feel?''

When he got home there was a telephone message from a Mr. Girod. Girod? The name sounded familiar. But he couldn't place it. He returned the call the following morning. Girod answered immediately; his voice possessed the smooth, assured tone cultivated only by a lifetime of privilege. He identified himself as being with the state Republican Party. Lockhart remembered meeting him with David Walsh.

"What can I do for you, Mr. Girod?"

"I wonder if we might have lunch one day this week."

"My schedule is pretty tight."

"I'm sure it is. But I'd like to explore an idea with you."

"Can you be more specific?"

"Yes I can," Girod replied easily. "We were impressed by your television interview and several other recent appearances. Very impressed. I'll come straight to the point, Mr. Lockhart. We believe you could have a great future in politics. Possibly at the top."

Lockhart had to restrain an almost overwhelming urge to burst into laughter. What an irony! They lose Walsh; they want Lockhart! Poor old David must be turning in his watery grave, poor bastard!

Macleod settled himself in the left cockpit seat. He fought the shivers that coursed through his body. He refused to give in to them, damn them! He wouldn't give them the satisfaction; wouldn't let them make him tremble and shake like some old steam engine on its last legs.

His eyes ran over the forward instrument panel. Then he glanced at Karen in the right seat. Looking eager as hell. And feminine. Instinctively, he ran his hand over the stubble on his chin. He felt grubby.

"All set?"

She nodded, smiling. He picked up the microphone from

its hook and began transmitting on the battery-powered intercom.

"Brad?"

"All set down here!" came the disembodied voice of the flight engineer.

"Okay, stand by to start."

He turned to Karen. She already had the checklist in her hand.

"Battery?"

"It's on," he responded.

Boost pumps, crossfeed valves, oil quantity, circuit breakers. . . .

Deep breath. Moment-of-truth time. He flipped the start selector switch to "high pressure" and raised the start lever to the idle detent.

Now for the start switch. Below, down in the freezing wheel well, air should be flowing out of the cylinder and toward the engine—if the system was still intact.

Yes, air pressure was getting to the air-driven starter.

But, God almighty, it was barely making the tachometer needle move! At this rate the cylinder of compressed air would be empty before the engine started!

"C'mon, baby," Macleod hissed. "Please. Just one more time."

He bit his lip as he watched the exhaust-gas temperature gauge. Nothing happening! Zilch! All those crazy fires on the ice were just a stupid waste of time! The damned cylinder just didn't have enough pressure left to do the job. . . .

Now the needle began to edge clockwise.

"I think she just might make it . . ." Karen breathed.

"Go, baby!"

Yes! Just! He released the start switch. The aircraft trembled slightly and momentarily as the engine spooled up, as the compressor took the air, squeezed it, and forced it into the burner cans. Success! In a moment the powerful engine had settled down to a steady whine.

"God damn, we really did it." Karen sounded almost astonished.

Macleod let out a roar of delight.

"You gorgeous thing, you!" he exclaimed as he turned to Karen.

She flushed and grinned. "Gee, thanks, Mac."

"No—I meant the engine and the starting system and all that . . ." He shrugged and grinned and reached across and kissed her on the cheek. "What the hell, I meant you too."

"Thank you, Mac," she said. "That was nice."

"I didn't think she'd make it."

"I had my doubts too," Karen confessed. She climbed out of her seat and went to Brad's panel.

"Everything okay back there?" Macleod asked.

"Looks good here."

Macleod smiled as he glanced at her back. Looks pretty good from here too, he thought. "Let's turn on the heat."

"Coming right up," she said.

Janet Spencer appeared in the doorway.

"Is everything okay now, Captain? Can we have some heat? And what about some power for the galley? Everyone's asking for something hot to drink."

"Anything your little heart desires," Macleod assured her.

She grinned. "My little heart desires to get the hell out of here. But in the meantime, I'm grateful for small favors."

"Thank *her*," said Macleod, nodding at Karen. "She thought of anchoring the tires."

"It was actually Mr. Lee," Karen insisted.

Brad bustled in, bundled in an overcoat and blankets.

"Good job," Macleod told him.

"No sweat."

"Stay with your panel for a while and keep an eye on things," Macleod told him. "I'm going down to make sure the ice is holding."

"I'd like to come, too," Karen said.

"Fine."

They went aft into the passenger cabin. The pale faces were wide-eyed with expectation. Would the heat and lights stay on now that the engine was running? When would they get something hot to eat or drink? Would the toilets start working again? One joker asked when the movie would start.

"Please be patient, folks," he told them. "You should start feeling the heat in a few minutes. That's all it'll take."

Macleod went down the slide first, to finish in an untidy heap at the bottom. He turned as Karen followed, reaching out and taking her hand, helping her to find her balance.

Did he hold her hand a fraction of a moment longer than was really necessary? And was she aware of it? The inconsequential questions darted at him like playful pets.

"Thanks," she yelled over the shriek of the engine.

"You're welcome," he said.

"There's no way to come down those things gracefully."

"Or up," he said.

She smiled.

He cleared his throat and turned to look at the engine. It was running normally, sounding as healthy as ever.

All ten tires seemed to be safely embedded; the poor, ice-shrouded 707 looked as if she had been an integral part of the floe, like some ice-age mammoth in suspended animation.

"It worked," he said.

"Three cheers for Mr. Lee," Karen said.

Macleod liked that. Straightforward honesty, giving credit where it was due. It was a quality he admired, yet found so rarely in women. "We'll be comfortable for a while."

She nodded. "And I'm sure they'll find us long before we run out of fuel."

"I'm sure you're right," he said.

"Really?" she said.

"No, not really," he said, slowly shaking his head. He frowned at the invisible sky. "Fog or no fog, they should have been here by now. Dozens of planes and ships. I just don't get it."

Karen said, "Maybe they're looking in the wrong place."

He nodded. "I was thinking the same thing."

At last the low cloud cover had dissipated; the sun sparkled on the ocean's surface. Perfect search conditions now. Visibility unlimited.

Blondheim, the navigator, came forward and arranged his lanky frame between the pilots' seats.

"Okay guys, this is it," he announced. "This is where the Mayday message said the seven-oh-seven went down."

Fleishman, the aircraft commander, nodded as he angled the Navy P-3C "Orion" into a shallow bank, the slender wingtip tracing a large, circular path about the unmarked spot of water. No debris. No oil slicks. No life rafts. No bodies. Nothing.

"I see something, sir!"

Sanfelici, from the radio operator's position. An instant later:

"No, sorry, sir, just a whale, I guess."

"Keep looking."

"Yes sir."

"Since it was shot down," said Blondheim, "there should be *some* debris on the surface."

Fleishman shrugged as his eyes kept traversing the bleak emptiness of ocean. Only a distant bank of stratocumulus cloud to break the monotony. Even if the 707 had dived straight into the ocean, it should have disintegrated on impact; again, pieces of it should be floating around, grisly mementoes of the tragedy. The object was to find them.

Blondheim caught his arm. He pointed. "Company."

It was a Tupolev Tu-95 "Bear," a Soviet reconnaissance aircraft, flying at almost the same altitude as the American machine, on a converging course.

"What the hell are they doing here?"

"I'd imagine they're looking for the same thing we are," said Fleishman.

"But they shot it down."

"They claim they didn't."

The Soviet aircraft was close enough now for the crewmen to be visible. At a waist window a man could be seen with a camera, taking snapshots of the U.S. Navy aircraft. Shots for the Kremlin or the family album?

Barton, the engineer, reported the presence of the Soviet aircraft to the Military Rescue Coordination Center. Correctly. Formally. Then he said longingly to Fleishman, "Ya' know, I wish to God I had a machine gun; I'd love to shoot down those bastards; let them see what it's like to take a high dive into the goddamn ocean."

"Knock it off," Fleishman ordered. But he knew how Barton felt.

The warmth was delicious, like soft, gentle fingers sliding around your collar, around each toe, across your ankles, caressing you, sending tiny tingles of delight along numbed nerves and aching extremities.

"I'm never going to complain about heat again," Brad

declared. "When it's ninety-eight and humid as hell, I'll remember this place."

Macleod smiled. "I think I'd rather forget it."

Karen worked her fingers, grinning at them as if they were novelties. "Nice to have you back," she told them. "I missed you."

Brad said he still had a couple of toes that hadn't reported in yet.

"Have you figured out how long the fuel will last?" Macleod asked him.

"Well, let's see now. With one engine idling, we're burning twelve hundred pounds per hour. So that should last us about fifty-seven hours."

"That should be long enough," observed Karen.

"Surely to God, they'll have picked us up by then," added Brad hopefully.

"Sure," said Macleod, with a glance toward Karen.

Brad turned on the taped music and piped it over the public address system. The syrupy melodies evoked a melancholy and genuine homesickness for real airports and civilization.

Macleod rubbed his eyes, suddenly sleepy now that his body was warm again. He tried to blink the sleepiness out of his eyes. No time for sleep, not now. There were things to be done.

But what? He couldn't think of anything.

He turned. A peculiar noise was emanating from the main cabin. What the hell . . . ? Janet Spencer opened the cockpit door.

"Thanks for the heat," she said, grinning.

Behind her, the passengers were applauding, cheering!

Embarrassed, Macleod waved at them.

"Can we have some galley power?" Janet asked.

"Sure. Tell everyone they'll be getting something hot to eat fairly soon. And open the bar. But you'd better limit them to one drink per passenger. We've got enough troubles with them sober."

Macleod sighed as he pushed his empty plate aside. "I didn't realize I was so hungry."

"Landing on ice floes gives one an appetite," said Karen.

"I used to like snow when I was a kid," Macleod mused contentedly. "Every winter it was a big deal that first morning when you looked out and the whole world was white. You'd spend the whole day playing in the snow; you'd get hot as hell from the exercise and your mother would say you were going to catch your death of a cold."

Karen nodded. "That's what my mother used to say too."

"All mothers say that. They're programmed to say it."

Karen frowned; she inclined her head toward the window.

"Hear something?"

"I'm not sure."

Macleod nodded to Brad; the flight engineer bolted out of his seat and ran aft to switch on the battery-powered emergency transceiver.

Macleod opened his window and listened. There *was* a sound out there, but it was hard to identify over the noise of the number three engine on the opposite side of the airplane. It seemed to be a distant, disinterested kind of sound. And apparently getting no closer. Was it an aircraft looking for them or was it merely one of the many that passed this way every day? The sound faded.

"I'm not even sure it was a plane," said Karen.

"Me neither," said Macleod.

"It could have been the wind. Or a rumble in the ice."

"I know," Macleod murmured automatically.

"I wonder how far we've drifted?"

"Not far enough to significantly change our position."

Brad returned, blowing on his freezing fingers. "Son of a bitch just went right by." He plopped himself back into his seat. "He wasn't even looking for us," he said. "He was just flying from point A to point B. Surely they know we're down, so why the hell aren't they looking for us?" There was a tone of apprehension in his voice.

"They certainly don't *seem* to be looking for us. I just don't understand it," said Macleod. "It doesn't make any more sense to me than it does to you."

Brad jerked a thumb rearward. "Those passengers aren't so dumb. They're wondering too. They asked me—and I told 'em the search planes would be coming soon."

"That's all you *can* say."

"Yeah, but how long can you make them believe it? It's so goddam frustrating."

"I don't know," Macleod told him. "And I hope we don't have to find out."

"I think the fog's lifting a little," said Karen, staring through her sliding window.

Macleod looked. Maybe she was right. Maybe the lousy, clinging crap was finally starting to break up. Maybe now they'd start searching the area as if they meant business. What the hell was delaying them? It was maddening, sitting, waiting for someone else to do something. Far better to get things going yourself. But how? What could he or any member of the crew do to hasten the rescue? Nothing.

Instinctively his gaze roamed the instrument panel.

It stopped at the compass.

He slid open his window and studied the misty boundary of the ice floe. Then he looked at the compass again.

"I think we've got an interesting development," he said.

The others looked at him expectantly.

"It looks as if the thrust from number-three engine is moving the whole chunk of ice," he told them. "It's pivoting very, very slowly."

"You're kidding," said Brad.

"No, no I'm not."

"Jesus, you're right," murmured Karen, studying the compass.

Macleod said, "I get it. We've anchored the plane in the ice. And now the engine is acting like a super outboard motor! See? We're on a ship, not an airplane!"

"Of course," breathed Karen. "We're going around in circles because of power from only one side of the airplane. I guess if an engine on the other side of the airplane were running, we'd be turning in the opposite direction."

"Exactly," continued Macleod. "But if engines on both sides of the airplane were running, we might not turn at all. As a matter of fact, we might even be able to control the direction of this ice cube. And maybe even move forward at the same time."

"And sail it home." She grinned wholeheartedly, delighted by the beautiful simplicity of the discovery. "Or at least sail somewhere."

"Right!"

"Great!"

"Sail? *Sail?* What the hell are you guys talking about? I don't believe this whole thing," Brad said, shaking his head as if not sure what he was hearing.

Macleod said, "According to our flight log we were somewhere over Baffin Bay when we came down. So we sure as hell wouldn't want to go any farther north. Right?"

"I'll buy that."

"Okay. But if we were to head south we'd probably get into warmer waters. And that isn't a very good idea when your ship is made of ice. Besides, the North Atlantic is down that way. We would miss land entirely. Same problem heading west. We've got the islands of the Canadian Northwest Territories. It'd be easy to pass between them. Hell, with his lousy visibility, we could pass within a mile of an island and never see it. Seems to me the smart thing to do would be to head east . . . toward Greenland. We couldn't miss anything that big."

Brad said, "Sure, but we'll never get there. If we start another engine, we'll run out of fuel twice as fast and freeze to death that much sooner. Besides, Greenland could be a few hundred miles away. No way we get there dragging all this ice."

"That's possible," said Macleod, "but we might be a lot closer to Greenland than you think. There's no way of really knowing. Besides, it's better than sitting here and doing nothing."

"Is it?" asked Brad. "How smart is it to use up fuel just to leave the place where they'll start looking for us as soon as the fog lifts?"

"The trouble is," Macleod declared, "I have a very strong feeling they're not coming for us, not here anyway. They've got to be looking somewhere else."

Brad stared. "Somewhere *else?* Where? Why?"

"I have no idea. But something is definitely wrong."

"When the fog clears, they'll be looking for us. *Here,*" Brad insisted.

"You could be right," Macleod told him. "But I don't think you are. I think we've got to get the hell away from here any way we can and hope to find land or at least get out of this fog so we can be seen by a ship or a plane.''

"You're crazy," Brad snapped.

"I don't think so," Macleod said, eyeing Brad. The flight engineer was getting shaky, probably imagining himself freezing to death somewhere in the wastes of the Arctic Ocean.

"No one's ever done such a thing before. It's insane. You'd be jeopardizing the lives of everyone on board.'' Brad's voice was biting.

Macleod shook his head. "No, I just want to get us out of here. In my opinion, it would be the best course of action, so this is the course of action we're going to take. Got it?"

Brad shrugged, realizing the futility of further opposition. "Okay. You're the boss," he muttered as he turned back to face the engineer's panel.

Macleod exchanged a quick glance with Karen. "Okay," he said, "let's get this show on the road."

He turned to the controls, satisfied to be doing something positive, taking definite action, instead of just sitting and waiting for something to happen. He reached up to the overhead panel on the ceiling between the two pilots' seats and set the start selector to "low pressure." At the same time, Brad moved the air source switches to "recirculation."

"All right," he said to Brad, "start the turbocompressor."

Steiner nodded and raised the toggle switch on his panel.

Karen advanced the number-three throttle. The tachometer needle of the turbocompressor moved steadily clockwise as the power built up.

Macleod watched the gauge. Okay; eighty percent rpm. Time to squeeze the start switch for number one, the engine farthest out on the left wing. Now the tachometer for the number-one engine registered fifteen percent rpm; he raised the start lever.

"Thirty-five percent," Karen announced several seconds later.

Macleod released the start switch as Karen retarded the number-three throttle.

Both engines were now operating normally. Sweet as could be.

"Glad that's over," he said, breathing again.

"It's going to seem dull starting engines the conventional way," Karen added.

"Dull, but easier on the nerves," Macleod commented. He slowly increased the power on number one. "Let's see how she steers."

"It's working," said Karen, her eyes on the compass. Her smile broadened. "Yes, now we're actually turning to the right."

Macleod watched the compass until the airplane was heading east. Then he adjusted the thrust levers, first number one, then number three, experimenting with each until he achieved a balance, until the incredible craft was maintaining an easterly course.

"Greenland, here we come!"

27

IT WAS SPONTANEOUS. At first it was simply a group of citizens. No more than fifty. Some in their teens, some in their middle years, one couple in their eighties. They all arrived at about the same time, a few minutes after eight in the morning. And for a short time they did nothing but stand in front of the White House, peering through the iron railings as if seeking an answer to some puzzle. They didn't even speak to one another.

Then, fifteen minutes later, a bearded man in a plaid shirt arrived. He held a large manila envelope. He tried to give it to the guard at the main gate but was told to take it to the side entrance. He did.

"There are five thousand, two hundred signatures inside this envelope," he told the guard. "We spent all night getting them. They come from just one little town in Pennsylvania. Just one town. And I want you to tell the President that he has the support of everyone in Boltonberg. And tell him not to give one inch to those sons of bitches in Russia! Not one lousy inch! Tell him this is it! No more bullshit! No more talking! No more retreating."

A reporter from a local radio station drove up. He caught some of the bearded man's words on tape. Within the hour they were heard by a quarter of a million listeners. By ten o'clock, the number of citizens that had converged on the White House had swelled to more than fourteen thousand.

They were angry, yet there was an undercurrent of unity.

"Hey, hey, make 'em pay . . . hey, hey, make 'em pay . . ."

A rhythmic chant. And it caught on. Thousands of voices repeated it over and over again. Not loudly. Not wildly. The chant was uttered in an almost conversational tone, all the more effective because it was unforced. It developed a peculiar, utterly distinctive beat. It spread like wildfire, radio and television reporters instantly recognizing its unique quality. Within hours it had crisscrossed the country and was being repeated everywhere.

Shortly after noon the center of Washington was jammed.

"The incredible thing about this demonstration," declared a television reporter, "is the spirit of camaraderie, the sense of common purpose. Citizens are arriving by car, by plane, by train, by bus, all determined to tell the President how they feel and to pledge their support. But the really staggering thing is the unanimity. Perhaps for the first time in recent history, Americans seem to be of one mind. Many are calling for retaliation! These people demand that Moscow understand once and for all that America is not a paper tiger and will protect its interests. This may be a turning point in U.S. history. After decades of passivity, these people are demanding action and they feel it is long overdue. There is a fervor here that is not to be underestimated. And there is a kind of elation among the demonstrators. I can even tell you that the threat of nuclear war will not diminish their demands."

He interviewed a few of the most vocal activists.

"The only language those bastards understand is force," declared a steelworker from Pittsburgh; he had driven to the capital after a night shift. "So we got to show 'em we mean business. Knock one of their goddam airliners out of the sky and see how they like it."

"An eye for an eye?" asked the reporter.

"Right on! Hit the sons of bitches where it hurts. No pussyfooting around this time. We've always been afraid to strike back. But not this time."

"Why don't we take over the Russian embassy. Hold *them* hostage for a change," declared a pert blond secretary.

"Send a strike force to Cuba!"

"Let *us* take the goddamn initiative for once," snapped a black accountant from Baltimore. "We've always had to react; for once, let's act. *Now!*"

"Screw negotiating!" yelled a construction worker from Trenton. "We negotiated with Iran when we should have gone in there and blasted the bastards off the face of the earth. We won't make *that* mistake again.''

A newspaper correspondent wrote that the scene reminded him of photographs he had seen of the cheering crowds in Munich's Odeonplatz at the outbreak of war in 1914. It was the essence of nationalism. Of singlemindedness. Devotion to country. A celebration of the State.

Afterward, no one could recall any orders being given, any discussion taking place. It simply happened, as if by divine ordination. The crowd, still growing at an extraordinary rate, formed naturally into neat rows. Still chanting as they moved, a vast army expressing their determination.

When at last the President appeared, there were no words, no exhortations. Not even a speech. He merely stood and acknowledged them, waving, nodding his approval. They waved back and cheered.

There was total communication.

MEMORANDUM TO: Arthur Connolloy, Vice-President, Production.

FROM: E. Lockhart, Chairman of the Board.

CATEGORY: Top secret.

SUBJECT: XB-3A

1. Advise within twenty-four hours how long it would take to initiate full-scale production of the XB-3A.
2. If necessary, I will order reduction of civilian projects presently in development or production. How much of the labor force and facilities could be diverted to XB-3A production and how long would the process take? What would be required?
3. When could we complete the first production aircraft?
4. What would be the rate of production within six months? One year?

(Signed) E. Lockhart.

''How serious is he about this Wanda person?''

Dorothy's face was chalky but she was sober. She held her hands tightly clasped in her lap. Her breakfast had consisted of tea and a single piece of dry toast.

"I don't ask about Mike's love life," Lockhart told her. "It's none of my business."

"You're his father."

"He's an adult, Dorothy. Has been for a long time. I have no right or reason to tell him whom he should or shouldn't be dating."

"What do we know about her?"

"Not much."

"She could be a slut."

"I don't think Mike would get involved with a slut."

"Why doesn't he ever bring her home?"

"Perhaps he doesn't want to."

"Why doesn't he want to?"

"Maybe he's afraid that you might be here . . . drunk."

Her head jerked as if she had been struck. "That's a vicious thing to say." It was incredible how persecuted Dorothy could sound at times: the innocent wife wronged by the wicked husband.

"It may be," he said. "But it's also true."

"How dare you say that my son doesn't want to see me."

She responded predictably, volumes of drivel about evil Lockhart plotting to drive a wedge between mother and son. It was familiar stuff. The curious thing was how little it disturbed him. Strange, how circumstance altered one's perspective. For all those wearisome years he had permitted himself to be harassed by her. It was as if he had been serving time, doing penance—God knows for what.

But now everything had changed.

Lockhart's gaze wandered to the afternoon newspaper on the table. He picked it up and skimmed the headlines. Column after column, article after article about the Trans American airliner; generous comments about David Walsh from editors who had vigorously roasted him while he was alive. His eye caught a story about the crew of Flight 902. Captain F. J. Macleod, 39; First Officer K. Dempsey, 29; Second Officer B. Steiner, 37; Flight Attendants . . . and photographs: dedicated professionals in a field so akin to his own.

Tragic they had to die. Sacrificial lambs. But in dying they had served their country far more than they ever could have in living. He studied the face of the attractive pilot, Dempsey. Her image caused him no pain. Her death was unavoidable.

"Why don't we ask her to dinner?" Dorothy suggested. Lockhart turned around. "Ask who?"

"This Wanda."

"What for?"

"To meet her, of course. Don't be obtuse."

"But what would that accomplish?"

She gazed at him, her eyes cold and calculating.

"You don't care enough about him—"

"Don't be ridiculous," he muttered, still reading.

Abruptly, she reached forward and tore the newspaper from his hands, flinging it away as if it were something unpleasant and dangerous. "Pay attention," she hissed."I'm talking about something very important."

"Only to you," he told her. He clenched his fists; the desire to hit her, smash her into silence, was almost over-whelming. But he restrained himself. He rose and shook his head despairingly. "I intend to leave you, Dorothy. There's nothing to be gained by continuing this sham of a marriage. I want a divorce."

For a moment there was no reaction from her. Then she raised her head and looked past him, out toward the ocean. "I will never divorce you," she said quietly and with some dignity.

"This is no marriage, Dorothy, not by any stretch of the imagination."

"I know you like to think that."

"It's a fact."

"Only because you have made it that way."

He assumed a reasonable, two-adults-in-serious-conversation tone. "But, Dorothy, what are we achieving by prolonging the agony? We're both miserable even if you won't admit it. Why make ourselves more miserable by continuing to live together?"

"I simply will not discuss it," she said.

"Because of your religion? Dorothy, for God's sake, don't be a hypocrite on top of everything else. When was the last time you saw the inside of a church?"

"It's none of your business." She shook her head, not looking at him. "I won't divorce you, Eric. I took a vow . . ."

"I'll give you grounds," he said. "We'll make it seem as though it's all my fault."

"I will not discuss it."

"There's someone else," he said.

She got up. "I know," she said. And walked away.

Anton Litkov yawned. His eyelids felt as if they were made of lead. He stared at the photographic print and it blurred; the lines wobbled and mingled, forming an intriguing but totally meaningless pattern; and then, for some inexplicable reason, he found himself playing soccer in the Lenin Stadium in Moscow, cheered on by tens of thousands of fans . . . an incredible run, darting with unbelievable skill between the challenging boots of the opposing team . . . the goal coming nearer, the goalie crouching in anticipation of the attack, his hands outstretched, fingers extended, ready to grasp the ball as it came hurtling at him with the speed of an express train. . . .

Good heavens! He straightened his spine with a jerk that stung. He had actually been asleep! His head had fallen forward and had been on its way to receiving a thoroughly nasty thump on the desk when he awoke. Just in time.

Guiltily, Anton reached for the next print.

But he had an uncomfortable feeling that his lapse had not been unobserved. Stazov, the supervisor, didn't miss much.

"Sleepy this morning, are we?"

Anton groaned. Just as he feared. Stazov's voice was one of nature's serious errors: a catastrophic blend of pitch and tone.

"I'm sorry," Anton mumbled.

"Bored with our work, are we?"

"Not at all, comrade."

Which wasn't totally true. Indeed, ninety-five percent of his work at the Soviet Institute for Arctic Studies was stupefyingly boring. It seemed to Anton that a graduate glaciologist might be put to more productive work than sitting around studying an endless series of satellite photographs of the Arctic, recording endless data, noting the tiniest changes in the character of the region, compiling countless volumes that went off somewhere to be filed, programmed and no doubt lost forever.

"Possibly you should get to bed early tonight," said Stazov. "Your own bed," he added with a hoarse chuckle.

Anton chuckled too. It was always wise to chuckle when your superior chuckled.

"I shall follow your advice, comrade."

"See that you do."

Why did Stazov never yawn? Never doze off? Could he really be as vitally interested in everything as he appeared to be? Was it humanly possible? The idiot spent his day strutting about, peering over everyone's shoulders, dropping sarcastic remarks here and there, apparently deriving the keenest pleasure from the endless process.

Dutifully Anton set about noting the facts revealed by the next infra-red photograph, studying the fog-blurred forms, recording all the dreary data on the correct form, neatly (there had been several complaints from Central Division in Moscow about his difficult-to-decipher writing).

Fifteen minutes later, Anton Litkov's boredom evaporated. He sat upright, as if propelled by what he had seen. Something terribly wrong. He frowned. Had the photographs been mixed up in Administration? It had happened before. Mix-ups were infuriating, making utter nonsense of the data. . . .

He retrieved the earlier photos and matched the sector numbers and the computer-grid designations.

No, nothing apparently wrong there. The sequence numbers checked out.

Was there some simple, plain-as-the-nose-on-your-face explanation? There had to be. But what was it?

"Something wrong?"

Stazov asked the question in an accusing manner, as if he had already decided that whatever was wrong was caused by the incompetence and sloppiness of one Anton Litkov.

"I wonder, comrade, if you would be good enough to look at these."

"Why?" What could possibly deserve the personal attention of the supervisor himself?

"I have been studying this series of satellite prints . . ."

"Splendid news," Stazov commented.

"There is a . . . peculiarity."

"A peculiarity?"

"I'm sure it's apparent to you."

"Of course . . ." murmured Stazov.

Anton smiled inwardly. The pompous little idiot couldn't

see it! It was so obvious . . . glaring . . . and he was missing it!

The beady eyes scanned the photograph again and again. Without success!

"What precisely . . . did you see?"

Capitulation! Anton had to control the wobbling of his lips; they longed to curl into a grin of sheer triumph. He scratched his chin elaborately and pointed to the tiny white dot in the upper left corner of the print.

"See here, comrade . . . and here . . . and here. You will note the quite distinct direction in which all of the ice is drifting."

"Yes, of course."

"Now, however, kindly analyze this particular ice floe on the sequential photographs."

"What about it?"

Cretin!

"Well, comrade, don't you see? It clearly is moving in an entirely different direction!"

28

A MOOD OF holiday gaiety had infected both passengers and crew members. They had been on the move and were at least making some progress. To hell with sitting and waiting! Greenland, here we come! They had crowded toward the flight deck, grinning delightedly at Macleod and the others. They were heroes, all of them! Someone had hung a sign on the forward bulkhead: "USS 902."

It was fun while it lasted but as the hours passed everyone had become quiet; they had little to do but stare out at the fog and feel the gentle swell of the sea beneath them. One by one the passengers had returned to their seats.

Janet Spencer appeared in the flight deck. "Captain, is there anything we can do with those toilets now? They still don't work."

Macleod glanced back at Brad. The flight engineer shrugged. "The lines are still frozen, I guess."

"How about seeing what you can do?"

"Sure," was the curt reply. Brad sounded somewhat less than eager, for which he couldn't be blamed; but he got up and went aft with the small tool kit he carried on every flight.

When he had gone, Karen said, "I'll keep an eye on his panel."

Macleod nodded. Sensible suggestion. He watched Karen settle herself in the engineer's seat, her eyes quickly noting the state of the aircraft's systems; fuel, electrical, heating, oil pressure. . . .

"I bet you thought you'd graduated from that seat forever."

She grinned. "It feels like home again."

Her back was to him. Just as well. After a few moments,

Macleod realized that he had been studying her. Thank God she didn't turn suddenly and find him at it.

He turned forward and peered into the sluggish fog. How fast was this contraption moving? Two knots? Five? No way to tell. "It'd be a gas to push those thrust levers wide open," he said. "What d'you think she'd do flat out? Fifteen? Twenty?"

Karen grinned. "Maybe twenty, with a tailwind. If we didn't capsize."

"After this, maybe I'll take up sailing."

"It's a lot more fun without all this ice to drag along," she said.

"You ever go sailing?"

"I've tried it a few times," she said. "I used to know a guy who was nutty about it. His idea of heaven was to sit in a boat with a glass of Scotch, listening to opera."

"And you?"

"Unfortunately, I was just as nutty about airplanes as he was about sailboats; you might say . . . we drifted apart."

Macleod acknowledged the pun with a chuckle. "When you fly, sailboats seem pretty tame."

"I know what you mean," she said.

"My wife hated airplanes," he heard himself say.

Now why, he asked himself, did you have to bring her up?

Karen said, "I don't think enough women really get a chance to appreciate flying. Most of them just sit and look out the window while some man does the flying." She looked up. "Have you ever done any soaring, Mac?"

He shook his head. "You?"

"I learned to fly in sailplanes."

"You still go soaring?"

"A little. There's a club near Kirkland. Just east of Seattle. You should try it sometime."

"Maybe I will," he said. "I might take a few lessons."

"I should warn you," she said.

"What about?"

"I have an instructor's certificate for gliders. You might find yourself being my student." Her hazel eyes were alive and bright.

He said, "I don't think I'd mind that at all. As long as you're easy on beginners."

"I've been told I'm very demanding," she said.

"That's the way to be," he told her. Suddenly he wanted to ask her about her family, her home, her school, her interests. But, hell, this wasn't the time or the place; in fact a less suitable time or place would have been hard to imagine. Besides, there was no future in it. She was sitting there chatting probably because she had nothing else to do. She was friendly enough right now, but when they got back to civilization, all the old hostilities would probably emerge. But her warmth toward him did appear to be genuine.

He frowned. The ungainly vessel seemed to be pitching a little more heavily. The ocean slapped against the edge of the ice, sending up a shower of ice spray.

Damn, he wasn't correcting for the northerly wind. She was probably drifting to the south.

More power was required from the number-three engine to maintain the easterly course.

He glanced at Karen. "The sea's getting rougher."

She nodded; she had noticed; no doubt she had also noticed that the increased power was consuming fuel more rapidly than a few minutes ago.

Sea spray spattered against the windshield, like tiny fragments of shrapnel.

"The wind does seem to be getting stronger," said Karen. "Maybe it'll blow away this fog."

And maybe it'll break this hunk of ice into smaller pieces, Macleod commented silently.

There was a frightening, splintering crack somewhere to the right. The aircraft lurched on its platform of ice, rolled to one side before righting itself. How much had broken away that time? Macleod eased back on the power again, to reduce the strain on the ice. But now forward motion was reduced to nil.

The chatter quickly faded in the passenger cabin. The motion of the sea was becoming unpleasant. Several passengers were sick, coughing and spluttering into their barf bags.

Brad returned to the flight deck, disheveled from his plumbing labors. "Jesus, this thing's rocking!"

"We noticed," Macleod commented. "Did you get the toilets working?"

"Only one. Now everyone's puking in it. Lovely."

"I kept your seat warm," said Karen as she slipped back into the copilot's seat. She stared ahead. "I think the fog may be lifting a little."

"A very little," Macleod grunted.

The fog seemed endless. At times it seemed to lighten a fraction; there was even an occasional hint of blue sky. Then the grayness closed in again, dense and implacable.

Another cracking sound from the rear. The crew jerked as if struck. The sudden sound had evoked images of a great fissure in the ice, opening up like a huge mouth, swallowing the aircraft and its occupants.

Macleod turned. "I think we'd better check on how well the landing gear is staying fixed in the ice."

Karen said, "I'll go."

Brad shook his head longsufferingly. "It's the engineer's job," he said, "like fixing johns." He shrugged his coat on and went aft.

"I'd have gone," said Karen.

"I know," said Macleod.

He adjusted the power settings once again, using more power to compensate for the thrusting of the sea. He shook his head in dismay. "Maybe we should have gone west."

"There's no way you could have known this swell was going to develop," Karen told him. "For all we know, the wind might have shifted and helped us along."

"And Howard Hughes could land here in his Spruce Goose and fly us all off to Hollywood." He scratched his nose. Why did his nose always itch at such inappropriate moments?

"They'll find us," said Karen. "They're bound to."

"Sure," said Macleod. But what if the next crack in the ice tips the 707 into the sea? How many of the passengers and crew would be able to get out and into the rafts before the whole thing went down? The passengers had been divided into teams, each to use a certain exit; the instructions had been repeated again and again. Everyone was supposed to know exactly what to do if the moment came. But it was one thing talking about emergency procedures, quite another carrying them out when the plane might be tilted downward at some frightening angle, rapidly filling with freezing water, full of terrified people clawing for escape. What was the alternative? Get the passengers out now, while the aircraft was still relatively stable, and have them await their fate while sitting in the life rafts? Maybe he should give the passengers a choice. The more passengers who decided to wait in the rafts, the easier it would be for the rest to get out if and when they had to get out. But who in his right mind would voluntarily sit in a raft on the ice in a freezing wind when there was a warm airplane only a few feet away?

Somebody should invent an airplane with fold-down sides, he thought. Then everyone could simply get up and walk out in five seconds flat.

The cockpit door opened. Brad came in, his face pale.

"So?" Macleod turned in his seat. "Everything okay?"

Brad shook his head. "I could only see the tops of the tires," he said. "They're almost submerged. The goddam water's sloshing right over them!" He lurched as the ice floe tipped momentarily. "I tell you, we're going down already," he declared, his voice harsh with strain.

Macleod shook his head. "No, we're not sinking. We're just riding lower in the water because we've lost so much ice that the weight of the plane is having more of an effect. We are not sinking," he repeated.

David Walsh finished the letter to his wife, sealing the envelope just as Milt Bryden returned to his seat and sat down with a sigh.

"Problems?"

Milt shook his head in vexation. "You know, Senator, there's nothing in this life more frustrating than to find a female who's ready and willing—and then have absolutely nowhere to go to oblige her."

Walsh smiled. Milt had been diligently charming that flight attendant for hours.

"You'll have to wait until we get ashore."

Milt again shook his head. "But what if we never make it to shore?"

"In that case there'll be no problem."

"But I'll go to my grave . . . horny."

"You'll have to be content with memories," said Walsh. He slipped the letter into his inside jacket pocket. If his luck held he would be able to tear up the letter in a few hours; but if it didn't, at least he felt good about having written it;

perhaps someone would find it someday. The letter told Pamela how much he thought about her during this ordeal; it told her that he loved her now in a deeper, more meaningful way than when they were first married, that she had contributed far more than she could possibly know to any success he had enjoyed in the past and might have enjoyed in the future. He wrote about the early days: the dance where the Woody Herman Band was performing, the leaking roof in the church where they were married, the Korean War days, the spurious report of his death in action, law school, state politics, the children. . . .

He massaged his chin. Maybe he would give the letter to Pamela even if he *did* get through this mess.

Vassili Kalinokov reflected upon the lunacy of world politics. The Soviet Union invaded Hungary in 1956, Czechoslovakia in 1968, Afghanistan in 1980. What did the rest of the world do? Absolutely nothing but make speeches and boycott the Olympic Games. Now, however, the Soviet Union seemed closer to war than on any of those occasions—and because of something in which the country was not even involved!

He reviewed his notes for the fifth time. Was there a clue that he had missed? A hint of a solution to the puzzle? It was known that the aircraft, a Boeing 707-320BAH, took off from Seattle-Tacoma International Airport at 0252 Greenwich Mean Time on Wednesday last. On board were one hundred and twelve passengers and a crew of seven. The only passenger of any significance was Senator David Walsh, the renowned anti-Communist. According to one informant the craft also carried an aging film actress by the name of Mrs. Lawson (whoever the hell she was) and a Negro pianist of some small reputation. The flight proceeded normally for about seven hours until, at a position of 65° 34' north, 1° 7' west, the pilot transmitted an emergency message. An attack by Soviet fighters. Then silence. No wreckage or survivors had been located, although this could hardly be considered of great significance, considering the enormous expanses and the possibility that the aircraft could have gone straight to the bottom without leaving a trace.

"Could David Walsh's political enemies have killed him?" he asked Morikilov. "Could they be that desperate?"

"It's a possibility, sir," was the predictable reponse.

"But if indeed that is what happened, why the mention of Soviet fighters?"

"That I do not understand, sir."

"That is what we had better understand. And quickly, comrade."

"Yes, sir. I know, sir," said Morikilov darkly.

Kalinokov sighed. His brain felt as if it had grown rusty, like some old piece of farm machinery that had labored too long and too hard without proper care and attention.

"How is your family?" he asked. He had not the slightest interest in the response, for all the Morikilovs possessed a similar level of wit and charm. But the weary piece of machinery needed a brief respite.

"They're all well, sir. Josef will soon be a naval cadet."

"Isn't that splendid. I'm sure he'll do well."

"I hope so, sir."

"Has he left home yet?"

"No, he leaves two weeks from this Friday, sir."

"I'm sure he will miss you all, the stimulating conversation around the table and, most important of all, he'll miss your good self, his father, the fulcrum of the family, always willing to impart the benefit of your years of experience with life's vagaries."

"Indeed yes, sir," said Morikilov, seemingly a little unsure of what precisely had just been said. "We intend to have a small family gathering a week from Wednesday, a send-off party, you might say, for the young man. If you would do us the honor, sir—"

"Most kind of you. A prior engagement, you understand."

"Of course, sir."

On the face of it, thought Kalinokov, the most likely suspects are ourselves. And yet we deny responsibility. Are we really being truthful? Is there a massive cover-up in the Kremlin? How could the Soviet Union benefit from this? Does anyone in Moscow really care whether Senator Walsh lives or dies? Then again, the whole thing might have been caused by overly zealous fighter pilots, having a little fun, scaring the Yankees, then accidentally shooting down the 707. Planes of both nations frequently intercept one another and missiles have been fired inadvertently.

"But what about the radar?" he asked aloud.

"Sir?"

"Sorry, I was just thinking. If other aircraft were involved we should have known about it from the satellite radar."

"Unquestionably, sir."

The telephone rang. The general. "Progress?"

"None, Comrade General."

"None?"

"We're still considering many possibilities."

"There is a body of opinion, you know, that some American fanatics may have been involved in this affair to create an excuse to launch a first strike against the Soviet Union."

"Anything is possible, I suppose—"

"You think it unlikely?"

"Extremely unlikely."

"Why?"

"It simply isn't consistent with American political behavior. Besides, they aren't prepared for such action."

"There are many important people who don't share your opinion. You should know that the armed services are going on Phase Two Alert immediately."

Kalinokov's innards lurched.

"I want results," said the general. "If I don't get them, you know the consequences."

"I understand," said Kalinokov. And indeed he did.

When the general hung up, the telephone emitted the characteristic humming of the security lines. Kalinokov gazed at the receiver and hung up. Perhaps the fateful decision was rapidly approaching. Others had defected before they could be humiliated and destroyed. It had always been a possibility for those in his particular profession. He had no wish to defect. He loved Mother Russia, infuriating as she could often be. But survival superseded all in importance. The Americans would be glad to have him. But God only knows whether he could ever make it to the American Embassy and get out of the country. He was aware of the close watch that was kept upon men like him. Morikilov himself would be only too pleased to pull the trigger on a despicable traitor. . . .

The telephone rang again. Morikilov answered it. He shook his head.

"No, he cannot possibly be disturbed. He is working on a

matter of the highest priority.'' His cheeks became flushed with anger: ''No, I've already told you, I haven't the slightest intention of interrupting him . . .''

Kalinokov sighed. ''Who is it?''

''Someone from the Institute for Arctic Studies. Says he has been ordered to talk to you by General Svetlanov. But I informed him . . .''

''Arctic? All right, I'll speak to him.''

Morikilov seemed hurt. He had done his best to protect his superior from disturbance and this was how his efforts were appreciated.

Kalinokov picked up the phone. ''Yes? This is Kalinokov.''

''Colonel, sir. We have a curious phenomenon that General Svetlanov thinks may be of interest to you. We have been told that it is taking place in the same geographical location where satellite radar temporarily lost track of the American Flight Nine-Oh-Two.''

''Yes, yes, please continue.''

''Colonel, we take series of infra-red satellite photographs of the Arctic. We study the changing meteorological patterns, the ice formations, their effect on weather and many other glaciological phenomena.''

''So I understand. Very important work,'' Kalinokov muttered.

''Well, we have discovered something that is most unusual. Most unique. It is an ice floe that appears to be drifting in a direction that is totally different from all of the others that surround it. And it is making good progress.''

Kalinokov blinked. ''How is such a thing possible?''

''We have not been able to determine that. But evidently some force is being applied to this ice floe. Something has to be making it move that way. Unfortunately, the area has been subject to a great deal of advection fog in the past several days; we have taken a rather large number of infra-red pictures; not quite so sharp and clear as we would like. But there is no question that this ice floe is moving eastward instead of south as are all the others!''

The noise was like a sudden, violent clap of thunder. It was felt as much heard. It jarred every nerve.

The aircraft pitched, thrusting its nose downward. A spray of freezing water careened across the windows.

For an awful instant it hung there. Baggage, clothing, books, meal trays, bottles, glasses went tumbling and splashing and smashing along the floor.

We're going to die," a man yelled hysterically.

But the airplane rocked back again, still solidly fastened to her icy platform. Creaking, squealing, the floe righted itself. More bangs, more sounds of disintegration, sounds of despair.

Macleod grasped the glare shield to brace himself as he eased back the thrust levers. He glanced around. Everyone seemed okay. Shaken but okay.

Karen managed a weak smile. Brad just stared.

The floe had settled down. But the aircraft was at a slight angle now.

Macleod pulled back his side window and peered out into the fog. Christ, how much of the ice floe was left? Three-fourths? A half? How long would it be before this ponderous ship would become a submarine?

He turned to Brad. "How long will the fuel last?"

"I can't tell for sure. But we're getting pretty damn low."

Macleod eyed the thrust levers. Damn it, he wanted to shove them fully forward, to urge every last pound of power out of this ridiculous apology for a ship, to do battle with the ocean.

But too much thrust from the jet engines would be dangerous, pulling, tugging, twisting the weakened floe. Too much power could also break the wheels loose from their anchored positions in the ice. And too much forward motion in this rough sea could drown the engines with salt water and flame them out, leaving the 707 drifting hopelessly as before.

Safer to be prudent. Not much fuel left anyway.

Hold together, baby, he pleaded silently.

29

THESE DAYS, TELEVISION newscasters all sounded the same: slightly breathless, as if they had run to their sets and had insufficient time to convey all the vital information they possessed. More acrimony between Washington and Moscow; accusation and counter-accusation, rumors of naval fleets, both American and Soviet, steaming toward strategic positions; demonstrations, incidents; Russian and American flight crews having an altercation at Yesilkoy Airport in Istanbul; lines of people buying rifles, shotguns, pistols, anything that would shoot; survivalists building bomb shelters; swarms of potential soldiers, sailors and airmen crowding recruiting offices all over the country.

"It's like the day after Pearl Harbor," said an elderly man interviewed on a Detroit street corner.

"The sooner we show our strength and stop talking with the Russians the better," declared a housewife outside a Minneapolis supermarket.

"I was opposed to the war in Vietnam," said a bearded physics professor from UCLA, "but this time it's different. We have to draw a line. If this kind of international piracy is to be brought to an end, the Soviets must know we are prepared to use force."

In Boston, the newscaster reported, a voice had been raised in protest; a man in a bar said there was no proof that the Russians had shot down the Trans American airliner. Enraged patrons hurled themselves on him; when police finally extricated the man, he had suffered four broken ribs and an assortment of abrasions and lacerations. "Rarely," said the newscaster, "have the American people been so galvanized.

And,'' he added, ''not since 1941 have we been closer to war.''

Lockhart flipped the remote-control switch on his desk. The television screen darkened; the cabinet door slid shut.

Roy Meyer, president of Lockhart Aerospace, shook his head in wonderment.

''I find it difficult to believe that all of this has taken place so quickly,'' he said.

''I don't find it difficult at all,'' Eric Lockhart commented. ''It's been coming for years. This, or something like it.'' He placed his hands squarely in the middle of the desk. ''Roy, I intend to initiate production of the XB-3A immediately.''

Meyer was startled. ''*Production?* . . . But we don't even have a contract—''

''I am well aware of that.''

''The board would have to approve such an unprecedented move—''

''I'll take full responsibility. I am firmly convinced now that we will get that contract. If we expedite production, so much the better.''

Meyer's gray eyes were troubled; he liked things done according to the book. ''Eric, it would involve a fantastic financial commitment—''

Lockhart nodded briskly. He felt exhilarated, marvelously alive, making things happen. ''I'm aware of that too. We've already drawn up contingency plans. We know how to convert much of our commercial production to the XB-3A. Now I want to know how soon we can get our line of credit from the banks. I want you to call a meeting of all the divisional vice-presidents. This morning. Get dates and times from them, then cut them in half. I want this to happen fast, Roy, faster than anyone would have believed possible!''

Meyer said, ''Eric, I know you're acting in a spirit of patriotism. But I do feel obliged to point out that if the government does not decide in favor of the XB-3A, it will mean the financial destruction of Lockhart Aerospace.''

''You're right,'' said Lockhart. ''But there's virtually no risk. The mood of the country and the Congress should be obvious to everyone. Senators and congressmen will be falling all over each other to approve this contract.''

When Meyer had gone, Lockhart crossed his office and

stood at the window, looking out over the construction buildings and the engineering offices. This was the apogee of his existence; all the countless events and the kaleidoscope of emotions and disappointments that constituted his life were culminating in this moment. This is what it was all about. This was his destiny, his purpose in the great scheme of things. He knew the American people better than all the pontificating politicians; speeches and treaties were fine for headlines, but it took *events* to capture the public imagination, *action* to stir the blood.

It was an exciting, bustling morning, a morning full of conferences, of decisions, of progress; a day of harassed executives and horrified comptrollers. By early afternoon a reasonably accurate timetable had been prepared: only those commercial aircraft already on the production lines would be completed; other orders would be postponed. In nine days they would begin to cut metal and the XB-3A production line would start to take shape. The many subcontractors also could be pressured into accelerating their production. Men of purpose would find they could do the impossible as a matter of course. When it was all over they would look back on these days, Lockhart thought, and they would call the whole thing a miracle. But they'd be wrong; there was nothing miraculous about it; there was only determination, dedication and good old American know-how.

At 1:15 his secretary called from the outer office.

"Yes? What is it?"

"Your son, Mr. Lockhart. He would like to see you."

Was it his imagination or did she sound uneasy?

"Very well. Have him come in."

When Mike entered it was clear why Miriam had been troubled. He looked like hell, scruffy and disheveled. And it was sickeningly obvious that he had been drinking. His eyes were bloodshot; he made his way a little too carefully to the chair beneath the portrait of Willard Lockhart. Then, for a few strained moments, father and son simply looked at one another. Mike seemed to be on the point of saying something, but the words apparently refused to come.

Lockhart said, "What's wrong, Mike?"

To his surprise, Mike emitted a weird, low-pitched giggle.

"Wrong?" he muttered. "Christ, what the hell could be wrong?"

"You've been drinking."

"That's very true," Mike admitted. "Since about two this morning, if you want to know the sordid details. Scotch mostly but with some beer chasers thrown in for good measure."

"Perhaps we should continue this conversation when you've sobered up, Mike."

"Hell, no," said Mike. "We wouldn't have this conversation if I was sober." He smeared a hand across his face. Lockhart grimaced; it appalled him to see his son in this condition. Even worse, he was worried about what his son might reveal publicly while so inebriated. "If I was sober I'd keep my mouth shut, because I'm scared of you, Dad. Did you know that? It's true. You scare the shit out of me."

"Go home. Sleep it off."

"Can't sleep," said Mike with a foolish grin. "Haven't slept since you-know-when. I keep trying. But nothing happens. Didn't know you could keep going so long without sleep."

"The doctor can give you something."

Mike shook his head. "There are no pills to cure what I've got."

Lockhart's innards were churning but he forced himself to respond calmly, rationally. "It'll pass, Mike. Time heals everything. In a little while you'll understand the greatness of what we've done. Together, we've achieved what no government has been able to do since World War Two. You must see the big picture, Mike, the global significance of it all."

"She knows," Mike said.

"She?"

"Mother. About Walsh. Everything."

Lockhart gazed intently at the silver model of the LC-4 on his desk, studying its details as if seeing them for the first time.

"What makes you think so?"

"She told me it was out of character for you to go and see David Walsh the evening he left for Europe."

"And?"

Mike shrugged. "There wasn't much more—"

Lockhart said quickly, firmly, "She doesn't know anything, Mike. She's just taking potshots in that alcoholic darkness of hers. The fact that I decided to see Walsh and he just happened to be on that plane was nothing more than a coincidence as far as she or anyone else is concerned."

"She asked what I was doing in the Arctic."

"She's just nosing around, Mike, nothing else. She's always been making all kinds of accusations about me. Mike, she resents how close we are and would love to drive us apart."

"She told me you have a mistress."

"Typical of her—"

"Mrs. Virginia Patterson, seventeen twenty-seven Meadowlark Avenue."

Lockhart moved his ivory pen-holder a fraction of an inch to the left. "Do you have a telephone number too?"

Mike said, "It's true, isn't it?"

Lockhart said, "I want you to take a few days off, Mike. Go up to the cabin and relax. Unwind. Do a little fishing. Take your mind off things."

"What about this Patterson woman?"

"What about her?"

"Well, is it true or isn't it?"

Lockhart forced himself to speak quietly. "Mike, I don't presume to intrude in your private affairs. Please afford me the same courtesy."

Mike opened his mouth to respond, but nothing vocalized.

Lockhart said, "Your mother doesn't know anything about the project. She may be wondering; she may be questioning. That's all. That's all she can do. You look terrible," he added.

"Do I?" Mechanical, disinterested response.

"You haven't even shaved."

"Haven't I?"

"You must get hold of yourself, Mike. Take some time off. You've earned it. You need it."

Mike stared at him. "Do you really think *fishing* is the answer to all of this?"

"Of course. You just need some relaxation."

"Jesus Christ! I just murdered one hundred and nineteen

people!" Mike pointed a finger. "It may surprise you to know that ordinary people can't turn their emotions on and off so easily. Ordinary people worry and wonder. Ordinary people have *feelings!* Ordinary people have consciences."

"You're my son, Mike. You're not an ordinary person."

"But I am, Dad. I hate to disappoint you but I am. And I'm scared to death by what we've done. We were wrong. Terribly wrong."

"No, Mike. We were right." Lockhart had to restrain himself from crossing the room to Mike and shaking him. "Don't be weak, Mike. Don't let fear destroy your resolve. We're engaged in the most important work of our entire lives. We've made the world wake up to reality. You and I did that, Mike."

Mike nodded slowly, sadly. "I know. That's what I keep telling myself. But for some reason it doesn't help."

"It will. I promise you."

Mike stood up, swayed, and caught an arm rest for support. "I'm gonna leave now."

Lockhart started to get out of his chair. "I'll drive you home."

Mike shook his head. "No thanks . . . Wanda's waiting for me."

"Okay. Are you sure you'll be all right?"

"I'm going to be just fine," said Mike.

"That's good."

As he opened the door, Mike turned. He seemed to be on the verge of saying something, then he took one last look at his father and left.

A moment later, Miriam, chubby face creased in concern, appeared in the doorway. "Is everything all right, Mr. Lockhart?"

"Yes. Why do you ask?"

"Well . . . your son seemed . . . not quite himself."

"He's fine. Don't worry about it."

The planning, production and engineering managers came in with an Everest of problems. Then Public Relations worrying about press releases. Then Legal, followed by Personnel, in turn followed by Finance and Engineering Design.

The message came late in the afternoon.

"Would you take the phone, please, Mr. Lockhart. He says it's urgent."

"He?"

"Someone from the sheriff's office, sir."

Sheriff? "This is Eric Lockhart. Who's this?"

"This is Sheriff Mald. Darwin County. It's about your son . . ."

"You can see him for a minute," said the doctor. "But only for a minute."

Lockhart went into the room—an antiseptic nightmare of white and stainless steel, punctuated by incongruously cheerful pictures on a wall.

Mike lay there, eyes closed, his skull and one side of his face heavily bandaged. He looked incredibly weak and disabled, and didn't stir when Lockhart approached.

Lucky to be alive, according to the sheriff. Car went off the road, ran between a couple of trees and over a cliff. Fell nearly a hundred feet and jammed itself against a boulder. Girl in the car? No, the sheriff had no information about a second occupant in the vehicle.

The prognosis?"

It was touch and go, the doctor said.

Lockhart shook his head. It was absolutely inconceivable that Mike might actually *die*. He refused to even consider the possibility. Mike would recover fully. In a little while they'd be reflecting on how dangerous it was to drink and drive. . . .

So much depended on Mike himself, the doctor said. He had to do the fighting, there in that hospital bed. He had to *will* himself better, force his body to respond. . . .

"Mike? Can you hear me?"

Did the eyelid flicker ever so slightly?

"You've got to get well, son. We need you. I need you."

Damn his throat for closing up on him. He held Mike's hand for a minute. Then he turned and left the room. He stood in the corridor staring out of a window overlooking an expansive lawn and saw nothing. God, it was only a few hours since Mike had been in his office . . . and now he was in that lousy hospital bed, helpless and fighting for his life.

He telephoned Virginia.

"Is there anything I can do?" she asked.

"Not right now. It's a small hospital but they seem to be taking good care of him. I may have him moved into town later."

"I'm terribly sorry, Eric."

Then he called Dorothy.

Ruth, the maid, answered. In her mechanical way she said Mrs. Lockhart wasn't feeling well and couldn't come to the phone at the moment.

Which meant she was blind drunk.

Relieved, Lockhart told Ruth what had happened. Her sharp intake of breath sounded oddly like an engine turning over an instant before ignition.

"Mr. Mike's going to be all right, isn't he?"

"Sure he is, Ruth, sure he is."

Lockhart hung up and walked slowly back along the shimmering corridor to the bench across from Mike's room. He sat down. The news media would soon get hold of this. Anything to do with a Lockhart was news. Thank God the sheriff hadn't mentioned alcohol.

He became aware of a presence beside him. He looked up.

"Mr. Lockhart, I'm very sorry to have to tell you that your son has just passed away . . ." the doctor said.

"The fog *is* clearing," Karen said, pointing excitedly.

Macleod stared. Yes, no doubt about it, the crappy stuff was losing its substance. "Maybe we'll actually be able to see where the hell we are!"

"Wherever we are," Brad interjected, "is about as far as we're going to get. We're damn near out of fuel. The engines are running on fumes."

"How much longer do we have?"

"Anywhere from a minute to half an hour. No way to tell. The gauges have bottomed out."

Brad, the ray of sunshine.

At times it seemed as if the aircraft were plowing along through the sea rather than riding on top of it. Water kept cascading over the ice floe, punishing the brittle platform, working at the tenuous grip of the landing gear.

Janet came in, white-faced, weary.

"Better cook whatever frozen food you have left," Macleod said.

"There isn't very much."

"I know. But we're almost out of fuel. Let's use the ovens while we can, okay?"

"Okay, Captain."

"Janet."

"Yes sir?"

"How's everyone doing?"

"Not very well, I'm afraid."

"Sorry to hear that. I guess they're getting pretty frightened. Look, the fog's beginning to clear. Maybe you and the other girls ought to pass the word around. Just in case they haven't noticed. It might cheer them up a little."

"D'you think the search aircraft will spot us now?"

"Sure hope so. If they don't I'm going to write my congressman."

"Me too," she responded.

"Great broad," he muttered when Janet had left. Then he smiled, realizing that he had made the remark automatically, thinking that another man was sitting to his right.

Karen said, "I think she's a great broad too." Then she turned forward. "Look!"

Macleod turned too. Incredible sight! The sun! Streaming through the last wisps of fog, burning them away. Gorgeous blue sky above.

The sun danced a merry jig on the water, sparkles of light bounding from wave to wave. Macleod couldn't take his eyes from the sight. It was the most delicious thing he'd seen in ages. Thank you, Lord. This was proof that there really was another world beyond the fog. There really was a sun that shone and a sky that was magnificently blue. There was hope. He glanced back through the open cockpit door to the passenger cabin. They had been similarly affected back there; they were all chattering again, pointing, grinning.

But in the distance, a sobering sight: more fog across the choppy water, a bank of it, huddled low like some vile reptile lying in wait for its victim.

Karen was searching the sky.

"See anything?"

She shook her head. "I thought I heard an airplane. Wishful thinking, I guess."

"You and me both. But keep listening."

"You can bet on it," she said with a smile. A charming smile. Funny how he never noticed it before. Funny how he never noticed a lot of other things about her before.

Janet came in with trays of leftovers.

"Chicken again?" Brad inquired.

"You should be so lucky. Just odds and ends," Janet told him. "You get half a baked potato and what's left of the maraschino cherries."

"At least it's edible," said Karen.

"We've had to improvise as best we could," Janet said. "There wouldn't have been enough to go around otherwise."

"Got enough coffee for everyone?" Macleod asked.

Janet nodded. "Maybe one cup for each passenger. But only if we make it weak."

"Then that's it?"

She nodded.

"Okay, might as well serve it now. Get everyone fed and warm." He turned to Brad. "Turn up the cabin heat a little, will you? Let's get them as comfortable as possible."

"Okay, but it won't be for very long."

Macleod stuck his head out of the cockpit window. He looked directly down to the ice. It was a less then encouraging sight. The water was flowing freely over the frozen surface, at times concealing it entirely so that the 707 looked as if it were floating on its landing gear. How long would they stay afloat? Who could tell? His gaze traveled over the wings sheathed in ice.

God knows how many tons that ice was adding to the weight of the airplane. But there was no point in wondering; they couldn't chop the damned stuff away. Now the sun was playing games with the ice, creating a bewildering array of glittering jewels that encrusted the aircraft's metal form.

Beautiful.

Brad started to say something.

He stopped, his mouth agape.

Beneath the aircraft the ice creaked, then squealed, then screamed in pain. A sound to chill the blood.

The babbling in the passenger cabin ceased abruptly.

For a moment the aircraft was unaffected; it still plowed on through the choppy water, nose gently rising and falling, rising and falling.

When the crack came it was again like a rifle shot.

Behind the 707 the ice snapped. The break seemed to catapult the aircraft forward, as if the rest of the ice had suddenly rejected the section on which the aircraft was perched.

"God . . . !"

They clutched at controls, glare shields, anything that was solid. The whole thing was rolling as if it was going to turn completely over!

Water smashed against the cockpit, exploding through the open window in a freezing deluge.

There was nothing they could do but hang on. And pray.

Painfully, reluctantly, the 707 righted itself, wobbling, swaying dangerously on the diminished platform of ice.

Karen gulped, her hands gripping the control wheel instinctively, although the flight controls were just so much useless weight.

"It's going," Brad croaked, white-faced. "The goddam thing's going to turn turtle any time now."

"I don't think so," said Macleod, forcing his voice to sound matter-of-fact. "But it's time to get on the life jackets." He eased himself out of his seat and nodded to Karen to take over. "I'd better go back and tell everyone the bad news."

They looked up as he approached: rows of faces, many of them now familiar, like lifelong friends. Senator David Walsh smiled briefly; his aide, Bryden, looked aggrieved, as if he blamed Macleod personally for what had happened. Flitch, the public relations man, was scribbling industriously. He had a hell of a story. Probably had visions of a Pulitzer Prize. Would he be there for the accolades?

"I've got good news and bad news," Macleod announced through the battery-powered megaphone. "The good news is that we're out of the fog. So we can be seen at last . . ."

"How soon are they going to rescue us, Captain?" An ancient, querulous voice.

"If it's not damned soon, I'll write my congressman," he reiterated mechanically.

No one laughed.

He said, "But the bad news is that we're almost out of fuel. And the ice we landed on is breaking up, as I'm sure you are all aware. I just don't know how much longer it's going to support us. Maybe minutes; or maybe it'll still be floating a year from now and become a hazard to maritime navigation. But we've got to face the fact that it could go under at any time. So just to be safe, I want everyone to put on their life jackets. The flight attendants have shown you how to do it. You may find them a little uncomfortable while you're sitting in your seats. Put up with it. Those jackets could save your life if we have to abandon ship. But don't inflate them while you're still in the airplane. You all know which life raft you've been assigned to—"

"How long could we survive in one of those rafts?" someone asked.

"A long time, sir, believe me. The trick is not to get too wet. Each raft has a canopy to protect you from the elements. In addition to the portable radios, each raft also is equipped with a set of signal flares: during the day use the orange flares; at night use the red ones."

"But who do we try to signal? There haven't been any airplanes around here."

"There will be now that we're out of the fog. I guarantee it."

"But there's still more fog all around us."

Macleod pretended not to hear the remark. He went on: "In addition to the flares, each raft is equipped with a water desalinization kit to convert sea water to drinking water . . . and a sea anchor and dye marker to color the surrounding water a brilliant emerald green to help the spotters . . . signal mirrors, flashlights, whistles . . . a first-aid kit, bailing buckets, sponges, water storage bags . . ." He didn't mention that each raft also had a religious book with the appropriate prayers.

"How about a bar?" asked Jarvis in Row 18.

Weak, shortlived smiles from a couple of passengers nearby.

"Next year's model will have a bar," Macleod promised.

"When will we have to get into the rafts, Captain?" Senator Walsh asked the question, making a noble attempt to sound completely unconcerned at the prospect.

"With a little luck, we won't have to, Senator. Maybe we'll be able to stay here until we're picked up."

"But we're running out of gas, so we won't have any heat, isn't that correct?" The speaker was a direct, no-nonsense sort of guy; he liked to get the facts completely clear.

"That's true, sir."

A middle-aged woman thrust up her arm. "Captain, if any more of this ice breaks off, we could go down like a stone . . . shouldn't we get into the rafts right now?"

"Hell, no," someone responded angrily. "We don't want to get into those goddamn things any sooner than we have to."

"If this thing goes down, I'd rather be in a life raft than sitting here, mister!"

They were scared now; their faces reflected fear. A sudden, shocking reminder of their plight: the ice emitted an agonizing groan. It stunned the passengers into silence. They waited for more sounds. Eyes darted from side to side, hands gripped seat backs and arms were braced in anticipation.

The aircraft rocked, then righted itself. "Shiiiit," said someone softly.

For some reason the comment struck Macleod as absurdly funny. He fought back nervous laughter. Was his sanity finally snapping like a rubber band pulled too tight too long? God, how much confidence could these poor bastards have in a captain with the giggles?

With difficulty he assumed a suitably commanding expression.

"I'm certain we won't be here much longer," he said.

That was when the fog enveloped them once more.

Two minutes later the engines cut out, one at a time, starved of fuel.

"I am now seven-point-two kilometers from the target," Commander Remizov reported to Leningrad on the ELF radio. His eyes were tired from staring through the periscope of his old World War II submarine, the *Eugen Onegin*, trying in vain to pierce the damned fog.

The radar operator reported the target still in the same relative position.

"Have you identified it yet?" the colonel in Leningrad inquired.

The man's voice irritated Remizov.

"Negative. It's not yet possible to identify. There is a great deal of fog in the area. I believe the target is aware of our presence, however. As we approached, our sonar detected some kind of noise-generating mechanism. Then it ceased. But the target is maintaining its position. We have it in radar contact."

"Can you tell us anything about the target? Anything at all."

They sounded worried in Leningrad. They'd be a damned sight more worried, those chairborne warriors, if they were here, under these frigid waters, shadowing an unknown type of vessel that might have the potential for destroying him at any time.

"I am unable to describe the target," he reported, "because it is enveloped in a dense bank of fog. But the radar does indicate that it is a very large vessel, the size of an aircraft carrier, perhaps even larger."

"Larger than an aircraft carrier? According to naval intelligence, there are no aircraft carriers or any other vessels of that size in those waters. Maintain radar contact with the target and keep us advised."

"I can add that the target is moving very slowly eastward," Remizov reported.

"I repeat: maintain contact with the target. At all costs."

Remizov sighed but acknowledged the order without further comment.

In Leningrad, Vassili Kalinokov sat back and stared at the ceiling of the communications center. Clearly the mysterious target had been aware of the approach of the submarine. It had shut down its power. He smiled to himself, realizing that he was thinking of the target as a reasoning creature, some kind of waterborne monster. But it wasn't. It had to be a large ship of some sort. Could it conceivably have something to do with the flurry of recent events in the Arctic? There had to be some kind of pattern to all these unusual occurrences. Was all of this some kind of deception to conceal a new type of naval vessel for Arctic operations? And to whom did it belong?

He telephoned the general.

"So you have no answers to this paradox either, Comrade Kalinokov?"

"Not yet," he replied sullenly. "We're working on it."

"You are doing a lot of work but obtaining very few results these days. When do you anticipate having some answers?" The general loved such questions.

"The fact is, sir, that in spite of our previous and extraordinary accomplishments, we are, alas, only human."

The general wasn't amused. He never was.

30

AS HE DROVE he heard the car radio reporting that extensive military preparations were underway by both NATO and Warsaw Pact countries. Elements of the United States Seventh Fleet were moving toward the Persian Gulf while the Soviet aircraft carrier *Kiev*, accompanied by a powerful flotilla, was reported moving from the Baltic into the North Sea.

Lockhart heard the words but they seemed to have no significance. They belonged to another world, another time.

He turned into his lengthy driveway. The two-story house was tranquil and clean, bathed in amber from the setting sun.

Dorothy's Jaguar was parked in the garage. It was dusty; she hadn't used the car for weeks, perhaps even months. Why not her instead of Mike? He shook his head; futile, thinking such things. His brain was numb and confused. Was this really happening? Was Mike really . . . *dead?* The idea seemed so horrendous that it was hard to comprehend. But, yes, it had happened; he remembered everything. And now he had to face Dorothy and break the news to her.

Ruth was in the kitchen. She hurried to the door.

"Hello, Mr. Lockhart. How is Mr. Michael?"

"Bad news, I'm afraid." When he told her she collapsed into a chair as if struck, dissolving into tears. He watched her, surprised at the intensity of her feelings. He had had no idea she was so fond of Mike; anyone might have thought he was a member of her own family. . . .

Ruth managed to convey that Dorothy was upstairs. Sleeping it off. But she had to be told.

Dorothy's bedroom door was white, bearing that ornate gold molding he had always hated, a frivolous thing, a jumble

247

of cherubs and bursts of buds. It had been suggested by her gay interior decorator with the velvet suit and the polished fingernails.

He shook his head. Why did everything seem so unreal, like a play in which he was performing a role? He paused before the door, listening. No sound. Was she still asleep? He knocked gently. No response. He turned the knob, opened the door and entered, closing the door behind him.

She lay sprawled on the bed, the covers rumpled and twisted. Her head lay at an awkward angle, her face buried in the king-size pillow. What was she dreaming about? Innocent childhood? Dancing the foxtrot? Ancient love affairs? Cases of Scotch?

He felt a twinge of pity. He could let her sleep on to dream her dreams . . . but, no, he had to wake her to brutal reality.

"Dorothy . . . Dorothy."

He touched her shoulder. She stirred, groaned, rolled her head to the other side; her hair stuck up in spikes.

"Dorothy, wake up." He gripped her shoulder more firmly. And shook it.

"You've got to wake up."

She opened an eye and closed it again.

"Dorothy, please."

"What . . . ?" She stared at him without apparently seeing him. Her eyes started to close again.

"You must wake up, Dorothy."

Now she knew who it was. "Wha' the hell . . ."

"It's about Mike, Dorothy."

"Mike?" She repeated the name as if it were unfamiliar to her.

"Sit up." He grasped her shoulders and dragged her into a sitting position. She didn't resist, but limpness made her heavy; hair awry, eyes puffy and bloodshot, she reeked of stale alcohol.

"Dorothy, I have something terrible to tell you."

"Terrible?" Her mouth twisted as if anticipating a blow.

"Dorothy, listen carefully. Mike . . . had an accident."

"What?" The watery eyes were uncomprehending.

"He's had an accident, Dorothy. A very serious accident. "He's . . ."

"Accident?" She shook her head as if to clear it. "Serious . . . ?"

"He's dead, Dorothy. He died a couple of hours ago . . . a car accident on the mountain . . ."

She shook her head again, but slowly this time. Her voice was a harsh growl. "No . . . I don't believe you. You're lying to me . . ."

"No, I'm not, Dorothy. I wish it weren't true. But you must accept the fact. Mike is dead."

Her eyes never wavered from his face. They had a lifeless quality; they stared but registered nothing. Only her mouth moved; she kept scraping her upper teeth over her lower lip. She still wore the remnants of the morning lipstick; smears of mascara stained her pale cheeks.

"He didn't suffer, Dorothy. He was unconscious until he died. They called from the sheriff's office . . ."

Suddenly, totally without warning, she lunged at him.

"You killed him!" It was a shriek, not a statement. It came from her throat, a primeval cry of rage, of hatred. Her fist caught him on the side of the forehead.

Surprised, knocked off balance, he toppled backward, slipping off the bed.

She was on him in an instant: hitting, scratching, biting, tearing. "You bastard, you fucking, filthy bastard, you killed my son . . ."

Her thin arms flailed. Bony fists struck his face. Her frightful eyes loomed at him. A whiff of foul breath. A hand holding something. Hurtling at him.

He rolled aside in time. The heavy china lamp smashed only inches from his head. A sharp fragment caught him on the ear. Her fists kept pummeling him, sharp, vicious, stinging.

But now he had recovered from the shock of the attack and reacted with the pent-up antagonism and resentment he had controlled for so many years. He hit her in the face. His knuckles struck her cheekbone. A sharp pain shot up his arm.

"You miserable bitch," he gasped. And hit her again, in the jaw this time.

Over she went, slumping against the bed, tumbling in an untidy heap beside it, blood bubbling from her mouth, spattering the carpet. She stared up at him.

"Bitch," he snapped again. "*You* killed him."

She moaned something; then she lay still and began to sob uncontrollably.

Panting, he stood over her. Her blood spotted the white carpet, like blood from a winter hunt, marring the bright fresh snow.

"Damn you," he gasped.

Eyes closed, she didn't respond. She just kept on crying.

Oh Jesus, Mike.

For a moment he had forgotten. He winced, hurt again, just as keenly, just as cruelly as the first time. Mike, Mike, Mike. Why, for Christ's sake, *why?* It shouldn't have happened to you. It was all wrong.

Dimly he became aware of someone knocking on the door.

"Mrs. Lockhart? Mr. Lockhart? Is something wrong?"

"It's all right, Ruth," he said. The voice was not quite his.

"But I heard something fall . . . I . . ."

"It's all *right*, I said."

"Yessir."

He sat on the bed and supported his head in his hands. He cried, remembering his son, picturing him, hearing his voice, his laugh. So young and full of life. For an instant it felt as if the sheer intensity of his misery would destroy him. But the feeling finally began to subside. He opened his eyes, the tears still flowing. He dried his eyes with a handkerchief, stood up, wobbled and straightened himself.

He glanced in the mirror. She had ripped his shirt; some of her blood was spattered on the sleeves and collar. She was obviously insane to have attacked him like that. . . .

God, again, for a few seconds, he had forgotten about Mike. The shock of remembering was like a physical blow. Was he, perhaps for the first time in his life, incapable of accepting reality?

He tugged the necktie out of his collar and walked out into the corridor and along to his own suite. He went into his bathroom and washed his face in cold water. He tossed his suit jacket and pants on a chair; the rest of the stuff went into the laundry hamper. He stood for ten minutes under a steaming shower and then dried himself carefully. She had punched him hard in his chest and the side of the face; bruises had already formed.

Damn her . . . Oh Christ, Mike. Again that stinging pain of realization. How long before the truth became part of him?

Numbly he took a plain, dark blue suit from his closet. There were things that had to be done, arrangements that had to be made. But it was so incredibly difficult to think. His head ached, a throbbing, jabbing pain; he felt sick and weak. Reaction, he guessed.

He decided to go to the office. He would make the necessary arrangements from there; infinitely better than staying in this damned house.

He went downstairs, straight through the hall to the front door. "I'll be at the office," he called to Ruth.

"Sir . . . yessir," came her voice from the kitchen.

Why did it have to be such a glorious evening? So damn perfect. It was cruel. He drove through the plant gates as swarms of Lockhart workers were finishing their shift, streaming homeward in their Fords and Hondas. Several recognized him; one or two smiled respectfully. He nodded. Korney of Accounting. Fariello of Purchasing. Acheatel of Engineering.

Thank God Miriam had long gone home. The IBM Selectric wore its somber gray cover. He sat down at his desk. Through his window he could see the employees still leaving, others arriving, thousands of them, white collar, blue collar, thinkers, craftsmen. Some geniuses, some morons. He picked up the phone and called Charlie Anderson, the corporate counsel.

"Hello."

"Charlie, Mike was killed in a car crash today."

Gasp. "My God, Eric . . ."

"I'd very much appreciate it if you would make the necessary arrangements. He's in a little town called Enumclaw, just northwest of Mount Rainer. The local hospital. He died there."

"Eric, please accept my sincerest condolences . . . and of course to Dorothy . . . I can't tell you how deeply shocked . . ."

"Thank you, Charlie, I know you cared a great deal for Mike. Can you do this for me?"

"Yes, yes, of course . . ."

"Thanks, Charlie. I knew I could count on you." He hung up.

Miriam had left mail for him, sorted in three neat piles as always: urgent, private and for information only.

Automatically he leafed through the letters.

An envelope caught his eye. The writing looked familiar.

It was Mike's! His heart leaped; for a magic instant the letter told him that Mike was alive, after all; there had been a preposterous error. . . .

A standard corporate internal-communications envelope, addressed to him but with the words PRIVATE AND CONFIDENTIAL penciled in after the name.

He opened it.

Mike had scribbled a few words on an interoffice message form. He had written the word "Dad" between the printed headings MEMO TO and FROM. The message was short:

> I can't live any more with the knowledge of what I've done. I'm sorry that I'm not as strong as you are. I don't want to be a disappointment to you. And I'm sorry. By the time you read this it will be all over and, thank God, I'll be able to sleep at last.
> Your son, Mike.

The words didn't make sense. They ran into one another, becoming a jumble, a hideous kaleidoscope of nonsense.

Mike took his own life?

Unthinkable. So absurd was the notion that the note was obviously some kind of sick joke, some ghastly prank. It had to be. He found himself nodding his head, vigorously, agreeing with himself, asserting his belief. But it did look like Mike's handwriting.

A forgery? Possibly, quite possibly; anyone with a modicum of such talent would have little trouble. More nods. But then he stopped nodding. It was as if Mike were there, standing beside him, recounting how he had left his father's office, had gone down to the main floor, had scribbled the note and had asked one of the girls for a standard interoffice envelope. He had written E. LOCKHART, 5TH FLOOR. Then: PRIVATE AND CONFIDENTIAL. After that he had simply dropped it into the nearest Out tray, left the building, entered his car and . . .

The telephone rang. Lockhart didn't answer it.

God, Mike, why?

The pain boiled inside him, searing every nerve and muscle, torturing him, tearing him apart.

He sat, wincing, sobbing, cringing.

31

"STUPID BASTARDS," HISSED Brad Steiner. "Why the hell don't they come? They could *see* us now, for Christ's sake!"

Macleod nodded understandingly. He knew how Brad felt. The damned sun was a mockery, shining down once more out of an empty sky, glittering so brightly on an equally empty sea.

"They *must* be looking for us," Karen declared, as if discussing some inevitability of nature.

Brad shook his head. "They've abandoned the whole damn search mission, if you ask me."

"No way," said Karen. "Not this soon. It stands to reason that they're still looking for us. Unless the civilized world has vanished since we took off, people have to be asking what happened to Trans Am Flight Nine-Oh-Two. And if they're asking, they must be sending planes to look for us."

"But *where* are they looking?" Brad asked. "They're sure as hell not looking anywhere around here."

Lots of questions, but apparently no answers.

There was more fog, a mile or so away, an evil gray bank of the stuff. And all they could do was sit and watch it loom larger as they drifted nearer, helpless to do anything about it.

Macleod tugged the blanket tightly around him. If the rescue aircraft were going to show up, they'd better hurry. It wouldn't be long before the fog enveloped the 707 again.

Or maybe the ocean would claim her first. It was sickeningly uneasy, the way she was floating now, forever on the brink of tipping over, perhaps turning completely upside down so that the 707 would hang like some monstrous fly from an icy underwater ceiling.

He shook his head, tiring of his own frightened mental ramblings. He told himself that he should be trying to think of ways to save his passengers' lives. But he could think of nothing else. He was weary and depressed, thinking it entirely possible that he would die within the next few hours.

The biting cold was in command once more. It had begun its assault the moment the engines had died. First the floor: chilling the feet, then moving on to fingers and backs, noses and ears. You could bundle yourself in blankets, curl yourself into a tiny ball; still the cold would find a crack in your cocoon; it sapped your energy and your will. You watched your breath condensing in silvery clouds, freezing on sidewalls and windows. Deadly quiet now. No engines, no rush of heat streaming in through vents. No din of aircraft coming to the rescue. Only the slopping of the ocean against what was left of the ice floe. A disconsolate, hopeless sort of sound.

Then they heard another sound. An airplane! Flying low! Unquestionably an airplane!

"You handle the flares," Macleod told Brad. "I'll handle the radio."

The two men scrambled out of their seats and hurried aft to the main rear exit. Passengers threw questions at them as they passed. Was this a search plane? Would they soon be taken back to civilization? How long would the rescue operation take?

"Stay in your seats! Please!"

Glimpses of aggrieved faces: passengers who seemed to feel that the captain should have stopped and discussed the situation with them in detail instead of dashing headlong for the exit and jumping out onto the evacuation slide that led down to the semisubmerged ice.

The rafts were floating now, pulling at their ropes like chubby pets anxious to run free.

Macleod and Steiner switched on the battery-operated transceivers and fired an emergency flare.

And watched the tiny speck of an aircraft disappear in the distance.

"I told you," Brad muttered. "The sons of bitches have

given up on us. That guy was just cruising along; he's not in any search pattern.''

Macleod shook his head. "It could have been someone who doesn't know anything about us . . .'' He trailed into silence, conscious of the apprehensive faces at the windows above him.

Senator Walsh stood in the doorway.

"Any luck, Captain?"

"Not this time," Macleod told him. "But there'll be another plane along soon."

"I'm sure there will."

"Like hell," hissed Brad.

"Have you ever lived in Cleveland?" Melvin Lee inquired.

Harriet Lawson shook her head. "No, why do you ask?"

"I've been watching you. I just know we've met somewhere before. It's been bugging me because I can't place you. My wife tells me to mind my own business and not to trouble people; she says I'm too nosey for my own good and, heavens, she's probably right. But I just had to get up and ask you. I hope you don't mind."

Harriet Lawson smiled. "No, I don't mind at all."

"Before Cleveland I lived in Baltimore; but that was way back, just after the war—the *first* war—and you weren't even born yet, were you?"

Harriet Lawson felt warmed by the words. How pleasant to meet someone *really* mature.

"I used to do some acting," she said with suitable modesty. "You may have seen some of my movies. My last one was called—"

Melvin Lee's eyebrows arched as if activated by a spring. "Don't tell me! Now I know your name! I knew it from the moment I saw you. Never forget a face. Never. Ever." He snapped his fingers, wincing with the effort of remembering. Then, triumphant, he pointed. "I know! Olivia de Havilland!"

Misty fingers seemed to reach out and once again usher the ice-laden vessel into the thick of the fog. In a moment the sun had again vanished, replaced by damp, freezing grayness that dimmed every hope.

A woman started sobbing, quietly.

Sam Coglin strode forward to the flight deck, demanding to know why no rescue aircraft or ships had appeared.

"I don't know," said Macleod, who was wiping his feet dry with paper towels, trying to get them warm after sliding down to the water-covered ice.

"Why the hell don't you know? You're supposed to know everything about emergencies. How come you can't do a goddam thing now, when it really matters?"

Macleod shook his head, slowly, sadly. "I'm sorry, sir. Believe me, we've done everything we possibly can. There is nothing else we can do but wait. I'm certain that help will be along soon."

"And how the hell are they going to find us in this crap? If we do manage to get off this goddam ice cube and back to civilization I'm gonna report you, mister, and tell the world how you really fucked up."

Suddenly Karen was on her feet. She slapped Sam Coglin on his left cheek with the flat of her right hand; in the small cockpit, the blow had the impact of a shot. "You idiot!" she shouted. "If it weren't for Captain Macleod you'd be dead! We'd *all* be dead. But you haven't got the brains to realize it! You should be thanking him for what he's done, not blaming him!"

He stared at her, astonished, one hand touching the reddening cheek. "You hit me," he said.

"You'd better believe it," Karen declared, her cheeks now as red as Sam Coglin's. "You deserved it."

Then she sat down. Arms folded across her chest. Staring angrily through the forward window.

For a moment there was silence on the flight deck. Everyone seemed to be waiting for someone else to speak first.

"You'd better go back to your seat," said Macleod finally.

Sam Coglin glared. "You're gonna regret this, all of you." He turned on his heel and went back to the passenger cabin, slamming the cockpit door behind him.

Macleod said to Karen, "That was noble of you. Very noble."

"But not very smart," she commented. "Anyway," she added, "it really felt good."

"I wouldn't worry about the consequences," said Brad flatly. "Chances are, we won't get out of this alive anyway."

"Thanks for the comforting words," Macleod muttered.

"I'm sorry," said Karen. "I shouldn't have done it. But he made me so damn mad."

Macleod looked at her as she straightened her jacket and patted her auburn hair back into place. He wondered briefly about the proper way for a man to react when a woman did battle on his behalf. Was there any established code of male conduct when he has a female champion? He didn't know and he didn't care. But he felt great about it. Did women feel this way when men defended them?

For a delightful moment he forgot where he was, and why. Then there was a rap on the door. Senator Walsh appeared.

"Are you having any trouble up here?"

Macleod shook his head. "I think everything's under control now, Senator. We had a little difference of opinion with Mr. Coglin."

Walsh nodded. "I saw some of it through the open door. I was sitting just outside." He glanced at Karen. "You have quite a right hook, young lady."

"I guess I lost my temper," she admitted.

"And now Coglin is going to sue the airline for a couple of million bucks," Brad put in.

"Which I suppose would not do First Officer Dempsey's career too much good," said the senator.

"It was worth it," said Karen.

"From where I was sitting," said the senator, "it looked very much to me as if your Mr. Coglin made the first move; if anyone asked me, I'd have to say that in my opinion First Officer Dempsey was merely defending herself." He glanced at Macleod and Brad Steiner. "Wasn't that the way it looked to you?"

They both nodded, speechless.

"Fine," said the senator. "Feel free to call on me if the matter goes further when we get out of here."

Harriet Lawson smiled to herself. It was nice of the old guy to mention that he recognized her—even if he did get the name wrong. If the book went into a second edition, maybe she would tell the story; it would be a pleasant human touch to add to all that sex and glamour—most of it a giant crock, anyway. She closed her eyes and thought of being curled up in front of a log fire with Clark or Franchot or Paul. Or almost anyone. Silly of her, worrying about being remembered. What the hell did it matter? Boy, she thought, there was nothing like facing death to learn about life. If, as seemed almost certain, she was to end her days here, how many would mourn her? Maybe there were a few fans left. Would *Time* mention her passing? "*Died. Harriet Lawson, 64*, erstwhile movie queen who specialized in showgirl roles in more than forty films in the '40s and '50s, in the crash of Trans American Flight 902 in the Arctic Ocean. Lawson, born Harriet Lipschitz in Brooklyn, New York, was thrice married, most recently to producer Joseph R. Santley, who died in 1978. The actress recently published her memoirs; the book died shortly before its author."

The sobs wracked Lockhart's body; the tears streamed, unchecked, unashamed.

Virginia cradled his head on her chest, stroking his brow, running her fingers through his hair, comforting him as a mother might comfort a child. "It's all right," she told him gently. "Cry. Cry as much as you need to. It's good for you."

At last there were no more tears. Lockhart rubbed his eyes. He felt empty. "I'm sorry," he said, looking past her. "I haven't cried since I was a kid."

"Don't apologize, darling. There's nothing to be sorry about. I know how you feel."

Yes, he thought, she really does. She understands.

"It was such a *wasteful* way for him to die," he said. He had told Virginia about the car crash. She knew nothing of the suicide note. No one did. He had destroyed it.

He turned to her. "There's no one important to me any more," he told her. "Except you."

She smiled. "It's sweet of you to say so, Eric. It means so much to me."

"I mean it," he said. "No one else matters. I wish we could just get away for a while, just disappear."

"You know how I would love that, Eric. It would be good for you too. We could go someplace where nobody would recognize us. But you've never gone on a vacation for as long as I've known you."

"I have a place in Mexico. Near Puerto Vallarta. I've never even been there. Dorothy used to go there once in a while. It's small but quite comfortable and has a spectacular view of the Pacific. I'd like to go there for a while, but only if you'll come too."

She studied him intently, as if trying to penetrate his innermost thoughts. She nodded. "Of course I'll come with you, Eric. I'd love it. But what about . . . everything here?"

"Dorothy? That's no problem. She doesn't give a damn about what I do anyway. As far as the plant is concerned, I can leave everything in Roy Meyer's hands. He's extremely capable and can get along without me for a while."

She shook her head in wonderment. "You never cease to amaze me, Eric. I can be ready whenever you are."

"Let's leave Friday," Lockhart said, "immediately after Mike's funeral. We'll fly down in the company Learjet."

"I don't know what to say."

"There's nothing else to say."

32

"WE'RE GOING TO sing," Macleod suddenly announced.

"Sing?" Karen stared, wide-eyed. "You gotta be kidding."

Macleod shrugged. "I don't think it's such a bad idea. I've seen it done in lots of movies. What the hell, what have we got to lose? It'll give us something to do and it may perk up everyone's spirits."

Brad muttered, "*Your* singing will perk up our spirits?"

Macleod glared. "What the hell do you know about my singing? Have you ever heard me sing? For your information, I was once in an a cappella choir."

"You?" Karen spluttered into laughter. She stopped abruptly. "Sorry—but I just can't picture you in a choirboy's suit."

"My mother said I looked cute as hell," Macleod declared. "What song do we all know? How about 'Coming' Round the Mountain'?"

Brad grimaced. "That old thing?"

"This isn't a goddam rock concert," Macleod answered. "Let's just sing." He cleared his throat. "She'll be coming round the mountain . . ."

Karen and then Brad joined in, self-consciously at first, then with increasing enthusiasm. Singing was a declaration of defiance, an affirmation of life. As they sang they felt the stirrings of renewed confidence.

Soon an accompaniment drifted forward from the passenger cabin. The sound swelled as other passengers joined in. Maybe those old movies were right, Macleod thought.

At the end of the song there was applause. They wanted more. Janet Spencer got to her feet and began singing "He's Got the Whole World in His Hands," clapping as she sang.

Quickly the others picked up the song and the hand-clapping. It was infectious. The rhythm pulsed through the hull, a beat of hope and a declaration of determination to survive.

Then the clapping slowly faded into silence; there was a rumbling from below. The airplane stirred uneasily.

A moment later it came: a violent, end-of-the-world sound as the ice snapped and cracked beneath the 707. The aircraft lurched, tipping to the left. Someone screamed. The left wingtip slapped the water and disappeared beneath the surface.

Everything loose went tumbling across the cabin—trays, plates, books, bags. Caught off balance, Janet Spencer fell, sprawling, groping in the semidarkness for something to grab onto.

Macleod didn't waste a second. "Get the exits open! We're abandoning the aircraft! *Now!*"

The words transformed the passengers from neat rows of seated figures to a massive herd, pushing, shoving, feeling, clutching in the dim light, struggling along the narrow aisle to the main and emergency exits, to the four slides that led down to the rafts.

The crew members bellowed instructions.

"Don't stop at the exits! Jump! Jump! Jump!"

"Inflate your life jackets as you leave the aircraft!"

The aircraft wobbled uncertainly, threatening to roll over completely.

The floor rocked beneath the passengers' feet, groaning, complaining.

"Get them into the rafts!" Macleod ordered the crew.

"Leave your baggage, for Crissake! There isn't room for it! Something sharp could puncture the raft!"

"I can't slide down that thing."

When necessary, crew members shoved passengers through the exits and into the slides. No time for ceremony.

"Get out! Now! Jump!"

They slithered helplessly down the slides, clawing for a handhold on the slippery rubberized surfaces, splashing into several inches of freezing water, gasping, bewildered, confused. They sprawled full-length as they tried to find their feet on the ice. Crew members shoved them unceremoniously into the twenty-five-man life rafts that bobbed about the stricken aircraft like toy boats in a bathtub.

"Everyone out?"

Macleod yelled along the great tube of the fuselage, now suddenly empty.

He turned. Karen was at the doorway.

"Get going," he told her.

"Aren't you coming?"

"In a minute!"

He ran the length of the fuselage, checking behind the seats and in the johns. Yes, everyone was gone. No passengers were left behind.

He began to retrace his steps toward the exit. He saw Karen, still standing at the doorway, still waiting. Why, for God's sake? Didn't he tell her to jump?

That was when, with a curiously weary-sounding crunching and groaning, the whole machine began to tip slowly farther to the left. He glimpsed the right wing through the cabin windows, lifting like some huge metallic limb in a hopeless gesture of supplication.

He saw Karen, arms thrust out toward him, falling to the left, hitting a passenger seat, losing her balance. Simultaneously, he struck a seat back; his legs buckled beneath him; he sprawled full length in the aisle.

Outside someone shrieked.

A babble of voices. Then more splitting and cracking of ice; more buckling of tired metal. He felt the movement around him; a massive, unstoppable shifting of what had been his whole world.

Quite calmly he thought: this is it. She's going to slip right off the ice and she'll go down like a brick, and if I don't do something as fast as hell we'll go down with her.

We.

Trying to move was like trying to lift the 707. Bodily.

Got to get up, simple as that, got to.

The cabin floor was at a crazy angle. Everything askew; anything not fastened down was falling, bounding, breaking.

"Karen!"

It was, he realized inconsequentially, the first time he had ever uttered her first name.

Where was she?

He had to scramble over the seats, fighting with seat-back tables that fell free and hit him as he went by, kicking aside cushions and hand luggage that tumbled capriciously under his feet and hands. A large book fell from an overhead rack and hit him sharply on the side of the head.

"Karen! . . . Karen!"

The aircraft slipped again, the hull twisting to an accompaniment of agonized shrieks from ice and metal.

There she was! Lying in a heap against a bulkhead. Bruise on her head. Must have been knocked out.

"Karen! Please! C'mon, you've got to help me!"

Jesus, he could hardly move her. Dead weight. No, not that, for God's sake, not that.

She opened her eyes and stared blankly at him. For an instant there seemed to be no recognition. Then she remembered. And realized. And began to react.

She nodded. And moved.

He grabbed her shoulders and pulled her from the corner into which she had slumped.

"We've got to get out! Right now!"

More nods from her as her eyes surveyed the scene.

The door was only a few feet away.

But it had become a trap door leading straight into the ocean.

The emergency slide was useless now, flattened against the side of the fuselage by the rising water.

He pointed. She nodded. No question about what they had to do.

Plunge into the frigid water and dive deeply to clear the aircraft. And quickly!

He grabbed her hand.

The shock of the cold was devastating. The blood seemed to congeal in his veins. Everything slowed. The frigidness pressed down on him, crushing him.

When at last he broke surface he had to think about where he was, fight the numbness, the strange lethargy that kept telling him there was plenty of time. . . .

He saw her, hair flattened across her forehead, mouth open, eyes wide and round. And blank.

He caught her about the neck as she started to go under.

"I've got you," he said.

But the words didn't come.

He felt a strange peace. The water wasn't all that cold now.

What was all the fuss about? Why the screams and the cries? The splashing? The hands? The hard fingers? Why was everyone always spoiling pleasant moments? It was so obvious that he and Karen would be one hell of a lot better off if everyone just left them alone.

He felt warm, both inside and out, as if he were cuddled in front of a fireplace after finishing a large, delicious plate of his mother's homemade haggis.

Then, shockingly, he was cold again, unbearably cold, agonizingly cold.

A face. Brad.

"I've got you," he said.

Somewhere, sometime, he had said the very same thing.

To someone else. To someone who mattered—

"Karen?"

"We've got her too," said someone. "She's all right."

He felt an odd, semifluid movement beneath him. It was the bottom of the life raft: a film of rubber between him and that awful sea. He sat up. Beside him, Karen sat up too, bundled in blankets. She smiled and rested her head against his shoulder. Her nose was red.

Behind them the 707 was at a lunatic angle, one wing plunged deeply into the water, the other thrust skyward. She was balanced on the remains of the ice, still anchored by her landing gear. The ice itself was equally on edge, part of it clear of the water, looking as if it wanted to shake itself free of the metallic creature that persisted in clinging on and on.

Brad said, "We've tied the rafts together in a chain."

Macleod nodded. He shivered violently, wondering whether it would have been preferable to have slipped away into the depths. Hell, he was on the way then; now he had an unpleasant feeling he was going to have to go through the same business all over again. . . .

"Jesus!" yelled someone. Someone in pain? It was hard to figure.

"Look!"

No, the voice sounded enthusiastic.

Enthusiastic about what? Macleod wondered in an uncharacteristically laborious manner.

Then he saw it. Sunshine! It sliced through the misty ceiling, a beaming stream of hope and life.

Karen sat up and grinned. Her fingers touched his arms, and tightened. Her smile broadened. She pointed.

They had drifted clear of the fog bank.

And there, less than a mile away, was an incredible sight: land, shimmering in the sunshine!

"The fog seems to be clearing in the area of the target," Commander Remizov reported to Leningrad. "I believe we may soon have visual contact."

"You are still submerged?"

"Affirmative."

Remizov grimaced. What the hell did they think? That he was going to surface and line the crew up along the foredeck? Remizov wiped the sweat from around his neck. It was stifling in this old tub. How long could a man remain healthy breathing the fumes of diesel fuel and his crew's body odor? He couldn't decide which smelled worse. Did he, Remizov, stink as vilely as Simonov? Did Simonov smell worse than Novikov?

Suddenly rambling thoughts of body odor vanished. The target was definitely emerging! His fingers tightened on the periscopic controls. He made a fine adjustment of the focus. There! His eyes ached with the effort of trying to pierce the misty distance. There! God, yes! At last!

He stared. Blinked. Blinked again. He was seeing things. His mind was coming unhinged.

"Simonov!"

The stinking lieutenant snapped to attention.

"Yes, Captain!"

Remizov indicated the periscope.

"Report what you see."

"Very good, sir."

A moment later Simonov turned, frowning, puzzled. "An aircraft . . . it looks as if it's *floating*."

Remizov heaved a silent sigh of relief; his mind wasn't going after all.

He took the periscope. Adjusted the focus once more. An airliner, by the look of it, apparently drifting like a ship. But, no, now it was apparent that the aircraft was on a platform of ice; one wingtip was under water.

Commander Remizov reported: "The target is a four-engine, jet-powered airplane. It is resting on an ice floe."

Somehow the colonel in Leningrad didn't sound as astounded as Remizov expected.

"Can you identify the aircraft?"

"I believe it to be a commercial airliner."

"Nationality?"

"I can't tell from this distance."

"Can you get closer and make a definite identification?"

"Yes, but we are entering very shallow waters."

"We understand your concern, Captain. But it's absolutely vital that we obtain an identification of that aircraft as soon as possible."

"Is it worth the loss of a submarine?" Remizov snapped.

The colonel in Leningrad didn't hesitate. "In this case, it very well might be, Captain. You must identify that aircraft."

"I will try, Colonel," Remizov reported. "I can tell you, however, the aircraft has been evacuated. I can see perhaps one hundred people in four life rafts."

"Has the aircraft sunk?"

"No, there is only one wingtip under water and the machine has come to rest in the shallows of the bay. I do not believe it can sink any farther."

The colonel asked again, insistently, "Can you identify that airplane?"

"Yes," said Remizov. "I believe I can now. There is something written on the side of the fuselage, just above the windows."

"Read it, please."

"Damn, it is coated with frost, but I think I can make it out. The letters are T-R-A-N-S-A-M-E-R-I-C-A . . ."

The colonel in Leningrad said, "Good work, Captain! Well done! Now tell me, are the survivors in any immediate danger?"

"Not as far as we can determine."

"Then I suggest you take a series of periscopic photographs, remain submerged and leave the area as rapidly as possible. We have what we need."

"You mean that we are not to offer assistance to these people?" Commander Remizov asked.

"Absolutely not. It is imperative that your boat not be detected within the territorial waters of Greenland, especially since the passengers are not in immediate jeopardy. We will notify the Americans and let them effect the rescue. Commander Remizov, we suggest you leave the area as rapidly as possible. *Before* the Americans arrive. The modifications made to your boat must not be observed. There will be no further discussion of this matter.''

Kalinokov sounded as nonchalant as if he were announcing the date of the next committee meeting. ''I have to report, sir, that we have discovered the American jetliner on an ice floe off the west coast of Greenland. The United States military has been advised of the fact. The passengers will soon be picked up by the American air force or navy. It is apparent that the Mayday call indicating that the aircraft was being shot down in the Norwegian Sea by Soviet fighters was a hoax. As to the reason behind it all, one can only speculate at the moment. This proves beyond any doubt, however, that the Soviet Union was not involved in any way.''

''Good,'' said the general. From him, the remark could be considered a veritable plethora of praise. ''Now we must convince the rest of the world of that fact.''

Kalinokov hung up. He was tired. Odd how the end of a difficult problem was like the end of a bittersweet affair: a relief to have it done with yet a sense of loss that something so significant has gone from one's life forever.

A knock on the door.

''Come in.''

A pretty brunette head. Sensual underlip; bright eyes slanting deliciously toward plump cheeks. ''Excuse me, Comrade Colonel, I must be in the wrong office. I was told to report to the Central Information Directorate. Number forty-three, they said . . .''

''Number forty-three, indeed. But not in this building. In the Nevsky Wing. That way,'' he added, pointing, noting with pleasure the girl's alert manner. Perhaps a brain as well as a body, this one.

''Forgive me, Comrade Colonel. I do apologize for disturbing you.''

''Nothing to forgive, my dear. A mistake anyone could have made. It just so happens I am walking that way. I'd be happy to escort you.''

She beamed; her cheeks colored charmingly. ''You're very kind, Comrade Colonel.''

"It is my pleasure," declared Kalinokov. Which it unquestionably was. Suddenly he was no longer tired. He felt on top of the world. This one was going to prove interesting; he could tell.

As he stood up, he glanced at his reflection in a window. Tall, straight, still an impressive figure of a man, he convinced himself. But that damned tunic was still not quite right. He would have Morikilov do something about it. First thing in the morning.

33

THE COMMANDER OF the United States Air Force Base at Thule, Greenland, was alternately smiling and frowning at Macleod and Senator David Walsh across his desk. Smiling because his helicopter crews had brought the occupants of Trans American Flight 902 to safety, frowning because he could have done it within a few hours of the crash landing, if only he had known the downed airplane was so close.

"You were supposed to be in the Norwegian Sea," he told Macleod. "Your emergency message got screwed up somehow."

"Emergency message?" queried Macleod. "We never made one. We couldn't. We had an electrical fire that shorted out the radios as soon as the thing went off."

The general's frown deepened. "As soon as what thing went off?"

"The bomb—or whatever the hell it was."

A captain of U.S. Naval Intelligence was present, Stephen Forrest, a bespectacled, scholarly-looking individual with a graying crew-cut. He said, "You mean, some sort of explosive device on board brought you down?"

"Of course," Macleod replied. What, he wondered, were these military guys driving at?

"But what about the Soviet MiGs?"

Macleod shrugged. "Soviet MiGs? We didn't see any Soviet MiGs. In fact, we only saw a couple of aircraft the whole time we were on the ice. They were civilian aircraft, by the look of them—"

Forrest persisted. "You mean to tell us that you *never* saw any Soviet MiGs at *any* time?"

"Russian fighters over Baffin Bay? No, of course not."

"None at all?"

Jesus, these guys were dense. "No," said Macleod, "as I said, some sort of explosive device went off in the forward baggage compartment. That's what caused the electrical fire and that's what brought us down. You see, one engine blew and the drag of the damaged—"

The general wagged a finger. "Are you sure that your explosion wasn't caused by a missile?"

"No. What the hell are you guys talking about?"

"And you didn't transmit a Mayday call?"

"No. We couldn't."

"Well, someone did," said Forrest. "Which led everyone in the world to believe you'd been shot down over the Norwegian Sea. And that is why all search-and-rescue operations were concentrated in that area."

"And," said the general, "the emergency transmission indicated that Soviet MiG fighters were attacking you. It's caused a major international crisis. The United States and the Soviet Union have been mobilizing rapidly; we've been heading for a major confrontation."

Macleod was stunned, speechless.

Senator Walsh sat back, astounded. "You mean to say that *we've* been the catalyst that could have led to World War Three?"

"Absolutely, Senator. We've probably been closer to a state of war with the Soviet Union than at any time in history."

"Because of *us*?" Macleod asked. "I don't get it. Why would anyone want to suggest that the Russians shot us down?"

"And who?" muttered Walsh thoughtfully.

There was a knock on the office door.

"Come in," the general barked.

The door opened. A young lieutenant entered carrying a small box.

"Sir, I thought you should see this right away. The frogmen recovered it from the wreckage of the seven-oh-seven. It looks as if these fragments are the remains of an explosive device, but there's no way to be absolutely certain at this point. They seem to have been blown from the forward baggage compartment into the electrical compartment beneath the cockpit. It appears that an advanced compound of C-4 explosive was placed aboard the aircraft, possibly in a bottle. We think it might have been in what's left of this bottle,'' he said, opening the box.

The glass fragments were green, small and jagged.

But one still retained a piece of a label.

David Walsh leaned forward and examined it more closely.

"Please be careful, Senator. Don't cut yourself."

"I'll be careful," Walsh replied. He picked up and studied the fragment of glass bearing the piece of label.

"Seems as though it might have been a wine bottle," said the lieutenant.

"Looks that way to me too," replied Walsh.

34

THE TELEVISION SET came on at precisely 7 A.M. Pacific Daylight Saving Time. The "Today" show was just beginning. It had been Lockhart's habit to wake up to the news every weekday morning. The familiar tones of the network newscaster aroused him immediately. But Virginia pulled the covers over her head, trying to prolong the last vestiges of sleep. She had no desire to be awakened abruptly to the harsh events of the day. But the urgency and import of the lead headline shocked her out of her drowsiness.

"We have just learned that the Trans American Airline Boeing seven-oh-seven reported to have been shot down by the Russians over the Norwegian Sea has been found just off the west coast of Greenland." Even the normally expressionless newscaster appeared genuinely startled by what he had just read. "Details are still sketchy, but a report attributed to a military spokesman at Thule Air Force Base in Greenland states that with the exception of one passenger—a Swedish national—all passengers and crew members survived the ordeal without serious injury. One of those survivors is believed to be Senator David Walsh, the leading Republican contender for the presidential nomination. A well-informed Pentagon source has stated that the airliner evidently was *not* shot down by Soviet jet fighters as was originally believed. We have no further information at this time, but stay tuned for the latest details as soon as they become available.

"And now a word from—"

The screen darkened and the audio went silent as commanded by the remote-control unit in Lockhart's hand. He was stunned, unable to utter so much as a word. But then his

273

mind began to pick up speed, accelerating frenetically as he grasped the impact of what he had just heard.

The airplane was *not* destroyed?

My God, Mike was wrong. But how could that be?

They *survived?* David Walsh was *alive?*

His heart pounded with the realization that his whole world had suddenly changed. It might even collapse around him. He began to perspire; rivulets of sweat began to trickle down his neck.

Would they be able to connect him with the incident? No, that wasn't possible, he assured himself. But what would happen to the Devastator? They wouldn't disapprove the contract, would they? An incomprehensible thought.

No, no one would ever know for sure that the Soviets weren't responsible for downing the airplane. The world situation hadn't really changed. There was still a desperate need for the XB-3A. The Senate would still approve production. Or would they? How would all of this affect the mood of the country now? Did Meyer tell him that corporate funds had already been committed for the Devastator? He couldn't remember; his mind was swamped with a nightmare of unanswerable questions.

He had to calm down, relax, and take each potential problem in turn.

"Don't you think so?" said Virginia.

He couldn't answer. He hadn't heard one word she had said in response to the news broadcast. How long had she been talking?

Without even acknowledging her, Lockhart threw off the covers and got out of bed. "Virginia, I've got to go to the office. Right now."

"Mr. Lockhart is so anxious to see you, Senator. Please go right in."

Miriam was shocked at Walsh's appearance. He looked so tired and pale and distraught. Even though it had been three days since Flight 902 had been found, she wondered what could be so important that he couldn't take more time to recover from his ordeal before seeing his old friend.

The senator wore a sport jacket, a Western shirt and cotton trousers. Miriam found herself trying to remember when she had ever seen the senator in anything less formal than a three-piece suit.

A determined David Walsh strode into Lockhart's private office. The two men were meeting for the first time since the departure of Flight 902.

Eric Lockhart literally ran around his desk to embrace the senator. "David, David. Thank God you're all right. I can't tell you how overjoyed I am to see you. But my God, man, you look so tired. Here. Please sit down."

Walsh remained unusually quiet and stoic. He sat down in front of the polished oak desk as Lockhart returned to his black leather chair. The two men sat in silence for a long moment, like chess players on opposite sides of the board. It was then that Walsh's anger and disappointment suddenly surfaced.

"I don't believe this, Eric," he said with a tone of incredulity. "You are absolutely insane. You try to kill me and more than a hundred others and act as though nothing has happened."

Lockhart was startled by this emotional outpouring, but quickly regained his composure. "David, what in the hell are you talking about?"

Walsh reached into the left inside pocket of his sports jacket and withdrew a small, clear vinyl pouch. He held it up in front of Lockhart. "This is what I am talking about."

"That? What the hell is that?"

"Doesn't it look familiar, Eric?"

"Familiar? No, why should it?"

"This is a piece of glass from the bottle of wine you gave me. I've carried it with me ever since leaving Greenland. There is no doubt that the explosion designed to destroy Flight 902 originated in a bottle of rather fine wine. It was a good year, Eric, but not for explosives."

Lockhart's throat was suddenly dry. He cleared it, noisily, painfully. Don't lose control, he told himself. Be calm.

"C'mon, David. Think clearly. There must have been all kinds of bottles aboard that jet."

"That's undoubtedly true, Eric. But you see, this piece of glass contains a small part of the label from the bottle of wine you gave me. Small, yes. But identifiable. It's the only part of the label that survived the explosion. And I seriously doubt if there was another bottle of 1945 Lafitte Rothschild aboard that flight.''

Lockhart sat back, attempting to recover from that revelation.

"The Naval Intelligence Laboratory is analyzing other fragments at this very moment, Eric. We both know what they'll find. And when I give them this piece of glass, it will be the last piece needed to complete their puzzle.''

Lockhart studied Walsh's face, his determination, his resolve. It occurred to him that, yes, they very well might be able to prove that the bottle contained C-4 explosive. But only David Walsh knew where that particular bottle came from. He reached out as if to calm Walsh. But his hand seemed to become an absurd object, hanging there between them, doing nothing.

Softly, he said, "David, what I did, I did for our country, for everything *we* believe in, for everything you and I have worked so hard to achieve. This was the only way to turn this country around. My own son was willing to sacrifice *his* life in this struggle—''

Walsh nodded his acknowledgment.

"—If I could have sacrificed my own life to achieve the same purpose," Lockhart continued, "I would not have hesitated.''

He stood up now and moved slowly around the desk toward Walsh. He loomed over him, his eyes boring directly into the senator. "How many times have we agreed that we would sacrifice our own lives and the lives of our families to save our country and our values for future generations?''

"I know, Eric. I believe that as firmly as you do, but I never implied that I would ever condone murder! My God, Eric, you tried to kill one hundred and nineteen people.''

Lockhart was not deterred. He ignored the accusation and continued his verbal barrage in an even more aggressive tone.

"Look, David, I'm overjoyed that you and everyone else survived this ordeal, genuinely ecstatic. What we have accomplished with this plan is beyond expectation. We have turned this country around. America is now receptive to everything we have fought so hard to achieve. We will build the Devastator. Americans haven't been this united since World War Two. And you, David, are going to be their leader, the next President of the United States. You're a hero. Everyone will rally around you. The liberals and the doves are crushed.

We have won! Under your administration, we'll have a rebirth of American vitality, American power and the will to use it."

Almost laughing, he continued. "What do you want to do, David? Throw all of this away, by making me out to be some kind of criminal? It could ruin *your* career, too."

There was no doubt that Lockhart's eloquence had an effect. The words had softened Walsh's chiseled expression of antagonism; they had taken some of the darkness from around his eyes.

"I understand what you are saying, Eric. But everyone knows now that the Soviets did not shoot down the airplane as was originally reported. Certainly this will temper all of that anti-Russian sentiment."

"On the contrary," snapped Lockhart. "Only *you* know about the label on that piece of glass. Only *you* know that I gave you *that* bottle of wine. With the fervor that is sweeping this country, Americans will believe that if Soviet MiGs weren't responsible for the incident, the Russians were undoubtedly behind the plot anyway. It's only right that the Communists be the scapegoats for a change."

Walsh suddenly became introspective. He had listened carefully to every word. "What makes you think that the public will continue to hold the Soviets responsible?"

"Because of you, David. You are the key. It's you the Russians fear and everyone knows it. Can you think of a better motive for anyone to have attempted to destroy the airplane?"

Lockhart placed a hand on Walsh's shoulder and said almost paternally, "David, we've won the battle; now let's win the war."

Walsh rose slowly, wearing an expression of confusion and uncertainty. Much of what Lockhart had said did make sense. It sounded so logical. Perhaps all of this should not be wasted. And there was no doubt that recent events had thrust him mightily along the road to the presidency. A lifelong goal was literally within his grasp now.

Sensing victory, Lockhart decided it would be best not to push the issue further at this time. He said, "David, why don't you go home and get some rest. Sleep on what I have said and we'll work out the details over dinner at the club tomorrow night.''

Acknowledging the invitation, Walsh said, "Yes, Eric, it is true. Our greatest duty *is* to our country and our fellow man.''

Warmly, Lockhart put his arm around Walsh's shoulders and escorted him to the door. Walsh closed the door behind him, wished Miriam a pleasant afternoon and slowly walked down the long corridor, deep in thought. He turned right toward the elevator and was met by three men dressed neatly in business suits.

Without saying a word, Walsh removed his jacket, lifted the tail of his shirt and removed the miniaturized recorder taped to the small of his back. He handed it to the first man.

"Thank you, Senator Walsh. As you know, the lab was unable to prove conclusively that the explosion originated in that bottle. You have saved the F.B.I. a great deal of trouble.''

35

"I RAN INTO Brad at the airport today," Karen said. "He told me that he's decided against the printing business after all. He's going to try for first officer again. I hope he makes it."

"I have a feeling he will," said Macleod. He sipped his Courvoisier and glanced up; a trio of sombreroed musicians approached the table, beaming like benevolent bandits as they strummed guitars. A black-haired girl with a formidable cleavage materialized at Macleod's elbow. She carried a beribboned basket of flowers. Would the *señor* like a beautiful rose for his lovely lady?

Macleod almost shook his head. He had never given a rose to anyone at a dinner table, for God's sake. But Karen looked away from the basket a little too quickly, her expression of bland disinterest quite unconvincing. Contradictory, complex creatures, females. Even female pilots. He took a pink rose and glanced up at the girl, expecting to be told the price. The girl flashed a brittle smile. There was an instant of indecision. Then he handed her a five-dollar bill; with a squeak of thanks she whirled away to the next table.

Karen took the rose and smiled at it, studying it.

"That was sweet," she said.

That was also highway robbery, Macleod thought but didn't say. "Another cognac?"

"My mother always told me to watch out for men who offered second cognacs."

"She was quite right. Still want another?"

She nodded, smiling that marvelously *total* smile of hers. It aroused a man to be smiled at that way, because the smile said: Hey, I've found someone I really want and I know that beneath that crusty exterior of yours, there's a hell of a warm, sexy guy and there's no one in the entire world I'd rather be with than you.

It was their sixth date in ten days. Three days had elapsed between the first and second. One day between the second and third. For the last four days they had been inseparable. That morning they had had breakfast together at her apartment; the previous morning at his place.

The incredible thing was how she had become an integral— *essential*—part of his life. She excited him; it was a consuming excitement, not jagged and unnerving as it had been with Angie. He had been genuinely astonished to discover just how intensely involved he was with Karen, whether he was in bed with her, in an airplane, a sailplane, or a restaurant, or simply walking hand-in-hand along a street. Why was that? What made this relationship so utterly unique? For the first time in his life, he felt complete. His life had suddenly become more than just aviation and career. He felt the strange awareness that he could trust her with his deepest feelings and emotions without fear of being hurt.

He said, "I bet no one in this restaurant would guess in a million years that you're an airline pilot."

"I think I'll take that as a compliment."

"That's what I had in mind."

She looked at him in her direct way. "On the other hand, Captain Macleod, even if you were sitting there in your BVDs, I'll bet everyone would know that you're an airline pilot."

He grinned at her. "Thanks. I like that."

"I thought you would," she said.

At this moment her eyes were blue with green flecks; yet on the way to the restaurant, Macleod recalled, her eyes had definitely been green with blue flecks.

He tried to remember the color of Angie's eyes. And failed.

She said, "It was a wonderful dinner. But the company was even better."

"Just being my usual loveable self."

She grinned. "There was a time when I thought you were

the nastiest, most arrogant man in the world, next to Attila the Hun."

He said, "Maybe Attila wasn't that bad when you got to know him."

"The thing that I can't help thinking about is, if it wasn't for that madman, Lockhart, we wouldn't be here. I wonder what they'll do with him."

"Put him away for the rest of his life, I hope."

"In his own perverted way, he probably thought he wasn't doing anything wrong," she said.

"So did Hitler," said Macleod. He glanced at his watch. "We'd better get going. You barely have time to pack a bag. Our flight leaves in a couple of hours."

"What flight?"

"The one to New Brunswick, New Jersey, with a quick connection at La Guardia."

"New Brunswick? We're going to New Brunswick?"

"Right."

"Tonight?"

"Sure."

"Do I get to ask why?"

"Of course."

"Okay, why?"

"Because there are a couple of people there I'd like you to meet. They're going to meet us at the airport. You'll like 'em. And I know they'll be crazy about you. By the way, have you ever tried haggis?"

"Haggis?"

About the Authors

HAL FISHMAN is an award-winning news anchorman for KTLA-TV in Los Angeles. BARRY SCHIFF is an airline captain with more than 16,000 flying hours to his credit, as well as a noted aviation writer. They both reside in Los Angeles.